Doghouse Blues 2

Clive Radford

Published by Rogue Phoenix Press, LLP
Copyright © 2021

ISBN: 978-1-62420-568-2

Editor: Amanda Armstrong

Dedication

To all satire lovers.

Contents

Chapter 1: Dr Fraser I Presume?

'If you want to keep your sanity,' someone told Roger Fraser long ago, 'don't let the world run you.'

Huh, he thought, *great maxim, not so easy to put it into practice.* Moreover, replaying some inauspicious social events to date from summer 2011, he concluded fate abided as the chief culprit behind his interminable misfortunes. Superficially never far from controversy, albeit even when he had not been the source of discord, or alternatively the need to play the peacemaker in the face of overwhelming odds, somehow the altercation always fruited in him getting the rough end of the pineapple and ending up in the doghouse licking his wounds.

Shaking his head in disbelief he wondered, *why do these damned things keep on happening to me, and why do I allow myself to get sucked into so many pulse-raising and unmanageable capers*? First, the infamous dongle incident became a significant *faux pas* when he assumed the article approximated a man's man-servant. Then the Fraser's notorious garden party segued into a newsworthy saga for peer Kappa Corinthians Rugby Club players to mercilessly lampoon him with, unrestrained. Those capricious occurrences were followed by various family related disputes, coming to terms with his new trouble-shooter role at The Firm, and jousting with *femme fatale* schoolgirls in order to preserve his freedom and stay out of jail, during his involuntary evening classes helping them to accomplish top-grade A-level business studies results.

However, the *piece de resistance* took place at Greenwich Park, when his wife Charlotte had a brush with the law consequent to a major disagreement with a Godzilla-sized woman about the 2012 Olympic Games. When people disagreed with Charlotte's often contentious views, she remained prone to side-lining her *de facto* responsible self in favour of fisticuffs. Though performed in an entertaining and often passionate manner, nonetheless Roger had encouraged her to curb her quick temper, particularly since James, the Fraser's ever resourceful son, retained a video of the episode captured on his iPhone. Holding it over both his parents as a means to gain blessings in the pocket money department and reduce his household chores burden, James lingered fireproof, at least *pro tem*.

Ensuing from a set of unforeseen circumstances, largely beyond their control, well, Roger's at least, for the first time in their twenty-plus years' relationship, Charlotte had empathised with her husband, realising they were both in the doghouse. She told him, when she found a way to delete the scandalous Greenwich Park video, James would be toast. Until then, she promised to be on her best behaviour, much to her husband's relief.

Still reeling from the unimaginable mishaps, he raised the bugbear of providence with wise owl friend Allan Mallory.

"Well, Roger, it's akin to age creeps up like molten lava imprisoning everybody in its wake. You don't notice the advent of its passage until actualisation sets in." Laying a kindly paw on his shoulder, Alan prescribed, "you need to put your minor tragedies and calamities into perspective."

"You mean, don't dwell on them?"

"More the case, don't allow them to become overbearing. Nothing you recited could be categorised as a grave cataclysm."

"Of course, in the workplace I'm unassailable, whereas home environs are invariably a breeding ground for my apparent hopelessness and haplessness. I find the blessed dichotomy disarming. I take your point, but—" He simpered. "It seems to me, to avoid the beartraps, there needs to be a change in my domestic and leisure-time approach."

Alarmed by the proposed upheaval, Alan assured, "you needn't modify your amiable personality and propensity for gaffs, intentional or otherwise. That'd be a shame. You wouldn't be the same person. Just accept the cavalier way you interact with people in the private sphere inherently results in the occasional, let's call it, *misunderstanding*. And I must say, it seems to be a family trait in that others within your clan, and don't take this the wrong way, also stray into a controversial sphere, more often than the norm."

"You make it sound like the Fraser family is cursed! Maybe we should be renamed, 'The Addams Family.'"

"I'd not go as far as that, although Charlotte would make a sensational Morticia Addams."

"*Hot damn*, that makes me Gomez Addams or worse still, Lurch!"

"Well, you brought up the subject of kismet, Roger."

~ * ~

As usual, Roger never had enough hours in the day to fulfil offbeat singular ambitions. What with the job, his family and of course Kappa Corinthians, every waking moment seemed to be consumed without any slack to tackle what he considered to be reasonable alpha-male desires.

In parallel with his investment banking career, he had partially-formed notions about starting his own British Touring Car Championship team with BMW, taking a three-months Route 66 road trip sabbatical with Charlotte and perhaps long-term friends the Hunts and the Andersons, and even exploring the upper reaches of the Amazon and the Blue Nile. Way back in his youth, Roger had briefly fostered yearnings about becoming an adventurer in the mode of Sir Richard Burton or Livingstone, tearing through the dense jungles of Brazil and Central Africa in pursuit of lost civilisations and priceless antiquities. Maybe he could even make a few bob out of the venture by writing about his experiences?

But all these activities relied on him sustaining his health and mental alertness. With the onset of middle age creeping ever nearer, plus additional trouble-shooter demands, those dual recognitions amplified his awareness time rested as the most valuable commodity at his disposal. Finite life coupled with the perception that the unexpected could rifle through and decimate any scheme made him deduce, sooner rather than later, he needed to augment his grand designs into plans. *I must make every minute count, let alone every hour*, he recognised.

Since graduating from Kings College Cambridge with a degree in economics and achieving chartered financial analyst status, Roger's life appeared to be one long white-knuckle ride through domesticity and career. There had never been an intermission when he could take a deep breath and make calm calculation about other things he'd like to fulfil before the grim reaper came knocking. His aspirational dreams persisted, caught in foggy flight, never quite distilling into discernible features he could grasp and make reality.

During his sometimes distinguished and enduring rugby career, he had suffered several injuries. But for the grace of god they could have incapacitated or more severely invalided him, as he had seen happen to fellow players. With advancing years, he became mindful any legacy injury might seriously affect his later life and thereby the opportunity to enact the halfway-defined objectives, occasionally creeping into the forefront of his consciousness.

When he discussed his latent vocations with Charlotte, she maintained there'd be plenty of scope for whatever he wished to effectuate when he retired from The Firm. Notwithstanding, despite the daily challenges with Essex boy traders in the bullpen and the generic vagaries of investment banking, calling for a constant reinvention of the *modus operandi*, Roger failed to see a demarcation ahead when he retired. Besides, the green trouble-shooting responsibility had put extra zip into his stride. Howbeit the complete irregularity of the tasks and their impact on his analyst function needed to be carefully managed, he found both twisters stimulating and very satisfying. In his prepossession, he saw himself jetting off to Tierra del Fuego, Kathmandu or Timbuktu to settle some thorny hang-up The Firm's London operation had run into for decades to come.

Most analysts had built up enough private equity investments to retire comfortably by age fifty-five, the strategy certainly applying to him. Roger had been making provision for retirement since his early twenties, assembling enough dividend-bearing assets to pull the ripcord and float gently down into his dotage when he hit forty. That landmark had come and gone, leaving him still motivated to make money and securing sufficient kicks out of investment banking's daily battleground to want more. But by sixty, even for a top-of-the-pile analyst, noises would be made at The Firm regarding forced retirement. If he could keep fit and healthy, once past the sixty cut off point, he estimated he might go on until seventy, at least in a casual consultancy capacity. Only the executive layer evaded retirement at sixty, with the likes of 'Ayatollah' Luther Bembridge and Toby 'Top Cat' Chalcroft upholding their careers for however long they desired. Some execs even went on into their eighties, or until their toes finally turned up on the job.

Revisiting the trouble-shooting province, he assessed it undeniably added another dimension to his career longevity. Based on Top Cat's appraisal for awarding him the job, it became vividly transparent the Ayatollah and he wanted experience coupled with drive and determination to succeed to broker whatever trouble-shooter undertakings were thrown up. Requiring Roger to call upon his diverse market knowledge and interpersonal skills to resolve difficulties and thereby conserve The Firm's precious business reputation, to date each engagement had been markedly different, with little repeatability of solution applicable from one tricky situation to the next. Reasoning, as he got older, wider familiarity would be supplemented to his canon, making his acquired currency even more valuable to The Firm, he felt self-assured if still fit and healthy at sixty, surely he'd not be put out to pasture?

Applying analytical techniques, he worked out his options. While still relatively young, it made sense to embark on all his fancies. Waiting until he enrolled in the part-time consultancy stage of his career might be too late. By then, what physical and mental shape could he be in, presuming he still lived? Jostling with all the variables, Roger finalised until siblings Wendy, James and Heather were safely off his hands in terms of economic and emotional dependencies, it'd be foolhardy to jeopardise his city career to bring off intimate cravings. 2025 rendered the earliest watershed date, when Heather, the Fraser's youngest child graduated from university, and he neared fifty-eight. That left little room for manoeuvre to cram in his perennial goals before he slammed into sixty, and possible enforced retirement.

Aiming to decipher the poser, he reflected on the immense names graduating from Kings; Robert Walpole, E.M. Forster, Rupert Brooke and Alan Turing among them. Even economics guru John Maynard Keynes came to mind. Having seen their disastrous monetary and fiscal effects justified by Gordon Brown, as a necessary constituent for creating the big state, Roger had denounced Keynes theories. Even so, he pondered if Keynes and the other Kings' luminaries had wrestled with the conundrum of family and professional career verses clandestine lodestars.

Setting about seeing to the callings of home and The Firm, the symmetries continued to confront Roger Fraser. His facsimile image of a latter-day Stanley discovering him in the guise of Dr Livingstone, ensconced in a vine and coconut laden paradise, away from the perpetually taxing and infinitely tangled worlds of creature comforts and high finance, hovered as a remote vision.

Chapter 2: Crimson Avenger and Hail Mary

Several people had asked Roger how his new stock analyst-trouble-shooter assignment was working out, including Steve Hunt, solicitor extraordinaire and a friend of his since childhood.

"So, how are you coping with the combined charge?"

"To my surprise," Roger certified, his peepers opening wide, "it has brought some startling and most welcome compensations."

"Very eloquent. For instance?"

"Equities Director Toby Chalcroft, insisted The Firm provided me with a top-of the-range, modern as he called it, multi-functional communication device."

"You mean," Steve began in a derisive accent, "a mobile, or as the septics call it, a cell phone?"

"Yes," he confirmed, self-conscious of his friend's shadily disguised mocking.

"Ha, ha, you're trading in your tin can and string system," Steve verified, "for, dare I say it, something from the twenty-first century?"

"Hhmm, very droll, as Gordon Anderson might say." Sneering and hissing in equal measures, Roger made his annoyance plain to the smiling provocateur. "Anyway, when I say top-of-the-range, that's not quite true," he admitted. "After I compared it with the iPhones owned by Charlotte, Wendy and James, but paid for by yours truly, I found it's about midway to being top-of-the range in terms of capability and features, but a huge improvement on the prehistoric device I previously used."

"*Dear god*, mobile phones are a hindrance to a solicitor," Steve alleged. Rocking on his heels, as if preparing to make an argument in the style of the Gettysburg Address, he advised, "I used to be able to hide from people I didn't want to talk to, chiefly over-anxious will beneficiaries fretting about their share of the deceased's jackpot, or voracious solicitors' representing the accused, trying to cut an unrealistic deal with the plaintive I defended. But—" Developing a despairing expression and hopping from foot to foot, as if readying Roger for more shocking news from the world of the wig and gown, he disclosed, "mobile services have given me no hiding place from their persistent and often avaricious advances. Even if I switch the damned thing off, it still gets flooded with messages." Grimacing, he explained, "under the conditions of the solicitors' charter, I am duty bound to respond to them, independent of how absurd or far-fetched they are."

"Dear me," Roger jested, relishing Steve's no-win predicament. "It's *such* a hard life in the legal profession these days."

"Don't tease, Roger," declared the burdened legal stalwart. "You'd build a steel barrier around yourself, if you had to cope with some of the grasping and gluttonous vultures descending on my office, petitioning for a resolution to an action yet to be heard in the civil courts." Screwing up his lineaments, he took on a more fraught demeanour. "Or even worse, and this really beggars' belief, some predatory housebreaker fiend, whose plea-pedlar solicitor claims he resided out of the country, when his client's fingerprints are all over the place, and my client is suing for unlawful entry."

"Ah yes, oh put upon one, but likewise, isn't it true, you once put a trained chimp on the stand to testify on behalf of one of your dodgy clients?"

"No, it's *not*, Fraser," Steve denied. "It was a parrot."

"Hah, I see," Roger wistfully corroborated. "Makes my daily duelling with the bullpen fraternity seem quite tame in comparison."

"You'd not credit some of the strokes these ambulance-chasing, so-called justice junkies get up to, to prove their client lingered nowhere near the scene of the crime." Waggling an outstretched finger, he pressed, "I had a case recently, where in front of the judge, a courtroom cavorter virtually wrapped his arms around his extremely attractive female client, and asserted she was not driving her Range Rover Discovery 4, when it collided with my client's house."

"*Really*!" Roger exclaimed displaying genuine astonishment.

"Phew, the damned silly old coot of a judge nearly believed her, and went on to recommend my client withdrew the action, until I presented irrefutable evidence she drove the car."

"Oh. Pray tell."

"I had one of our investigators track down her male accomplice. Apparently, while attempting to keep control of the car with her right hand, she pleasured his crimson avenger with her left hand. When he climaxed, his gentleman's relish flew up onto the windscreen preventing her from seeing ahead."

"And," Roger anticipated, "she crashed into your client's house?"

"Precisely. But she even tried to make out the house moved into her path and caused the crash!" Hands on hips, he developed an improbable countenance then scorned, "that's just the tip of the iceberg. I could bore you for hours with tales of brief-bandits intercepting juicy cases—"

"We call it insider trading in financial services," Roger interjected.

"Quite." Frothing, he extended his tale of courtroom woes, annexing, "fee-fanciers and statute-sticklers involved in duplicitous activities bordering on the criminal, ponsified legal eagles pulling statute touter tricks…"

"I have," Roger commenced, oblivious to his diatribe gush, before Steve came in again.

"…Justice joy-riders acting as so-called, no-win-no-fee noblemen, using prince of precedents tricks to bamboozle juries, looking like they've been selected from a who's who of international criminals themselves..."

"I have," Roger tried anew, bored with the incensed tirade, Steve trumping him for the nth time.

"…Full-facts fanciers and judgement-jockeys more suited to the

Old Vic than the Old Bailey, with their theatrical antics and last moment witnesses popping up out of thin air. And, *worst of all*, sentence-sellers contending their client came from a so-called disadvantaged background, and thereby could not be held responsible for their heinous crimes." Hyperventilating, he wiped his forehead. "Believe me, Roger, the list goes on and on and on."

"Have you finished *now*?" Roger cross-examined, his resonance a blend of irritation and amusement.

"Yep, rant over."

"Returning to *my* theme," he cautiously nominated. "I have only ever used a mobile phone for basic communications, but The Firm has issued me a brand-new Blackberry Curve 8520. My older-than-old Ericsson SH888 is archaic in comparison. I used to get a lot of heat about its age from those feral Essex stock traders I've told you about, such as Lawrence Springs."

"*Lawrence Springs*!" Steve gushed, simpering with disdain. "What kind of a half-assed name is that?"

"Yes, I know," Roger eagerly agreed. "I've always ascribed it to be a made-up moniker compensating for his real birth name, probably Arthur Sludge or suchlike. Anyway, he'd come into my *sanctum sanctorum*, pick up my Ericsson and say, 'You've really got a state-of-the-art, up to the minute piece of crap here, Roger.' Then he'd sarcastically enquire, 'Where does the coal go?'"

"Cheeky sod. You should have decked him," Steve proposed in his no-nonsense, kill the bastards while they sleep solution to all problems.

"You think so?"

"*Yeah*. You should have torn him another arsehole, and shoved his napper up it."

"Quite," Roger reluctantly acknowledged, never prone to using such drastic means to extract vengeance, but nevertheless in tune with the sentiment. "However, he's not the only person to mock my Ericsson. Miss Saunders, the old biddy living at the capacious house adjacent to High Elms Golf Course—"

"Who?" Steve interjected.

"Miss Saunders," he echoed. "You must know her. She looks like Barney Rubble out of *The Flintstones*."

"Oh yes, the cranky dear with the permanent five o'clock shadow. The one who makes the occasional, unwitting goof."

"How do you mean?"

"She was at last summer's village fete conversing with some other ladies on the organizing committee, when I happened to be waltzing by. They were talking about local councillor Dick Pennell, acting as emcee. In a fit of outlandish praise, Miss Saunders unashamedly voiced, 'Oh, I really like Dick,' spouting it with such conviction that I burst into laughter, but the indiscretion appeared lost on her confederate committee members. They just glared at me, as if I'd poured scorn on their precious organisational work."

"*I really like Dick*," Roger iterated, grinning broadly. "Holy crap, talk about the innocents mixing in with the unintentional-blooper-challenged."

"Quite."

"Anyway, Miss Saunders had a go at my Ericsson SH888 when I bumped into her in the village general store, saying a man in my position ought to be better equipped to communicate with others. She then produced a brand spanking new I-Phone from her handbag and proceeded to bore me to death demonstrating its usefulness. If Charlotte hadn't come along, I swear I'd have never got away."

"Right, so you're pleased with your Blackberry?"

"Oh yeah. Now I can jerk-off, if you'll forgive the phrase, with the best of them. This baby has got everything from multi-media functionality, a high-res camera, to Wi-Fi worldwide web services. Hell, I've even learnt to text, although that method of communication is alien to my sensibilities. It's also got more apps than you can shake a stick at, not that I'm going to waste my time on any of them." Tossing his noggin in the air he gibed, "it's such a powerful piece of kit, I could remotely control the *Starship Enterprise* with it."

"Jesus, Roger, next you'll be twitting, as in the Twittersphere!"

"Huh, more like the *twattosphere*; the cult of fake celebrity inhabited by a bunch of cyberspace gossip junkies getting high on made-up news and false accusations of sexual indiscretions."

"Ohh—" Steve leered provocatively. "Perhaps you have something to offer in the latter domain?"

"I shall neglect that unjustified innuendo. Besides, aren't you meant to be the doyen of erotic imprudence, constantly sniffing out the *demi-mode*?"

"Mmmm, maybe."

~ * ~

Irate solicitors and jerk off mobile devices apart, during early October several developments in the Fraser household tested Roger's receptiveness, and even his constitution.

Eldest daughter Wendy maintained a kind of experimental if not benign connection with her friend, Sly. Howbeit passive, it still gave her father qualms, Roger unable to come to terms with 'some Neanderthal' as he called him, 'grunting around his daughter.' If it went on, the Purdey would have to be retrieved from the loft, Roger ending up in jail for shooting him.

Continuing to play the voyeur with the opposite sex, James and his gang of teenage malcontents seemed to be locked into peeping Tom syndrome, but crucially, Roger's son had started to look into girls' mince pies instead of staring at their chests. He even talked to them subsequent to Roger giving him Queens English coaching lessons and exercises in ocular movement self-control, all in an attempt to improve his image with Wendy's friends, and, the gorgeous Michelle, a near neighbour's freshly graduated daughter, transfixing James with her every bodily movement whenever she came anywhere near the Fraser's house.

Updating her TV game show contestants' disciplinarian regime, especially for her version of *The Weakest Link*, youngest daughter Heather had hatched a scorched earth policy to permanently excommunicate failing stuffed animals from her enactments. As Roger had guessed, she press-ganged him into acting as referee for some of the more outrageous punishments she intended to inflict on recurrently offending and thereby deficient combatants. About to flick the control setting to cremate, he had rescued Miss Piggy and Kermit the Frog from a literal roasting when Heather imprisoned them in the gas cooker.

Moreover, these relatively trifling domestic disputes and arguments paled into insignificance compared to a gastronomic test. Much to Roger's chagrin, Charlotte had played a double-bluff, recommencing her fondness for veggie food from their happening event at Tunbridge Wells. Imposing the austere eating drill on the entire family, plus any guests happening to stumble over the Fraser house threshold seeking sustenance, it had become a daily endurance course, if not a blunt attack to the digestive tract.

Explaining to dining guests Gordon and Rachel Anderson, their recent New Age enlightenment became the culprit behind Charlotte's latest crusade, Roger further informed them mulch stew followed by root vegetable puree inhabited the menu at least once a day.

When Charlotte exited the dining room to fetch some New Age gluten-free bread, Gordon gazed down at the witches' brew placed before him, and crossed himself right to left and up and down. Flaring his nostrils, he then bent forward as if sensing for flesh-devouring creatures lurking beneath the surface of the concoction.

"You're not even a Catholic," Roger reminded him.

"I might go in for a quick conversion before consuming this," Gordon cited. "It looks similar to the kind of stuff Linda Blair fed on before she rotated her head 360 degrees in *The Exorcist*."

"*Gordon!*" Rachel remonstrated, her acid tone having Roger reckoning his associate Kappa Corinthian was in for some intense tongue lashing when the Andersons returned home. "Have the good grace to consume what Charlotte has lovingly blended for us."

"But it's bubbling," he protested. Taking off CJ from *The Rise and Fall of Reginald Perrin* he complained, "I didn't get where I am today by feasting on tadpole and terrapin soup."

Sniggering, Roger craved he had made the uncharitable but

perfectly punctilious comment.

"Everything all right?" Charlotte questioned, re-entering the dining room, having heard Rachel's raised voice.

Taking charge, Rachel assured, "oh yes, Charlotte darling. My, this is awfully interesting. What is it? I mean, what's in it?"

"It's er," Roger interposed, "best you don't know, Rachel." Sensing his wife's black lour, he quickly supplemented, "that'd spoil the surprise."

Gordon crossed himself afresh.

"Are you cultivating a religious twist, Gordon?" Charlotte ventured.

"No, I, er—" Gordon initiated then glanced across at Roger, his 'help me' sign flashing like a neon beacon all over his boat race.

"We, er," the equally flustered Roger took over, "we were just reminiscing about a childhood experience, weren't we Gordon?"

"Yes, that's it, a childhood experience," he confirmed, familiar with Charlotte's intolerance of anyone pouring cold water on her newly acquired modernist outlook, and not wishing to be the recipient of one of her, 'turn to stone you bastard' stares, accompanied by a very long lecture on the positives to be profited from espousing a politically correct attitude to all things in life.

Sensing an inappropriate tale on the near-horizon, Charlotte's scowl became a frown. "About religion?" she catechized, gaping at her husband. "You, and Gordon?"

"Yes," Roger enthused, his ultra-creative mind kicking in under potentially volatile repercussion conditions. "Trent Whorlow, a mutual friend of ours, and a left-footer."

"A left-footer," Rachel piped up. "What's that?"

"A Catholic," Gordon articulated.

"Quite," Roger concurred. "One fine summer's day, we were talking to Trent and some of his Catholic mates about football, when their priest Father Ignatius forged into view. Instantly, Trent and his affiliate cat-lights—" Hesitating, he noticed Rachel's curiosity flowering again. "That also means Catholics."

"Oh, I see," Gordon's wife accepted, knowing the penny should have dropped sooner.

Resuming, Roger detailed, "Trent and his pals immediately became subservient, bowing their heads as the priest approached. After exchanging a few words with all his junior parishioners, he wheeled to query Trent voicing, 'And who are your friends?' He replied, 'This is Roger and Gordon.' Surveying us up and down, the priest gabbled to me, 'And are you a good Catholic boy, Roger?' Well, of course being a smart-arse, I retorted, 'No, Father, I'm a Christian.'"

"That bout of impudence cost him six our fathers and twelve Hail Mary's," Gordon trumpeted.

Nodding his appreciation of Gordon's comeback, Roger then revolved to confront Rachel and Charlotte, detecting both remained stony-faced.

"Oh, Roger," Charlotte scorned, "you lacked diplomacy even when you were a boy."

"Yeah, he perpetually babbled indiscreet utterings," Gordon remembered.

"I told the story to help you out, Anderson," Roger yelped. "The *least* you can do is support me."

Suspicious of her husband's story-telling motives, Charlotte contested, "why did Gordon need to be helped out?"

"Because," Roger inaugurated, desperate not to let Charlotte cotton on to Gordon's revulsion of her New Age culinary delights. Then his mouth dried up.

"Yes?" she pressured, her phiz burgeoning into a glare.

Thirsting to be somewhere else, Rachel stared at the ceiling. Correspondingly, Gordon cleared his throat and cast a despairing gander at his friend.

"Because," Roger duplicated, then stopped, realising an invaluable liberty had arisen for a third party to buttress his gripe, bemoaning his wife's New Age menu could seriously affect the stomach lining and irretrievably damage the taste buds.

"*Well?*" Charlotte inveighed.

On the verge of telling her the truth, Roger's faculty for propriety and the need to uphold his conjugal rights surpassed his desire to confine the pureed Soya beans and curdled nutmegs diet to the dustbin forever.

"*Ohhh*—" Defeated yet again, he vigorously shook his head. "Great *balls* of fire! Pass me the cursed condiment."

Chapter 3: Halloween Horrors

Invited to a Halloween party at Tania Woodrow's house, the entire Fraser family had great expectations of the bash for weeks beforehand, Heather in particular expressly seeing the juncture as a forum to reconnoitre her dark side, and test out her developing people skills, meaning, get her own way with strangers.

One of the very few members of Charlotte's arty-farty crowd Roger genuinely cherished, he beheld Tania to be tremendous fun, a good conversationalist and unlike so many of his wife's cultural elitist friends, hadn't got her noodle all the way up her own rectum, trying to be politically correct. God knows what had attracted her to a trendy arts and crafts course at Orpington Technical College, Roger often cerebrated. Judging by her persona, she'd be more suited to running a gaming den than finding commonality of purpose with the clay and paint set. Even better, her husband Matthew fitted Roger's preferred type; excellent sense of humour, didn't bore about his job and enjoyed a few sherbets. He also thought Roger was wonderful, something else they had in common.

Everybody lured to the festivity from the tech took the ghosts and goblins celebration reverently, Charlotte fathoming her student chums sparing no expense to manufacture a golden impression, leaving other party goers gasping. Equivalently wanting to make a spectacular entrance and not be upstaged, she proclaimed the Frasers should deck themselves out in exotic Halloween costumes.

~ * ~

"I must say," Roger testified during final preparations for the bash in the lounge, "we do look like a real scary bunch."

"It takes one to know one," Charlotte retaliated, unable to resist a cheap joke at her husband's expense.

"If the occasion arises," he went on, ignoring the dig and reflecting his wife making jokes boded well for a pleasant evening's enjoyment, "I might use my own get-up to scare the living daylights out of those I come across on my, 'to be avenged against list.'"

"Just as long as you don't indulge in any of your robust world angles," Charlotte cautioned, her light temperament changing to watchful.

"Whatever do you mean?"

"I know you enjoy ribbing people you dislike at socials," she elucidated, "above all, when you've had too much to drink and you disagree with their political opinions."

"It's just part of the cut and thrust of everyday social intercourse, darling."

Glaring at him she whined, "and *don't* use that phrase in close proximity to my arts and crafts friends."

"What, 'social intercourse'?"

"Yes, it sounds very vulgar."

"It's an entirely normal phrase to use when describing social interaction."

"There's another contentious one," she howled.

"What?"

"Social interaction. It can be misconstrued as well."

"To mean what?"

"The same as social intercourse."

"*Really*, Charlotte," Roger castigated. "Your friends have got lewd minds."

"Now don't do anything to embarrass me this evening, Roger," she instructed, her jocular voice upgrading to the matronly *modus operandi* she adopted before social soirees. "You know Tania has some special entertainment planned, and I don't want you getting into a sarcastic modulation and making disparaging comments."

"Disparaging comments," he innocently parroted. "You mean, this play they intend to enact might not be word perfect?"

Glowering, Charlotte then became passive. "Tania and those playing the parts have been working very hard to polish the performance," she promoted, glistening, and evidently in sell-mode Roger contemplated. Pouting, she regressed to her uncompromising disposition. "So, let's have no sniggers or catty remarks if it's not up to Drury Lane standard."

"Yes, my little nest of vipers," Roger whispered under his breath, unable to stop himself sliding into neo-*Fawlty Towers* lingo.

"What did you say?"

"Just establishing my undying commitment to be on my best behaviour, darling."

"Good." Pricking up her ears, she heralded, "I can hear the children coming down the stairs, so let's set a good example to them in terms of the conduct stakes."

"Your wish is my command," he condescendingly fended.

"Roger!" she admonished. "*Enough.*"

Sweeping into the lounge, Wendy led the Fraser junior Halloween brigade.

"How do I look, Mother?" she explored, searching for favourable feedback.

"*Oh*, darling," Charlotte settled, "absolutely fine."

"What about me, Mum?" James canvassed.

Raising her eyebrows at her son's manifestation, his mother verified, "spine-chilling."

"And me, Mummy?" Heather lastly chimed in.

"Even dressed in a horrific outfit," she bubbled, "you're still adorable."

"What's your take, Dad?" Wendy queried.

"Well," her father began with a very straight mug, "you all look positively hideous." Breaking into a vibrant smile he clarified, "in the nicest possible way of course."

"Yes," Charlotte endorsed, "I'm sure no one is going to upstage the Frasers when it comes to the Halloween garments department."

"Oh, Mother, you do look entrancing," Wendy opined. "I bet none of the other mums will look as good as you."

"Thank you, darling," she purred.

"Yes, I'll have to keep a tight sentinel on your mother this evening," Roger warned, winking at the children. "She's quite the fetching siren in that get-up."

Penetrating the utterly ravishing domain in a scarlet and black *Bewitched* raiment Elizabeth Montgomery would have been proud of, Charlotte glowed with contentment. Very short and exceedingly tight, it exposed her elegant, long, shapely legs and trim figure, sheer, twenty-denier, tan pantyhose and burgundy, spiked high-heel boots adding to the effect. Normally, her hemline finished just above the knee, but tonight's outfit neared the daring, barely covering her apple-shaped derriere; Roger recollecting, in spite of being just over forty and bearing three children, his wife still had the body of a twenty-year-old and the legs of a baby gazelle. Echoing bees around a honey pot, he foresaw men clustering around her, licking their lips.

Going conservative, Wendy had opted for a gothic bride ensemble. Now tied, at least platonically speaking to Sly, during dressing she told her mother she had by all accounts to be off the market.

James being James, he had been as outlandish in his attire as Charlotte allowed. Masquerading as a Hellraiser, replete with synthetic ghoulish mask, he told his family he'd not be taking any prisoners in simulated horror movie enactments.

Morphing into Medusa, dear, sweet, butter-wouldn't-melt Heather had her blonde curls made into serpents by her mother, and her optics shadowed with blues and greens to enhance the supernatural bring off. Earlier, she'd informed her parents that she intended to capitalise on her martinet skills to make sure she got a fair crack at the apple bobbing. If unfairly treated by competitors, she plotted to feign a little girl lost act to give her an advantage. Failing that, she'd turn them to pillars of stone with one twinkle of her Medusa stare.

Transforming himself into the very incarnation of Lord Lucifer, the master of the house had crossed out Lord Lucifer on his ensemble and emblazoned 'Lord Roger' across his chest. Apprising the rig suited both his garish joke telling skills and public perception of his professional status, Charlotte insisted the Devil did not reside in Hell, but instead, the Isle of Dogs financial district housed his lair, along with all the other fiends and depraved spirits.

"Do I look really malevolent?" James interrogated, blazing garishly and holding up a fake head in one hand, whilst drawing a plastic knife across its throat with the other, both dripping congealed imitation blood.

"You don't need a gaudy outfit to prove that, James," his mother specified. "The way you applauded those onlooker-requested best bits of *The Inbetweeners* Thursday night, would convince anybody of your potential for evil."

"Oh, *Mum*," he defended, his put-on villainous semblance cascading into disbelief. "It's just comedy, more coarse than black humour."

"I don't see the difference," Charlotte countered, hands on hips and plainly verging on taking the contention further, until Heather jumped in with her latest pearl.

"Anyone watching evil programmes," she announced in a hostile voice, "should be locked up and the key destroyed, especially if they are being nasty to animals."

Perplexed as to the proclivity of Heather's outburst, Roger rubbernecked his wife with a quizzical mien.

Shimmying her head, the *Bewitched* charmer expounded, "she's been scrutinising a documentary on Channel 4 about how a dead hippopotamus gets eaten by other animals, while the TV crew record it. Heather thought it evil."

"That's right, Mummy, humans should not get enjoyment out of seeing animals eat each other."

"I must say," Charlotte backed, "it did transpire as unfeeling and very macabre."

"That's right, Mummy," Heather pushed, "the film crew should be punished."

"Right, I see," Roger accepted, conjuring up visions of his own candidates to be punished for the iniquity they'd put on him.

Whilst edifying Heather's hostility to TV film crews, Charlotte had also been studying her husband's apparel. Vigilant as ever and already in policewoman mode, acting to ensure the Fraser family survived the gala without incurring any controversy, she advanced towards him.

"Roger." She pointed. "What's that you have on your lapel?"

A hanging taxman motif had been appended to her husband's Lord Lucifer rig.

"Ahh, it's my own individual accessory," he bragged.

"What?"

"It's a symbol of rebellion at odds with oppression."

"Roger, what on Earth are you on about?"

"I bought it from a street dealer, selling anti-capitalist stuff at Canada Square. Couldn't help but fall for this emblem of taxation revolt."

Leaning forward, Charlotte scrupulously audited the badge. "Is it meant to be a tax inspector hanging from red tape?"

"*Yes*," he jubilantly authenticated. "You have it in one. It will be fitting for the demonic nature of Halloween night, and I know many people at the jamboree will appreciate the irony."

"Hhmm, I see you're already getting into the spirit of the function."

"Yes, for once," he cheerily expressed, "I'm going to display my discontentment of the system in general and authority in particular."

"Are you going to blow up the Houses of Parliament like Guy Fawkes, Daddy?" Heather quizzed.

Picking her up, Roger kissed his youngest daughter on the cheek. "No, my little bundle of joy. I have reserved that delight for the 5th November."

Preserving a wicked gleam, he replaced Heather to the standing posture, then rotated his outstretched hands in a *Night of the Living Dead* facsimile before snapping into a grisly chuckle.

"You're very buoyant tonight, Dad," Wendy commended. "Anyone might think you'd won the National Lottery."

"Now you know I don't bet, Wendy, at least not on games of chance." Moving nearer to the gothic bride clad teenager, he explained, "earlier today, I got a call from Henry Jacques saying Gary Delaware will be visiting The Firm next week. That's why I feel quite effervescent."

"What's the significance?" Charlotte probed.

Twisting to address his wife Roger advised, "I used to work with Gary at J P Morgan Chase. Henry knows him as well."

"I still don't see why it has made you so happy."

"Gary and I had some rare old times together in our formative years, so it will be good to see him. He went to work for Chase in Manhattan over twenty years ago, but having taken a job with Studwick Harley, a private bank and a major player with The Firm, I got word he'd returned to England in May. He's coming to Canary Wharf to discuss some mutual business."

"So, I suppose," Charlotte suggested, a suspicious slant plastered into her lineaments, "you're going to relive some shared experiences with him?"

"Yes, and to use Wendy's word, it's put me in a very 'buoyant' mood."

"I trust it won't involve any shenanigans," Charlotte forewarned.

"*Shenanigans!*" he single-mindedly copied. "Why Charlotte, what do you take us for, a couple of immature, recently graduated, fly-by-night, *Sin City* congeneric characters, out to paint the town red?"

"Yes."

Chapter 4: A Poignant Play for Today

Drawing the short straw in the abstinence stakes, Charlotte drove the MPV from the Fraser's Hazelwood house to Well Hill, the location for the gory celebration. Pulling-up at traffic lights in Farnborough, the Fraser junior bloodsuckers proceeded to scare a brace of traffic wardens. Wandering back to 'Bastardo HQ', to use a Latin American term Roger had picked up on his trip to Guatemala, after a productive day slapping parking fines on motorists daring to park outside their own houses, they tarried startled as the MPV drew away, Roger acclaiming the kid's antics, and making a rude gesture at the despised agents of unwarranted law and order. Though incurring his wife's displeasure, not caring about the consequences, he threw caution to the wind, urging Charlotte to chill out and loosen up. For Roger, the brash but hugely enjoyable episode set the meter of his attitude for the evening.

Unusually warm for the autumn season, the MPV's passengers took advantage of the balmy night, tilting their heads upwards out of the windows to gain a better sight of the cloudless firmament above. Providing Charlotte with a running commentary of the wondrous starry constellations, they enabled her to jell together their vivid descriptions to form a representation of her family's source of fascination. Priming the Frasers for their impending Halloween party, the eerie passage through West Wood along Chelsfield Lane complemented the ambience of the sky spectacle.

Sparky and stimulated with excitement, on reaching their destination everybody anticipated estimable recreations to be offered by their hosts.

"I'm heading straight for the apple-bobbing," Heather pealed.

"I'm going to find Jenny and Rebecca," Wendy declared.

"What about you, James?" his mother grilled, ever cautious about her son's often debatable intentions.

"Oh, I'm sure Wendy's friends will keep me amused," he answered.

"Oh no they won't," Wendy blasted. "You're to steer clear of them. After you and your gang leered at them and my other friends during the garden party, they think you are all pornographic."

"*Pornographic*," Roger repeated. "Are you sure you are using the right word?"

"Yes. Roxanne Harrison saw Billy Swan taking pictures of us on his iPhone."

"Oh, I see," Roger acknowledged, narrowing his snoopers at James.

"Only a bit of fun, Dad," he assured, holding out his hands registering contrition. "Billy deleted the pics afterwards."

"Daddy," Heather softly cajoled.

"I know what's coming. You want to know what pornographic means."

"Yes."

Aloofly striding away from the MPV, he delegated, "your mother will tell you when we get home."

"*Roger*!" Charlotte blurted, miffed at the imposition.

Both hallmarks of the eve of All Saint's Day, candle lit Jack-o-lanterns made from scooped out pumpkins furnished the Woodrow's house porchway, and wispy gossamer over the doorway gave the illusion of ghostly fog. Playing up to his intolerant Lord Lucifer mantle, Roger boldly rapped the front door knocker. Moments later, a Michael Myers kindred spectre materialised out of the murky light complete with fake flashing blade to confront him. Lunging forward, Myers buried his knife above Roger's left-side clavicle, his victim taking the blow without flinching, knowing its rubbery edge to be harmless. Bouncing upwards into Lord Lucifer's hood, the blade tip ended halfway up his snout, making him produce a ghastly *"aarrgghhh"* holler.

"Roger…is that you?"

Straightaway, he identified Matthew Woodrow's voice.

"Yes, Matthew, it's definitely me," he evinced in a broken, shrill voice, ahead of removing the rubber blade from his hooter.

Taking him in, Matthew contended, "didn't recognise you in your devil's outfit. Most appropriate for someone from the financial services sector. After all, you're all pariahs now." Cackling at his own joke, he shook Roger's hand. "Don't take offence, I just couldn't resist, and it is open season on bankers anyway, isn't it?"

Unoffended by the swipe, Roger imparted a warm smile. "It's always open season on bankers." So used to his business sector being the butt of acidic buzz, it became an expectation from friends and foes alike. "And I know my wife agrees with your sentiments."

Emerging from the shadows, the *Bewitched* siren came into Matthew's perspective.

"Hello, Charlotte," he purred. "My, you *do* look captivating." Turning to the more junior Frasers, he greeted, "hello, young ones. Come to bob some apples and tell some bloodcurdling stories?"

"Hello, Matthew," Charlotte reciprocated. "I see you're in character already."

"Yes, the festivity has been in play for a few hours already, so I'm more Michael Myers than Matthew Woodrow. Wait until you see Tania, she looks fantastic in her Midnight Mistress rig."

As the Frasers piled into the Halloween den behind Matthew, he took a slash at a few unsuspecting bystanders dressed as the Minister of Death, Midnight Vampira and the Phantom of the Opera. Seeing Charlotte advancing, Midnight Vampira said "hi," took her arm and whisked her into the dining room, lavishly laid out in the fashion of a medieval banqueting hall. *Obviously,* her husband conceptualised, *Charlotte's going to be dished out the latest, who's being doing it with who gossip from the arts and crafts class.* Beckoning to them, 'Roger and the young ones', as Matthew called the Fraser clan, followed him into the kitchen, a plethora of graverobbers and ghosts shrieking, gargling and rattling their chains at them, the junior Frasers responding in kind.

Greeting her latest guests, Tania swapped a few gregarious words about the Fraser's Halloween costumes and the night's amusements agenda.

"What have you done with Charlotte?" she polled.

"Oh, Midnight Vampira purloined her on the way in," Roger notified.

"*Midnight Vampira*," Tania retorted. "I wonder who she really is?"

"Charlotte seemed to know her, so I assumed she's one of the arts and crafts set."

"Jeepers, there's so many people here incognito, masquerading as their alter egos, or in disguise to avoid recognition." Furrowing her brow, she confessed, "I have no idea of their identity."

"Isn't that the whole notion of Halloween?"

Considering for a jiffy, she assigned, "yes, you're right. God knows who I've been talking to under the illusion they are someone I know, when in reality, Matthew has invited them."

"It's at least half the fun of these wingdings. You could be making overtures towards a delectable chanteuse decked out in a revealing getup, only to find when she removes her mask, she's your best friend's wife, or even graver, your own wife!"

Tania glared. "You haven't done that have you, Roger?"

"Good god, *no*. If I had, you'd have attended my funeral long ago."

"Charlotte still keeps you on your toes then?"

"My dear Tania, that is such an understatement as to be facile without contradiction. I can confidently predict, as for any other social event, at some stage this evening my fractious wife will round on me for the most insignificant of misdemeanours. She might have latterly adopted a liberal philosophy, but she has retained a keen taste for correctitude." Leaning into her he confided, "I sometimes muse she has puritan blood and her ancestry incorporates Witchfinder General associations."

"Could be pretty useful at a Halloween carnival."

"Quite, but I wouldn't test it. You might be disturbed by what her investigations expose."

"Oh, Roger, you make Charlotte sound like Sybil Fawlty."

"Funny you mentioning that."

~ * ~

Refreshments and Halloween themed bits and bobs were dispensed to Roger and the young ones by Matthew, his knife frequently coming into play to fend off other vampires keen to make the Frasers their artificial quarry.

Whilst Roger talked to Matthew, Heather joined more sub-ten-year-olds at the apple bobbing, Wendy and James scuttling off in search of young adults to fill their comfort zone.

"Memorable show," Roger enthused. "And Tania looks really spectacular in her Midnight Mistress garb."

"Yes, she does. We decided if we were going to have a Halloween bop, it'd be one to remember. We went to one her sister trialled a few years ago. It never really took off and ended up as a damp squib. So, intending to make this fandango go with a bang, we learnt from the experiment. By the way, how's the punch?"

"Oh, mouth-watering," Roger certified. "It must be 1,000 percent proof. I could gorge on it all night," he disclosed, gawking towards the dining room and pondering *what's keeping Charlotte so long? The goings-on at the tech must be more fruity than usual*, his wife shocked by whatever Vampira told her, and thereby needing to drill down into the controversy, just to make sure it didn't comprise any transgressions by her immediate friend set, or god forbid, her own family members.

"It's an old recipe we got from one of the neighbours…very rich, very tasty."

"What, the neighbours or the punch?"

"As it happens, both, dear boy. He's a big cheese in the software business, and she's chief accountant at Pearson and Gower."

"The package holiday outfit for senior citizens?"

"Yes."

"Weren't they done for granny exploitation?"

"Indeed they were."

"A scam to do with charging for nursing facilities?"

"Mmmm. Pearson and Gower got too greedy maximising profits and minimising costs by employing nursing staff from Eastern Europe not conversant in English. One poor old dear got allotted heavy-duty laxative, when she really requisitioned indigestion tablets. She spent most of her Rhodes holiday enthroned on a commode, unable to move for fear of flooding her room with excrement."

"Yes, that's it," Roger endorsed. "Does make the blood curdle, doesn't it?"

"It does. We'll all have to be very careful of whom we trust when we're in our dotage."

"Quite."

Examining Roger, just as Charlotte had done at home, Matthew became fixated by his vestment personalisation.

"You're not going to make a remark about my hanging taxman motif, are you?" Roger catechized.

"No, I noticed it when you arrived. Very good, incidentally, we should all be wearing them."

Peeking down at his chest, Roger solicited, "what is it then?"

"'Lord Roger'," Matthew verbalised, persisting his exploration and signifying to the lettering Fraser had annexed to his livery. "Hhmm, does it mean, you are Lord of rogering?"

"I'd love to imagine I used to be, but alas, my conquests have been far and few between."

"Not many notches on the bedpost then?"

"Barely a handful."

"Ohh, Roger." Encoring his supervision, Matthew drilled, "a handsome, well-built, alpha male like you ought to have logged scores of bedpost notches, before you were twenty."

"Well, I headed for the land of plenty," Roger bemoaned, "but then I met Charlotte."

"I bet your horizontal samba hit-rate improved then, didn't it?"

"Oohhh yeeaaahhh," he dreamily frothed. "She was, and still is, some kind of woman in that department."

"*Really*!"

"Nothing short of a miracle happens once the bedroom door shuts. She becomes the classic *femme fatale*, pandering to my every need."

Exhilarated by the disclosure, Matthew begged, "tell me more."

"You've heard too much already!"

"Crikey," he uttered. "I never realised before tonight what outstanding legs she has."

"Yep. They've always been one of her best features."

"They just go on and on and on."

Still drifting vacantly, the lord of *soi-disant* extensive and varied rogering agreed. "I know."

"Well, she really looks sensational. You don't want to let her stray too far from your side," he recommended, "or one of these young bucks will be after her."

"*Jesum crow*. She'd eat them alive."

"Yeah, but what a way to go," Matthew crooned then mooned, making Roger give his pal a sideways ogle.

Protracting their chat, at the same time Roger scanned the horizon scoping for anyone he knew, or at least fancied he knew. Very difficult to be certain with costumes disguising organic features. Then his gaze fell on someone more recognisable to him.

"Is that Martin Gayle I can see in the garden?" he broached.

"Yes, it is," his host settled. Slapping his forehead, the light came on. "Of course, you're both with Kappa Corinthians."

"I didn't know you knew Martin."

"I don't really. His wife Claudette is pally with Tania."

"Ahh, I see. Wheels within wheels making for an ever-shrinking world."

"Very prophetic, Roger, sorry, Lord Lucifer."

"It's 'Lord Roger' actually," he gleefully corrected. "Yes, sporadically I dovetail into graphic metaphors. I promise it won't happen again this evening."

Continuing to gawk in Martin's direction, as fortune had it, his Kappa Corinthian cohort saw Roger and waved, beckoning him into the garden.

"My club captain needs me," Roger avouched. "Do you mind if I exchange a few words with Martin?"

"Not in the least, my dear fellow. I have to go and mingle anyway, well, cut some more flesh with my rubber blade. But before we part, can I ask you a personal question?"

"Seventeen inches."

"What?"

"You were going to ask, what's the length of my todger."

"What! *No*. Besides, it's not seventeen inches."

"How do you know?"

"Well…"

"Ahh." Raising a cautionary finger Roger entreated, "best not to table personal matters. They could lead to the unexpected. Wouldn't you agree?"

"I still say your appendage is not seventeen inches."

Roger began to release his belt buckle.

Conservatively pushing his hands up, Matthew bleated, "okay, okay…seventeen inches."

"See, I knew you'd agree."

~ * ~

"Martin," hailed a fast approaching Roger, "I just about recognised you through your Red Devil attire."

"Hello, Roger," he interchanged with his usual convivial smile. "I ventured you'd be at this fling. I see you're the devil as well."

"Lord Lucifer, actually, well, I'm re-branding it as 'Lord Roger.'"

"Oh, do forgive the slur."

"Ha, ha, only kidding."

"I adore the hanging tax inspector," Martin flattered, his tribute dripping in irony as he betokened the dangling social menace. "Certainly gets my vote."

"Thanks. I rationalised it'd draw more admiring comments, but apart from Matthew, you're the only person to even distinguish it. However, the night is young, so maybe some poor napping businessman, stung with a tax bill as big as Manhattan, will see it and applaud loudly."

"More the case, it will probably have him in tears."

"Yes, you could be right. I've had to comfort several smash-and-grab tax casualties over the years. It's always pitiful watching them whimper, then as realisation sets in, they concoct ways to extract revenge."

"That reminds me," Martin hatched, "do you recollect when we played the Inland Revenue Office at Carshalton in 1997?"

"Indeed, I do. Still at the height of my peak performance, I played right wing."

"You got a quartet of tries, didn't you?"

"Yes," Lord Roger validated, pride jingling in his modulation. "Sadly, it ended up as the ultimate match I scored more than two tries in. But my enduring imprint of the encounter is the Kappa Corinthians boiler house taking no prisoners in the scrums."

"And every tackle made akin to a life or death decision," Martin augmented.

"Hhmm, I recall a number of our players having antipathy against the Inland Revenue went into a Billy Two Rivers Mohican-style war dance in the dressing room before kick-off shouting, 'I'm gonna cut me out a tax inspector's liver.'"

"Yes, a lot of blood on the pitch during that faceoff."

"And most of it spirting as tax inspector red."

"Happy days."

"Oh, the best."

"Anyway," Martin readied, laying a protective mitt on Lord Roger's shoulder, "you do realise, we must be on our best behaviour this evening?"

"I do, no rugby club japes here…I suppose."

"Stiff upper lip tonight, Roger," his club captain half-ordered. "Let's show these people, er ghouls, there's more to rugby players than beer and barneys. Besides, no doubt Charlotte has apprised you to conduct yourself properly in the presence of the arty farty set, like Claudette has me?"

"Oh yes," he fixed, resigned to a prank-free evening. "I've been pre-warned not to be disparaging about this play Tania has arranged for our delectation."

"Me too."

"By the way, I understand the common factor is Tania knows Claudette and Charlotte."

"Yes, I only found out when Claudette referenced the connection during our journey to Well Hill."

"Where is Claudette?"

"Ahh, she's actually part of the pageant."

"Mother of god," Lord Roger babbled, surmising he might have put his foot in it.

"Relax, Roger," Martin petitioned. "I'm just as sceptical and got a roasting for it earlier on. Claudette is in the throes of finalising for this ripping yarn they're going to enact. She co-produced the play and is acting as prompter. How about Charlotte. Where is she?"

"Midnight Vampira waylaid my darling wife on our way in. Someone from the tech I surmised. Anyway, enough of the hum-drum of the amateur dramatics group." Sheepishly flexing his cheek muscles, he propositioned, "may I pose a problematic enquiry?"

"Go ahead."

Issuing him a philosophical stare, Roger posed, "do you ever get the feeling you're not in control of your own destiny?"

"Specifically?"

"I mean, do things come at you out of nowhere, you have no control over, albeit how much you try to evade them?"

"Specifically?"

"Do effects keep on happening, making a massive dent in your well laid out plans?"

"Specifically?"

"Okay." Roger took a deep breath. "Someone once told me, 'If you want to keep your sanity, don't let the world run you.'"

"Got it. You mean, despite your best endeavours, domestic occurrences tripping you up?"

"I do. You see—" Plainly perturbed by the perspicacity, his top lip curled slightly. "In the main, I'm unassailable in the workplace. I'm calm and collected, the epitome of imperturbable serenity. Conversely, often I flounder around in household situations, travailing to find an anchor point to manage the hoary dispute creeping up on me, through no fault, or at least little fault of my own." He puckered his lips as if craving understanding. "Sound familiar?"

"No."

"*What*!"

"I'm kidding. It resonates, and it happens to me, but I must say, not with the regularity it hits you."

"Right." Opening his hands, a subdued lour spread across his kisser. "Maybe I'm just unlucky?"

"Maybe you just unwittingly put yourself in the firing line?"

"Hhmm, maybe, but it does suggest a lack of vision and forethought."

"True. You need to refine your look-over-the-horizon capability."

"Sense what's coming," he interpreted, "and take evasive action before the beast fastens its jaws onto my arse?"

"Precisely."

Rocking on his heels, Roger emanated a relieved dial. "Okay, my captain, I'll try to enhance my perceptive powers."

"That's the spirit."

"Thanks." Grinning, he queried, "reverting to expected social protocol, what have you been up to this week?"

"Ohh—" Martin's countenance spouted compunction. "I landed early this morning, after a business trip to the West Coast."

Formerly Marconi Avionics at Rochester, Martin's sales manager role for BAE Systems had made him into a latter-day Alan Whicker, globetrotting around five continents in pursuit of customers to buy the company's military defence wares.

"Been selling your ultra-advanced, black boxes to the septics?" Roger gibed.

"Yes, did some good business, but as usual, *huh*—" He cracked. "Los Angeles threw up some weird people."

"How?"

"Oh, flaky, obtuse we'd call it, larger-than-life oddballs and misfits."

"Ahh, I know what you mean. The Firm has a branch in San Fran. Some of the barnstormers and clowns I've met from that neck of the woods are pure Hollywood, by way of they seem to be acting out their lives as dysfunctional extras in some dopey septic soap opera."

"Peculiar, you referring to Hollywood," Martin opined, his simper mushrooming. "Let me tell you what happened."

"Please, I sense this could have real entertainment value."

"Well, Los Angeles is still reasonably hot during mid-autumn, so after my business with Boeing, heretofore the Douglas Aircraft Company, at Long Beach. I went to my room at the Marina del Rey Marriott, dumped my laptop, took off my jacket and headed for the bar where I gorged on a cold Michelob. You get the picture?"

"Sure. Marina del Rey is the flake capital of California - Beverley Hillbillies, surfing Casanovas, eccentric rock stars—" Delaying, he stepped closer, then in a pseudo-derisive inflection attached, "and limey businessmen."

"Quite." Martin sanctioned, not reproaching Roger's gentle dig. "Here's what happened. Minding my own business, I sipped on my Michelob. The guy on the next bar stool says, 'Say buddy, are you an airline pilot?' Perplexed, I challenged, 'What makes you think I'm an airline pilot?' He appraised me from head to foot then rejoindered, 'Well you sure as hell look like an airline pilot, and you're dressed like an airline pilot in those black slacks, white shirt and black tie.'"

"Sounds like a top-of-the-pile flake," Roger assessed.

"For sure. So, this goes on for about fifteen minutes, with me admitting my attire including the slacks, as the septics call them, could be mistaken for an airline pilots' rig. But irrespective of what I said, I couldn't convince the guy I wasn't an airline pilot. Finally, in desperation I hauled out my BAE Systems business card and presented it to him. 'There,' I pleadingly coaxed, 'Martin Gayle - Sales Manager BAE Systems.' Swaying on his stool to take a broader peek at me, he rubbed his chin with his free hand, the other hand permanently wrapped around his beer glass, then with disbelief still stamped into his lineaments, he says, 'Well are you an airline pilot in your spare time?'"

"Hah, ha, ha," Roger cackled. "I envisioned things agnate to that only happened to me."

"Yes, so did I…but, it wasn't the end of it."

"How?"

"The dude then asks me, 'What part of Australia do you come from?' Exasperated, I squawked, 'What makes you think I'm an Australian?' 'Your accent,' he says. Bewildered, I told him I was pure-bred English. Zanily gazing at me, he yowls, 'Well why are you speaking with an Australian accent.'"

"Beggar's belief."

"Absolutely, not even when I showed him my passport did he believe me, and I had the devil's own job getting away from him."

"Astonishing. What happened next?"

"The following day also proved to be a boiler. I'd been with Lockheed Martin at the Burbank skunk works where the F-22 Raptor stealth fighter is made. Again, subsequent to the business, I dumped my laptop and jacket in my Marriott room and ambled to the bar, being careful to make sure the guy from the previous day did not dawdle about. So, there I am, sat on a stool at the bar sipping my ice-cold Michelob, happy no one conceives I'm an airline pilot."

"Manifestly, it's best not to take any risks in septic city central," Roger crooned, as if he too had experience of Marina del Rey's legendary weirdos.

"Quite. Anyway, a group of eight people were clustered around a large table, just a few feet from the bar. I figured from their elated conversation they were TV or film people celebrating having just been awarded parts in a movie. Then a fella from this group came to the bar to make an order. Cognizant I'd overheard their boisterous palaver, he sat on the bar stool next to me and prattled, 'Say buddy, are you in the film business as well?' Staring blankly, pondering I might be caught in another instance of misleading career identity, I replied, 'No, I'm an Australian airline pilot.'"

"Golly gosh, ho, ho, ho," Roger chortled. "Superb, Martin. Wish I'd been there. But your contretemps is not surprising. The City of the Angels is overpopulated with brain-cell-deficient, freakish, whack jobs."

~ * ~

After gobbling down more of Matthew's fabulous punch, Lord Roger moved on from his ebullient Kappa Corinthians captain to seek out Heather, finding her vying for supremacy with a group of similarly rowdy youngsters at the apple bobbing in the kitchen. Observing them trying in vain to get their still-developing mouths around Granny Smiths steadfastly refusing to co-operate and slipping aside when they made contact, had him snickering at the display. Seeing her father, Heather waved him over, obviously keen to get him involved in the maddening activity.

"Feasting on fruit, Heather?"

"Daddy, I'm not Heather this evening," she admonished. "I'm Medusa."

"Okay, feasting on fruit, Medusa?"

"Yes, Lord Lucifer. Have a go."

Making a disgruntled aspect, he muttered, "do I have to?"

"Yes."

Honestly, Roger meditated, *if it's not Charlotte or Wendy telling me what to do, it's my youngest daughter. Women are explicitly the bane of my life, but I do love them.*

"Very well," he conceded.

Kneeling over the inflatable paddling pool, his north and south unlocked, he nosed onwards, chasing a chosen apple, but no matter how he rearranged his mouth, the blessed thing failed to find its way between his jaws. Inevitably, much to the amusement of the gaggle of small children witnessing the woeful exhibition, he ended up soaking his Lord Lucifer cloak and hood. Persevering, more through luck than judgment, he fastened onto the side of a target he'd managed to wedge up along the side of the pool. Assaying to take a bite, he ended up with more lukewarm water down his throat than apple.

"You're doing it all *wrong*, Lord Lucifer," Heather informed as an apple segment got stuck to the roof of his mouth and he spluttered out a mouthful of water attempting to remove it.

"Well if you're so clever, Heather," he squealed, "you have a go."

"*Medusa*," she insisted.

"Medusa," he duplicated.

"Found your natural intellectual level, Roger?" he heard someone say.

Still on his hands and knees, gawking up he saw Tania goggling down at him.

"Yes, thank you, Tania," he blathered, tepid water dripping from his upper body garments as he affected the vertical, just in time to see Charlotte coming his way with Midnight Vampira, the creeper purloining his wife on their way in. "Oh, no, that's all I need."

Discovering her husband drenched above the waistline, Charlotte broke into giggles. "Oh, Roger, you're all wet."

"Don't *you* start," he whooped, as a stray piece of apple leapt from his mouth.

Other ghouls, ghosts and goblins gathered in the apple bobbing area, many keen to have a go and show Roger their winning techniques. Rubbernecking in wonderment, he saw Meat Man, Alien Invasion and Batwing Vampire demonstrate apple bobbing made as easy as falling off a log. With each waterless-soaking success, his embarrassment heightened.

Then, a large woman dressed as Bleeding Beauty got a bit too greedy trying to consume an even larger apple in one. Swallowing as she rose to her feet exultant with triumph, her respiratory apparatus refused to accept the stomach-bound sphere. Turning purple, it took onlookers a while to realise she was choking.

"Somebody *do* something," Tania shrieked, panic emblazoned across her mush. "The last thing we need at a Halloween party is death by asphyxiation."

Coming to the rescue, a Crypt Crawler impersonator slapped Bleeding Beauty in the middle of her dorsum repeatedly to relieve her blockage. Regrettably, it just resulted in her complexion transforming from purple to blue.

Taking in the multi-coloured, choking woman, Roger quipped, "ooohh, very pretty."

Coming to the rescue, the Woodrow's neighbour Ben Andrews dressed as Disco Dracula claimed command. Forcing Bleeding Beauty's napper over her stomach he instructed her to cough, but the step merely swelled up her pop-art, day glo cheeks like a balloon, though Roger calculated it more resembled Auric Goldfinger being sucked out of a de-pressurised aircraft, after fighting with James Bond in the penultimate scene from *Goldfinger*.

In the end, a Grandpa Munster tribute act intervened, dispensing the Heimlich manoeuvre. After several compression attempts making Bleeding Beauty's eyes bulge, matching those of the dastardly foreign agent in *Stingray*, out popped the offending apple, its terminal velocity carrying it across the apple-bobbing zone straight into Madame de Sade-attired Cynthia Stewart's ear. Yelping, Madame fell rearward, elbowing Teresa Thomson masquerading as Malice in Horrorland in the ear, and pushing her headlong into the inflatable paddling pool.

Chortling, Roger whirled to tease Tania and Charlotte. "Easy when you know how, isn't it!"

~ * ~

With Heather and the other young children still in hysterics at the Bleeding Beauty mishap, Charlotte and Roger exited the planet-apple battle zone in search of Wendy and James, the teenager hunt eventually finding their offspring in the lounge. Redecorated in a London Dungeon likeness, it had been embellished with plastic chains, devices of torture and even a simulated prisoner cell, all in preparation for those wanting to avalanche away from the Halloween theme and indulge in group S&M activities, replete with PVC clad mistress domination. *Interesting*, Roger deliberated, *I must check out this attraction later in the evening.*

"Ahh, there you are," Charlotte pealed. "Enjoying the bash?"

"Even better than I imagined," James enthused.

"What about you, Wendy?" Roger probed.

"My guise really needed to be more daring," she admitted. "Jenny Jeffries has come as a Hocus Pocus Hottie and Rebecca Sumner as Immortal Mistress. In comparison, my Gothic Bride outfit is drab." Holding out the sides of the gown, she emphasised the disparity.

Just about to say, 'It's fine, darling,' as Roger's lips commenced moving, Jenny and Rebecca bounded into the London Dungeon, tittering like deranged and inebriated budgerigars. *If I didn't know they were seventeen*, Roger considered, *irrefutably, they'd pass for at least twenty-one in those revealing outfits.*

Totally immobilised, James drooled over the scantily clad young mantraps, his chin nearly hitting his knee as he originated a comparable statue pose, barely able to breathe, much less speak.

Clocking his son's languor, Roger warbled, "oh no, not another trance-inducing zombie incident."

"Hello, Mister Fraser," Rebecca silkily jawed, doubling for a preying Venus flytrap, as he came across her sight line.

Attending his extra-curricular business studies evening sessions at Wendy's school, Chelsfield Grammar, the trope of her suggestive cavorting and membership of the vixen pack disrupting the seminars with their sexual innuendo routines still remained fresh in his memory.

"Hello, Rebecca," he guardedly reciprocated.

"So, you're the famous Mister Fraser," Jenny chirped. "I've heard a lot about you." Espying Missus Fraser had adopted an overbearing demeanour, she broke off into formality. "Er, Rebecca says you're a good teacher."

Whilst not taking A-level business studies herself, chronicled into fable rather than fact, the Fraser folklore had gone feral around the lower sixth form, Roger's inability to prevent the girls funnelling his court into a forum for lewd and lascivious tomfoolery, flying about senior student circles faster than a Lamborghini Aventador on rocket fuel.

Using adult concern to steer around the evening class saga, Roger lectured, "I credit you've not been drinking alcohol, girls."

Holding her hand to her mouth, Rebecca guffawed, almost bringing up most of the punch she had gobbled down. "No, not us, Mister Fraser," she affirmed, smirking at her evenly playful companion. "We're *good* little girls."

Collapsing into giggles, the postulated miscreants became delirious with joy, their intoxicated movements shifting fastenings on their costumes, exposing more flesh than they realised. Regaining a measure of decorum, Rebecca grabbed Wendy's arm and the threesome departed the dungeon for the kitchen, James' blinkers slavishly tracking each step his sister's friends took. Lifting his son's lower jaw, Roger replaced it into the mouth shut position. Still totally transfixed by the two alluring young ladies, he doubted James even noticed. *So much for his,* 'I will talk to girls' *regime,* Roger reflected.

"What's *that* all about?" Charlotte demanded to know.

"Nothing, darling," Roger verified. "Just girls being girls."

Squinting at him, his wife emanated a preachy warning. She had her suspicions about the extracurricular school initiative, notwithstanding, nothing happened apart from Roger being baited, as Wendy could confirm. Regardless, in Charlotte's hyperactive mindset, even mild mistrust warranted careful dissection, engendering just as much pain to her husband as an in-coming tackle from an eighteen-stone prop forward.

This could get tricky, Roger anticipated. *Time for an exit strategy.*
Smartly spinning on his heels, or perhaps as Roger would say,

Lord Lucifer's hooves, his vision fell on a well-known, if not disconcerting, spook. "Oh...isn't that your chum Brigit, dressed as Cruella de Ville?"

Sustaining her intimidating glow, Charlotte made a mental note to revisit the topic, then twisted around to absorb her friend. "Brigit," she spouted, her mouth gaping wide at the effusive extravaganza before her. "Is that really you?"

"Or is it the *real* Cruella de Ville?" Roger whispered under his breath.

"Hello, Charlotte. Yes, categorically it's me." Taking her in, she praised, "oh, you do look ravishing." Then giving Lord Lucifer a critical gleam, her top lip curled as she wittered, "hello, Roger," the acid virtually leaping off her tongue.

"Brigit," he icily traded. "Are you well?"

She eyed him circumspectly, as if discrediting the sincerity of the enquiry. "As it happens, I've not been feeling at all well of late."

"Nothing trivial I hope," he murmured as Charlotte said "hi" to a passing troll.

"*Pardon*!" Brigit retorted in a rasping upper register.

Inventing on the hop, one of his better talents during social intercourse as he called it, he rendered, "I asked if you have recovered from your recent outdoor bath?"

'A real Miss Shagnasty, Germaine Greer and Diane Abbott rolled into one', as comrade Kappa Corinthian Steve Hunt once caricatured, Brigit Hammond had hob-nobbed at the Fraser's summer garden party a few months earlier. As one of the unfortunate bystanders inadvertently caught up in the water wars melee, she had got a proper drenching as hostilities erupted. Seeing her name on the guest list, Roger had joked to Charlotte, 'I'll put some garlic over the front door,' only to receive the inevitable turgid response from his wife. Often misconceived by those not sensitive to her unique brand of communication, she shot back Brigit was a lovely person, Roger responding, 'So was Stalin', only to suffer more haranguing from his wife's whiplash tongue.

Breaking into a reproving frown, Cruella vented, "yes...thank

42

you," a touch more vitriol in her return. "And I see you've had an unaccustomed rendezvous with H2O yourself."

"Yes," Lord Lucifer confessed. "Got a dousing apple bobbing."

"*Good*," she blurted, emitting a smile of complete satisfaction.

Sarky bitch, Roger brooded, as an involuntary counter-smile covered his physiognomy.

By virtue of his wife's totally unfounded suspicions about the business studies evening sessions, he felt the need to store up some brownie points, hence his pleasant body language with Cruella. Erstwhile, he had found it best to err on the safe side when it came to the possibility of incurring Charlotte's disfavour in all contentious affairs. To deflect potential wrath and stay out of the doghouse, he had assimilated any good book entries lessoned the tongue lashing and subsequent penance.

Decidedly on the dark side of puritanical, and disliked by all her friend's husbands and boyfriends, Brigit Hammond had experienced bad karma with the financial services industry, blaming the chance fate exclusively on Roger, albeit she had never had any contacts with investment banks, let alone The Firm. As the septics' say, she seemed to constantly have a bug up her ass, though the reason, or more probably, multiple reasons behind her rectal aggravation, eluded Roger and others she treated with consummate disdain.

Intrinsically sensing his wife expected him to re-build bridges with her friend, he decided to furnish the olive branch and be civil with the shrew. "Did you enjoy the food at our garden party, Brigit?"

"Oh, Charlotte's dishes were fine," she declared, rotating to and fro about her hips, her chin smugly thrust forward, patently attempting to browbeat him. "But yet again, you over-cooked the meat, and it had little flavour."

First a sarky bitch, now a cheeky blaggard, Roger reviewed. *Just because you got a soaking, doesn't give you the right to impugn my chef skills.*

Fancying herself as a bit of a culinary expert, Brigit had carped on about Roger's barbecued delights in the past. Developing into the fountain of pretty much perpetual friction, not insomuch his meat offerings were in any way uneatable, nonetheless, Brigit used it as a superficial vehicle to offend him. Rebutting in a rash of unadulterated abandon, with Charlotte out of earshot, Roger had articulated tongue-in-cheek, 'Cooking requires no intelligence. Were it not so, women would be no good at it.' Purposely designed to infuriate Brigit, she had let loose with a tirade of misandry that bounced off Roger without him incurring the slightest psychological mark.

Fuming at her latest insult, and in defiance of the sure knowledge he'd get lambasted for his impudence when the Frasers went home, he blabbed, "*look* Fanny Craddock, if I had known you wanted *cordon bleu* standard, I'd have entreated Gordon Ramsey to cook for us."

"No need to take offence, Roger," she cattily whined. "Charlotte, my dear, you really ought to put your husband on a leash." Sending another perishing burn in his direction, she demanded, "and have him frequent some temper control councils."

Glaring at Cruella, he wanted to borrow his wife's x-ray vision so he could melt her marshmallow spiky visage and watch her dissolve into nothingness as he howled with gladness.

Clearing her throat in an attempt to diffuse the fast-growing conflict, Charlotte tattled, "changing the subject, what have you been doing this week, Brigit?"

Taking the invite to pontificate, she charged headlong into a tedious, dull and pretentious set of accounts regarding her arts and crafts activities, and her exhaustive trials to get her horse, Muffy, to behave himself in public. Apparently in the habit of taking a dump on car bonnets when Brigit trotted around the lanes of Kent County, Muffy had provoked endless embarrassment for her. During the momentous exposition, every detail became a paramount stop-press item, not even *Newsnight* stalwart Jeremy Paxman could subdivide into finer detail.

Dovetailing into numbness with tedium, the seconds passed, resembling centuries for Roger, the minutes approximating entire epochs of life development, Brigit the instant cure for chronic insomnia. She could bore for England. Ultimately, she got down to the vinegar strokes with a half-assed story about some youth jumping on her car trailer.

"What did you do?" Charlotte surveyed.

"*Ohh*, I tossed him off," Cruella stipulated with vigour.

Chuckling at the double entendre, Roger blustered, "oh yes. Did he enjoy it?"

"Roger!" exclaimed his wife, giving him a dig in the ribs.

Suddenly a fly had the impertinence to traverse around Brigit's head. Wafting her hands at the seed of her annoyance, she trumpeted, "I hate anything that buzzes."

"Does that encompass electric dildos?" Roger mumbled.

"What was that?"

Spurred on with conviction brought about by resistance, he reiterated, "I said—"

Before he could get more out, Charlotte interceded with another rapier dig to his ribs, ensuring Brigit floated free from hearing the provocative question, and leaving her husband smarting.

Observing from the wings, when Lord Roger excused himself from the fray and moved off to get some fresh air, Matthew Woodrow joined him.

"I must say, Roger, you took a beating there."

"Yes, it's a perennial punishment when I meet Brigit 'Cruella' Hammond. Dreadful woman."

"I'm thinking under the auspices of Halloween, its witchcraft."

"Holy kamoly, more like *bitchcraft*."

"For sure."

"To use a quaint Royal Cheshire phrase, she wants her arse feeling. It'd make her less objectionable and more subservient."

"Oh, Roger—" He roared. "You do come out with them."

"To say she has an extremely large mouth is an understatement."

"Is it true, she once opened it so wide, a passing leaping bullfrog landed on her meaty tongue?"

"Maybe."

Pondering, Matthew conjectured, "I wonder if she spat out or swallowed the frog."

"Knowing Miss Shagnasty, she probably crunched the critter then swallowed it whole!"

~ * ~

After the Frasers engaged in further acts of social intercourse, Roger finding the lovely phrase guaranteeing to bring the ladies out in a hot flush, if expressed beside them, the evening's headline undertaking at long last loomed, a play to be performed by members of Charlotte's arts and crafts group. Enthralled with anticipation, most partygoers amassed in the large hallway and stairwell, the sweeping area having been converted into a mini-stage, with seats laid out in a U-shape to accommodate the audience.

"Where's Wendy, James?" his mother grilled.

"She's horsing around with Jenny and Rebecca," he signed. Then in a lowered voice, appended to no one in particular, "wish I was horsing around with Jenny and Rebecca."

Hearing the melancholy plea, his father smiled. "Don't fret, James. Your time will come with the girls."

"*Phooey*," Charlotte griped. "He'll have to smarten up his ideas for it to happen."

Discouraged, James transfigured into a glum aspect.

"Don't worry, son," Roger urged. "Soon they'll be all over you like cows in—"

"Yes, Roger?" Charlotte broke in, about to blow a fuse.

Sucking in breath at the near obscenity, Lord Lucifer swiftly changed the topic. "By the way, you were a long while with Midnight Vampira. What kept you?"

"Oh. Felicity Raeburn, aka Midnight Vampira, had some interesting news about Pablo Pringle."

"What, your arts and crafts teacher, also doubling as the martial arts instructor?"

"The very same."

"Don't tell me, he's glued his syrup to his skull after what happened at our garden party."

"No, but he's *not* forgotten the soaking Steve gave him during the water fight, resulting in his toupée coming off." Pausing, she rifled Roger with a razing sulk. "He's moving on to a new appointment in Dundee. His fiancée lives there and they're getting married."

Recoiling, Roger advised, "Dundee is right in the heart of Jockland. He'll have to learn to speak Jock, if he's going to communicate with the locals."

"Odd you mentioning communication. Evidently, sometimes he has trouble understanding what his fiancée says. Felicity heard that the fiancée made a marriage proposal in principle, but Pablo misunderstood."

"How can anyone possibly do that?" Roger disputed. "Language barrier or not."

"Deeming he had okayed an invitation to a family kali, when he touched down in Dundee, he found his future in-laws were geared up for the pre-marriage nuptials."

"So no getting out of it?"

"No, his fiancée's brothers and cousins saw to that. In their evaluation, he'd gone for the proposition and stayed duty bound to fulfil his obligations."

"And presumably, the martial arts stuff didn't help him out, I mean to make an escape?"

"He planned to propose anyway. Just let's say, his fiancée brought the proposal forward by a year, so he decided to do the decent thing."

"Just goes to show, and I'm always telling those delinquent Essex boy traders at The Firm the same thing…qualify the opportunity and read the fine print before you press the commit button."

"Mmmm. Anyway, Pablo takes off at the end of the autumn semester, and we'll see his replacement in the New Year."

"Do give him my best felicitations," Roger unconvincingly conveyed. "Oh, and tell him Steve sends his fondest regards."

Folding her arms, Charlotte posted, "I'm *sure* he will appreciate it."

"Just resurrecting the evening's grand finale, what's this play about?"

She explained, "it's an adaptation of *The Rakes Progress,* set-in eighteenth-century London."

"I see. Who's in it?"

"Irene and Bernard Pascoe, and Linda and Neil Green. Irene produced the play with help from Claudette, Martin's wife."

"Yes, he told me." Puzzled, Roger queried, "what does it have to do with Halloween?"

Giving him a sideways rebuking flare, Charlotte verbalised, "nothing, but it's not the point. Don't be picky, Roger."

"Yes, my sweet," he tamely acceded.

"And none of your customary sarcasm, thank you," she pleaded.

Can't win, can I? Roger mulled.

Spying about, he saw the play's four participants in the doorway to the dining room, still in their Halloween attire and trading what he guessed were eleventh hour thoughts apropos the dramatisation, the two men explicitly agitated and jumpy, the two women toiling to calm their nerves. Roger knew Bernard from other socials, and had bartered a few jovial words with him after the apple-bobbing episode. Sometimes Roger bumped into the normally frothy Neil at Saint Mary Cray rail station. Like Bernard, he emerged less than pleased to be delighting the Halloween party goers. He had waved to Neil earlier in the evening from across the garden as he talked to Martin Gayle. Echoing his friendly gesture, nevertheless, he seemed to be internally absorbed. Then Linda surfaced, glinted a gregarious smile at Roger, grabbed Neil by the arm, and led him inside the house. Deducing nothing untoward, Roger carried on his conversation with Martin. Now, he figured all might not be hunky dory with the thespians.

"They've been rehearsing for a few weeks," Charlotte told her husband. "Well, when Bernard and Neil were available."

"Bernard and Neil don't appear to be very happy."

Also observing unrest developing at Shakespeare HQ, she gurgled, "no," anxiety in her voice making her agreement prophetic. "I do hope it all goes alright for them."

"Daddy," Heather probed, "is this going to be the same as the play we saw with Uncle Barry and Aunt Beverley in Leeds?"

Her father unfastened his mouth to answer, but as on so many occasions Charlotte beat him to the draw. "No Heather," she rectified, "that was a farce, this is a serious play."

"Does anyone get their head chopped off?" James cross-examined, dribbling with relish at the prospect.

Again, Charlotte retaliated with a lightning quick reply. "If anyone is going to get their head chopped off, it will be you, James." Glaring at him, she berated, "I haven't forgotten you are still blackmailing us after my inauspicious Greenwich Park affair."

Glistening, he shrilled in a satisfied voice, "yeesss."

"Ohh, really cool, Mummy," Heather complimented, "you're truly getting into the spirit of Halloween night."

"Really cool," her mother replicated. "Where did you hear that phrase?"

"Oh, Mummy," Heather intoned, "I am seven, and I'll be eight soon."

"Yes, I know, but where—" She stopped, outwardly depleted by insensibility as if lost for words. Periodically, not even Charlotte could decipher the stimulus flowering in any of her children when they came out with the unpredictable. Regaining coherence, she enquired, "where was I?"

"Chopping off James' head," Roger prompted.

"I didn't mean it literally, I meant as a…oh…never mind. Everyone just sit down and behave yourselves."

"Me included?" Roger buttonholed.

"Especially you," she confirmed.

Pitching a mournful gloom at his father, James became lost between the desire to play hunt the one-eyed, wonder weasel with Jenny and Rebecca, and the certain knowledge, someday his mother would find a way to access the offending file on his mobile, chased by extremely rapid and painful retribution befalling him.

Giving him a wink, Roger whispered in his ear, "best not to bait your mother when members of her arty-farty crowd are about to entertain us, son."

Out of the blue, Wendy materialised beside her father with Jenny and Rebecca in tow, the latter pair cackling wildly.

Radiating a disapproving lour at them, Lord Roger interrogated, "are you sure you two haven't been drinking?"

Squinting at each other, the sparsely clad sirens smirked, smothered developing laughs with hands over their mouths, then tolled together, "oh no, Mister Fraser, we've not been drinking."

"Then what's making you guffaw so much?" he pumped.

"We've just seen Mister Wiggins relieving himself in the garden," Jenny informed.

"And *so*?" Roger prodded. "We're all caught short once in a while."

"Well," Rebecca clarified, "he had difficulties with his zip and—" More chortles and cackles leapt from the taken-for-granted, inebriated pair.

"Yes," Roger pressed.

"And he...he...nearly got his thing caught in his zipper," Rebecca soldiered to get out before all the girls broke into laughter.

"Oh, is that all?" Roger jeered. "Hah, I speculated you were going to say something *really* funny."

Dissolving into more uncontrollable mirth, Lord Lucifer's satirical riposte went straight over their heads.

"Sssshh," Charlotte badgered, shooting a vaporising glance at the girls. "It's overtures and beginners. They're going to start soon."

Gaining control, the girls sat down on the floor in front of Charlotte and Roger, Jenny and Rebecca either side of James. Shining and purring at the patronage, he flaunted ecstasy, Wendy amused by her brother's reaction.

Tasked with getting the play underway, Midnight Mistress, Tania, arrived at stage centre for her MC stint to much encouraging yelps and claps from the assemblage.

Holding up her arm to quell the barking and baying, she smiled then announced, "ladies and gentlemen, boys and girls, we now come to the climax of the evening's festivities, an adapted enactment of *The Rakes Progress.*"

As the crowd noise subsided, Matthew got to play sound and lighting engineer. Throwing a few switches, the emulated stage area became illuminated by two parallel red-light beams, and an eerie soundtrack filled the background. Entering from the dining room, Irene and Bernard began the introductory act, Linda and Neil following a few moments later.

Intending to portray country squire, Tom Rakewell (The Rake), his milkmaid lover, Anne Trulove, Nick, Shadow the Devil, and Mother Goose, a whore, Roger weighed with Bernard in his Klingon outfit, Irene decked out as Alice the Living Dead Doll, Neil imperious in his Thriller Werewolf costume and Linda as Morticia Addams, they were more comparable to a bunch of miscast space bandit reprobates, time-slipped from a Hammer Films house of horror film set into Hogarth's Hanoverian England. Cast as Anne Trulove, notably, Irene looked more analogous to a frenzied Dorothy from *The Wizard of Oz* rather than a Georgian milkmaid. Already, other people were making the same connections, and in place of the placid expressions anticipated for a heartfelt play, their complexions beamed into glee.

Everything went spiffingly well until the next act, when Neil lapsed into memory loss mid-sentence, gargling like a psychotic duck bumbling for his words. Gawping at Claudette, acting as prompter in the wings, he beckoned the line. She obliged him almost syllable by syllable, hoping Neil caught on, but he remained bereft of recalling the text. Instead, he came across as twinned with a demented parrot, duplicating its owner's words. Sitting cross-legged beside the adults, some of the sub-ten-year-olds embracing Heather sniggered at the unintentional comedy. Despite quietly admonishing their disrespect, their parents also erred into merriment as Neil's ordeal continued.

Logging like their children, some parents found it laborious to sustain control, Lord Roger simpered at their contorted dials, just about holding in the laughter buried deep in their stomachs, but not far from surfacing. Sensing a farcical catastrophe on the near horizon, his mug muscles lifted into the elated pose, Charlotte despatching the habitual dig in his ribs trailed by a decimating scowl on sighting his joy.

Regaining script take-up, Neil handled the partial disconnect well. Winking, he received a small ripple of patron applause and carried on.

Then in the third act, with her arms outstretched in a loving stance, Irene gazed to stage right, expecting Bernard to spring up. Hearing her husband reciting his lines from stage left, shocked, she spun around, making a solemn scene appear comic. Having given up on child control, this too drew titters and semi-smothered laughs from the adults. Threatening a volcano-like eruption, Charlotte held her hand over James mouth to prevent his laughter escaping, his hands holding firmly on to his mother's chair, so to stop him catapulting upwards in one giant articulation of hilarity. Consecutively, James' dilemma had Wendy, Jenny and Rebecca in a frenzy, all three cowering down behind Charlotte and Roger, so as not to be seen trying to repress their jollity.

Perspiring, flushed and on the edge, their nerves jangling, by act four Bernard and Neil felt worse for wear. Holding the play together, Irene and Linda perpetuated their parts with determination to adhere to the script, the only facet keeping the representation going.

Approaching the pivotal act, when Neil was meant to say, 'Oh, fair maiden, I have come to rescue you, and fill your life with joy,' instead, with his concentration ebbing he delivered, "Oh, fair maiden, I have come to roger you, and fill my wife with toys."

At the onset, not quite taking in the misreading, the spectators whispered, 'What did he say?' Then it sunk in, the gory clinker of guarded cheer rising as the intrepid players reciprocated perplexed gleams.

Realising the *faux pas* had not gone unheard, opening his hands in a gesture of apology, Neil gaped at Lord Lucifer. "Sorry to take your name in vain, Roger. No offence intended."

"None taken," he assured, the unforeseen ad-lib dialogue evoking more giggles and hoots disrupting Bernard's absorption.

With his next line scheduled to be, 'Hark a pistol shot!', the gathering lost collective control, when instead, holding his sword aloft, the line became, "Hark, a shistol pot, I mean a postel shit, er, shostol shit…ah, cowshit, horseshit, bullshit, I didn't want to be in the bloody play in the first place!"

Breaking into bellyaching laughter, adults and children alike, bent over in irrepressible rejoicing contortions, their countenances reddened, and their larynxes sent into overdrive, developing a cornucopia of guffawing and snorting. Many of those seated fell off their chairs, rolling around the floor with the junior cacklers.

Prompter Claudette tried in vain to reengage the actors with the correct lines, but to no avail. Still game to rescue the play, poor Neil and Bernard got a rocket from their respective wives, the foursome's archetypal English farce display only serving to add more fuel to the mirth fire.

Gurning at Charlotte, Roger remarked, "heavenly to be around people all pretending to be grownups, isn't it?"

Struck dumb, his wife had become white-faced and aghast at the extraordinary spectacle, Tania and other prominent arts and crafts set members equally horror-stricken at the unpremeditated sequence of events.

With accusation written all over her puss, Charlotte found her voice, fixed her gaze on her husband and cried, "did you set this up, Roger?"

"*Me!*" Lord Lucifer squawked. Folding his arms, he slowly shook his head. "Not guilty. I'm just an innocent bystander."

Chapter 5: The Ayatollah's Adversary

Whilst in the middle of parsing Euro zone gilt-edged securities and figuring out the least risky course to offer corporate investors, Fraser heard a knock-knock on his office door and a smiling Gary Delaware loomed into view.

Tilting his napper up from his work, he chimed, "Gary, how the devil are you?"

"I'm fine, Roger."

Exchanging a warm handshake, the old friends then settled down in two easy chairs, hugging cups of gourmet coffee, and taking a cursory reconnaissance of each other.

"You haven't changed at all, Gary."

"Nor have you."

"Hot damn, you're being too kind. Since we were at J P Morgan Chase, I've put on a few pounds…well at least a half a stone, maybe more—" He grimaced. "And, as you can see, my once dark hair is now approximating a greyer tint."

"It suits you, Roger."

"Funny you saying that, my wife Charlotte infers the same." He rested. "You never met her, did you?"

"No."

Glimmering, Fraser jabbered, "a lot of water under the bridge, Gary, lot of water."

"Yes, our nascent days in the square mile seem consonant with an eternity from today. Sometimes I can't believe twenty years have coasted by."

"By George, they were glorious junctures," Fraser reflectively set forth. "Say, do you remember old Joss Errington?"

Backtracking for a split second, Delaware imparted, "I do. Joss imprinted an indelible stamp on all the analysts and brokers. I joined two years ahead of you, so I saw a lot more of his unsubtle humour."

"Do you recall the name of the secretary he always went after?"

"Chevonne Mobley, otherwise known as 'Tasty', because of her feminine attributes."

"Oh yes, a right little prick teaser. Without doubt we all had wet dreams about Chevonne."

"For sure. I can also cite, being a good ol' northern boy, Errington brought in jam tarts to eat during the day. Holding a tart in his right hand, he'd attract Tasty's attention, jab at the tart in his left hand and arraign, 'You're a tart, a tart, a jam tart', in a leery, dripping voice."

"Yeah," Fraser reacted, slowly chortling, Delaware also joining in. "He came up to me once, tapped me on the shoulder, marked Chevonne and snarled, 'She wants shafting by a woolly-bull.' It had me in fits of laughter. I couldn't conceive a woolly-bull image, but nonetheless had no qualms conjuring up a scene starring Chevonne and a berserk bovine. The vision has persistence."

"The classic Errington howler that has stuck with me revolved around Bethany Hatton. Do you recollect her?"

"The uppity woman in corporate accounts," Fraser wagered. "Very fair-faced, but a total pain?"

"You've got it, and by the way, Joss called accounts, 'the sales prevention department.' One day, he wanted credit extending for a particularly errant client, but Bethany had put a stop on their corporate account. Joss whined, 'Just because they don't pay their bills, doesn't mean to say we can't extend their credit,' but she lasted adamant. Bursting into the bullpen, crimson with anger, he bawled, 'Bethany Hatton needs locking in a small shed with six rampant sambos. They'd teach her some respect for seasoned traders.' It brought the floor to a standstill, people falling over or doubling-up in uncontrollable jollity, his sentiment savagely poetic, but totally illogical. You could see why

Bethany had dropped the boom, but Joss had none of it."

"I heard about the episode, however, the one coming to mind with Bethany, involved Joss depositing a doll's eye into her bottle of green olives. She freaked out when she forked it out, supposing she had skewered a real eye."

"Oh yes, I recall the prank. Didn't she make a formal complaint to HR, and they set about hunting down the culprit?"

"Indeed they did, and Joss told HR they should be seeking someone missing a false eye."

"Of course, riling ugly women was his other forte. He'd come up to his unfortunate patsy flaunting a flabbergasted deportment and boldly blast, 'Good god, have you got a license to be out in public with a scary face like that? In Wales you'd be done for sheep scaring!'"

"Yes, on one occasion, the ugly woman's pal said she was not well and needed a doctor. Joss replied, 'It's not a doctor she needs, it's a plastic surgeon.'"

"Ha, ha, ha, ooh wicked. Shucks, they don't make Joss Errington types anymore, do they?"

"No, it's a shame. Happy days though, Gary, happy days. Of course, today, such innocent japes always culminate in a witch hunt, the guilty ostracised if not sacked on the spot."

"Yes—" Grimacing, he shuffled uneasily in his seat. "We live in different times, and not ones I care for. Compared to twenty years ago, they are austere, restrictive and tediously dull. When the PC brigade took over running Western Europe and North America, repartee became outlawed, sacred cows instituted and a puritanical discipline applied to every sphere of society."

Fraser's ex-colleague went on to recount his career at Chase in Manhattan, and what made him take up the head of private equity fund management duty with Studwick Harley. Still getting his feet wet, finding out about Studwick Harley clients having a parallel bond with The Firm, it led to his sojourn to Canary Wharf.

During the explanation, Fraser reassessed his earlier impression of Delaware's appearance, recording subtle alterations in his lineaments and physique had developed since they worked together at J P Morgan Chase. When he initially knew Gary, he possessed the same angular phizog and hairstyle fingerprinting thespian Nigel Havers, but now as they talked, he logged Manhattan had taken its pound of flesh out of him. Not so much beaten down by the stresses of investment banking, but drawn, as if some invisible force had reshaped his clock into a map symbolising all his trials and tribulations, Fraser esteemed the New York experience must have been testing.

"So," he accorded at the end of Delaware's recap, "you've been in discussions with Henry?"

"Yes, I also met your trading floor sales manager, Ricky Henshaw." Stopping, he became business attuned. "Perhaps I can get down to the purpose of my visit."

"Go ahead."

"I need some help with one of our private investors. Henry and Ricky told me you've got this trouble-shooting mandate now, so I want to take advantage of your skills in that domain."

"They're being over-complimentary. It's a recent nomination and I'm still in a pickle coming to terms with why The Firm discerned I could discharge trouble-shooting tasks."

"Maybe trouble-shooting is too strong a term for this challenge, but it does need someone with vision and good interpersonal skills."

"I'd have to clear it with Equities Director Toby Chalcroft. Do you know him?"

"Only by reputation."

"Well, I still report to Henry for my stock analyst duties, but for my 'Jim Phelps' doppelganger, I have a dotted line to Chalcroft for trouble-shooting requirements. Why don't you tell me about the poser, then I can brief Top Cat?"

"Top Cat?"

"Yes, Chalcroft has the same initials as Top Cat, the TV cartoon character, hence his colloquial nickname at The Firm."

"Is he conscious of his moniker?"

"Probably, but I'd not test the assumption. He can be *very* explosive."

Outlining the business puzzle, Delaware enlightened Zicon General, one of Studwick Harley's principal clients, had sent out signals suggesting they were considering jumping ship in favour of another UK based private bank, probably Coutts or C. Hoare & Co, but stubbornly refused to outline the motives as to why. Zicon also hinted their investment portfolio with The Firm had also come under review, providing the foremost driver why Delaware came in to see Henry Jacques.

"Strange, Zicon dropping the hint to you," Fraser commented, "instead of contacting The Firm directly." Confused, he scrunched up his features. "*Why?*"

"I didn't stop to dig deeper, Roger, but yes, it did equate with oddness to me, as if Studwick Harley were being used as a covert messenger."

"Hhmm," Fraser uttered. "Nothing happens by chance or without a cause in investment banking. What could it be?"

"God knows. Anyway, with Studwick Harley being a business partner of The Firm, and thereby having a shared mutual interest in Zicon General, we'd welcome your help to resolve whatever the deadlock is."

Clearly perturbed, Delaware's light demeanour transposed to serious, Fraser detecting he had inherited a can of worms, and needed to sort the Zicon problem before confidence in him started to ebb with his new employers.

Sensitive to his predicament, Fraser radiated. "Okay, this might fall into my trouble-shooter remit, but because the client is a big hitter, I'm sure Toby will give it the thumbs up."

~ * ~

After Delaware set up a meeting with the client, Fraser and he waited in the Walbrook Street Zicon General reception, not far from the world-renowned Mansion House, TC having sanctioned the trouble-shooter's support.

Arguably as mysterious and secretive as The Firm, and invariably cloaked in rumour, scandal and controversy, but with an acceptable civic-shop window commensurate with philanthropic and charitable exploits, Zicon General had become the fount of perennial fascination to the financial sector at large. Not a public company, and thereby under no obligation to disclose accounts or board member names, let alone the true complexion of their core businesses, Zicon endured as a spring of conjecture in news circles, enterprising journalists forever digging to unearth what lay below the prevailing facade, and governments worldwide having their security services monitor the ever-growing behemoth.

Some voiced Zicon General were a holding company for several international blue-chip corporations, used to screen and channel liquid assets into the investment markets without incurring heavy taxation losses. Others theorised the company operated as a confederation of billionaires and cardinal industrial conglomerates, converging together for mutually beneficial business gambles. Not quite a cartel, more a giant business monolith, capable of setting global trends and affecting government decision-making worldwide, the Zicon mystique had become self-perpetuating.

Whatever the truth of the matter, towering security mechanisms and procedures coupled with legions of not-up-for-negotiation, robust, pug-ugly security officers, doubtless having 'Terminator' Schwarzenegger and 'Rambo' Stallone running for cover, deterred those flying too close to their fiery sun. Moreover, an army of corporate lawyers made sure anything contentious or illegal never saw the light of day in a court of law.

From The Firm's and Studwick Harley's perspective, Zicon General delineated an investment portfolio of over £5billion in assets, but they were by no means the only investment team to play ball with Zicon, the company spread betting their risk with at least five other consortia Fraser knew about. Consequently, Delaware's and Fraser's concern centred on the investment business, rather than dissecting the more dubious dealings of their mutual client.

When Delaware attempted to make the appointment, he found their normal routes into the Zicon investment management team had been curtailed without rationalisation. Familiar with the nature of the beast, he had not sought as to why. To get the ball rolling, Charlie Kelcher, a kind of middleman between the inner sanctum of the Zicon General corporate structure and the outside world was nominated to take the meeting. Demonstrably, Delaware concluded Kelcher had been designated to keep them at bay, until Zicon distinguished what The Firm and Studwick Harley wanted.

After going through an intense security check, putting NASA's rigorous procedures in the shade before a Cape Kennedy space shuttle launch, and a body search inspecting every orifice, Delaware and Fraser were sent to the Zicon reception area to await their contact.

"I heard tell," Fraser allotted, "they even frisked Blair and his entourage a few years ago, when he came in for a meeting."

"Huh, at their New York fortress," Delaware exchanged, "the President got the same treatment."

"Hhmm, I marvel how they'd deal with God?"

"Probably tell him to sign in like mere mortals, saying deities were not exempt from Zicon security regulations."

"Hi, I'm Charlie Kelcher."

Rubbernecking up, Delaware and Fraser then glinted at each other, more than a little bewildered someone had managed to invade their space without them noticing. Both found the prospect of Charlie Kelcher incongruous and amazing.

"Good morning," Delaware felicitated. "I'm Gary Delaware from Studwick Harley, and this is my associate Roger Fraser from The Firm."

"Ah yes, the legendary Firm," Kelcher sardonically articulated. "An establishment even older than Zicon General, and one, let's say, having junctures of controversy, even notoriety."

"Quite," Fraser acknowledged, tittering at The Firm's less than saintly hoi polloi perception, then scowling at Kelcher's gall to censure his employer, when Zicon General were hardly in a position to be critical.

Taken aback because they expected Charlie Kelcher to be a man, what Delaware and Fraser shook hands with seemed to be of indeterminate sex, neither obviously male nor female, Kelcher having a short but not entirely butch hairstyle, feminine peepers, perfectly flat chest, as good as androgynous and very thin. Dressed in a Missus Thatcher dubbed *Spitting Image* pinstripe suit only added to the prognostication regarding gender.

"This way gentlemen," showed the nondescript, levitating its arm towards the lift atrium.

Marching off at a brisk pace, Delaware and Fraser followed the life form a few steps behind, imparting the obvious body language 'what is it?' to each other. By the time they were ensconced in a tenth-floor meeting room, the visitors were still hedging their bets. Normally at a primary meeting with a client's delegate, protocol craved the seller addressed them as Mister, Missus or Miss, before being invited to use Christian names. On this day, the callers were risk averse, petitioning the being on the other side of the negotiating table as Charlie from the off, on the intuition it could not offend.

Labouring to ascertain why Zicon General were leaning towards changing investment house jockeys, the glowing, vibrating vision before Delaware and Fraser stayed intransigent, not divulging anything plausible or business-based.

Deciding to utilise an above the salt business value rationale, Delaware led on behalf of the selling team, sketching the business case for staying with Studwick Harley and The Firm, leaving Fraser to derive the hidden agenda and what really drove the dissociation waves. Finishing his summary pitch, reiterating the pedigree of The Firm and Studwick Harley, Delaware then let Fraser loose with a few exploratory inquests about futures, but in typical Zicon General fashion, Kelcher batted them away on the basis the possible answers were company confidential. The longer the tennis match went on, the more Fraser became convinced the enforced impasse was a deliberate ploy designed to get them out to play, but for what purpose? If he posed the right question, maybe it'd unlock the gate to the real issues.

"Charlie," he initiated in a soft restrained voice, "may I ask, are there any indirect obstacles causing Zicon General to scrutinise this possible change?"

"That's a good intuitive query," Kelcher complimented, leaning forward, as if the key to the standoff would become transparent. "Maybe The Firm and Zicon General have more in common in terms of subtleties than we envisioned."

"Is there someone else worthwhile talking to," Fraser persisted, "perhaps affected by oblique quandaries?"

Smirking, the organism's inscrutability relaxed into tangible openness. "Hhmm, okay. I'm going to put the possible transfer of our investment business to another private bank and investment house on hold *pro tem*." Lingering, as if enjoying keeping Delaware and Fraser on tenterhooks for a twinkling longer, Kelcher then avowed, "I will set up a meeting for you with Mister Dwight Armstrong, our Director General of Global Investments. He might be able to guide you further."

Fraser had been in the same room as Armstrong twice, but never had any proceedings with him, his Zicon General contacts exclusively residing in the portfolio management side of the business. Though reporting to Armstrong, the Director of Global Investments kept all his supernumeraries at arm's length, and Zicon's financial services providers even farther from his sphere of direct contact.

"That's fine," Fraser corroborated. "Thank you."

"Oh, by the way," Kelcher chirped, virtually as a throwaway comment. "Mister Armstrong knows your Mister Bembridge."

Hhmm, a very heavily weighted hint, Fraser resolved. "Yes, we are mindful of the association," he gingerly muttered.

Finalising the conference, Kelcher returned the callers to reception, Delaware and Fraser keen to immediately critique the meeting as the being jogged away.

"Okay, I'm dying to know," Delaware cackled, "what was your take on *the creature*?"

"You mean, was it a man, or a woman, or perhaps a tranny?"

"Yes, yes."

"Well, Gary," Fraser budded, "I've attended thousands of

business meetings on five continents, but I've never seen anything comparable to that before. In reaction to your vexation, it could be either and I don't propose to do a below the waist survey to verify its sex. Even then, it might not necessarily authenticate its psychological gender."

"Cripes, very funny, Roger. I too have seen some strange individuals in New York, but they were out on the street, not in the ivory citadel of a major blue-chip company. And the way the creature snuck up on us in reception undetected was eerie, like a chimera popping-up out of thin air."

"Yeah, must have taken lessons in stealth from *Kung Fu* David Carradine."

"For sure."

"It's immaterial anyway," Fraser maintained. "In all frankness, we shouldn't care less if whatever we talked to had a trunk and pink hair, so long as they're authorised to conduct business."

"Yes, you're quite right. Hey—" He frowned. "Who is this Bembridge fellow?"

"I ruminated when you were going to float that. Luther Bembridge is The Firm's VP Investment Banking for the London operation."

Placing the exec, Delaware yowled, "of course…but what's the connection with Armstrong?"

Cogitating for a trice, Fraser then generated a contorted aspect. "I don't know, but I've got a suspicion it could be the provocation behind the current glitch."

~ * ~

Needing to report the staggering development at Zicon General *vis-à-vis* Bembridge, and consult with the equities director to see if he knew anything about the Armstrong-Bembridge linkage, back at the ranch, Fraser headed off to see Toby Chalcroft.

"So," Top Cat remarked, his croakers flashing, indicating he chomped on the brainteaser, "Zicon are playing ducks and drakes, and you guess Bembridge might be axiomatic to it?"

"Mmmm."

"And this creature—" Lifting his upper lip Humphrey Bogart gangster fashion, he then grimaced. "What was the name?"

"Charlie Kelcher."

"Right," TC took in, rubbing his chin as if trying to recall the name. "This er, Charlie Kelcher gave a hulking hint Luther and Zicon's want-away hunger are somehow connected?"

"Correct, Toby. Got any theories pertaining to bad blood between Bembridge and Armstrong?"

Shooting a quizzical gleam at the trouble-shooter, Chalcroft groaned, "I met Armstrong many years ago at a Bank of England convention...strange bird, very strange."

"How do you mean?"

"I got talking with him about how Zicon General had become a client of The Firm way before Studwick Harley came upon the scene, and certainly long before either of us were born. Howbeit observant of the relationship's durability, he saw it as nothing more than an inherited investments channel. Communication with him took a lot of hard work, and I never felt comfortable in his presence. Can't quite quantify why, other than a feeling of semi-hidden resentment."

"About what?"

"I never got within hearing distance to find out, Roger. Their business is a massive cash-cow for The Firm, so not wanting to upset the apple cart, I simply let sleeping dogs lie."

"And the affiliation with Bembridge?"

Beetle-browed, TC grouched, "hhmm." Meandering over to his executive suite window array overlooking the Isle of Dogs financial district he clenched his fists, a sure portent he'd been troubled by Fraser's briefing. "I don't know, but I suspect it's on the personal clash side of the equation. The conundrum is—" He glowered at Fraser. "How to table it to Luther without raising his hackles?"

Signifying an underway imminent mutation to his identity, Chalcroft glimpsed at Fraser with his all too familiar chameleon countenance. Nodding and mouthing something Fraser could not quite hear, his mannerisms transformed from reasonable businessman to hard-hearted overlord, his idiom a mass of counter estimations to be executed by a third party without scope for debate, meaning delegation of a thorny complication rotated in his cranium.

Uh-oh, Fraser speculated with trepidation, *there's a Mission Impossible assignment coming my way. I hope you're not going to ask me to do battle with the Ayatollah.* As if uncertain about his strategy, Chalcroft focused on the window outlook again then marked Fraser, his locution still caught between multiple shades of solution option and their discharge.

Exhaling noisily, as if tempted to offload a delicate if not dangerous task, he became reticent, mumbling indecipherably, before saying, "I'll request a consultation with Bembridge this evening. We'll have a few drinks in the boardroom, then I'll casually dovetail into the snag. What do you think, Roger?"

I think, thank god you didn't instruct me to do that, he mentally sanctified. "First-class approach, Toby," Fraser joyously commended.

Resuming the seated attitude at his huge executive desk, he scrutinised Fraser mischievously. "On the other hand," he coldly proclaimed, "it might be better coming from you, in the guise of a trouble-shooter perplexity."

Already Roger could see Bembridge metamorphosing into his Lizard King natural state, like Henry Jacques and he had surmised at the Bembridge's Cheyne Walk social a few months earlier. If the possible enigma demonstrated to be contentious, and he pushed the wrong buttons, he had visions of the Ayatollah consuming him whole.

"Hhmm, perhaps not," Chalcroft updated after fresh rumination. "Its best coming from me, chain of command and so forth."

Relief rushed from Fraser's inner being. "Yes, you're right, Toby. It'd be the wisest course of action."

~ * ~

Early on the Wednesday morning, still inbound to London Bridge on the 07:40 from Saint Mary Cray, Fraser got a call from Top Cat's PA instructing him to see Toby straight away on his arrival at Canary Wharf.

Ushered into his inner sanctum by the PA thirty minutes later, Fraser found Chalcroft zonked out in his executive chair, ashen, his eyes glazed over.

"Good morning, Toby," he jangled, in an effort to drag the equities director out of his malaise.

Breaking from a palpable trance, Chalcroft goggled at the trouble-shooter. "*Jesum crow*, is it?"

"I take it your meeting with Bembridge turned out to be problematical."

"*Problematical*!" TC repeated. Fleetingly shutting his snoopers, as if travailing to blot out a recurring bad daydream, he declared, "we've got a *real* dilemma here, Roger, and what I'm about to tell you goes no further, not even to Henry Jacques."

Flicking his fingers, he betokened Fraser to sit down in the chair facing his desk. Invariably, the trouble-shooter had the inkling sitting in the chair eventuated an artificial breaking of wind noise through the rear passage, duplicating the embarrassment CJ causes Reggie Perrin, but it had never happened. He also endlessly awaited TC to say, *I didn't get where I am today by*…but that had never happened either. Long ago, he settled the fancy had been created because Top Cat's singularities, speech patterns and the timbre of his voice often bore an uncanny resemblance to Reggie's nemesis. Albeit, fixing in no way did Chalcroft try to imitate or even emulate CJ to preserve the advantage with underlings such as him, he conceded he could be incorrect.

"Go ahead, Toby."

"This is definitely trouble-shooter territory," Chalcroft attested.

"What makes it so? Surely this is an internal, if not a private article."

"True, but if we don't manage this hitch properly, it could have as grave consequences for The Firm as the Guatemalan business, had you not sorted it out."

"So, what's the squabble between Bembridge and Armstrong?"

Disgruntled and frustrated, Top Cat grabbed the arms of his leather-upholstered executive chair. "Conspicuously, it has more to do with the Bembridge Foundation than The Firm."

Often when flustered, principally by *prima facie* insoluble affairs landing on his desk unannounced, Toby became mobile. Assuming a walking stance, he paced up and down behind his desk, his arms essaying to find a suitable carriage to help evidence his burgeoning consternation, his prickly agitation overwhelming any sense of unhurried deliberation. In his ordered mentality, personal emergences had little to do with management quandary solving, and even less with running a flourishing investment house, Fraser sensing he converged on an explosion.

Waggling a finger in Fraser's direction while still on the move, he tersely bellowed, "do you know what this is, Roger?" Before the trouble-shooter could respond, Top Cat imparted, "this is a conflict of interests and egos between professional and domestic components." Coming to a halt, he grabbed the top rearmost section of his executive chair, squeezing its soft foundation with both mitts until his knuckles became white. "It transpires our illustrious VP of Investment Banking has let his ego drive get the better of him." Releasing the grip on his chair he leaned over it, looming large in Fraser's vision. "Earlier this year, the Bembridge Foundation became the recipient of an endowment worth up to £750k per year for the next three years from the Ripley & Mortimer Group." Rattled, he peeped to the heavens, as if wanting a deity to help him keep control of his temper. "Like Bembridge, Armstrong is a philanthropist and chairman of his own charity, 'The Armstrong Institution', a fund also under consideration for this hefty endowment." Gripping the chair firmly again, his knuckles glowed even whiter as he came to the point. "I believe we can safely deduce; this is the incitement behind Zicon General's semi-veiled threat to jump ship."

Seething with irritation, he practically collapsed into his chair. Peering at Fraser square-on, he assigned, "Bembridge and Armstrong were at Charterhouse together. According to our temperamental VP, there has been an on-going competitive standoff between them ever since."

"What rendered it?"

"Apparently, and you will find this beyond rationality; some form of wager or juvenile my-dick's-bigger-than-yours type quarrel. Bembridge failed to be more specific, but since then, their paths have crossed several times. At every rendezvous, hostility has passed between them conserving the grudge." Lingering to try for more control over his anger, he shared, "Bembridge winning the prized endowment for his foundation has proved to be the latest source of competitive resentment. Counteracting, Armstrong seems to have upped the ante on this occasion by bringing the occupational interconnection into play."

"Did Bembridge envisage Zicon General might jump off the wagon placing their investment portfolio elsewhere?"

As if reliving the prior evening's testing boardroom encounter with the Lizard King, Chalcroft flunked retorting at once.

"Toby," Fraser lightly stimulated.

"Let's just say, based on your meeting, he put two and two together."

"How did he take it?"

"Furious is an understatement," TC bemoaned, his spiers blooming wide. "You know how rapidly he can alter?"

"Oh yes."

"Well, I'd adjudge this one was cataclysmic. Quickly quantifying Zicon's threat blossomed as a backlash from Armstrong wanting revenge for his Bembridge Foundation endowment success, he went ballistic." Clenching his fists, making them radiate white yet again, he attacked his desk *Tai Chi* style to vent his rage. "He wants us to, and I quote, 'handle the situation, and make sure there is no fall out.' Unquote."

"Can I take that to mean, make sure Studwick Harley and by implication, The Firm, keep Zicon's business, whilst not risking the Bembridge Foundation's endowment?"

"Exactly, Roger, exactly," TC substantiated before relaxing his gripped hands from what Fraser imagined to be Bembridge's metaphorical throat. "I want you to treat this as an external trouble-shooting duty," he huskily instructed. "Keep me informed twice daily of developments."

Tempted to say, *I thought both of us were going to manage this thorny labour*, he demurred, shrewd to it being a hollow gesture. While still extinguishing flames from the Ayatollah's vicious tongue, the instant he exited the boardroom the previous evening, Top Cat had probably made up his mind to assign the undivided enchilada to the trouble-shooter.

~ * ~

Fraser set up a 12:30 meeting with Dwight Armstrong through Charlie *Kung Fu* Kelcher, then called Gary Delaware to say The Firm had Zicon General covered and to cool his jets for a few days and bear with him. Summarily, Delaware discerned a modifier had happened behind the official scenes. When he referred to Bembridge, and what the poser with Armstrong amounted to, *quid pro quo*, Fraser fed him a bumper dose of bull. Knowingly, he swallowed it, but finished the call with, 'Whatever you are doing, Roger, make sure Studwick Harley comes out clean.'

Once again, the androgynous cherub ostensibly materialised out of nowhere in front of The Firm's man in the Zicon General reception, escorting him to the executive suite where Armstrong waited.

Making their mutual introductions, Top Cat's depictions of Armstrong resurfaced in Fraser's cognizance. His flabby handshake and cloyed body language seemed perfunctory, congeneric to only taking the meeting through professional courtesy, but his posture betrayed a much more onerous brute hid barely beneath the veneer.

During former occurrences Fraser happened to be in the same space as Armstrong, he never got within sniffing distance of him, pronouncing on his physical hallmarks not coming into play.

Now with him less than a few feet from Armstrong, the Director General of Global Investments way above average height became imposing. At six-one, Fraser could claim to be tall, but he rated

Armstrong to have at least six inches on him. Taking him in fully, Fraser chronicled he had developed a rangy build, but not necessarily through dedicated athleticism. His craggy mug with skin tones greyer than pinkie-white and dusky pupils where usually blue is presumed, signified an ex-smoker who had seen the light, but not before doing irreparable damage to his respiratory system. Most of his hair had gone, but what lasted shone black in an austere brushed off his forehead fashion, doubling nineteen-thirties Wall Street bankers. Reminiscent of Davros, arch adversary of Dr Who, and creator of the Daleks, Fraser hypothesised what horrific offspring he might have fathered, or more accurately created to also test the good doctor. Apart from the less than weighty handshake, he also perceived Armstrong appeared formidable, impenetrable, and probably unrelenting in his sentiment of how the entire universe should submit to his vision.

"Thank you for affording me the opportunity to discuss Zicon General's investment portfolio with you," Fraser conveyed in his best business tenor, a necessary opener under normal business-to-business conditions premeditated to engender confidence and mitigate risk.

Not replying, incontestably Armstrong expected Fraser to lay out whatever absorbed his inclination before deigning to speak. Detecting the reluctance to mesh in bi-lateral conversation, The Firm's emissary went for a lateral ploy to coax Armstrong out of his austere stance.

Clocking a series of family photographs on a sideboard adjacent to the exec's paramount desk, one portraying a young man in rugby garb, kneeling and clutching a trophy, he ventured, "is that you in the rugby kit, holding a silver cup?"

Chiming, "huh," Armstrong then sneered, as if Fraser had out-foxed him with a clever chessboard play. Moving to the sideboard, he picked up the photograph and examined it. "Yes, it's from my Charterhouse days."

"We have something in common then," Fraser interchanged. "I still play rugby."

"Yes," Armstrong icily endorsed, not fluctuating his gaze from the photograph. "For Kappa Corinthians."

Startled, before Fraser could ask how he knew, Armstrong volunteered the wisdom.

"You're probably reckoning," he submitted, prying deep into Fraser's optics, through his cranium, into his brain and on deep into his soul, "how do I know."

Feeling his life essence being drained and sucked dry, for Fraser the sensation corresponded to Superman being exposed to kryptonite.

"I know everything about you, Roger, from your birth in Middlewich, your school and university records, your domicile in Kent, your marriage to Charlotte Stevens, the names and ages of your three children…even which rugby club you play for."

Hauling himself out of malaise, Fraser contrasted, *if the Ayatollah had a predilection to descend into the darker recesses of the Malcolm Tucker character, then Dwight Armstrong epitomised the even more calculating Frances Urquhart.* Though most of The Firm's more sensitive clients probed representatives they were doing business with, needing to play along with Armstrong a bit more to get the measure of him he raised his eyebrows feigning solicitude. "Hhmm, you have been busy," he congratulated.

"We have files on all the principal players at The Firm managing our investment portfolio, comprising Toby Chalcroft, Henry Jacques, Ricky Henshaw, yourself and even—" Stopping abruptly, he sneered. "*Luther Bembridge.*"

Anticipating a retaliation at the mention of Bembridge's name, he narrowed his blinkers at Fraser. Not biting on the lure, the trouble-shooter tarried calm, only offering stony features.

"You're not surprised," Armstrong tested.

"On the contrary, I'd have been surprised if a predominant blue-chip investor like Zicon General did not audit its investment houses' senior officers." Desisting, his expression became contradictory. "However, I'm a little taken aback you've come as far down the chain of command as me."

"Don't be modest, Roger," Armstrong antagonised. "It doesn't become you. I hear you are destined for high office at The Firm."

"Well, if it's true," he offset opening his arms. "I am unaware of it."

Gone the next second, Armstrong broke into an ephemeral smile.

"Charlie Kelcher said you were diplomatic, and I can see why The Firm appraises you so mightily." Staring at the facsimile of his younger self as if searching for lost horizons, he replaced the framed photograph on the sideboard. "Now…what can I do for you today, Roger Fraser."

"Well, Mister Armstrong," he birthed.

"You can call me Dwight in the privacy of my suite," Armstrong granted.

"Well…Dwight, I want to understand why Zicon General is contemplating a move from The Firm and our business partner Studwick Harley."

Facing Fraser again, Armstrong's arrogance bubbled up. "Why do you *think* we're mulling over such a move?"

"It's what I'm here to find out."

"Don't be coy, Roger. I know you've done your homework in advance, including talking to Toby Chalcroft about our possible intentions. Consecutively, he addressed Bembridge. From 1922 onwards, The Firm has administered the majority of Zicon General's investment portfolios. Since then, Zicon has seen some explosive earnings on our investments." Segueing into a conciliatory deportment, he sought, "so why are we contemplating a change now?"

"No doubt you're going to tell me."

Partially pacified, Armstrong sat down at his jumbo-sized executive desk, so large, and even dwarfing the insignia of potency used by Toby Chalcroft, Fraser became swayed there must be a bus facility to ferry people up and down its extreme length. Settling in to his identically huge executive chair, *ad modem* to a stalking beast, Fraser's antagonist fixed his stare on him as if about to dissect The Firm's ambassador.

Preserving parity of intent, Fraser eyeballed him, the short hairs on the back of his neck aroused in response. Just as intimidating as Luther Bembridge, he mused Zicon's Director General of Global Investments also housed the capability to shape-shift and transform into a lizard proportionate creature, feeding on the tasty vitals of captured prey, stock analysts and latter-day trouble-shooters inclusive.

"No, Roger, I'm not going to tell you anything. You're going to tell me."

"May I be frank?"

"Of course."

"It has nothing to do with The Firm." Delaying, he beheld Armstrong full on. "It might be a more intimate ingredient."

Incensed, the allegation brought Armstrong sharply to the vertical. Traversing the huge space around his desk, in Fraser's flight of fancy, he vanished into the distance before re-emerging on the horizon and in due course coming to rest by the side of the trouble-shooter. Hovering over him agnate to a pterodactyl about to eat its lunch, his snorting hot breath congealing on Fraser's colder dial, he demanded, "*go on*," his pronunciation reflecting the gravitas of a royal directive.

Feeling comparable to Howard Roark under the scrutiny of Gail Wynand in Ayn Rand's *The Fountainhead*, Fraser could not persuade himself that dissimilar to Wynand, Armstrong had a hidden softer side. Reeking of dominance, revenge and subjugation of the many required to bend unrelenting to his will, his uncut personae jack-knifed with vitriol. If he had to make a comparison from literature, O'Brien torturing Winston Smith in Orwell's *Nineteen Eighty-Four* totalitarian state came to mind, his Davros physical likeness having him halfway there already. He could almost hear him saying, 'Power is tearing human minds apart and putting them back together in new shapes of your own choosing', and, 'If you want a picture of the future, imagine a boot stamping on a human face – forever.' Spiraling, Fraser began to see Gordon Brown's idiosyncrasies in Armstrong's mush, his many long-held suspicions about the ex-PM's ulterior sinister motives for world dominion over all human life resurfacing. Conjecturing up what lay behind the doors leading further into Armstrong's executive suite, he rotated his peepers to take in the far periphery. Did a 'Room 101' beckon to those unwilling to submit to the Director General of Global Investments will? *Stop it,*

Fraser told himself. *You're losing it. Pull yourself together.*

"I'd say," he fathomed, "it has to do with your association with Luther Bembridge."

"Spot on, Roger," Armstrong confirmed, grinding his teeth and clenching his fists.

"With respect, Dwight, whatever it is between you two, do you really believe bringing our mutual business into the equation is going to help?"

Retracing his steps, after a long trek around his gargantuan-sized desk, stopping off for refreshments at his drinks cabinet in Roger's fantasy, he occupied his seat directly opposite The Firm's man.

"I have the puissance to put Zicon General's investments where I evaluate they will get the best returns," Armstrong unequivocally upheld. "Right now, I'm unsure about The Firm's, and thereby Studwick Harley's credentials to prolong our business liaison."

"Why do you say that?"

"Fundamentals, Roger." Cocksure, he inclined forward. "Risk verses confidence."

"How?"

"Confidence is based on belief, notably, belief in the executive structure being able to deliver on promises." Dwelling, he eyed his opposite number awaiting a riposte. None came, Fraser deliberately mothering a poker mien. "I am no longer self-assured about Luther Bembridge's prudence. Thereby my confidence in The Firm has diminished."

"Aren't we still talking about a private aspect?" the trouble-shooter persisted.

Another transitory barbed smile leapt from Armstrong's phiz. "Okay, I've had my fun fencing with you. Yes, it is of a domestic nature, and yes, it is intimate, and yes, the hang-up is your VP of Investment Banking."

"Explicitly, what has Mister Bembridge done to incur your displeasure?"

Fraser's question broke the levee, Armstrong's fist coming down heavily on his desk, its few surface contents fleetingly levitating and a pencil on the edge of a notepad taking flight. Both watched the trajectory of the object, in the end coming to rest in a pitcher of water on his sideboard, a matchless shot. Fraser didn't know whether to laugh or extend a sober outlook. Howbeit, Armstrong's penetrating stare demonstrated levity to be a mistake. With superhuman exertion, Fraser managed to control his habitual tendency towards mirth and resided focused on the pickle in hand. A spark of sheer staccato godsend in an otherwise sterile environment, it illustrated how the profound and the funny often co-exist in the same space-time coordinates.

"No more jousting, Roger," the Davros ringer ordered. "I know you know what the issue is verbatim. So, let's have it out on the table. Bembridge stitched me up with a major-league endowment that ought to have gone to my philanthropic enterprise, not his."

"Surely," Fraser countered, "Charities vie for sponsorship and funding continuously. It seems to me, to be as competitive as the financial services sector in terms of wooing noteworthy contributors. Why is this competition any different?"

Renewing his obdurate stance, Armstrong enlightened, "because it's Bembridge, and he's been causing me grief since Charterhouse."

"I suspect the price for keeping Zicon General's investment profile with The Firm is Mister Bembridge's head on a platter?"

Gleefully, Armstrong hailed, "what a gorgeous thought." Ceasing, Fraser surmised he inwardly visualised an effigy of the Ayatollah's upper story skewered on a silver platter. "Either his head or he cancels the Ripley & Mortimer Group endowment, and they adopt the Armstrong Institution."

Certainly attractive to many at The Firm, Bembridge's napper on a platter did not equate as a realistic option.

"Doubtless, if you had the equivalent donation from another patron," he gauged, "it'd quell your desire for revenge?"

Relaxing into his custom made, leather-bound executive chair, Armstrong purred in a glossy voice, "you're very innovative, Roger. You should come and work for Zicon General." Fraser didn't react.

"Mmmm—" Thrown by the proposal, he swung about in his chair. "I hadn't weighed an alternative contribution as an option. Can you make it happen?"

"Can you leave it with me?"

~ * ~

Giving TC the SP on ZG and DA, dependent on his level of excitation or agitation, Fraser witnessed Chalcroft's countenance ebb and rise between horror and disbelief in response.

"'What you're saying," Chalcroft reiterated, "is if The Firm and Studwick Harley are to keep Zicon General's investment portfolio, and Bembridge is to keep his Ripley & Mortimer Group donation, as well as his head, then we'll have to find an equal donor for Armstrong."

"Exactly, and it presupposes hell will freeze over before Bembridge gives up the Ripley & Mortimer Group donation, and drills them in the direction of the Armstrong Institution."

"A pretty fair assumption," Top Cat agreed. "Whatever the reservoir of this long-running feud between Bembridge and Armstrong is, the other night I got the distinct affection Luther would resign or be fired, rather than see the endowment go to Armstrong."

"Yes, I'd already come to the same deduction. I also concluded if Bembridge were to go, it'd be bad for The Firm. He's very influential with most of our important clients, and I can see the likes of JP Morgan Chase, Merrill Lynch and Morgan Stanley offering him a VP post, and they're our primary competitors." Stopping, he let his synopsis sink in with Chalcroft. "Under such a development, Bembridge might take some of our clients with him." Again, he momentarily halted, Top Cat nodding in agreement. "I think when you met with Luther, maybe, just maybe, as you outlined the Zicon General deadlock, he concurrently rated his water-tight position at The Firm held steadfast, and another solution needed to be found to satisfy Armstrong. It's primarily why I piloted the temperature of the water *vis-à-vis* an endowment substitute."

"I can see your logic, Roger, but the hitch remains, where do we find another benefactor? Using The Firm is impossible, contravention of the financial services code definite, the SEC undoubtedly interpreting it as tantamount to bribery. Our parent company would never stand for it anyway, heads undeniably rolling far and wide."

"Apart from a few loose notions regarding some form of *quid pro quo*, I've not set out the entire explication yet."

"How do you mean?"

"Well, we need to identify an organisation wanting to do business with The Firm, having a lot of cash on their books, some of which can be donated to a charity in exchange for a corporation tax credit."

"Yes, that'd do it…but who?"

"Let me work on a resolution over the next few hours, and I'll let you know."

Chapter 6: The Mancunian Way

Vacating Chalcroft's executive suite, Fraser headed straight for The Firm's London HQ chief analyst, Henry Jacques. Tapping into Jacque's database, they searched for clients seeking investment funding over the next quarter and having cash on their books set aside for philanthropic crusades. When he became inquisitive about the exercise, Fraser felt vaguely supercilious telling him Top Cat had earmarked it as trouble-shooter territory and wanted restriction on a need to know basis.

Working together for fifteen years, they'd struck up a goal-directed relationship from its inception, Fraser deeply admiring Jacques and valuing his counsel and friendship. His boss for the stock analyst function, he'd actively encouraged him to take up Chalcroft's trouble-shooter placement. Being worldly and ego-free, he had seen it all before, residing acquiescent and cooperative without enquiring any further as to the disposition of the request.

Albeit out of loyalty, Fraser painted some broad brushstrokes about the paradox, hinting at the personalities involved and consequences for The Firm if a resolution could not be found. Ingesting the intelligence, Jacques threaded the loose ends together reconstructing the total picture. Smiling before Fraser had finished the review, he'd already worked out the play.

"You've, er, got the gist then, Henry?"

"I have, but rest assured, if Chalcroft asks me if you filled me in on the problem, I shall say, what problem?"

"Thanks, Henry, you're a pal."

After trawling through half a dozen candidates, none quite fitting the bill, Jacques enunciated, "ah, here's a feasible prospect." Ogling up from his computer he shined, an air of victory written into his erudite facade.

Studying the screen, Fraser saw the name Western Goodricke underscored on a spreadsheet.

"I don't know them, Henry. What's their line of business?"

"They're a subsidiary of Foxley & Chapman."

"Oh yes, F&C I do know."

An industrial conglomerate plc with heritage and longevity in heavy machine manufacturing, Foxley & Chapman also owned a portfolio of other manufacturers and non-core businesses encompassing biotech Western Goodricke.

"What's Western Goodricke seeking in terms of investment?"

"Well, they're entangled in a microbiology project needing more funds to shore up and complete the research."

"Stem cells perhaps?"

"I'm not sure. Biotechs are not one of my strong suits, but the summary brief says it's an embryology product aimed at improving the yield from farm animals and is predicted to have huge export potential."

Better not tell Heather about that, Roger meditated. *She'd be appalled and probably contact some pseudo-military animal rights group to blow up the Western Goodricke labs.*

"Why have they failed to secure investment funds?" Fraser explored.

After reading the opportunity notes, he replied, "transpires our assessors are not convinced it is a viable investment."

"Mmmm, are there any other capable candidates?"

Returning to the spreadsheet, Jacques recommended the search. "There are at least three other subsidiary companies seeking investment this quarter, but regrettably, their parent companies do not have cash on their books to devote to a charity."

"So, Western Goodricke are our best bet?"

"Yes."

"Why won't the parent company bankroll the research?"

"The Foxley & Chapman business model is based on self-sustaining P&L centres. F&C will put human resources into their non-core businesses, and in this paradigm the parent has injected some capital in the form of technical support services into the embryology research undertaking, but according to Western Goodricke, F&C's cost limit has smacked the buffers."

"So how does this work, Henry? I mean, in a trade-off, if The Firm nominates this biotech to our investors, how's it going to induce F&G to become a corporate sponsor to an external philanthropic foundation?"

"Ah," he retorted. "That's going to need some of your trouble-shooter magic."

Recoiling, Fraser complained, "Jesus, Henry, you're beginning to mimic Toby Chalcroft. He, too, conceives I'm some kind of magician, pulling deals out of a top hat on demand!"

"Well, Roger," his boss candidly expounded, "in essence, it's what this new capacity of yours calls for."

Gleaming wryly, he canvassed, "what magnitude of investment are they after?"

Clicking the Western Goodricke name on the summary of investments spreadsheet, a hot-link led Jacques to their company file. Rifling through the dossier to its summation page, he enumerated, "they already have £35m in venture capital funding, most of from F&C, but they need an extraneous £20m from the investment market."

"It's not a lot," Fraser remarked. "What's the best terms we can grant them?"

"Before I answer, let me clue you in on their business plan." Scanning the proposal, he advised, "the extra investment is for materials, and plant meaning scientific instruments, plus additional human resources over the next year. On the premise their brand is first to market, Western Goodricke forecast a return on investment of at least £400m in licensed production sales to top pharmaceutical manufacturers such as Astra Zeneca, over the subsequent five years."

"So," Fraser capped, "it also gives an investor a knock-on good fortune to invest directly in F&C stock, where the biotech revenues reside?"

"Yes. Investing in the manufacturing pharmas also presents a dormant blue bird to investors."

"Quite right. What about the terms?"

"The capital plus investment rate interest maturity happens eighteen months after the cash injection, so we applied a fairly hefty interest rate of 8.5 per cent annual equivalent rate, making a gross profit of £2.55m on the twenty."

"And presumably," Fraser argued, "we'd spread the risk among corporate and private investors."

"Naturally."

"So, our risk is if another biotech beats Western Goodricke to the punch, they become a follower?"

"Bang on, and under such a regime, our payback could take far longer, unless the debt is called in, but that'd bankrupt Western Goodricke, with investors seeing little of their capital refunded."

"Plausibly, back-to-back t's & c's with the parent company has not been allowed by F&C?"

"Correct."

"Hhmm, so based on mainstream inflation projections, when does the investment fall into negative equity?"

"Just let me re-check." After making a few key strokes, the numerics became displayed on his computer screen. "Based on accumulating interest, at the twenty-fourth month mark," he stipulated.

"I begin to see why our investment assessors were so cautious," Fraser accepted. "I wonder what else became a contributing agent?"

To unlock the reservations behind the Western Goodricke investment rejection, Fraser went to see Head Investment Assessor, Roslyn Joyce.

With The Firm for at least a century, or so it seemed to both her and the generations of analysts and brokers consulting her over the years, when Roslyn joined she had a trim waist, but after many decades of being entertained by prospective clients seeking investment, she had developed a fuller figure. Reminding Fraser of Connie Sachs, the MI5 intelligence officer in le Carré's *Tinker, Tailor, Soldier, Spy*, she possessed the same sharpness of intuition, instant recall of archived information and appreciation of all current business under scrutiny, whereas other investment assessors needed to troll through reams of data to get the same illumination and make calculated conclusions. Accordingly, Roslyn had become a Firm legend. Consequently, if free, Fraser always approached her when he needed erudition fast.

"Well, Roger, Western Goodricke have some very smart people and a reasonable business profile," Roslyn thrashed out, "but the research they are engrossed in is open-ended."

"You mean, they're unable to settle an end date for project conclusion?"

"Yes, though I will admit it is chicken-and-egg. If The Firm pumped funds into the business, the end date would happen sooner. It's the organic law of scientific research, expressly within the biotech field. But what they're evaluating, and it's in the embryology part of the biotech spectrum, is also being researched by other biotechs. By the time the research is consummated, some other biotech might have already come up with a commodity."

Just what Henry and I concluded, Fraser cerebrated. *No need to labour the point.*

"I see," he vouched. "So, to get The Firm to invest requires a management decision to override a reasoned business valuation."

"Yes," she settled, curiosity embracing her features. "And?"

"I'm brooding, it needs a rational justification."

"If you mean a business case, yes."

"Right, thank you, Roslyn."

He revolved to skedaddle.

"Roger," she called.

Fraser faced her.

"Be careful. My nose tells me your usual robust business ken is being compromised by other coefficients."

Inbound to his own hideaway, Fraser digested Roslyn's salutary words. Nevertheless, his optimism persisted. After contacting some independent investment appraisers to gain a helicopter view of the up-to-date biotech market, he copied-off the Western Goodricke profile and scooted to Chalcroft's executive suite. Explaining the only viable option they had to get Bembridge and thereby The Firm and Studwick Harley out of the nasty stuff, centred on a transaction with the F&C subsidiary, the Director of Equities took in his plan.

"You're implying," Top Cat reviewed with a sense of elation tempered by prudence, "if The Firm approves an investment in Western Goodricke, then we can go to Foxley & Chapman with a *quid pro quo* proposal?"

"Yes, that's the idea, Toby. In exchange for The Firm investing in the biotech, F&C get some cash off their books by becoming a corporate donor to the Armstrong Institution and in the process, qualify for tax credits as a corporate donor to a registered charity." Pausing, he exulted, "*everyone's a winner.*"

"What! What's that?"

"Sorry, I lapsed into Del Boy talk. It's the effect of being around those damned Essex traders for too long."

A rare gregarious smile shone from Chalcroft's normal poker visage. "I see. Well, the next stage is to meet with Foxley & Chapman."

"I anticipated your approval," Fraser disseminated. "I've already set up a meeting with F&C Corporate Investments Director, Frank Appleby, for tomorrow, and made the seminal proposition."

"Good," Top Cat enthused. "We won't do anything precipitous with this planned Western Goodricke investment until you've felt out the parent company."

~ * ~

Ostensibly, one of the founding fathers of industrial scale manufacturing, Foxley & Chapman's corporate HQ had been at Trafford Park since William Foxley founded the company in 1895. Since inception, F&C had established a strong prosperity pedigree in the business world and reverence in the wider social community.

All companies have their own culture, mission statement, business models and corporate governance procedures safeguarding stability, persistent growth and business practice codes set by the board, and adhered to by employees at every layer in the operational structure. No exception, F&C adopted these precepts and had acquired a reputation for plain speaking and fairness of trade, two crucial facets ensuring the company's protracted tenure. Fraser expected Frank Appleby to mirror the code.

Starting discussions over breakfast in the F&C executive dining room, they felt each other out before the cardinal bout to take place in Appleby's office.

Gnarled and grouchy but in a very pleasant way, the Corporate Investments Director came across as a seasoned campaigner, his understanding of money models impressing Fraser. Unmistakably a good ol' northern boy, brought up on bread, dripping and tripe, he had fully embraced the Mancunian subculture in all its varied and many splendid forms, from gurning to gulping gallons of lukewarm Boddingtons. Swiftly taking to him, Fraser conjectured at company outings to Blackpool, Appleby probably wore clogs and a handkerchief on his noodle to blot out the Sun, replicating the Gumby buffoons in *Monty Python's Flying Circus*.

"How long have you been with F&G, Frank?"

"I believe it's coming up to thirty-three years," he tallied. "Might resonate as considerable, but most folk at Trafford Park have worked here all their lives. Foxley & Chapman are fabulous employers, retaining the same empathetic employee care schemas William Foxley introduced at the company's launch. It's a well-known differentiator. Many of the mid-range FMCG and light engineering manufacturers in the area provide higher basic wages, but their businesses are not as stable. Coupled with employee loyalty, it has seen successive generations from the same family work for F&C."

"Not too much resource churn then?" Fraser praised.

"No. As I say, employee loyalty is a significant determinant in preserving a steady workforce, and thereby attaining and passing on skills. We have third and fourth generations of families working for us, uppermost in the Trafford Park area, but it's an identical story at our plants in Sutton Coldfield, South Shields and Bristol."

"I suppose," Fraser chanced, "in terms of employee care, F&C are consonant with Lever Brothers."

"On the dot," the genial Mancunian confirmed. "We don't have the equivalent of Lever Brothers Port Sunlight village to house workers, but the company does own properties all around Manchester, rented out to employees at very judicious rates."

"It must make for a very happy workforce?"

"It does. The work is rewarding, and so long as City or United, preferably both, win at the weekends, productivity is always ahead of forecast."

"Jeepers." Fraser smiled. "As a constituent of common interest, I actually hale from Middlewich, and originally, my father from Bramhall and my mother Alderley Edge."

"Well, you do surprise me, Roger," Appleby kiddingly gibed. "When I heard your accent on the phone, I took you for a southern Jessie."

"I've spent most of my life in Kent," Fraser clarified. "So, any trace of a Cheshire accent got cleansed out of me at junior school."

"But," Appleby germinated, "and here's the acid test, are you a City or a United patron?"

"My great grandfather on my father's side supported Newton Heath."

"Good god, the prototype moniker for Manchester United."

"Mmmm, and both my mother and father champion United."

"So, you must back the Red Devils?"

Sparkling at his host, he defended, "no."

"City then?"

"I'm afraid not, Frank. Being a lifelong Liverpool devotee, I'm the black sheep of the family."

"*Ohh!*" Appleby cried out. "I won't hold it against you, lad, but be careful who you touch on with your allegiance around here. Some folk opine it symbolizes going over to the dark side. Mind you, you have an angle in common with our present-day Group MD for the diesel-generator division. He also adores Liverpool FC."

"How do you cope with his leaning?"

"He's based in Sutton Coldfield but comes from Heswall and grew up watching Liverpool FC."

"Yet another Cheshire man."

"Oh yes," Appleby ratified with an air of absoluteness and justification. "It's the one constraint the board impose for executive nominations...unofficially of course."

"Of course," Fraser duplicated.

"We don't want those bloody civil rights do-gooders plummeting on us from the Department of Employment, insisting we diversify our exec appointments outside the county. Lancashire is about as far as we go, and there hasn't been a Lancastrian on the executive board since 1983, when the previous incumbent passed on."

"Nobody from Yorkshire then?" Fraser hypothesised.

"*Blimey*, wash your mouth out with soapy water, Roger. East of the Pennines is definitely alien country."

"How do you get around the do-gooders, as you call them?"

"Oh, the short-list is always drawn up from solid Cheshire bedrock," Appleby substantiated. "Some are from our competitors, and they might even patronise foreign football clubs, indisputably foreign to Manchester, but our HR people will have corroborated their birth right. It's served Foxley & Chapman well for over 110 years, so we don't intend to change our policy because a bunch of southern Jessie's desiring to ingratiate themselves with so-called minority groups want to impose their insular doctrines on us."

"You were illuminating about your Group MD," Fraser echoed, trying to get the staunch Mancunian to recommence on the relevant matter.

"Oh yes. Sorry I got side-tracked. The vista from the fifth-floor executive boardroom of this building we're in now, gives an unobstructed spectacle of Old Trafford Football Ground. The club's bright red Manchester United insignia can be seen very clearly indeed. When Group MD for the diesel-generator division John Brookes visits us, conscious he's an ardent LFC advocate, we purposely put him in a chair overlooking Old Trafford Football Ground. As if vexed by some external force, he usually budges around in his seat for a while, then he moves the chair, so to avoid confronting the window. 'That's better', he usually says. Of course, he's in on the joke, and having a sturdy fabric, takes it in his stride without falling for the incitement bait."

"Hah, I'm pondering," Fraser originated, "what happens, if a newly appointed F&C executive turned out to be say, an Arsenal aficionado?"

"*Arsenal*!" Appleby blurted. "We do have our limits, Roger. Liverpool is bad enough, but the thought of one of those Flash-Harry, here today gone tomorrow, namby-pamby southern Jessie teams being lauded by an F&C exec—" Discombobulated by the notion, he shook his head. "Why, it'd be too much to bear."

"You should have a section on your employment application form entitled, 'football team supported'," Fraser suggested.

"We do."

~ * ~

With the introductory period over, Fraser and his host retired to his den to get down to the business in hand.

"From what we can gather," Appleby reiterated, "The Firm is proposing to invest in our subsidiary Western Goodricke, and correspondingly, F&C are obliged to aid the, er—" Stopping, he scrutinised the brief Fraser had emailed him after they'd talked on the phone. "The Armstrong Institution as a corporate sponsor."

"Precisely."

"You didn't mention what ration of sponsorship the Armstrong Institution is seeking."

"It's what I want to address today."

"Right. Let's get it out in the open and see if we can accommodate you." Hesitating, he audited the trouble-shooter. "Then I wish to comprehend why The Firm is investing £20m in Western Goodricke. That is not explicit." Smiling a, 'I will need to know smile', Appleby catechized, "how much are you after?"

"In return for the £20m capital investment, £850k per year for the next three years," Fraser tabled, pitching the sum above the equivalent Bembridge received from Ripley & Mortimer, knowing F&G would beat him down.

"Hhmmm, we were contemplating more along the lines of £700k," Appleby thwarted.

"Too low for The Firm, Frank."

"Very well, £750k."

"Make it £780k, and we're in business."

"Done," Appleby verbalised, "subject to final terms and conditions." Moulding a satisfied sparkle, he appended, "right, that's the easy part. Now, Roger, just what's driving this sudden patronage investment in Western Goodricke?"

"Forgive me for being coy, but I can only say, it's wheels within wheels and they encompass some degree of company confidentiality."

"You mean—" Appleby studied for a moment. "The Firm has a secondary agenda contingent on our parleys?"

Shrinking at Appleby's insight, nonetheless, Fraser held onto a positive frame of mind. "I can see you've done this kind of thing before."

Sniggering mildly, as if sensing the game taking on an unforeseen twist, Appleby peered at his opposite number. Resting his elbows on his desk, he transitioned into combat mode, his laugh mellowing into a perky bearing, all the signs of supreme confidence to be seen, echoing he had just made an advantageous chess move.

"I must have at least fifteen years on you, lad. The higher up the corporate ladder you get, the exposure to, let's call them, non-linear transactions, come more into your frame of reference. I've been party to some pretty creative affairs in the corporate investment director stratum, not necessarily fitting into conventional business routines but were axiomatic to closing the agreement." Engendering a prudent stance, he cautioned, "and don't go imagining, just because we speak with a provincial accent up here, we're not just as smart as the metropolitan London glitterati."

"Quite," Fraser consented. "I'm in a difficult position apropos what I can say. I'd deem it a favour, if you could desist from testing this particular line of enquiry."

"So, your hands are tied. Hhmm, may not be an influence anyway. It's just if you were in my role, I'm sure you'd want to know the ins and outs of any deal."

"For sure." Dallying, Fraser begged, "can I count on your indulgence, at least for the interim? Once the whole thing is in play, you might be able to work out what's happening in the background. By then, it will no longer be a confidential issue."

"Seems a bit nebulous," Appleby criticised, on the brink of pressing home the grilling. "But…because you are of good Cheshire stock, and at least the rest of your family are partisan to United—" Dawdling, he intentionally prolonged Fraser's agony. "I'm willing to provisionally run with it. Now, let's talk about Western Goodricke."

"Fine," Fraser welcomed.

"You're probably mulling over why, with so much cash on our books, Foxley & Chapman has not bank-rolled the last year of their research?"

"We assumed because there are other pursuits in the F&C rostrum ahead of them in the queue."

"Quite right. True, diversification from our core businesses has been a crucial plank in our long-term strategies for well over thirty years, but F&C still give priority to what we know, and that is manufacturing. Besides—" Halting to ruminate, he then supplemented with a hint of irony, "Western Goodricke has already been the recipient of a substantial cash and human resources injection. Our interests in telco, IT and biotechs come second to our core business. Right now, our cap-ex and op-ex budgets are fully absorbed in other ventures. Howbeit Western Goodricke could be a long-term cash cow, we're not willing to jeopardise core business investments by placing more capital with them now."

"Right, so can we close the deal?"

"Yes, we can, on this basis. As you know, Western Goodricke are a stand-alone SBU, and the parent company has little expertise in discerning the vagaries of the biotech world. It's another component prompting cautiousness with internal investments. Now—" Leaning rearward he quivered his brow. "The Firm has access to a wide array of experts giving guidance about your prospective investments."

"True."

"We want The Firm to commit to using one of your experts versed in the world of biotechs and pharmaceuticals to oversee the remainder of the research programme, embodying clinical trials. Can you do that?"

"We already have a strategy in play along those lines to protect our investment," Fraser validated.

"Good, then both our interests will be insured. You have a deal, Roger."

~ * ~

During his taxi ride to Ringway Airport, Fraser made a mobile call to Henry Jacques, requisitioning Dr Adam Kendrick, The Firm's resident biotech and pharmaceutical consultant, accompanied him to a meeting with Western Goodricke.

A professor of life sciences, Kendrick had worked for several blue chip pharmas before retiring and transposing into an industry consultant. Fraser had only exchanged a few words with him at The Firm's socials, but Jacques convinced the trouble-shooter of the specialist's steadfastness, and howsoever no way a businessman, he did have a grasp on the concept of profit and loss and a taste for a good investment.

Twenty-four hours later, Kendrick and Fraser were at the Western Goodricke Cambridge science park labs to conclude the investment part of what had become a very convoluted undertaking, and make sure there were no accidental side contentions. Sometimes covenants faltered at the ultimate hurdle, unpredicted skeletons in the closet and ghosts in the machine emerging to inhibit good business practice, inexorably resulting in the trade burning and crashing down.

Before the meeting, Frank Appleby had been on the horn to Western Goodricke Managing Director, Vaughan Edwards, telling him the good news and to expect a come by from Fraser to go through the terms of the pact, before The Firm's contracts people descended on Cambridge. When Fraser telephoned the MD, right off he got the intuition of someone not too tightly wrapped commercially, his confabulation unbalanced in terms of investment valuation, and his voice swinging between soprano and tenor, according to his interpretation of the terms Fraser outlined.

Taking The Firm's team into the boardroom, Edwards and Director of Research, Garfield Curbishley, engaged them in debate about the financing package, Fraser's initial negative take of the MD solidified by his airy-fairy sentiments concerning money elements. As the interchange proceeded, he formed the opinion Edwards and Curbishley were screwball fruitcakes, decidedly odd in the context of people he'd daily interface with in the business federation, but perhaps more typical of the head-in-the-clouds, time-stands-still-for-me, lab faction.

Bordering on the archetypal mad professor stereotype, with his huge spectacles and spooky hairstyle, presumably achieved through plugging himself into the mains each morning rather than combing his mop, Fraser's less than complimentary telephone impression of Edwards heightened with each response he made to The Firm's investment prospectus. As a responsible financial advisor, irrespective of how much Fraser tried to imprint upon him the ramifications of defaulting on the treaty, he dismissed them as minor stumpers, his only interest, securing the funding for his precious microbiology project.

Categorically a graduate from the school of the terminally doddering, when replying to Fraser's inquests regarding investment utilisation, Curbishley rose from his seat and moved around the boardroom with a curious gait, legs slightly akimbo, similar to one of Frankenstein's creations, murmuring a fractured response through a stuttering voice.

Neither exec imbued Fraser with a fortitude of confidence. However, sent to him by Frank Appleby before the meeting, their CVs revealed both to be Cambridge PhD post graduates, and exalted with almost idolatrous reverence within the sanctified halls of academia, Fraser finding the contrast between the glowing adoration of their peers and their sub-junior schoolboy cognizance of financial premises not just a dichotomy, but wholly disconcerting. How was it possible to become doyennes of the biotech fraternity concurrent with lingering adjacent, even oblivious to money fundamentals? The more the colloquy opened-up, the more Fraser had grave misgivings about risking the investment.

On the benefit side, Dr Adam Kendrick trumped the pair in terms of leading light worship, his reputation as a life sciences guru going before him, Edwards and Curbishley nearly breaking into a 'we are not worthy' exultation, when the four meeting participants pressed the flesh in the Western Goodricke reception. Musing the execs were going to bow and curtsey until Kendrick waved a dismissive self-effacing hand, Fraser had not witnessed such graphic apotheosis since Bill Beaumont delivered a one-man show at Kappa Corinthians clubhouse, having the entire club drooling with admiration, himself included.

Exploiting the deference as a vehicle to minimise risk, the trouble-shooter's work became easy when the execs swooned at the intimation Kendrick oversaw their work, to help guarantee the fabled embryology research was finalised in no longer than twelve months. Buoyed up by their enthusiasm, he tabled Western Goodricke pick up the tab for the professor's consultancy services. Taking it on without even ascertaining his day rate bonded Kendrick's reputation as a powerful piece of manpower, his very presence safeguarding Western Goodricke doing everything necessary to meet the end date for the production criterion microbiology offering, thereby equating with maximising confidence and minimising investment risk, the dual cornerstones all investors sought to ensure projected return on investment became reality. For the sake of business ethics, Fraser entreated Kendrick to quote his day rate, the amount not perturbing his admirers in the least, they willingly signed up for the professor's services on the spot.

As the paying homage to immensity conversation ran on, it cemented Fraser's evaluation that despite having no doubts about their biotech know-how, neither of the Western Goodricke execs manifested themselves as business savvy, the deficit deciphering why they were behind schedule on the research labour, independent of the required capital injection. Based on his antecedent excursions into the pure research brotherhood, primarily in the aerospace and energy verticals, Fraser had speculated this might be the case. Though an Einstein-class intellect endured essential to vision-out pioneering scientific theories, those same aptitudes were often disconnected from business reality in terms of financial and timescale factors, few pure research exertions ever delivering on-time and invariably over-budget. Notwithstanding, pure research formed the stock-in-trade bedrock for biotechs and the mainstream pharmas. Often costing £billions, the earnings on the necessary MO could be astronomical, as demonstrated by Glaxo Smith Kline and Astra Zeneca with their lofty FTSE one-hundred stations over many decades.

With these conflicting assessments in mind, Fraser had to make a judgement *vis-à-vis* the Western Goodricke capability to follow the trend. The more the talks unfolded, the more he erred to the conviction, at heart Edwards and Curbishley were pure-bred scientists, possessing only the slightest of business acumen, their natural constituency the lab, as opposed to the boardroom, and explicitly a tendency towards open-ended endeavour timescales. Under such a prevalent set of circumstances, it could signify disaster, not only for Western Goodricke, but the scheme to solve the Ayatollah's impasse with Dwight Armstrong.

While Kendrick went into chapter and verse about how he'd add value to the biotech undertaking, Edwards and Curbishley greedily lapping it up with a fork and spoon, Fraser mulled over durable project management skills would help to realise the research timetable. Further qualification of the microbiology enterprise exposed someone called Eric had been appointed to the tax, but the way the Western Goodricke execs intrinsically skipped over the elemental function, strengthened Fraser's earlier conspectus pertaining to them being more motivated by the research load as a piece of pure science, rather than warranting it succeeded in deliverables making money.

With this upstairs and being constantly motivated to minimise The Firm's and thereby their investors' risks, Fraser put on his best-selling persona, tabling Perry Fleming, another of The Firm's consultants with thirty years chemical industry project management experience, be contracted to inspect progress and help manage output. Anything protecting the continuance of the initiative, the execs readily agreed to, Fleming to be hired for one day a week, until the research culminated in the fabrication paradigm brand for volume licensed manufacturing. Sharing Western Goodricke were already in discourse with several pharmas relating to licenses, Edwards neutralised Fraser's trepidations around volume production, and thereby return on investment, while Curbishley verified UK Government certification had been built into the embryology research effort; the necessary conclusive proof-positive of fit for purpose stamp before the commodity went into production.

With all the bases screened, Kendrick and Fraser departed Cambridge in a far more buoyant frame of mind.

~ * ~

Later at Canary Wharf, Fraser met with TC to review the convoluted instalment.

"So, we're in the clear then, Roger?"

"Yes, it appears to be so. Foxley & Chapman will act as corporate donors to the Armstrong Institute, The Firm's investors will bankroll Western Goodricke, Zicon General will step up their business with The Firm and Studwick Harley, and Bembridge gets to keep his Ripley & Mortimer endowment."

"Good, I'll get Ricky on to our investors to start the ball rolling," Chalcroft advised, then tarried as if hit by a thunderbolt, a disconcerted expression splashed across his lineaments. "Let's hope Bembridge and Armstrong keep their on-going grudge rivalry well away from the business in the future. I could do without this kind of accessory overload wrecking other business openings."

"Yes, it did wipe out most of my scheduled work plan for this week."

"Well, it's the nature of trouble-shooting assignments," Top Cat argued. "They will come from left field, unannounced and unplanned for. You're going to have to get used to it, Roger."

"For sure, but it puts a whacking great hole in my normal day job responsibilities, and in defiance of Henry having no insurmountable reservations about my trouble-shooter mandate, he is disturbed about how it affects my analyst productivity."

"Don't be too spooked," Chalcroft petitioned. "I can always make sure Henry Jacques has cover to take on your analyst duties." Going into his pacing routine, Fraser wondered what bothered him now. "Tell me, Roger, are you enjoying these trouble-shooting escapades? Are they stimulating, motivating?"

"Yes, to all the above," Fraser affirmed. "I find they call for a skill set I didn't realise I possessed. The pressure seems to somehow generate tenets and innovations not necessarily emerging from my analyst work. Moreover, as is well known at The Firm, I have a low threshold of boredom. Irrespective of parsing the world's stock markets stirs up exhilaration, the trouble-shooter toils are on a loftier plane of challenge and thereby sequent satisfaction."

"Good, I'm glad you said that," Chalcroft enthused, "because over the next two quarters, I foresee some business jams arising that could go pear-shaped and will need rescuing."

Oh no, Fraser redressed, *in my eagerness to extol the virtues of the trouble-shooter province, what have I got myself into*? Yes, his latest dance with the devil had been an enthralling intrigue, but he didn't want to be snagged every time the peculiar came along. Indubitably thrilling, it still took its toll, Charlotte and the children cool about it, but he foresaw if trouble-shooter pursuits began to dominate his work programme, it could become a source of domestic conflict.

"Perhaps a team of trouble-shooters is needed," Fraser blurted, "so as to share the load, and allow for day jobs to be serviced professionally."

Stopping in his tracks, Top Cat enounced, "hhmm, an interesting notion. And maybe if demand increases, you could find yourself with an assistant."

Certainly not his weighing, he still felt compelled to lamely respond, "any ancillary resource to help shoulder the burden is welcome."

Squinting at Fraser, as if recognising he had misinterpreted the trouble-shooter's recommendation, Chalcroft qualified, "am I right in surmising you have apprehensions about your analyst work, or is it headaches outside the work domain?"

"A bit of both, Toby," Fraser certified.

"Leave it with me. This trouble-shooting venture is still in its infancy. Maybe it does need a bit more study." Approaching Fraser, Top Cat searched his physiognomy for any hints of reservation. "Let's re-examine the crux on the next occasion you have to don your Superman suit. In the meantime, enjoy the additional earnings you are generating. I'm sure Charlotte is never short of ideas on how to spend your supplementary income."

~ * ~

Fraser never did get to find out the embryonic instigator of the conflict between Luther Bembridge and Dwight Armstrong, other than a few days after the Western Goodricke business went through, the Ayatollah summoned his saviour to his executive suite, Fraser musing something might become uncovered.

"Roger," Bembridge hailed, cheery and obviously pleased with the upshot. "Please come in and make yourself comfortable."

"Thank you, Mister Bembridge," he brightly interchanged, knowing a cheerful disposition always sits well when the big boss man is pleased with your performance.

Briskly making his way over to the Ayatollah's bespoke, three-piece executive suite, he sat down, his attention immediately caught by a silver framed photograph of Bembridge receiving a cheque from Ripley & Mortimer the VP of Investment Banking had added to his trophy cabinet.

"I see you're perusing the Ripley & Mortimer presentation."

"Yes, Mister Bembridge. Congratulations."

Cladding Fraser in a gleaming smile, the Ayatollah then went over to his immense drinks cabinet, pulling out an ice bucket cooling a bottle of *Dom Perignon*, champagne being the *de facto* standard tipple for celebrations in financial services. Hearing the cork pop, Fraser glanced at the VP as he returned with two glasses of bubbly.

"I ascribed we ought to get together to toast your success," Bembridge extolled.

Taking one of the effervescing glasses, Fraser uttered, "you're too kind," his natural modesty ensuring he did not froth in front of the VP like a first-time weekly revenues trading winner from the bullpen.

"Well, Roger, incontrovertibly you are making a raging blockbuster of your trouble-shooting craft. I'm extremely pleased with the outcome of the Zicon General affair."

"Thank you, Mister Bembridge," Fraser diffidently appreciated.

Bartering more pleasantries, Bembridge being careful not to broach the foundation of his antipathy with arch-rival Dwight Armstrong, instead he resumed his salutation of Fraser's triumph, and how The Firm had always come through arduous trials with lateral formulas allied to good interpersonal skills.

Made partially merry by the *Dom Perignon*, when Fraser exited Bembridge's executive suite, he lasted none the wiser as to the origins of what sparked the spending of a humongous series of cycles by several firm employees, principally his, to resolve the business bugbear its knock-on effect had caused.

Later, he called Gary Delaware at Studwick Harley to give him the good news about the business as usual message with Zicon General.

"Say, Roger," Delaware probed, "did you divine Charlie Kelcher's gender?"

"No," he replied. "We'll just have to put it down to a species of unknown origin!"

Chapter 7: Guy Fawkes Fright for Sly

After yet another testing work week, largely dominated by the Bembridge-Armstrong episode, at Friday's close of business, Fraser awaited a cordial, relaxing weekend, free from controversy and the yoke of domestic servitude. Unhappily, he'd clean forgotten about Guy Fawkes Night, Wendy and James having invited some of their friends around to pay veneration to the gunpowder plot at a Saturday night celebration, or more properly, 'remembrance', as his son had quipped.

Reaching home, Charlotte reminded her husband of the impending shindig and specifically, Wendy's beau, the geekish Sly, attending. *Splendid*, Roger ruminated, *my life is over-brimming with completeness.*

"Now, Roger," Charlotte requested, "you will be civil to Sylvester, won't you?"

Contemplating if he'd be able to resist 'tossing', to use a Brigit 'Cruella' Hammond word, Sly on the bonfire, he reproached, "of course. How else do you expect me to behave?"

Detecting derision, she informed, "you're going to have to get used to Wendy having boyfriends, you know."

"*Boyfriends*! You're using the plural," he articulated. "I suppose it's not so much the concept I object to, more this distinct example of its embodiment."

"Oh, he's not that bad," Charlotte defended.

"So, you admit, there is an element of badness?"

"You're taking my comment out of context and into the literal. You know exactly what I mean."

"He's just *too* good to be authentic," Roger berated. "He doesn't drink, he doesn't gamble, he doesn't even swear." More corrosively, he catechized, "does he have a heartbeat, or is he really the mechanical android I've taken him for?"

"Oh, Roger, you're so intolerant of Sylvester. I think he's a nice young man with impeccable manners."

Not on receive, Charlotte's tribute failed to connect with her husband. Instead, carrying on his Sly destruction regardless, he blistered, "he doesn't even rise to the bait when either Heather or I lay it out upstream of him to catch him out! For a nineteen-years-old, he's excessively clever and skilled in the art of self-control and concealment. It's the kind of guarded behaviour I see every day in the financial services world, practised by people substantially older but just as devious. If this, this—" Unable to say the object of his disdain's name, he scrunched up his cheek muscles.

"Sly," she chimed in.

"If this…*Sly*," Roger repeated, curling his lip to emphasise his everlasting revulsion, "is a smooth operator now, what will he be like in ten years?" Raising his eyebrows, he blasted, "a right-regular, conniving spin doctor in the mould of Alastair Campbell."

"Oh, Roger," Charlotte scoffed, laughing at his ludicrous appraisal. "You're being far too fanciful with your unsubstantiated opinions and fears." Shaking her noggin and parading matronly window dressing, she placed her hands about her slim hips. "You're also being overly cautious, and letting your imagination get the better of you. It will be a short-lived courtship, you'll see."

At the unleashing of the word, 'courtship', Roger gave the Sly defender an alarmed sulk.

"I mean, relationship," she rectified. "Wendy is just exploring. She will dump him before you know it."

"I guess so," he conceded.

Despite recognising his overreaction, the prickly teenager in false love situation ceaselessly gave Roger grief. Notwithstanding Sly heeded Heather's warning at their primary meeting, that if he changed his name to 'Trustworthy' he'd evade her daddy shooting him, nonetheless the LSE student had totally failed to appreciate the gravity of the threat, misinterpreting the youngest Fraser daughter's words as just playful black humour. Not even when Roger stipulated he'd be purchasing a Rottweiler if he showed up again, did Sylvester construe his loathing for him. Instead, he had shielded with, 'Wendy said you had a wicked sense of humour', then proceeded to guffaw in a maniacal baboon fashion. Also only seeing it as a posturing tease, Wendy had joined in the devil dog threat ridicule of her father.

"Who else is coming?" Roger dug.

"Oh, the usual; James' gang members, and some of Wendy's A-level friends."

Ahh, must be careful, Roger deliberated, again recollecting the wrecking siren, man-baiting enacted by frisky A-level students at his business studies supplementary evenings, during the germinal weeks of the autumn term. Seeing the sultry Rebecca Sumner at the previous weekend's Halloween party, fixed his resolution along the lines of avoiding her on Guy Fawkes Night. When the Frasers got home from the Woodrow's bash, he had fully expected Charlotte to take him to task for calling Brigit Hammond, Fanny Craddock, and to also cross-examine him about Rebecca's and Jenny's schoolgirl innuendos. Albeit, fortune flew into the stratospheres for him that night. Engrossed in other topics, his wife did not revisit either peccadillo. Propping serendipity, he concluded she must have forgotten with all the fallout from *The Rake's Progress* debacle still fresh in her grey matter, and the half-accusation he had somehow conspired to engineer the farce with third parties. For once, the God of Bad Karma focused on some other poor sod, and not exclusively on him.

~ * ~

Arriving resplendent under a baleful moon with a mild chill in the air, ideal environs for the festivity and its bonfire centrepiece, the necessary preparation for Guy Fawkes Night had caused Roger the usual headaches, finally culminating with him setting up an area for a firework display and feasting facilities to beguile their guests in the afternoon. Like for the summer garden party, he solicited help from his children, but Wendy claimed she had to polish a business studies homework assignment for the eternally wet-behind-the-ears Mister Bryant, and James alleged duty-bound endeavours to make appropriate arrangements, whatever they might be, for his guests took precedence. Even more dubious, Heather apprised she had a full roster of punishment to administer to stuffed animals failing on her version of *Britain's Got Talent*. She also asserted she had to write a letter to David Cameron to complain about live animal exports through the port of Dover, and he should resign over the case.

As evening beckoned, ravenous as usual, James bounded into the kitchen, his tongue hanging out not because he'd seen a pretty girl, but because he'd smelt freshly baked savouries and desserts being laid out by his mother.

"Are those for the Guy Fawkes party, Mum?"

"Yes," she confirmed, crisply smacking his hand as he stretched towards the delights. "So keep your grubby mitts off them for now."

"James," his father gibbered.

"Yes, Dad."

"I suppose you've got the usual bedraggled suspects coming around this evening?"

"Yep. Neville Matthews, Jeremy Payne, Billy Swan and a few others. Actually, they're free-wheelers."

"Don't you mean, free-loaders?" Roger adjusted.

"Hah-hah, very good, Dad."

About to say more, James breathed in pure ambrosia from Charlotte's cooking deeds. Fastening his eyelids, he daydreamed about raiding the Guy Fawkes celebration spread in a few hours. Taking no chances, his mother ushered him aside from temptation, James backtracking to the present.

"*Oh*, by the way," he announced, "Billy's bringing a girl."

Stopping Charlotte dead in her baking tracks, the jaw-dropping news hit her like a thunderbolt. Equally floored, Roger stared in amazement at his son.

Discriminating his parent's disbelieving consternations at the hold-the-presses report, and realising they presumed he must be kidding, James reaffirmed, "it's true. He met this girl at Bluewater and he's bringing her to the Guy Fawkes commemoration."

"*Billy Swan*," Charlotte cried out, with enough incredulity in her voice to satisfy Roger's forethought of the macabre prospect as well.

"Yes, *you'll* see," James glorified, jam-packed with confidence.

"But, but, but, he's hardly human, let alone a lady killer," Roger contested.

"Oh, Dad, you're being unfair," James protested. "Billy does have a sensitive side."

"So has a rattlesnake, but I still won't let Billy get within touching distance of Wendy."

"Dad-dy."

Heather, Roger registered, and gauging by her wavering voice, he scented a spiny investigation coming on.

"Why didn't you let me invite my friends?" she remonstrated.

Having gone through two baptisms of endless w-questions with Wendy and James when they were Heather's age, the moment Roger heard a query even remotely up for an epic Q&A session and multi-layered until the cows came home from Heather, instantaneously he gave his wife full control.

"Your mother can answer that one," he proposed.

Rolling her blinkers whilst psychically lamenting her husband always delegated tricky child responses to her, Charlotte pressed her lips together then discharged him a biting gloom.

Ever the guardian of gumption, when not lambasting Greenwich Park preservation protestors, Charlotte made her explanation during her banqueting duties.

"With having a bonfire," she maintained in her most gentle, but compelling voice, "and only your father and myself to act as marshals, we thought allowing a lot of young children would be dangerous."

Dangerous, Roger cogitated, *what, for us or them?*

Circumspectly, Heather developed an unconvinced detachment, her father perceiving an imminent onslaught of unabated interrogation.

Conscious Heather had not rejoindered, Charlotte cocked her loaf of bread up from pastry preparation. As per her husband, she anticipated Heather's silence to be only a feint, and if not nipped in the bud, she'd still be explaining as to why for the rest of Guy Fawkes Night.

Inventing on the spot, Charlotte offered, "it's a Health & Safety regulation, darling."

Oh, very good, Roger mentally applauded, *persuasive and approaching a master stroke*, although Heather still bore mistrustful signs.

Having finished the usual marathon mobile gossip with one of her friends, Wendy joined the family assemblage.

Sensing a delicate affray in the making, she tested, "what's happening?"

"Your mother has just described to Heather why we can't have a load of young children running around the bonfire," Roger reiterated.

"But I'm not persuaded," Heather contended, issuing her parents an acrimonious pout.

Taking the initiative and hoping Heather let sleeping dogs lie, he canvassed, "who's attending from your set, Wendy?"

"Sly, obviously," she acquainted.

Twisting sideways, Roger muttered, "gghhhrrr."

"And Abigail Mortimer, Patricia Ellison, Rebecca Sumner, some others, and oh, your business studies class favourite, Roxanne Harrison."

Oh no! Roger almost expressed out loud.

Trying to control Roxanne's amorous advances in the classroom had become bad enough, but under the free reign of a social without any school restrictions, it could spell the end for him. Then he had an even scarier deduction. Had jailbait Lolita been invited as well?

"What did you say, Wendy?" Charlotte surveyed, breaking from her work at the mention of 'class favourite'.

Holding his breath and shutting his snoopers to temporarily shut out reality, Roger awaited the feedback.

Grinning at her father, Wendy blustered, "oh, nothing, Mum. Just a bit of schoolgirl banter."

Opening his optics, Roger saw his wife pinpointing him, her x-ray vision scouting his entire body, searching for evidence of malpractice. As Heather inevitably reengaged on the health and safety blitz with a barrage of w-questions for her mother, Roger cinched he must have come out of the surveillance clean, because she resumed food preparation while simultaneously fending off her youngest daughter's assault.

Skulking off into the garden before his fictitious misdemeanour could come to the front of Charlotte's mind afresh and the mini-drama reignited, he pretended he had to check the bonfire content lasted dry, ready to burst into flame.

Soaked with the distinct sensation, for some rationale beyond the scope of his brain for understanding female logic Charlotte had given him the benefit of the doubt, he rambled up the garden path crowning, *good, justice for Roger Fraser.*

An hour later, Wendy's and James's guests arrived. None of legal drinking age, Charlotte offered them a selection of non-alcoholic beverages to sip on while they waited for Roger to light the bonfire, and more expectantly, commencement of the celebration banquet. Having set up the beacon at the garden bottom on some grass-free land used to store weather-proof materials, and for conservation reasons at least fifty yards from the house, he intended to use it for roasting potatoes and chestnuts. Not ginormous by any stretch of ingenuity, more a token gesture to Guy Fawkes, its construction had been a tiresome burden, Roger having to hunt far and wide for fallen branches and disposable wood the prior Sunday.

Initially needing some coaxing, James helped him to get a sea of flames ignited with the aid of a massive squirt of lighter fuel. Bursting into life, the house and surrounding trees became silhouetted against the flames, Roger and James fleetingly distracted by the spectacle before resuming their outstanding chores; erecting foldaway garden chairs

Roger had borrowed from the rugby club to form a U-shape around the bonfire, and placing ten rows of fireworks, ready to be let off, once all the guests had settled in.

Returning to the kitchen, James and Roger were met by the flaunt of Billy Swan showing off his girl Tracy to his envious friends, and the astonishment of Wendy's. Their mouths breaching wide at the showcase of Billy's luscious conquest side-by-side with him, Abigail, Patricia, Rebecca and, of course, Roxanne, broke into hushed whispers and girly giggles, the incongruous combination reminding Roger of Esmeralda and the Hunchback of Notre Dame.

Proudly making the introduction to James's parents, he heralded, "Mister and Missus Fraser, this is my girlfriend Tracy."

Charlotte and Roger welcomed Billy's new found joy, she reciprocating with polite thanks in a perfect neutral English accent.

"Very impressive," Charlotte murmured to Roger.

"Yes, an awfully attractive girl, and so well-spoken."

Crowding around King Billy and his newly enthroned queen, Neville Matthews, Jeremy Payne and other James gang members unreservedly gushed praise for the lady killer's recent acquisition to his otherwise half-witted and imbecilic testosterone driven lifestyle, their universal homage to *The Inbetweeners* taking a lower place in the boy's affections.

Having bestowed his own 'we are not worthy' salutation on Billy, James sauntered over to his father.

"What's your take on Billy's girlfriend, Dad?"

"She's very pleasant and pretty, but she's not what I expected her to be."

"Oh, what were you expecting her to be?"

"Blind and deaf."

~ * ~

Making his splashy entrance late, Sly wore an LSE scarf around his neck, providing the evening's foremost temptation for Roger.

Accurately reading his brainwaves, Charlotte intervened, pushing him aside, and went forward to receive Wendy's friend, their eldest daughter on his arm.

"Hello, Sly, glad you could make it," she greeted with an endearing smile.

God knows why she's so hospitable to the cretin, Roger brooded.

"Good evening, Missus Fraser. Thank you for inviting me," he blarneyed with a capacious toothy leer.

Oh no, Roger discerned, *he's in ingratiation mode. What a toad.*

Seeing Roger gazing upwards to the house loft, the politico-in-waiting knew Wendy's father kept his shotgun there, Heather's foregoing inference apropos his potential to come face to muzzle with the Purdey, sheltered the need to keep his hands off Wendy, if he wanted to survive the evening.

"Hello, Mister Fraser," Sly prattled, hoping to avoid another thinly disguised warning. "Business good?"

"Yes," Roger dryly acknowledged. "Exceedingly good."

Continuing to inadvertently invite more encounters with both the Purdey and a Rottweiler, they flipped a few more words, forced on Roger's behalf, Sly still craving Roger's astringent antipathy towards him equated to an echo of his own special brand of black humour. No matter what Roger said to convey his distaste, Sly remained upbeat, the offensive slithering off his impregnable shell while he parried with defusing sentiments and narrow compliments. Not able to categorically authenticate if Sly's corporeal cleverness imbued him with a credit of invulnerability, Roger assessed it could be a cosmetic front, and under his polished gloss, plain stupidity prevailed. Still pondering the alternates, Charlotte told Roger chow time beckoned and bid him to fulfil his carbohydrates cremation duties.

With the bonfire budding blast furnace temperatures, he inserted potatoes and chestnuts on a long-handled spade into the cauldron's core. Less than five minutes later the chestnuts were ready and, shortly after he pulled out the potatoes, both marginally overdone. Pleased *cordon bleu* cook Brigit 'Cruella' Hammond had not been invited to condemn his culinary skills yet again, he handed the scorched, calorie-rich chunks and nuggets to Charlotte. Popping them in the oven with the other hot items to keep warm, she then called for everybody to go into the garden for the firework exhibit.

Congregating around the display area, James and Roger let off salvo after salvo, the girls hooting at every rocket launch, the boys more enthralled by the fire crackers. Becoming more demanding, the onlookers egged on father and son to play duellists with roman candles at twenty paces, until health & safety inspector Charlotte brought the boom down firmly on the want, the firework management team reduced to convention for the residue of the pyrotechnic parade. For an investment nearly bankrupting the Fraser monthly entertainment allowance, Roger deemed the fireworks afforded very limited value for money. Within what emerged as a very short intermission, whirling Catherine wheels stuttered to a standstill, and the final battery of sky-bound rockets vanished, audience oohs' and arghs' ebbing as the projectile's burst cluster decayed into nothingness. Ensuring the festivity's rapid pace did not flag, Charlotte announced commencement of their *al fresco* banquet, as ever, her party timing impeccable.

After filling their paper plates with Charlotte's tasty goodies and Roger's burnt offerings, the guests made their way to the top of the garden and surrounded the bonfire. Attacking their food congeneric to ravenous wolves, the James gang stuffed as much meat and savouries down their throats as their stomachs could bear, Billy Swan particularly keen to show Tracy he had a healthy appetite, should the opportunity to shed some calories through boy-on-girl action occur later. Adopting a more ladylike posture, the girls nibbled graciously and dabbed their lips with paper napkins, none confessing to being insatiably hungry, the need to sustain as near to a zero-dress size paramount.

Noting their guests were having a dandy stint, Roger assumed Roxanne and the other little foxes from the business studies class were going to behave themselves, and not aim to destroy his marriage. Enduring civil and courteous with Charlotte and himself, not once did they resort to anything bawdy or lewd, their conversational topics persisting as genteel and decorous. What took place in the classroom, apparently stayed in the classroom. Howbeit, Roxanne gave Roger a few unsubtle winks during the course of the evening, unnerving his constitution.

Whilst Charlotte and Heather stuck with the Wendy set, Roger nattered with the boys, quizzing how they were finding the new school term, and what they'd been doing socially. Interestingly, keeping the gender demarcation perfectly symmetrical, Roger observed Billy Swan occupied the ultimate chair in the boy's quarter, and his girlfriend Tracy started the girl's province.

"We've got a new physics master," Jeremy assigned.

"Oh," Roger yammered. "What's he like?"

"He looks like a griller," Billy recalled.

"You mean, a gorilla," Roger corrected.

"That's right," he verified, "a griller."

Glimpsing at Tracy, Roger noticed she hung on Billy's every word. Jerking his head up, he ruminated *what does she see in him*?

"He is very hairy," James annexed.

"Undeniably," Jeremy approved. "His body hair sprouts out from his shirt collar and his wrist cuffs. It's not natural"

"Maybe he's a werewolf," Roger jokingly propounded.

"Do you know, Mister Fraser, you could be right," Jeremy accepted. "Verily, he has a pointed snout and the beginnings of all-over facial fuzz."

"And I suppose," Roger mockingly docketed, "you're going to tell me he howls under a full-moon and has no mirror reflection?"

"You shouldn't joke about these things, Mister Fraser," Billy exhorted, espousing an esoteric riposte for once in his narrow life. "I have a very hairy distant uncle. He ended up being confined for a while."

Now I know where he gets his Lon Chaney junior looks from, Roger calculated.

Aware of her newcomer status and that she might be experiencing out of place notions, Charlotte and Heather went over to talk to Tracy. Clocking their presence, Roger reckoned his wife was as curious as him to hear why this very pretty, and he conjectured intelligent girl, had the hots for big, bad Billy. Balancing the adult participation amongst the group, Roger made his way over to the other girls. Nearing them, he audited their young and sometimes not so innocent frontages glistened against the bonfire glare.

"Plenty of room among us, Mister Fraser," Abigail tendered. "Come and sit here, and tell us what you have in mind for the business studies evening set next term."

"Ah, you're jumping the gun a bit there, Abigail," he objected. "I've not actually agreed to do any further symposiums."

"But Missus Greenwood said you'd do another session," Roxanne implored.

"Yes," Roger concurred, "but your headmistress also jumped the gun."

Catapulting foiled flashes at each other, the girls then directed accusing frowns at Roger, attempting to make him feel guilty.

"I'm not promising anything," he indicated, feeling about as popular as Benedict Arnold at a Brotherhood of the American Revolution meeting, "but—" They're features lit up. "Dependent on my work commitments, I might be able to squeeze in one or two workshops…but don't hold me to it."

"Oh good," Rebecca trilled, "Zoey Dunbar will be pleased."

Quaintly staring at Rebecca, Roger probed, "which one is she?"

"Oh, you *must* remember Zoey, Mister Fraser," Patricia prompted. "She's one of the year-thirteen students…" *She means the upper sixth to anyone on the wrong side of forty*, Roger chewed, *me included*. "…joining us the second week of the evening course." Judging by the symbolic poser hanging over his head, Patricia realised Roger had not made the connection. "You know," she goaded, "the one asking all those suggestive questions."

As Wendy's friends giggled, the penny dropped. "Lolita!" Roger croaked under his breath.

Whilst the man-baiting carried on, Roger's eldest daughter gave him a disapproving lour regarding his risqué secret, thereby compromising his personal security if monogamous puritan Charlotte were to hear about the indiscretion, unpremeditated or otherwise.

"Mister Fraser," Roxanne injected in a low husky voice. "What do you think of Wendy's boyfriend?"

"Oh, Roxanne," Wendy scolded. "I hope you're *not* going to embarrass me."

Not waiting for the reply, she got up, went over to Sly, grabbed him by the hand, and they made a hasty retreat to the other side of the bonfire.

Caught in a quandary, Roger mulled over, *Do I tell the girls I want to torture him with red-hot irons, or do I make the habitual bountiful response*?

Deciding to go for the middle-ground he allotted, "well, I do have some reservations, but…" Lost for the right words, the sentence hung incomplete, the girls sensing his qualms.

Taking the lead, Abigail chimed, "we all think he's an out-and-out dork."

"Yes," Rebecca endorsed, her malice barely concealed. "We envisaged you'd have chased him off by now, Mister Fraser."

"Hhmm," he gurgled, "do I detect there is no love lost between you girls and Sly?"

"It's a terrible name," Roxanne denounced. "Hardly one engendering assurance, is it?"

"Funny you saying that," Roger replied. "Heather admonished him on his shortened name, when Wendy first brought him to the house."

While Charlotte, Heather and Roger had been chatting to Wendy's and James's guests, the *Love Story* pair had moved from the bonfire to a more secluded part of the garden.

Perusing to his right, Roger saw the object of the girl's tongue lashing cuddling up to his eldest daughter. Drawing his dander, he had the crushing desire to make a journey loft-wards to fetch the Purdey, or phone the Rottweiler emergency delivery hotline.

His business inventiveness skills coming to the fore, Roger hatched a plan. *How about if I got James to tell Sly, Billy's girl Tracy had the hots for him? Sly approximates an egotistical sod, so he probably wouldn't be able to resist moving in on Tracy when Wendy is out of sight.* He could then nudge Billy, tell him the geek plotted to steal the girl of his dreams, resulting in Billy tossing Sly on the bonfire, Brigit 'Cruella' Hammond style, thus saving him the bother of dealing with the lothario, and crucially keeping him out of jail. Still refining the plot's fine detail, he felt a jab into his midriff.

"Roger," Charlotte summoned, "can you help me with the desserts, please?"

"Certainly, darling," he signalled, exhibiting willing. "Excuse me girls."

Walking to the house hand-in-hand with Charlotte, he gave his Machiavellian contrivance additional consideration, hoping to entrap Sly via his own variation on the renaissance Italian philosopher's methods.

"You're cogitating," professed his ever-vigilant wife. "What about?"

"Oh, just wondering…"

"Yes?"

"Er," he unconvincingly recommenced, "if the crocuses will be out early next spring."

"*No, you weren't,*" Charlotte argued. "You were contemplating ways to scupper Sly's linkage with Wendy."

Jumping up in real surprise, he cooed, "how could you possibly know that?"

"While you were talking to Wendy's friends, I saw you surreptitiously surveilling him."

"You know, they don't like him either?"

"Oh, that's just a touch of peer-group jealousy."

"*Jealousy!*" Staggered by the retort, he came to a standstill. "Over the king of dorks?" Bemused further, he upheld, "not so, Charlotte. It's genuine concern for our Wendy's wellbeing, shown by her very caring and loyal school friends."

"Oh, Roger," she censured in a governess-matching voice. "You're really getting this Sly thing out of all proportion. He's hardly the

Casanova type intent on eloping with Wendy to Gretna Green, is he?"

"A-ha!" Roger jeered as they coasted into the kitchen. "*Belle tournure* also failed Casanova, but that didn't stop him seducing his conquests with a Svengali-adopted comportment."

Scowling at him dismissively, she reprimanded, "*really*, Roger. Casanova, Svengali, you must fancy I'm simple to buy into such an analogy?"

"Listen, my girl, I know more about Casanova than you do about amorous LSE students," he touted, his confidence growing, "and I'm telling you—"

"Daddy."

Losing his train of thought, Roger gawped down at Heather. "Yes, darling. What is it?"

"Daddy, you'd better come quick. One of James' friends is fighting with Sly."

"*What!*" Charlotte roared, panic spreading over every contour of her dial.

Oh, joy of joys, Roger subliminally saluted, looking to the heavens, *my prayers have been answered. Oh, thank you God, I'll never vacillate over your existence again, and I promise to go to church tomorrow.*

"Well Roger, you'd better hop to it," instructed his trouble and strife.

"Oh…" Dismissively shrugging his shoulders, he intended to yield maximum opportunity for Sly to be slayed. "I'm sure it's nothing serious. Just young alpha-male rucking."

"James's friend has got Sly's head in the bonfire," Heather primed.

"*Roger!*" Charlotte blurted, hands on hips and baring a threatening dial.

"Oh, *alright*," he assented, "I'll go and see what all the commotion is about."

To let whoever had become Sly's nemesis finish the job, he wandered through the garden as slowly as he could, but fast enough to give Charlotte the vestige of him being on the case. Sure enough, when he reached the battleground, knight in shining armour, Sir Billy Swan, had Sly by the head, crusading to bake it in the bonfire, much to everyone's amusement, apart from Wendy. Beating on Billy's torso, she squawked to let her beau go, but so devoured with his task, the knight hardly felt the blows or heard her plea.

Seeing her father out of the corner of her eye, Wendy shrieked, "*Dad*, come and get Billy off Sly."

"Right," Roger expounded in as enthusiastically a voice as he could artificially muster.

Also having little interest in Sly's survival and keen to see the excitement, Heather had followed her father into the garden.

Glimpsing at her, he mildly bossed, "go to the kitchen, Heather. This is no place for an impressionable young girl."

"But I want to see what's happening, Daddy."

Before he could counter reply, Wendy screamed, "*Dad*, come on."

Continuing to move as slowly as he could, hoping to give Billy enough scope to cremate Sly's head, he gave up on harrying Heather to the kitchen.

"Just keep away from the bonfire," he commanded.

It hadn't occurred to him before, but as he appraised the kafuffle to his front, he took onboard Billy had developed into a big, strong lad. Charging rugby forwards would bounce off him. Not wanting to end up doing an involuntary Joan of Arc portrayal himself, Roger decided to go for the gentle, gently option with Billy the Mountain.

"Billy, old son," he trumpeted, his voice timbre in neutral, not really wishing to interrupt Billy's baking lesson.

Swirling towards Roger, Sir Billy the Geek Slayer kept a secure grip on Sly's head.

"You'd better let him go. His hair is about to ignite."

"But Mister Fraser…"

Hankering he'd protest catching Sly *in flagrante delicto* with Tracy, Roger cultivated impartial physiognomy.

"...he spilled his Red Bull all over my brand-new Wranglers. Made me look a right Herbert."

Solid motives for severe retribution, Roger gauged, soiling a man's jeans tantamount to gobbing on the Archbishop of Canterbury, although he knew many alleging they'd do worse to the sitting, trendy-lefty, Welsh Druid incumbent, for recurrently making the Church of England look like a bunch of wet wusses.

"Well, I commiserate with your annoyance, Sir Knight, er, I mean, Billy," Roger intoned. "But deep frying Sly's noggin is going a little too far."

"You want me to let him go then, Mister Fraser?"

No, I want you to complete the job and consign the worm to his maker, Roger telepathically imparted. "Probably best," he superficially supported. "He's turning purple."

Applying a renewed enforcing grip around Sly's scrawny neck, Billy whispered something in his ear along the lines of, 'Cross me again, punk, and I'll carve my name on your forehead, twinning what Brad Pitt did to Nazis' in *Inglorious Basterds*', then released the panic-stricken LSE student. Dropping to earth, Sly gasped for breath and whinged about half his hair still being alight, a fretful Wendy extinguishing the flame remnants by beating his noodle with a used paper plate, the exploit unintentionally embedding food scraps into Sly's scalp, much to everyone's amusement.

Still enthralled, the glorious, even gallant, flicker became a Saint Paul on the road to Damascus epiphany for Roger. He had a new god to worship, his name, Billy the Sly slayer. Roger's love and respect for him raneth over. Welcome to chew the cud with him anytime, and share his premier wines, when old enough to partake of alcohol legally, Billy the Mountain attained nobility and distinction in Roger's lexicon of the good and the great.

Conversely, Charlotte rested furious. Rushing down the garden path, she berated Billy about controlling his temper, insisting he made contrite apologies to Sly.

"But, Missus Fraser," Sir Billy whined, "It's me brand new

Wranglers." Addressing his friends, he beseeched, "tell her lads."

Bolstering the hero's cause, Neville Matthews reinforced, "he's right, Missus Fraser. I accompanied Billy when he bought those jeans from Topman at Bluewater. They were very expensive."

"Yeah, Wranglers are top dollar, Mum," James buttressed. "Billy had to save up for ages to buy them."

"Cost is not an ingredient here," Charlotte stipulated, arms folded, bearing judge and jury duties. "The nub is unnecessary violence and a disproportionate response to a heedless accident."

After the Greenwich Park massacre, you're a fine one to throw stones, Roger reflected.

"Not sure about that, Missus F," Jeremy Payne argued. "Messing up a man's Wranglers is strictly a no, no."

"Definitely," Neville approved. "It's a hanging offence. Sly got let off lightly."

While all the bi-directional for and contra to the exultation of Wrangler jeans banter went on, with an isolated Charlotte emanating snowballing disenchantment, Wendy's girlfriends had a whale of a time. Reluctantly concealing their mushrooming laughter behind hands brought in front of their mouths, they attempted to retain some nuance of decorum.

As Wendy comforted Sly, still coughing and spluttering from his close encounter with Dante's inferno, King Billy looked mightily pleased with his retribution act, his mates championing of his handiwork imbuing him with an acuity of justice.

Knowing she had little backing for chastising Billy, Charlotte gave her husband the eyes signal to pull proceedings into normality again.

"Okay everybody," Roger extolled, "the shows over. Let's restore the celebration and dive into the desserts."

After what evolved to be the acme mark of the evening in terms of Roger's pleasure and Sly's embarrassment, the balance became pedestrian, regular social topics and conventional behaviour sterile in comparison. Towards the witching hour, the Fraser's guests departed,

King Billy giving the Wranglers spoiler a parting withering sneer. Responding, Sly rubbed his scalp, rekindling scorching memories of what had happened a few hours earlier.

~ * ~

As a postscript to the evening, apart from Heather, the Fraser family plus Sly retired to the lounge for coffee and a nightcap. Tired, she bid them goodnight after Charlotte and Roger had smothered her in hugs and kisses.

"I presume you have fully recovered from your contretemps with Billy Swan, Sly," Charlotte enquired, still jittery Wendy's friend might have lost half of his hair in the cleansing flames.

Seeing James leering, Roger longed that his son had not cracked, because it made him develop an ever-broadening grin he tried to hide behind his brandy glass and out of Charlotte's gaze.

"Oh, I'm fine, Missus Fraser, but I must say, the yob's reaction to an unintended accident flabbergasted me."

Peeping at each other, James and his father both deliberated, *should I tell King Billy, Sly called him a yob*?

"Have you lost any of your hair?" Roger's wakeful wife investigated.

Touching his scalp, Sly articulated, "no, only the ends have been singed. I'm going for a haircut next week anyway, so little harm done."

"Pity," Roger muttered.

Unconverted, Wendy ploughed through the Sly thatch, searching for cinders. "Billy ought to learn to control himself," she bemoaned. "Sly's hair has taken a beating."

Entirely ignoring her plea, Roger legitimised, "oh, he was just being his normal alpha-male self in the presence of his girlfriend." Wrinkling his nose indifferently, intending to make any excuse he could find to justify Sir Billy's heroic brush, he tendered, "it's very hard at his age to take it on the chin in the neighbourhood of your girl, and not react."

Glaring at her husband's macroscopic sanctioning, Charlotte

changed the subject. "How's your course going at the LSE, Sly? What is it you're studying?"

"Political Science."

Cocking his napper up in disgust and tutting in James' direction, Roger brooded *that's just what the country needs, another political psycho*. "And what," he polled, "are you going to do when you graduate?"

"Probably, I'll become a researcher for one of the lobbyist companies."

"You mean," Roger persisted digging deeper, "you'll end up as what's called a political adviser to an MP, or even a minister of the crown?"

"Yes, but I really want to go into mainstream politics as soon as possible."

"As an elected proxy?"

"Yes."

"In *Parliament*?" he ejaculated, his incredulity gauge banging against its stops.

"Yes."

"But," Roger queried, "what are you going to bring to the job in terms of real work and life experience?"

"*Roger*!" Charlotte barked in a familiar rebuking fettle, meaning, back in your kennel.

"Oh, it's all right, Missus Fraser," Sly safeguarded smiling. "I'm getting used to Mister Fraser's acerbic attacks. I know he's only engaging in his penchant for cynicism and black humour."

Am I? Roger weighed.

"Dad's right," James supplemented. "Get a real job and your hands dirty, so to speak, before putting yourself up for election."

On the spot, Sly distinguished career politicians were ranked to be fully disconnected from real life and universally despised by the general public for their, 'do as I say, not as I do' rhetoric. "Politics has become a vocation over the past twenty years," he merited. "Long gone are the days when people from the trades and business professions became politicians. Most of the new breed adopt the political science degree path and lobbyist route, before applying to become a party candidate."

"And you think it's morally right?" Roger interpolated, narrowing his peepers.

"Whether it is morally right or not, is academic. That's the way it is."

"By Jupiter," Roger exclaimed. "Hardly a democratic or even a demographic delineation of the nation, *is it*?"

"Yes, for once I agree with Roger on a political issue," Charlotte declared, jolted by the concurrence of their opinions. "Representation befits coming from within communities in a democracy, meaning MPs sincerely digging their constituents' beliefs will stand for them in Parliament, and not be subservient to the party whip."

"You know, Sly," Roger inducted, "what my wife says is unconditionally valid. Until the rise of the political classes, palpably you want to join, MPs were selected by local constituency parties from candidates living and working in the locale. For example, in Attlee's post war government, MPs came from the shop floor, mining, farming and other private sector occupations, as well as the business callings, such as engineering and management. Most had perhaps twenty to thirty years of working life behind them, and thereby were able to draw on life journals as their passport to act for constituents. Since Blair took office, effectively, it's been replaced by candidates exclusively from party organisations, media pundits, self-interested lawyers, social workers and various other Nancy boy pursuits, having no connection whatsoever with the people they want to elect them to Parliament." Really getting into his stride he ridiculed, "even more astonishing, by age twenty-five they surmise this strikingly parochial life intimacy entitles them to be an MP." Stopping his recap, he glared at Sly. "Now, tell me, does it really seem sane to you?"

Going into a long diatribe, Sly justified the recent strain of politician, and why his own ambitions in the given direction were warranted, the Fraser family taking in a stream of double-standards, flimsy self-seeking pretexts for tax-payer funded political parties and sideways swipes at English tradition with mounting scepticism.

"None of what you said is moving in the least," James argued. At last in grownup mode and using the normally dormant organ between his ears, he shone, his observational and analytical skills pulling apart Sly's sneaky and egocentric plans. "You're defending joining this bunch of societal leeches, whilst simultaneously flying the caring, sharing vote trapping flag. My generation aren't going to fall for such shenanigans."

Well done, son, Roger inwardly congratulated with immense pride, *you're doing my work for me*. So delighted, he made a mental note to review James's allowance.

Counterattacking with attempts to vindicate why the BBC's executive structure is dominated by middle-class, PC pinkos living in the nuclear free-zone of Islington, the rise of the metropolitan political classes producing an elitist sect, and why he saw no ethical contradictions to the civic service code by joining their greasy, sycophantic, stiff-necked ranks, Sly became a social pariah as far as the Frasers' were concerned.

Shocked, Wendy's rose-tinted glasses regarding his wonderfulness clouded over. Unwittingly, in terms of exposing a trait objectionable to his eldest daughter, her father might have stumbled on Sly's Achilles' heel. Comprehending exit visas were imminent for Sly, the slimy toad, Roger noted her becoming incrementally alarmed by his bombast. All the same, he anticipated he'd not have the enjoyment of watching her ditch him, the joyous courtship guillotining, joyous at least to him, happening when they were next alone.

Conceivably oblivious to her negativity, the more Sly's duplicitous lecture went on, the more Wendy sunk into downheartedness, even anger. Unable to resist lambasting the Frasers with his one-world vision of everything condensed down to a single entity, with the State doing all citizens cogitating and decision making for them, it reminded Roger of David Miliband's future vision of a new world village order, without nations or individual identity, governed by an unelected, overarching worldwide body of mediocrities and narcissistic chancers, humanity reduced to ultra-low IQ drones and robotic androids, existing in an infallibly, sanitised world, pre-programmed to obey their overlords and regurgitate PC sound-bites verbatim. Without motivation, pride of purpose, or any tangible basis to exist, other than to breathe stale air and eat tasteless food, they'd shrink into nothingness.

Even left-of-centre, modernist doctrines advocate Charlotte appeared perplexed and disenchanted by Sly's autocratic control countenance for the future subjugation of those opposing the totalitarian, liberal-fascist regime he beheld to be right and just.

Encapsulating everything, from subsuming England into one gigantic international behemoth beyond the wildest fancies of the EU, to introducing more draconian laws limiting freedoms, all in the pilgrimage for political correctness, Roger decided not to quiz his mammoth manifesto further. Instead, he chose to let him become hoisted on his own petard. Having few interpersonal skills, Sly flunked distinguishing the Frasers were not buying. By the time, the Gordon-Brown-in-the-making discovered they were not sold on his twenty-first century vision and he had no allies, it was too late, his kinship with Wendy irrevocably damaged.

When Charlotte went to the kitchen for more coffee, her husband logged their eldest daughter whispering in Sly's ear. Whatever she said had a blistering effect. Unhesitatingly, he morphed the rap into student goings-on at the LSE, at length unmasking he had entered the alliance termination zone, Roger no longer inviting him to spend a few hours playing tag with a Rottweiler, or gazing upwards to the loft contemplating using his trusty shotgun. Sly's osmosis of self-importance and favouring an Orwellian future had led him into *harakari* mode. Wendy might not apply the conclusive *coup de gras* that evening, but it'd be soon.

As the LSE student withdrew, Roger couldn't help but say, "do come and see us again soon, Sly. I'm sure Billy the Mountain relishes making your reacquaintance."

Chapter 8: 'Cool' Salesmen and Karaoke Prophets

In a moment of compassion, if not weakness, Fraser agreed to a software salesman coming to see him at The Firm's Canary Wharf skyscraper. Patently immune to salesman repellent, the somebody at issue had managed to get through several layers of secretaries and administrators failing to fend him off with barge poles, stun guns and tasers. Through a convoluted route, he found his way to Fraser's landline number, made his elevator pitch and proposed a short meeting. Normally, the stock analyst crowed anything to put salesmen off. 'I've got yellow fever and I'm in quarantine,' or 'my pet gerbil has been bitten by a rabid dog and I have to take it to the vets,' typical. Remaining highly sceptical *vis-à-vis* the salesman's claims about the revolutionary stock market analytical package he hawked, all the same, he caught Fraser in a generous mood. Being a good ol' boy, he acceded to give the tenacious salesman twenty minutes of his, to quote him, 'very valuable time.'

'I must sound like a right halfway up my own arse prick,' Fraser had murmured as he replaced the handset on its cradle, but then reversed his stance deeming the border-repulsing defence to be necessary. Any feebleness shown to marauding predators instantly became interpreted as a fortuity for making money. Before the buyer knew it, other quarterly sales revenue-driven creatures descended on him, intent on plugging in their laptops and subordinating him to death by PowerPoint. Moreover, frailty on behalf of the buyer often culminated in the rapacious go-getter setting up camp outside his retreat, and staying there until the buyer signed a purchase requisition.

Software salesmen get suckered into supposing if they spin the wheel of the latest solution selling or target account selling technique, out will pop an order at the end of the process. About ninety-three percent of software sales comes from customers not actively out to buy, but nevertheless having a latent need, the skilled salesman unlocking such opportunities. However, without a need generated by a business pain, a compelling event, or a legitimate business driver, there is no opportunity. Salesmen are perennially slow to grasp this reality, often harassing prospects to the brink of distraction. Induced to meet goals himself, Fraser understood their motivations, even empathised with them, but prescribed walking out and finding someone with a real need, rather than beating on a door perpetually shut to them.

Ken Carter, the gentleman in hand, represented HAL Financial Solutions, a premier brand, global player with a proven pedigree and a lineage going as far back as The Firm's. 'Gareth Cheeseman' wannabe Ken had the same attitude and mindset for trafficking with customers as the Steve Coogan character, short on content but long on unforgettable makeup gusto. During their fleeting telecom, Fraser minuted Ken had shortened his birth name from Kenneth in the belief the catchier Ken Carter resonated as slicker, accordingly sticking in the buyers' mind. Whether authentic or just fantasy, it subsisted as a detail of conjecture beyond the realms of empirical measurement, psychology more the determinant germinating a good seller-buyer affinity rather than glassy monikers.

Undifferenced from a rutting stag, Ken bounded into Fraser's hideout, the glow of 'I'm not withdrawing until I have a deal' dripping from his IT *de facto* yardstick temperament. Capturing his mark's attention, to Fraser, his overly clean-shaven phizog flushed through excessive smoking, brought on by the need to constantly have an article between his fingers to conquer his nerves, and maybe a cocaine habit he just couldn't kick, were indicative of the software sales breed. Making Fraser remember a heavy-hitting HAL divisional director had been caught with cocaine lines in his office, and as a consequence had to resign and go solo, he hoped Ken did not equivalently end up with his P-45. A comprehensive crew-cut and an oversized body brought on by an ultra-abundance of calories intake, rounded out the factory paragon clone, 2011 model, or using software jargon, version 1.0, release 1.0. Attired in regulation *Men in Black* apparel, comprising shoes so shiny Fraser stayed sure Ken could check for emerging hair growth up his hooter before participating in a meeting by merely noting the reflection in his mirror-projecting feet warmers.

In Ken's daydream, he saw himself putting down a deposit on a top-of-the-range, colleague-impressing Subaru Impreza from the commission he aspired to earn on the transaction. Through his success, he already owned a C63 AMG, Mercedes latest puny attempt to compete with BMW's class-leading M3, but the Impreza tarried as a fun-packed status icon, a must-have for top software salesmen to win the admiration of their plastic associates.

Even before Ken opened his mouth, Fraser saw he gushed with over-eagerness, the sensation of selling his software package geeing-up adrenalin rush to the stratum whereby it could be safely theorised, mandies or some other uppers stimulant had passed his lips just prior to the sales call. *If we could bottle such ever-optimistic essence,* Fraser calculated, *it'd be far more valuable than anything the software industry has to offer to lighten our workload.*

Returning to perusing Ken's persona, he ruminated, *why is it, the software industry believes it helps to emulate a retired storm-trooper to meet surmised business place etiquette, and thereby sales will automatically follow?* Always finding the discipline hard to fathom, Ken the intrepid sales hunter symbolised the notion. If a passel of software salesmen had been waiting outside Fraser's sacred shrine, champing at the bit for under-starters orders and ready to impart their spiel, they'd have transpired no different in outlook to Ken. Hard to differentiate one from the other, their cloned conformity clinched no idiosyncratic features, just like probing a herd of Friesian cows and trying to identify the one called Daisy.

Competence and perhaps a little bit of memorable selfhood were the only significant instruments the buying fellowship sought in salesmen. Because they buzzed and dressed exactly the same, they corresponded more to pre-programmed robots, rather than the distinctive entities they tried to portray. Even before opening their mouths, half the battle became lost, because buyers had heard it all before from the exact same archetype, with the same hairstyle, wearing the same suit, and the same nasal-hair-exposing shiny shoes.

'If they could slip themselves into the financial services world,' Fraser often coveted, 'and understand our business drivers, the pressures determining decision making and the peculiarities of the investment banking fraternity, it'd count for a lot more than the cheap sales talk, inflated product claims and failed attempts at situational alignment usually fingerprinting them.'

"Good morning, Roger," Fraser's visitor bellowed in a deep reverberating voice, his intention to demonstrate confidence, professionalism, even kudos. "I'm Ken Carter with HAL."

Everyone in the software industry used Christian names on initial introduction, even if they were addressing Lloyd Blankfein, CEO of much hallowed Goldman Sachs. Investment banking stalwarts, Fraser typical, found the over-familiarity quaint. Allowing the presumption, they considered it symptomatic of a relatively new industry, compensating for narrow permanence by pressing the person-to-person skills button far too swiftly.

Handing the mark, meaning Fraser, his business card, the stock analyst reciprocated the salutation and they shook hands.

"Okay, I know we've only got twenty minutes," Ken recapitulated, "so let's get right down to what HAL's market analysis competencies can do for you. What I'm going to tell you about, is a really *cool* piece of software…"

Off he went, alleging unprecedented return on investment and total cost of ownership figures, backed up by a flurry of endorsements and references. Taking little of it in, Fraser still cringed at the term, 'really *cool* piece of software.' Uniformly spouted by telecoms and IT salesmen, the word 'cool' described anything from data routers through to ISO 15022 compliant trading application servers, the inference being, the adjective will be perceived as synonymous with quality, performance, even elegance, and most importantly, the universal panacea to any business obstruction inadvertently created by man, or nature. 'Cool software' promised to make the lives of those owning the business paradox easier and more manageable. Better still, wondrously, return on capital investment achieved before the end of the working week! A modern miracle in the making, comparable to God handing down tablets to Moses on Mount Sinai, and Moses thereafter parting the Red Sea, who in his right mind wouldn't invest in such 'cool' merchandise?

In Fraser's opinion, cool should be exclusively reserved to describe Miles Davis, Steve McQueen, Jackie Stewart and other world-renowned luminaries; genuinely super-cool, trend setting, inventive dudes, their photographs found in the Oxford English dictionary next to the word, cool. Howbeit, the same dictionary entry did not have any telco or IT commodity entries listed beside it, yet salesmen seemed to think by prefacing their offering with the word 'cool', it somehow moved their standing substantially up the pecking framework, the buyer miraculously imbued with a light-going-on apocalypse, subsequently signalling a large value order. Software might be efficient, effective, even elegant, but never, 'cool'. Though buyers didn't say it outright, they condemned the 'cool culprits' as schmucks for assuming a keystone word unlocked the door to the treasury, and bundles of readies flooded out in their direction.

Wrapping up his patter in precisely twenty minutes, Ken attributed no latitude for Fraser to ask questions, not to mention be given scope to table any current business bothers and operators. Already hungry traders formed a queue in his doorway, all seeking leads to go into sales mode with their clients. Unlike Ken, he craved they'd be on receive as well as transmit. Ironically, he categorised Ken's product to be pretty good, and yes, if the right enquiry had been made, he'd have discovered cap ex in the departmental budget for analyst tool enhancements.

Nodding to the wolf pack in his doorway, Fraser graciously flagged Ken's slot had expired, and he needed to carry on with the business of the day. Dejected, Ken put away his 'cool' toys and made ready to depart, order-less.

Clocking his fitfulness, Fraser got the sudden urge to be a good Christian.

"Hey, Ken."

"Yes, Roger," he mournfully replied, surmising he had blown it.

"Give Andy Drabble a call in IT systems support. Tell him I want your software package evaluated from a technical perspective, to see if it fits in with our business systems strategy."

Ken's puss lit up. "Yes, sir."

~ * ~

Notwithstanding his misgivings, sometimes Roger's connections with the software industry rendered remarkable bouts of humour. Requested to furnish white-knight motivator services by an eminent supplier of financial services software and professional services, when recalling the adventure to family, friends and co-workers, he renamed the company, The Prophets, to keep their real name out of the trans-continental gaze.

Out of the blue, The Prophets invited him to guest at their quarterly team talk for sales, marketing, technical and ancillary staff, to give an anecdotal, state-of-the-union conferral on the investment banking sector. Beefing up the team's inhalation of well-being and urgency, the colloquy intended to hone their appreciation of the challenges affronted by investment bankers, and help them tackle more proactively in the sector, a facet desired by Fraser and others on the buy-side, hence his approbation of the invitation. Additionally, The Prophets offered to cover his subsistence expenses, and to feed and water him during the congress, so with Henry Jacque's permission, his assent became validated by The Firm.

Relishing the respite from the Isle of Dogs financial district and after verifying the weather angle in advance of the convention, to make sure there were no imminent hurricanes forecast for either side of the pending day, Fraser took the good fortune to exercise his BMW M3 - a truly 'cool' car - to travel to The Prophets UK HQ in the Thames Valley.

Wanting to meet and greet him and other spokesmen in the evening to substantiate the next day's programme, their hosts arranged accommodation at a local hotel, Fraser duly driving from Hazelwood to Reading the previous early afternoon.

Due to hold ups on the M25, the journey did not go as planned. Before even reaching Reigate Hill, Radio Surrey reported traffic at a standstill due to a cow on the westbound carriageway at Leatherhead. Just how the cow had got there, the announcer did not explain, nor did he confirm if the beast abided dead or alive. Dashing to the scene, the entire Surrey Police motor patrol force brought the M25 to a stop in both directions under instructions from health and safety experts, causing tailbacks to both the Dartford Tunnel and Heathrow.

Resigned to such daily occurrences, road users amused themselves reading, fooling around with their mobile phones, or blowing kisses to attractive lady drivers. As the drudgery expanded, engines were switched off and the motorway fell silent. Inevitably, those caught short retreated from their vehicles holding their crotches, and stood on the tiered embankment schmaltzy with blessed release relieving their straining bladders, only to be chastised and ushered to their prisons on the road by plod. After an eternity of inactivity, two of the motorway's four lanes reopened in the westerly direction. Crawling past the Leatherhead junction, Fraser saw the offending bovine tethered to a fire engine and mooing at the legions of emergency services workers gathered around to feed her grass, torn up from a nearby field.

Just what the role of the fire service had been in the multi-dimensional, cross-service, nerve-jangling rescue, Fraser could only speculate about. Secondary to police, ambulance and fire service vehicles, he also saw RSPCA, Ministry of Agriculture and Farmers Union vehicles parked up along a mile stretch of the hard-shoulder, the two inner lanes lingering cordoned off with millions of cones. Gyrating his upper story in disbelief at the cow rescue circus of way over the top use of community resources, he concluded the escapade probably cost the taxpayer at least £50,000, and the economy must have suffered a downturn in GDP as an upshot of business being held up, or even curtailed. In conclusion, he adjudged it a marvel that the armed forces had not been called out to add their assistance.

During the fracas, mobile news units from the BBC, ITV, Channel 4 and Sky News somehow managed to get in on the act. Later, their early evening main stories were dominated by the M25 cow rescue. Holding a news conference, the Chief Constable of Surrey explained Molly the cow decided on a daytrip to see some friends to the west of Leatherhead, and had barged her way through a rotting wooden fence before nonchalantly strolling onto the M25, her companion herd members wishing her *bon voyage* and a safe journey. Mischievously, a Sky News reporter ironically explored, 'Was she trying to thumb a lift?' Scowling, the Chief Constable informed the politically incorrect reporter, 'An incomparably momentous matter had occurred, having the best minds in the South East's combined emergency services and associated QUANGOs parsing the quandary, and developing schemes for the better part of half a day to extract Molly safely.' So used to hearing such beyond common-sense retorts, Fraser didn't even report the outrage to his cohorts knowing they'd be far from surprised.

Later, when he enrolled at the hotel, his host, Bill Patterson, The Prophets VP of UK Sales, came over to reception to greet him. Forthwith, Fraser found out other white knight motivators had also been held up on their journeys by Molly, and the TV news central story rapidly became the focus of elongated contention, with parallel incidents retold to the shared amazement of the crowd.

Aware Heather would justify the D-Day landings scale operation to ensure Molly's survival, on the basis to do less was anti-cow and a flagrant act of human crime against animals, Fraser had already decided not to raise the subject in her vicinity when he went home the succeeding evening.

Amounting to a series of investment banking anecdotal yarns and lessons learnt from fruitless business campaigns, Fraser gave his dissertation at the motivational team-talk conclave the next day. With their intuitive probes and general interactive participation, he found the attendees to be sparky and distinctly up for the white knight session.

Usually, such talks were a bilateral exchange between orator and audience, avoiding the formality of delivering a paper or a sermon. Rather than an investment banker taxed with motivational objectives, he felt akin to Dave Allen telling his hilarious stories. Dissimilar to the powwows he did with clients, or at The Firm, he didn't stand behind a lectern, or gesticulate to a back-projector screen with a laser pen. Walking slowly around the elevated stage of the Prophet's lecture theatre, he merely compressed a hand-held toggle-shift to increment his PowerPoint briefing slides, each one having a humorous or poignant theme he extemporised on to make his points and boost listener assimilation.

Underwritten by The Prophet's hierarchy to improve business empathy and customer facing skills, all the same, he adopted a light-hearted and easy-on-the-senses approach. More of a group discussion, rather than the formal lecturer-student liaison Fraser had employed at Wendy's school for the A-level business studies evening confabs, it fruited elation for both himself and his eyewitnesses. Enjoying it so much and in danger of overrunning his duration slot, self-control got the better of his inborn song and dance man inclination and he finalised on schedule, drawing thunderous applause from those on the receiving end, imbuing him with self-satisfaction.

Sitting down in the front row of the assemblage with other guest white knight motivators and the Prophets senior management team, he awaited the residual of the symposium.

Now an independent consultant to the motor vehicle industry, the next motivational speechmaker, Joe Starling, used to work for Jaguar. Hitting the stage with a zestful bounce and perceptibly charged up for the colloquium, he doubled Fraser's bilateral routine, The Prophets brethren fascinated by his yesteryear tales of cherished Jaguar cars, such as the D-Type and the E-Type.

Towards the conclusion of Starling's talk, it developed into an unpredicted and notable keepsake. Finishing one Jaguar remembrance, he divulged, "we ended up at the Grand Hotel."

Before he could go any further, some wag in the seminar sang,

"It died with an awful sound."

Rubbernecking up, he heard from perhaps seven or eight people, *"when some stupid with a flare gun, burnt the place to the ground."*

Recognising the lines from Deep Purple's immortal rock anthem, *Smoke on the Water*, Fraser's ears pricked up.

About thirty more participants then came in with, *"Frank Zappa and the Mothers, were at the best place around,"* accompanied by what must have been virtually everyone from row two rearwards, rallying with a Karaoke-like, *"Smoke on the water, fire in the sky, Smoke on the water, fire in the sky."*

Lastly, imitating Richie Blackmore's fabled guitar riff, the aggregate congregation incorporating the Prophet's senior management team and guest speakers then broke into rapturous applause and laughter.

They might have got the words and lines mixed up verse to verse, but the spontaneity stuck in Fraser's consciousness. He could never imagine old school, blue chip investment house employees breaking into tune off the cuff *a la, Smoke on the Water*, in an analogous forum. The software industry might be young and often unsubtle, he refereed, but such impulsive and unprompted bursts of exuberance compensated for immaturity, and surely established the source for the pantheon of its ground-breaking inventions.

Chapter 9: Businessmen Behaving Badly

Waltzing past the bullpen after a powwow with Top Cat and Ricky Henshaw, Fraser bumped into Tarquin Stevenson, an ex-Firm dealer freed on seeing the light, and going off to work as a business development consultant for Kirkland Austerberry, one of The Firm's long-term clients.

"Tarquin, how the hell are you?" Fraser canvassed.

"Hello, Roger. I surmise you're going to ask what brings me to The Firm."

"It did cross my mind."

"I've just come out of a meeting with the investment assessor people."

"Roslyn Joyce?"

"Yes. I presumed the old buzzard had retired by now, but she's still going strong."

"*Huh*." Grinning, Fraser articulated, "Roslyn will never retire. She'll simply fade into the fabric of the huge data library she's been compiling for the past forty years and haunt The Firm forever."

Cheery at the notion, Stevenson ceded, "you're probably right. Say—" He glanced at his timepiece. "Have you got time for a beer or whatever your alcoholic beverage is these days?"

"For you, Tarquin, and since you were one of the very few brokers I could ever stand, it'd be a pleasure." Slapping Stevenson lightly on the arm, he catechized, "how's your business development life going at Kirkland Austerberry?"

"*Heavens*! It remains a far cry from those hedonistic days flying around the bullpen like a blue-arsed fly, but I just had to get out, Roger.

It drove me crazy."

"Yes, not many traders go on to make retirement age, do they?"

During his Firm tenure, newer members had deduced from his peacock-related Christian name, Tarquin was old school. They were right, but he did not pretend to be an aristocrat, just a well-spoken, grammar school graduate, not in the least bit snobby. Cheerfully talking to anyone, the sheer magnetism of his personality broke down artificial social barriers. Classically handsome and a dandy dresser, when he passed into his middle years, unlike Fraser, he had managed to control his weight, nurturing a surfboard proportionate build. Flawless decorum, an optimistic outlook and a cavalier tendency to life, all endeared him to Fraser. Those same distinctive attributes had also made him one of The Firm's best dealers.

After nearly twenty-five years working chiefly in commodities and gilts then derivatives stock, Stevenson left The Firm in 2003. Making a shed load of wonga during his term and no longer spurred on to compete against the new breed, barrow-boy method Essex coterie, he decided to exercise his Firm share options, and bale out into calmer waters, Kirkland Austerberry, a blue-chip FMCG conglomerate embracing him with open arms. Finding the shift to be *au fond* monastic in comparison, but most welcome, he liberated himself from the tremors and anxieties accumulated with The Firm.

"Come on, we'll go down to Brodies," Fraser promoted, hustling him away. "It's always quiet in the late afternoon, so we can talk without some damned stock trading jockey coming up and hassling me for leads."

Pitching up in a corner booth, replete with beer and peanuts, the old friends talked about wine, women and song. With no joint business issues to distract them, after making the usual mutual enquiries about each other's family's health and well-being, they free-wheeled into the oddball domain.

"Tuesday, I went to my son's prize giving night at his school," Stevenson recollected. "Strange affair, if I didn't know better, I'd have sworn some of the pupils were on the juice."

Glimmering, Fraser probed, "in what way?"

"Well, one boy said in his acceptance oration, 'I'd like to thank my parents, particularly my mum and dad.' I fancied I'd misheard, but I audited my wife and she swore I hadn't."

"Mmmm, a substantiation of the bleeding obvious. It's the same as saying, if history repeats itself, we can anticipate the same thing again."

"Yes, but I found it weird no one else twigged, let alone the teachers. It was as if the boy had been taught the belt and brace corroboration of his parent's status as his mum and dad equated with a normal clarification."

"Hhmm, they have some curious ways of teaching these days, but the misplay on words does remind me of Julian Dicks' season with Liverpool FC, when an over-effervescent BBC commentator, probably that arse-licking dick in his own right, John Motson, blurted, 'Julian Dicks is everywhere. It looks like there are eleven dicks on the field.'"

Astounded, Stevenson charged, "you're kidding."

"No, I might still have it on VHS tape."

"An interchangeable one I recollect centred around Andy Roddick. Some lady tennis announcer uncovered live on BBC television, 'One of the reasons Andy is playing so well is before the final round, his wife takes out his balls and kisses them,' then she added, 'Oh my God, what have I just said?'"

"It's a miracle the holier-than-thou BBC didn't bleep it out."

"For sure, they're also great, big PC dicks."

"True. The one always making me smile," Fraser recounted, "is on BBC News when they say, 'And this report has some flash photography.'" Lingering, he became flustered. "On first hearing the apparent warning, I couldn't work out if they were boasting about their photographic prowess, or bleating more goody two-shoes, nanny-state, PC bollocks."

"Oh, unequivocally it's the latter."

"Yes, my ever-ready, in-tune with anything PC wife confirmed it."

"I get the PC malarkey from my eldest daughter," Stevenson

accredited.

"I get it from my *two* daughters, as well as my wife."

"I'll say a prayer for you," he offered, sensitive to his friend's torment.

Snapping his fingers, Fraser gushed, "I've just conjured up another one." Halting abruptly, he warbled, "we sound like Mel and Griff, don't we?"

"Good grief, we're even wearing white shirts."

"Yes. Anyway, an American boxing pundit, can't place his name, blundered out, 'Sure there have been injuries, and even some deaths in boxing, but none of them were really serious.'"

"Jeez, there's no end to it?"

"Yep, my accidental gaffes are tame in comparison. Albeit, revisiting misplay of words but in the mispronunciation sense, during my A-level summers I worked as a gofer for a Dartford shipping company. Met an old matlow there named Bill Howe. Ipswich supporter with a conspicuous East London come Suffolk accent. Bill was always banging on about Ipswich centre-half Alan Hunter, but perennially dropping his h's, he pronounced the surname, 'unt-a'. So, taking the mickey I asked, 'is that apostrophe-u-n-t-a-apostrophe?' He replied, 'yeah, *unt-a*.'"

"Oh dear."

"Lovely chap though, wonderful storyteller."

Getting into their stride, the pair discussed more examples of incongruous speech before Stevenson renewed the theme.

"Tell me, Roger, are you a Gary or a Tony?"

Not catching on, Fraser cross-examined, "how do you mean?"

"You know, as in the comedy *Men Behaving Badly*."

"Oh, I see." He grimaced. "I'm not sure. You kick it off."

"Ooohh, after much cerebration, I'm a Tony."

"Really. I'd have pegged you more as a Gary; work ethic, marriage, babies, etcetera, etcetera."

"Your right, but beneath lays a Tony-style latent waster, dying for the easy life."

"A bit hard on the Tony character, isn't it?"

"Yes, in retrospect, unnecessarily brutal," he conceded. "Tony has many endearing traits. But for the path I chose, I might have mimicked them." Lodging his tongue deep into his cheek, he indicated the fancifulness of the pipedream. "So, Roger, how about you? Are you a Gary or a Tony?"

"I'm a bit of both, and I must say, I've always enjoyed *Men Behaving Badly*. Their antics make some of my social misdemeanours Charlotte complains so vehemently about seem tame in comparison." Suspending, a sparkle came into his pupils. "I'd watch an episode, see an outlandish transgression and think, well, at least I've not done that. But you've got me meditating wider now."

"I have?"

"Yes, what about Bob and Terry?"

Shuffling into the reclined posture, Stevenson worked out the connection. "As in *The Likely Lads*? The gregarious, fun-packed Newcastle pair, preceding Gary and Tony."

"*Correctamundo,* as the Fonz used to say."

"Mmmm, adds a rosy dimension. Terry approximates to Tony and Bob to Gary."

"Yes, but are you a Bob or a Terry?"

"The answer to that reflects the choice between being moderately responsible, and still having a good time…"

Losing his thread, Fraser helped him out. "Like Bob and Gary."

"…yes, or being a free-wheeling, live for today layabout."

"Like Terry and Tony, but I'm being supercilious towards those celebrities."

"The point is, Roger, we're either natural or socialised Bob's and Gary's, alter ego compelled to earn a crust, pay our taxes, bring up a family and in general be lifelong responsible and law-abiding citizens."

"Absolutely true."

"But what is so bad about being a Tony or a Terry? Why do we see them as good mates, but worthless in terms of their contribution to society? Who commanded we were put on this Earth to work and procreate, with recess for good behaviour to play rugby in your case, and go sailing in mine?"

"Ahh…well, Tarquin, we're in too deep to backtrack now. People make a decision regarding if they're going to be shakers and movers, or wasters and lamebrains in their late teens, and few change horses in life's mid-stream, do they?"

"No, but your resolution is robust," Stevenson avouched. "And on the upside, *Men Behaving Badly* and *The Likely Lads* provide a bit of escapism for real life Bob's and Gary's."

"They certainly do for me."

"Me as well. I've always found *Men Behaving Badly* to be the antidote to all the new man, caring sharing bull initiated in the early nineties." Throwing an expansive smile at Fraser, he declared, "my wife Cecilia ranked it to be unmasculine and false. There's a world of difference between buying into all this trendy human rights and Green stuff, just to be seen to be PC, and extending traditional good manners and courtesies to women."

"And yet normal alpha males brought up on good manners, respect for women and high ethical standards got castigated, and are still getting the rough end of the pineapple today. It's saying, 'You're too good to be true, so I'm not taking any chances, and will bring you down as often as I can.' It's a kind of double, double-bluff, but doesn't achieve anything."

"Apart from pandering to attitudes invented in the media," Stevenson supplemented. "And, by the insatiable rise of politically-correct zealots."

"Assuredly. How on Earth have people, not just women." He stopped. "That didn't transpire quite right, did it?"

"Afraid not," Stevenson attested, twinkling at Fraser's unmeant phrase jumble.

"I mean," he said, labouring again, "how has it got to the threshold, whereby we're afraid to speak our minds for fear of being overheard by the PC thought police and contravening their do's and don'ts code they've enforced on everybody?"

"I blame all those politicos and media mad pundits for the

dysfunctional society we now live in. They're a tiny minority, but they hold enormous sway over the political classes, and consequentially the public at large. I used to ignore it, turn a blind eye, demean them as just priggish upstarts sounding-off, but—" Unnerved, he furrowed his brow. "They have infiltrated all the cardinal societal institutions, principally government and the media, to the extent whereby they're literally running our lives."

"Hhmm, you've really cogitated long and hard about this."

"As a bullpen jockey, my life flip-flopped between work and domesticity, with little spare bandwidth to register external overarching outcomes affecting all our lives. However, since joining Kirkland Austerberry I'm not under as much pressure, so my acumen has logged other things. I've grasped for the past twenty-five years I'd been walking around blind, blandly presuming the people I voted into power did my bidding, and I could go about my professional and home life secure in the knowledge they worked in my best interests." Beetle-browed, he condemned, "it's not so. They have their own insular agendas to accomplish, and if it means cosying up to the PC brigade and betraying the voters, they do it."

"Never heard you talk this way at The Firm, Tarquin. For my part, I'm still largely in the work-home cycle more or less exclusively, with the occasional pass-out for good behaviour. Although of late, I've begun to develop some dreads about the future, especially the world my children are going to inherit."

"Yes, I recognise the cycle, and share your concerns." Screwing up his face, more unease surfaced. "Some things, or more precisely, some people, have really started to aggravate me."

"In your business and privy domains?"

"No. I'm talking about those in the political and media spectrum, impacting our lives by superimposing their schemes on us, and we have little recourse to do anything about them. They're immune from criticism and insulated from accountability."

"For example?"

"Oh, there are so many." Parsing for a trice, Stevenson then tabled, "here's one I find really obnoxious - Shami Chakrabarti."

"*Who*?" Fraser indignantly queried. "Sounds like a wash leather."

"She runs Liberty," Stevenson verified. "She's a right little, nauseating, loathsome, insufferable, condescending, holier-than-thou, I'm right and you are all wrong, PC bigot. She tells us how we must think, what we can say and can't say, who we must like and who we must dislike." Flinging a searching glitter at Fraser, he blathered, "you *must* have seen her. She's always on *Question Time* spouting her parochial, self-centred syllabus. I can't conceive why these slimy creatures from the political classes have so much sway and influence, and why they're granted so much airtime by the BBC."

"I see what you are driving at," he authenticated. "For me, it's been Gordon Brown in recent years."

"Dear lord!" Stevenson snarled. "I can't stand him."

"Quite, but before you go off on one, let me explain why. Just the other week, I served at an exceptionally testing meeting with one of The Firm's private investor representatives. I can't tell you the name of the person, but odiousness and he fitted in tandem. As I listened to his thought and action control rhetoric, the Freudian spectre of Gordon Brown popped into my cognizance *vis-à-vis* Big Brother incarnate. The more this guy banged on, the more in my inventiveness, his gloss became transformed into a Gordon Brown guise, and his voice became the low guttural yowl associated with the ex-PM. I found it quite disconcerting."

"I can just imagine it. Brown does have a Stalin cognate persona, cuddly on the outside but vicious beneath the veneer. Do you envisage other people have the same agitations about PC zealots and the direction the country is headed?"

"In quieter spells of meditation, undoubtedly, but it seems to me democracy is dead. What the majority want and vote for is not delivered. England, as we once knew it on the other side of the millennium, doesn't exist anymore, irrespective of how much Cameron pretends it does. The packaging, meaning the window dressing might be equal, but the content is radically different, and precious little of it is English. With the realisation the political classes have recalibrated the world exclusively in their favour, and their affiliation with the masses is only touched upon during elections, conversations such as we're having become academic. Once adopted, they dictate what they want, and are only influenced by the diktats of minority pressure groups, not the neglected majority." He stopped. "*Blimey!*"

"What, what is it?"

"I've suddenly realised, I'm parodying my mother-in-law's gospel."

"Something neither of us would have admitted to twenty years ago."

"Worrying, isn't it?"

"It's definitely a foretaste, Roger," Stevenson projected. "Those older than us have seen it all before, and are well placed to strike the Claxton warning bell. Trouble is, nobody takes any damned heed, belittling them as old fogies."

"Yes—" He faltered. "Where was I?"

"Minority pressure groups."

"Oh yes. It's really an inversion of the norm. Up to the late nineteen-seventies, governments habitually collapsed if they didn't deliver on the majority's bids. Since then, the majority view has been slowly but effectively obliterated from policy decision making. You're right in saying the political classes, notably the metropolitan elitists, have twisted English democracy into their own fiefdom."

"Doesn't make for a pleasant or palatable admission, does it?"

"No." Perturbed, Fraser surveyed about. "Do you know what, Tarquin?"

"What?"

"We're mirroring Gary and Tony, in one of their couch-bound, midnight hour, blokey discussions, after consuming several gallons of lager and a cheap takeaway."

"Well," Stevenson inaugurated, "we'd better complete the picture by tossing our beer glasses over our shoulders then."

Chapter 10: Corinthians and Crusaders

The quarter finals of the Kent Veterans Cup competition saw Kappa Corinthians draw Cranbrook Crusaders away, Fraser picked to play outside centre, with his mates Steve Hunt at hooker and Gordon Anderson at fly half.

A chequered history between the two clubs ensured the fixture resided as an antipathy match. Donkey's years ago, when Fraser played for the first team, Corinthians literally took a beating from Crusaders. Not only did they lose the contest, they withdrew from the field of play resembling survivors from a Taliban booby-trap, returning to Farnborough black, blue and bloodied, Fraser with a deep cut in his knee resultant from a flying Crusader boot leaving a scar. Others had suffered self-same disrepairs, the injury list long and distinguished, with some of Corinthians' best players side-lined for weeks on end.

Up to then, relations with Crusaders had always been cordial. Sometimes players could flare in the heat of the wrangle, capping with punches being thrown, but what had happened at Cranbrook stemmed from a primeval instinct to win at all costs. Sin bins had not found their way into the game at the time, and whilst many players were cautioned by the referee, officials were loath to send-off reprobates, cogitating number imbalance led to poor competition and could even exacerbate the enigma. By the closing whistle, three Corinthians had been substituted anyway, their injuries just too severe to allow them to carry on.

Why the unforeseen bloodletting had happened tarried as a mystery to Corinthians, the shocking ruck forging fierce debate apropos future on-field retaliatory practices.

For the season's counter fixture, Corinthians extracted vengeance on the men from Cranbrook. Nothing too vicious, never touching on the ultra-violence of *A Clockwork Orange*, just enough Crusaders claret flowed to give the Corinthians parity with what had happened to them at Cranbrook. Nevertheless, in abiding rugby tradition, what went down on the Farnborough field of play remained on the field of play. Unlike today's whinging professional footballers calling each other names, then going public in the press and complaining to the authorities, crowning in innocent players being set up on false charges to appease those of a politically correct bent, no complaints were made by either side.

Since then, all clashes between the two clubs, ranging from the colts to the mighty vets, had been filled with rancour bordering on malevolent warfare.

~ * ~

Forever motivated to win, Fraser and his teammates were prepared to give blood for their club, and if they died in the endeavour, their wives and girlfriends had been petitioned to give them honourable burials. Meeting at their Farnborough club house, fifteen players, five substitutes, coach Mason Harvey and his training staff, plus left-wing Damien Chapple's Great Dane, Attila, made ready for the assault.

Last to arrive, as Roger and his buddies neared the sacrosanct ground, Dusty Maltman came down the clubhouse steps to greet them.

"*Jesus*!" he blasted, hands on hips and coming across as masterful. "Coach Harvey isn't going to authorise you three out-of-condition old-timers to play, is he?"

"Back in your wallaby cage, or more accurately, wannabe cage," Steve responded, "you under-grown, sawn-off, Australian sheep-shagger."

"Yeah," Gordon endorsed. "Go and take a long walk off a short Australian pier and play with the Great Whites."

Snickering at the artificial abuse, Dusty clocked Roger. "Well, Fraser," he ventured, divining a full trio of insults, "aren't you going to have a crack? You usually do."

"Mmmm," Roger reacted. "My esteemed compatriots have conveyed everything which needs to be said, except…"

"Yeah?" prodded the playful Antipodean.

"…may I cordially suggest," he beseeched in his best Queen's English, "you try to keep a civil tongue in your head, until we are at least out on the field of play."

"*Phooey*," Dusty bellowed, playing the part and looking disgusted. "You can stick your civil tongue right up your civil jacksie and choke on it, you overgrown, prematurely-going-grey, pompous sack of Pommie excrement."

All four of the Corinthian comrades broke into laughter, the trenchant but playful exchange more or less typical for when they met up socially, or for a fixture.

"How the devil are you, Roger?" Dusty probed, thrusting out a hand to give Fraser a pulled punch in the solar plexus.

"I'm fine, but all the better for seeing you," he assigned. "Now tell me, Dusty, how many tries are you going to get today?"

Smiling, the genial Aussie stipulated, "it entirely depends on how much quality ball you give me from the centre."

"Well," Roger rebutted, "I'm dependent on Gordon's facility at fly half to fulfil my charge."

"And I," Gordon clarified, "with Hunt the Hooker doing as many turnovers in the scrum as possible."

Staring at Steve, they all envisioned a pithy response.

"Look, you flash bastards," he growled, "when we real men in the forwards win the scrums and the line-outs, just make sure you do the business in the backs, instead of waltzing around the pitch like a bunch of pregnant prima donnas."

"Yes, sir, General Hunt," Dusty guaranteed, saluting the hooker. "Say—" He winked at Roger and Gordon. "Didn't you play the principal in *Patton: Lust for Glory*?"

"No, George C Scott had the honour," Gordon right away amended. "Steve starred in Hooker: Lust for Pussie."

"*Bollocks*, Anderson," rebuked the unhappy hooker.

"Now don't go winding him up prematurely, Gordon," Roger forewarned. "We want him at the height of aggression just before kick-off, not before being confined with twenty other lunatics for the next hour on a coach having little scope for a raging bull-elephant." Smirking at Gordon, he supplemented, "besides, you know he's not well-balanced with chips on both shoulders, like Dusty."

"Now look here, Fraser," the infuriated bushwhacker barked, "if you cheeky Poms get my dander up, I'll give all three of you a seeing to right now."

"Ha, ha, ha, ha," Fraser chortled. Placing a reassuring arm around the Aussie he begged, "no insult intended, Dusty. You must forgive me. I just couldn't resist bringing the old skeleton out of the closet."

Further good-natured joshing took place before the Anglo-Aussie contingent joined their peers for a pre-match fitness test from Coach Harvey. Filled with keen resolve, the entourage then climbed aboard the coach taking them south to Cranbrook.

~ * ~

Like Dusty Maltman, five years older than Roger, Damien Chapple had stayed incredibly fit for his age, his body weight well in check. Developing an exhaustive exercise routine carried out daily, he also observed a strict calorie intake regime and had abstained from alcohol, apart from limited consumption at rugby club events. Consequently, as his contemporaries' eyes became bloodshot with the onset of middle age, accelerated by an inability to refrain from red meat and booze ingestion, his had survived fully translucent. Retaining muscle tone, his body zinged with stamina, his complexion shone with health, and his blond hair sustained its strength and congenital colour.

A dog devotee, Fraser dwelt unflinching he loved Attila more than his wife Julia. Parking himself beside Fraser on the coach, Chapple proceeded to smother the giant hound in a flurry of kisses, much to the dog's yelping and howling embarrassment.

"*Holy Moses*, Roger," he griped, "I really missed Attila while I was abroad. I called Julia nearly every night to make sure she fed him properly."

"I must say," Fraser complimented, "he's in good shape."

"He should be, with the amount of prime American rib he devours. No pork chops for him."

Familiar with the term, at the mention of prime American rib, Attila howled, his set of muscular vocal chords easily duplicating his immense strength in terms of decimating product, Chapple receiving calls to 'shut that mutt up' from incensed rugby players either composing themselves for the contest or engaging in dialogue.

"Alright you lot," he rebuked, "if you don't pipe down, I'll set him on you."

Making a kind of yawning yap at the end of his peal, Attila licked his lips as if imagining sinking his teeth into the steak, then settled down in the aisle.

Tapping Fraser on the forearm as if priming him for a jolt, Chapple revealed, "a neighbour of mine has got a bloodhound. When I landed from the Middle-East, Julia told me the neighbour, Missus Mallinson, a real peculiar, old goat, had become convinced her dog had gone rancid."

"*Rancid*! You mean, rotten as in stale food, not rabid as in rabies?"

"Yeah, you got it, rancid. Anyway, she'd locked the canine in a shed and called the police to come over to shoot it."

"*Shoot it*!" Fraser echoed, exclamation marks metaphorically bobbing over his head.

"Yeah, it does seem draconian, doesn't it? Anyway, deducing the old coot had lost her marbles, along came the police. They went to the shed, took a gander at the dog and yes, they concurred with Missus Mallinson he smelt terrible, but the police were not empowered to shoot dogs, rancid or otherwise, and proposed she called a vet. Out came the vet, gave the dog the onceover and told her, he's probably eaten stale meat, and what she can smell is coming out of every orifice in his body, howbeit, the dog is unremittingly fit. Missus Mallinson contended the pooch had gone rancid and demanded the vet shot it. He told her, vets don't shoot dogs and destroying a perfectly fit animal, smelly or not, is unlawful and the pungent smell would fade in due course. Well—" Bashfully, he tittered. "Julia asked me to examine the offending animal to see if I could see a cause the vet hadn't picked up. So, I go over to Missus Mallinson's house, and find the dog still in the shed, fit, but very smelly and even more mournful. He kind of whimpered at me, as if to say, 'What's up doc?' Bugs Bunny style. When I'm on my way to see the old coot to say, I know a farmer with a shotgun who'd do the dastardly deed for her, I heard Attila barking from the top of her huge garden bordering on open countryside. I rushed up to see what had got him all riled up, then I saw it."

"Saw what?"

"Someone had dumped a rotting sheep carcass, and it smelt exactly the same as the dog. I told Missus Mallinson what I'd found, and set forth her bloodhound must have been rolling in it, hence the cause of his all-over body odour. She gaped at me, as if I'd just dropped down from outer space and persisted, 'Well, I'd still like him shot.'"

"Wow," Fraser blurted. "Almost makes you glad to be human, doesn't it?"

"Quite."

"So how did it end up?"

"Missus Mallinson brought in an industrial cleaning firm to vacuum wet clean the canine." Fabricating a capricious mug, he halted. "*That is*, when they eventually got hold of it. Continually running for cover, the fetid monster sensed a cleansing bout awaited. But it had to be that, or taking the hound to a car wash."

"Better than being shot then," Fraser attested. "Mind you, there's a few rancid human beings I'd apply the shotgun solvent to," he specified, his least cherished person Sly coming to mind.

"Oh, incontrovertibly. Anyway, give me the SP on Christian Bowcott's stag night," he requested.

On assignment with his media company covering Middle-East developments, Chapple had missed the shindig. Keen to find out what happened, he insisted Fraser gave him chapter and verse about the riotous evening.

Qualifying his recollections to be alcohol impaired, Fraser narrated everything he could still remember. Sitting ahead of them, Steve and Gordon filled in the gaps. Aggrieved to have missed the do, Damien stressed if another spate of Middle-East unrest conflicted with the next rugby club stag night, his company needed to send someone else to cover it.

"Say, Roger," Chapple delved. "Changing the subject, have you seen that lightweight dummy, come airhead twinkie heading *Film 2011*?"

"Erm…not sure, Damien."

"Camellia Wankerman…oh, she's terrible."

"Ah, I think you'll find its Camellia Wakeman."

"Yeah, that's her," he sneeringly accredited. "She's so embarrassing, it's *ad modem* to beholding a badly trained baboon. She's just too immature even for children's TV."

"Oh, I know what you're driving at now," Fraser testified. "As you will recall, my mother used to be the film review correspondent for the Evening Standard. She has also expressed congruous sentiments. But I must say, I really lost faith in the programme when the noble Barry Norman retired. I haven't tuned into it on a regular basis since."

"Ah well, now you're talking," Chapple applauded. "Barry set the gold yardstick. Comprehensively honoured by the film industry, it showed he really knew his craft. What I don't get is why they have that total arsewipe Camellia Wankerman filling Barry's shoes."

"Wakeman."

"Yeah, Wankerman," he misreported. "I mean, if you're going to have a girl presenting a premier film review programme, it should be Lauren Laverne. Real easy on the eye, foxy, and—" He waggled an outstretched finger. "She knows what she's talking about."

"Lauren Laverne," Fraser replicated. "It's a marketer's flawless name, just rolls off the tongue *ala* Marianne Faithful or Marilyn Monroe. You couldn't make up a catchier, more sinuous name, could you?"

"You're right on that one, Roger."

"She has good pedigree as well. Her commentaries on *The Culture Show* are outstanding, and as you say, she is cheesecake coupled with intellect, even gravitas. Yeah, she gets my vote."

"There was another totally all-the-way-up-his-PC arse who used to anchor *Film* for the BBC. Can't cite his name."

"Oh, you must mean one of my least favourite people, Jonathan Woss."

"That's him. Another prize wanker not fit to fill Barry's shoes. What an unmitigated twat, worse than Camellia Wankerman."

"Wakeman."

"And another thing," he appended, ignoring the revision yet again, "why is she done up to emulate Dracula's daughter?" He frowned. "All black clothes and panda-spiers, hardly Cathy McGowan in the allure steaks, is she?" Giving Fraser a sideways gleam he speculated, "I suppose Cathy's a bit before your time."

"Cathy McGowan. You do keep coming out with them, Damien," Fraser extolled, snuggling into his seat and purring. "Cathy McGowan," he parroted. "Mmmm, conjures up some early memories. I listened to Cathy on Capital Radio as a kid in the seventies. My elder brother Colin had a gigantic poster of her in her *Ready Steady Go* days on his bedroom wall. Very much a cult heroine to his generation, wasn't she?"

"Oh, for sure. My eldest brother Vince is an enormous RSG fan. When I was still on the rusks, he talked about her incessantly with his mates. Years later he told me, she's the first girl he ever fell for, and his launching wet dream pivoted on the delightful Cathy McGowan."

"Mine centred on Joanna Lumley," Fraser thrilled, "but that's another story."

"Anyway, I don't know why they don't get Mark Kermode or Andrew Graham-Dixon to do *Film 2011*. They're the real deal when it comes to film critique."

"Yes, either could fill Barry's shoes."

"Hey, here's a bit of salacious news" he suddenly coughed up. "You know Warren Anson?"

"What, the human walking, talking penis, and I award the

description in a complimentary way. The quintessential nobsman of legend. He who played blindside-flanker extraordinaire for us?"

"Yes."

Furrowing his brow, Fraser positioned, "he moved on to Blackheath, didn't he?"

"Yes."

"Never heard of him."

"*Hah*! yes you have."

"What about him?"

"Someone told me he nearly got married. Well, I say married, but before the happy union, he tried for carnal knowledge of his bride to be. Wanted to give her a monster mash as he called it, but professedly, she nearly jumped out of her skin when she saw his manhood in full bloom, and dived for cover."

Laughing at the image, Fraser then submitted, "on a former occasion, wasn't he done for possession of an offensive weapon?"

"He was. Citing the public protection laws, some beak wanted to put a cage around his artful throbber."

"I must say, being in the communal bath with him after matches had its downside. I contrasted it to a python loose and on the prowl in the water. Crikey, talk about carrying an offensive weapon!"

"Quite. Well, after the shock, his intended drove him to go under the knife."

"You *mean*—" Aghast, Fraser's mouth unfastened. "Consent to open-hampton surgery?"

"Yeah," Chapple gleefully validated. "She'd never seen a womb raider before, and in her wildest nightmares, she hadn't foreseen the anaconda-dimensioned specimen before her when he whipped it out, the bell end virtually bouncing against his kneecap. She gasped, screamed *aarrgghhh*, then fainted. When she came around, his bride to be ordered he had a dick reduction operation, before she'd acquiesce to him guiding a ring onto her third digit, let alone doing the business with her."

"Did he do it?"

"Did he bollocks. He came dangerously close, but decided to

ditch the girl, keep his fantastic sergeant-major intact, and find a girl not frightened to death by it."

"Sounds a bit 'dick-tatorial' to me."

"Ohhh," Chapple yammered, creasing up. "Good one, Roger."

"Actually, Warren's *pre-dick-ament*—" He twinkled. "Puts me in mind of Monty Moreton, who was in the same year as me at Chelsfield Grammar. A small youth blessed with a huge yogurt slinger, when he started putting it about, he felt himself blacking out towards the climax of his exertions. It got so bad he went to see his GP about the nauseous sensation. The doc told him, during the act of coupling so much blood rushed to his muff marauder that it made him light-headed."

"You mean his dick size to body weight ratio was diminutive?"

"You've got it. So, he asks the doc, what's the solution? The answer comes back, if you don't want to ultimately peg out on the job, either put on some weight or have your appendage reduced!"

"So, what did he do?"

"He loved what God or nature had bestowed on him, so he went on a crash course of eating to vastly increase his dick size to body weight ratio."

"Did it work?"

"Oh yeah, but he ended up looking like the 'Michelin Man' with a ten-inch schlong sticking out of his nether regions when he got ready to perform."

"Ye gods."

"Anyway, when Warren played for us, he told me about some sexual encounter he had in his early twenties," Fraser opined. "Professedly, his conquest felt exhausted by his efforts, and bleated, 'Oh Warren, I can't take any more.' He pushed, 'You must, take this,' and the dong-champion resumed to the bitter end, the girl nearly split asunder by his rampaging weapon, but—" Grinning, he affixed, "my everlasting memory endured as the evil, leery, lour on his kisser, as he recounted the tale."

"Yeah, I can imagine. It's approaching Gentleman Gerald Evans exploits," Chapple advanced.

"What, the well-known, licentious lothario, and author of the books *How to Pick Up more Girls* and *The A to Z of Industrial Scale Shagging?*" he posed. "Aid memoirs to help out the dim-witted and the downright stupid in their quest to attract the opposite sex."

"The very same."

"He was also the author of that celebrated sex maniac's manual, *How to Achieve a Better Orgasm.*"

"With a girl or solo?"

"Both, I think."

"Huh, when it came to hanky-panky, he always did have all the bases covered."

"Yikes, another rare blast from the past. I've not seen Gerald Evans in centuries. His catch phrase to girls hinged on a variant to the Mars advert, substituting nobbing for Mars. 'A nobbing a day helps you to work, rest and play.'" Lingering, Fraser praised, "good player though. He went to Blackheath as well, didn't he?"

"Merton."

"Ah, yes, you're right, and it must have been over fifteen years ago."

"Affirmative, but we're getting off the point."

"Sorry, what were you going to say about Gerald?"

"You may recall, he had an oversized gentleman's sausage as well, not as humongous as Warren's, but still a mighty specimen."

"Of course, it's why he got the moniker Gentleman Gerald Evans, also known as 'the rampant rice giver', because of his mountainous sexual appetite. He certainly had a license to thrill."

"Did you ever see his private business card?"

"Private business card," Fraser aped, dubiety littering his modulation. "No."

"He had these business cards made up to help market his sexual prowess. If memory serves, they were embossed with 'Gentleman Gerald Evans - Stud Merchant,' then a hook line saying 'Ladies, experiencing problems of a sexual nature. Still can't get satisfaction. Need to be nobbed? Look no further, professional nobbing service available online.'

Then some contact details followed."

"Mmmm, he once told me, he really got a liking for it as a kid. Evidently, he didn't do bob-a-job week, he did nob-a job week." Pausing, he then polled, "did he get any takers?"

"More than he bargained for," Chapple confirmed. "And they weren't all dollies either. Some were dogs. Even Attila would reject them!"

Aroused from his shallow slumber at the chiming of his name, the Great Dane rose up on his front legs, then jumped onto his master and licked his schnoz.

"Get *down*, Attila," Chapple pleaded. "I'll feed you some essence of Crusader later."

An unmistakable reference to Kappa Corinthians on-going grudge with Cranbrook Crusaders, it brought several banshee equalling howls of approbation from those overhearing the comment.

"You mean, Coyote ugly?" Fraser grilled. "Three baggers."

"Precisely. His reputation going before him, he also got a Dear John thank you letter from a girl who'd tried him on for size. It finished with, 'Finally, may I congratulate you on your sexual intercourse technique. I found it to be very stimulating and satisfying.'"

"You're kidding me."

"No, it's true," he boomed. "Making him very proud of his natural endowment, Gentlemen Gerald used the letter as an endorsement for more trade. He even stuck a copy of it up on his message board at work." Ceasing, he then whispered, "he got more takers and even applied for the Queen's Award to Industry for nobbing recognition."

"You don't say," Roger replied. "Good work, if you can get it."

"Unconditionally. It's equivalent to Bret Michaels, the vocalist from the rock-band Poison. He had a TV series in which he got to road test prospective companions for the season, purple on pink. Really stupendous work because Brett's contestants were all attractive. Anyway, Gerald held the same enviable position. Girls sauntered up to him at rugby club do's, making no bones about their craving to road test his equipment."

"Well, GG had all the credentials," Fraser proclaimed. "Not every man is so lucky."

"True, I'm more in the mid-range size myself."

"Yeah, me too."

"They say, it's not how big it is that counts, it's how you use it."

"Perhaps, but all in all, wishful thinking, Damien. It's tantamount to those guys with pug-ugly, other halves saying, 'They're all the same in the dark.'"

"Yeah, you're right. If you've seen her face, then even if it's pitch black when you're on the job, the likeness sticks in your knowingness. I couldn't raise a stork for a three-bagger, could you?"

"No. Just makes you realise how some men are so brave to facilitate the desires of those, who let's say, have not been smiled upon in the beauty stakes. I couldn't do that."

"Ugly birds scare the living daylights out of me anyway, especially the economy-sized jumbo variants."

"*Holy cow*! Why?"

Exhaling noisily, as if regretting making the statement, Chapple became flustered. "I had this er…really bad occurrence in my early twenties."

"What, you got a chubby three-bagger?"

"No, no, nothing so spine-chilling," he qualified, becoming shy and withdrawn.

"Come on," Fraser nagged. "It can't have been that bad."

"Well—" he unsteadily birthed. "I used to knock around with this guy Nick. We were both assistant reporters at the *Daily Express* in Fleet Street. Nick developed into a real terror for ugly girls." Chortling, he then cited, "he'd go up to one in the huge, open plan offices we worked in, smiling and cheerily say, 'Good morning. How are you today?' His target cordially rejoindered with, 'I'm fine, thank you for asking,' and they'd share a few more civil remarks. Then, fixing his victim seriously, he'd say, 'I see you've been on the ugly pills this morning.' Of course, the girl dissolved and called him all kinds of unkind names in response, while her female pals clustered around to give her comfort. The battle went on with Nick batting back the insults and saying, 'Yes, I have got a prodigious hooter, but you still haven't told me how long you've been on the ugly pills?' Irrevocably, the poor girl collapsed into a flood of tears, her mates berating Nick and beating him about the bonce with any heavy object they could find, as he prolonged his, 'How long have you been on the ugly pills?' explorations."

"An amusing story, Damien," Fraser exulted, "but I don't see how it affected you?"

"Mmmm, I hankered you'd not ask."

"You've come this far. You might as well take it all the way."

"Very well." Licking his lips, as if what he was about to reveal still evoked mental grief and palpitations, he informed, "one night after work I went to a pub off Fleet Street with Nick. We were sitting in a booth when in walks economy-sized Serena, a literally super-huge, grotesque three-bagger, working in the paper's distribution centre. She also had a fart on her like a 650 Norton, really foul and ear-piercing."

"What, foul like Missus Mallinson's 'rancid' mutt?" Fraser gibed.

"Put it this way, when she let rip, she cleared the entire work area. Anyway, Nick went into his ugly bird routine, but, made of sterner stuff, Serena didn't rise to the bait or crack-up blubbing. Eventually, Nick gave up. Later, she came over to play the one-armed bandit next to us, Nick deciding to have another attempt at riling her. He carped, 'Careful not to lean too heavily on the machine, or you'll crush it.' Unambiguously the last straw for economy-sized Serena, she swivelled on her heels to confront Nick and spout some repellent verbals, lost vertical control and toppled towards the booth we were sat in. Nick and I gaped in horror as she plunged in our direction, but we were too dumbfounded to extricate ourselves from the booth. When the runaway blubber mountain came crashing down, I got the full force of her impact. Winding me, straightaway I regurgitated a couple of pints of London Pride all over her, making a bad standing even worse. Once she had regained the vertical, using our boat races to lever herself up, she mopped off the beer debris from her huge chest, then extended both hands and made a play for my throat. Quickly leaping from the booth, she came after me with the motive of inflicting pitiless pain on my personage, even though I screamed out my innocent bystander status."

Flushed by his salutary tale, Fraser affirmed, "I begin to appreciate your dread of fatties, ugly or otherwise."

"The episode gave me nightmares for years," he confessed. "And I still have a phobia about colossal, fat women toppling over and falling on me. If Julia and I are out for a drink in the Kings Head or the Cricketers, and a female lard-arse walks in, and heaven forbid comes anywhere near me, I break into a sweat with visions of economy-sized Serena crushing me again." Glinting at Fraser, he confided, "makes me feel all giddy just mulling it over. Can we talk about something else, Roger?"

"Coincidentally, on the anathema of nightmares, I recall another school contemporary of mine, one Corwin Bagley, had a momentous shock when he managed to get a girl between the sheets for the first time."

"Why?"

"Corwin had little knowledge of female physiology prior to the watershed. His shy playmate asked him to put the lights out before she undressed and got into bed. Obliging, Corwin then got his kit off and slid into the sack. Cuddling up to her, he felt a furry article tickling his meat popsicle, so he says to the girl, 'There's a ferret or a squirrel in bed with us!' Leaping out, he puts the light on, throws the sheets back and is confronted by a gargantuan hairy mott! Shrieking at the unexpected hellion, he fled. The experience gave him nightmares for decades and put him off sex completely."

"Doesn't surprise me, an overgrown ladies garden is a paralysing spectacle. It's very off-putting to the male of the species, rendering copulation impossible. They should be kept neat and trim. Personally, I've never been keen on cunnilingus. Pussies are for pumping, not making inspections at ultra-close quarters."

"Quite."

~ * ~

On their arrival at Cranbrook, Kappa Corinthians received the traditional opposition welcome, good hearted boos mixed in with intentionally over-forceful slaps on the shoulders. Whilst rugby protocol stipulated servilities were maintained off the field, knowing the significance of the engagement and with old scores still to be settled, sharp and penetrating sulks were interchanged by players from both camps.

When Corinthians last entertained Cranbrook, the fur really flew, claret and broken bones everywhere. After the match, one particular truculent Crusader, loosehead prop Andy 'Thick-neck' Heseltine, so named because his chin rested on his chest with no discernible evidence of flesh where his neck should be, still held deep resentment. As each Corinthian went by him, he hissed and snarled, Damien Chapple reversing the intimidation by having Attila roar at Thick-neck on his master's command, the Crusader recoiling before reciprocating at the Great Dane. Faultlessly pleasant with his retail bank manager hat on, when Thick-neck donned the Crusaders colours, a mind-blowing transformation took place. He became a cross between Doctor Crippen and Hannibal Lector.

"Hey, Chapple" he warned, "if you don't want that flea bag to end up as sausages, keep him out of my sight."

Howbeit sturdily built, he could not compete in Thick-neck's league, when it came to sheer horsepower grunt. Nonetheless, Chapple squared up to him. "Touch my dog, and *you'll* end up as sausages."

Baring his teeth and growling just like an irate Diane Abbott, Attila supported his master's threat, Thick neck accordingly retreating.

Gathering around Mason Harvey in the away team dressing room to review the coach's tussle prosecution instructions and win strategy, the Corinthians mentally prepared themselves for their clash with destiny.

"Right, gentlemen," he inaugurated. "We all know Cranbrook Crusaders has a special significance for us, don't we?" Scanning around his players, already changed into their crimson and royal blue shirts and black shorts strip, he saw unwavering casts and heads nodding in response to the premise. "Now, let's all try and keep calm and spotlighted throughout the match. We don't want anyone being sin-binned, do we? We're here to win, not participate in a blood-letting feast." Resting, he raised his eyebrows. "*Clear*?"

"Yes, boss," came the replies.

"Albeit we head the Kent Veteran's league table, Crusaders are third and have two games in hand, so they'll be out to crucify us today. If they can get some of our key players injured, and we falter in the league, they might just overtake us for the title, moreover—" He grimaced. "If Crusaders beat us today and go on to win the Kent Veterans Cup competition, it will mean they will have won the trophy as many times as Corinthians." Smacking his lips, he glared at his team. "We don't want that to happen, *do we*?"

A chorus of no's came back at him.

"Right, here's what we're going to do." Walking slowly amongst the players, he explained his scheme. "Forwards, make sure there are no turnovers against the head in the scrums, and we win all our line-outs. Steve—" Hunt the Hooker gawped up. "That's going to be largely down to you. Keep your concentration, and don't concede anything. Are we crystal?"

"Aye-aye boss," Steve responded, annexing a salute to his blessing.

"Half-backs, let's have some well-gauged feeds to the backs. Gordon and Carl—" Fraser's mate Gordon Anderson, and Corinthians scrum half Carl Francis eyeballed Harvey. "Additional to conversions, when the inevitable penalties arise, let's have the kicks right between the posts every time."

Nodding, Gordon and Carl acknowledged their cardinal roles, knowing, as playmakers, by and large the contest outcome rested on their performance.

"Backs," Harvey continued. "You're going to have to be on your mettle this afternoon, because those rampaging Crusader forwards will be on you before you know it. Roger, let's see some of your legendary body swerves."

"You got it, boss," sealed the outside centre.

"If Dusty is going to stand a chance of racing through for tries," Harvey exhorted, "he'll need you to supply quality ball. The same goes for Damien and Frank on the left wing."

"Boss, can I ask a question," Corinthians inside centre Frank Sterling enquired.

"Sure."

"I know you said to avoid confrontation in Farnborough, but judging by the comments and inferences we heard from some of the Crusaders on the way in, they could have a different agenda."

"Quite right, Frank. I discerned it as well. However, control and focus will win through for us today. So, let's not get into any fisticuffs. *Got it?*"

"Yes, boss," all team members including the replacements echoed.

"And everyone," Harvey ultimately implored, "let's keep our discipline, and make sure our play is tight and slick. I want to see creation coupled to craft today. They're good on the loose ball, so try and avoid rucks, a core Crusaders strength. To avoid rucking, make sure the passing is accurate and to hand, no fanciful lobs over the top which can be intercepted. I expect this to be a relatively low scoring affair for tries, so when we do get an opportunity, let's make it count."

More positive responses came from the players.

"Right, Gareth, have you got any final thoughts?" Coach Harvey balloted.

Kappa Corinthians vets fifteen captain and openside flanker Gareth Ross scoured around the team, his granite veneer possessed of inflexible resolve, the shine of 'they shall not pass' in his blinkers. A giant of a man, despite his size, he could still run as fast as most forwards half his age. Coming to the club from Askean RFC in his late teens, he had represented Corinthians at every senior level. Very popular with boiler-house merchants, principally Steve Hunt, Gareth had developed a reputation for a 'never say die' attitude on the field of play. Even if Corinthians were losing with instants to go, he drove the team on relentlessly.

"What I have to say is very simple," he conditioned. "As Mason designated, there's a lot resting on the match today. If we win, it will send a signal to Crusaders, they will have to go some in the league to overtake us to win the title. And, it will herald a warning message to those other teams coming through the cup quarter finals that Kappa Corinthians have disposed of the favourites. So—" Delaying, he developed an uncompromising expression. "Let's have the club chant to get our adrenalin going. We're going to *win* at Cranbrook today."

A huge cheer went up from the Corinthians before they broke into the club chant.

~ * ~

Instituting the play-off, Gordon Anderson sent a drop-kick spinning into the Crusaders half. Rushing onwards, gushing a banshee cry, his unique way of announcing himself to the opposition, Steve Hunt made a crunching tackle on the Crusader nabbing the ball. Running loose, the two sets of opposing players piled into a ruck. During the rumble, the referee penalised a Crusader for holding onto the ball while on the ground. Penalty to Corinthians. Scrum-half Carl Francis took the spot kick and over she flew. Three points to Corinthians with only two minutes on the clock.

"Superb start," Mason Harvey shouted from the touch-line.

Setting the tenor for the entire first half, both teams transgressed multiple times, too many close quarter crunches and scant flowing rugby topping in loose pick-up play, rolling mauls petering out, a lot of penalties, but no tries by either side. Separate from his defence duties tackling opposing backs on the charge, Roger saw little attack play, apart from when the Corinthians pack won the ball in scrums or line-outs feeding it to Gordon at fly half, and he curled a pass to the outside centre. If Roger avoided incoming tackles from Crusader forwards, he passed it out to Dusty Maltman for him to bring off his magic down the wing. Nevertheless, those opportunities were far and few between. Driving mauls and crunching tackles by both sides distinguished the play, but apart from a few uttered verbals and scowls, no one got significantly injured or ended up in the sin-bin.

At half time the score levelled at 15-15, allowing Coach Harvey's team talk to be upbeat and encouraging.

"Keep it up," he urged. "We can go home as winners."

Early in the second half, a scrum just inside the Crusaders half permitted Corinthians' scrum half Carl Francis the put-in. Marginally crouched, Roger made ready to receive the ball, if it came to him from Gordon. As the scrum jostled, the players heard a cry of pain coming from its centre. Hunt the Hooker's noodle bobbed up.

"*Aahh*, he's biting my ear," Steve screamed.

Blowing up, the referee had robust words with Steve's opposite number at hooker for the Crusaders, reprimanding him for taking a bite at the Corinthian's ear, and saying Billy Hayes caricatures, when the American prisoner bights off a Turk's ear in *Midnight Express* were strictly verboten.

Dressing down over, the scrum reconvened, but again a deafening yelp emanated from its midst succeeded by Steve braying "you *cuntasaurus rex*," at the top of his voice.

Collapsing, the scrum became a melee of flailing arms and legs. As the players got up, the Crusaders' hooker smiled, coughed, spluttered, and spat out a bit of Steve's ear. Then the dull thud of fist on chin established Hunt the Hooker had eased the offending Crusader.

"*Steve!*" Mason Harvey hollered from the sideline, the unhappy hooker rotating towards the coach. "Less of the fisticuffs. Remember, discipline."

Revealing teeth marks on his ear, Steve whined, "but boss, he almost bit my lug-hole off."

Intervening, the referee upheld if the Crusaders hooker tarried hungry, he should have had a bigger breakfast. Expressly wanting to retain control, and not give the players any grievance excuses for bursting into fight mode, he read the riot act but refrained from furnishing sin-bin cards.

Grimacing and grousing, Steve made threatening gestures at the offender. Ignoring the portent, the ear biter smirked with contentment.

With the scrum reset, a determined Steve Hunt hooked the ball against the head, the Corinthians boiler house making a concerted surge towards the Crusaders' twenty-two-metre line, Carl Francis collecting the ball from the scrum trailing edge and feeding Gordon a precision pass, the fly half then spectacularly dive-passing the ball towards Roger. Taking the ball on the move, he skilfully swerved past a Cranbrook forward, who to use an American football term had already sacked him fourfold, and rampaged on. Totally focused on his task, he failed to see man-mountain Andy Heseltine bearing down on his track, Thick-neck running over him Challenger 2 tank style, burying his snout and mouth in the earth, Roger flattened agnate to the coyote in a *Roadrunner* cartoon. Losing his grip on the ball, it flew up into the air, but the onrushing Cranbrook players were caught off-side, the ref blowing up, before prancing over to the Corinthians stricken outside-centre.

"You all right, son?" he examined, his gaunt phizog amassed with anguish. "You caught a real beamer there."

All rugby officials on the field of play called players, 'son.' Often younger than the injured player, for some inexplicable reason, referees felt obliged to enter the, 'there, there, referee will kiss it better' zone.

Still removing a large patch of turf rammed down his throat during Thick-neck's assault tackle on him, Roger whooped, "yeah, I'm fine, ref," spitting out the remnants as he spoke.

A few yards away, Thick-neck glared and grunted at Fraser, given the opportunity, a sure sign of more on-field muggings to come.

At the half midpoint, another scrum won by Corinthians saw fly half Gordon Anderson reverse pass to the blindside, the play graduating in sharp interplay among the Corinthians backs to avoid Crusaders tackles before the ball came to Roger. Keeping an eye on Thick-neck, after feinting to his right, then body-swerving around an on-rushing Crusader's tackle, he saw Thick-neck plummeting on him like a runaway train. Neatly outfoxing him by reversing inside again, the Crusader tackled fresh air. Free from the human juggernaut, Fraser thundered through the ranks of Cranbrook's defenders, handing them off like confetti, before delivering a terrific pass to grease-lightning right wing, Dusty Maltman. Flying down the wing, the Corinthian smoothly outpaced the Cranbrook chasers for the visitor's opening try in the corner, Carl Francis converting, the men from Farnborough going 15-22 up.

On a roll, Corinthians racked up further points, Fraser getting on the score sheet with a try between the posts, resultant from a magnificent move among the backs from a line-out.

With the meet boiling over again, Thick-neck had a set-to with Damien Chapple after the Corinthians' left wing had skipped around most of the Crusader's defence to score a splendid try in the corner. Breaking free from the Corinthians' training staff, Attila bounded off to rescue his master. Seeing the hound from hell approaching, Thick-neck withdrew his grip from around Damien's throat and took flight. No equal to the Great Dane, Attila brought him down on the Crusader's twenty-metre line, then proceeded to enjoy an early lunch, his jaws firmly clamped around his chump's ankle, pulling him towards the Corinthians bench to consume the prey, Thick-neck kicking and screaming under the attack. Racing over to relieve the Crusader from his man-trap ensnarement, Thick-neck squawking that dogs tackling players is not allowed in the rules, the gamekeepers shouted their agreement. Just as they reached him, Damien whistled and the Great Dane released his grip on his master's adversary, bounding away to a gaggle of loudly cheering Corinthians players.

At full time, Corinthians ran out 25-38 winners, an infrequent phenomenon for the travelling veteran's team at Cranbrook. In archetypal rugby union tradition, what happened on the park, stayed on the park, Thick-neck not complaining afterwards about foul play, Attila not sin-binned, never mind red-carded.

~ * ~

Heading to Farnborough on the team coach, the conquering Kappa Corinthians were in a boisterous and jubilant mood, Coach Harvey and team captain Gareth Ross parading up and down the aisle, congratulating their triumphant team and shaking hands with them. Stories and jokes about singular achievement flew from player to player, backs ceremoniously slapped, and kisses planted on receding hairlines, the coach creaking and expanding with the reverberations of happy warriors returning to their loved ones with the scent of victory still fresh in their nostrils.

"Are you tuning into the Barbarians match later this afternoon, Roger?" Gordon quizzed.

"Who are they playing?"

"Australia."

"No, I don't think so."

"Australia will crucify them anyway," Steve prophesied.

Ogling along the aisle Fraser, sanctioned, "yeah, but don't let Dusty hear that, or he'll be dining out on it for weeks at our expense."

"I'll be riveted to it," Damien Chapple guaranteed. "What with work demands and Julia involving me in her social activities, I don't get much scope to sit down in front of the box these days. But you're right, Roger. The Barbarians won't have a prayer against Australia."

"Yep," Fraser reasserted. "But it's not the issue for me."

"How do you mean?"

"Well, if it's not England or Harlequins, I don't really have any interest. It's purely academic, about as pulse racing as seeing Botswana verses Bulgaria, and—" He winked at Chapple. "Nowhere as exciting, as watching Attila tackle Andy 'Thick-neck' Heseltine."

"True."

"Besides, I'm committed to garden work this afternoon and as a reward Charlotte is making shepherd's pie for dinner, one of my favourites."

"What goes into making a shepherd's pie?"

"Well shepherds of course, just like cottages go into making cottage pie."

"Seriously."

"How the hell should I know. I'm an analyst. I just eat food. I have no idea what's in it."

Chapter 11: Old Coffee Pots and *Shiksa* Farms

Allocating Fraser to attend the annual, three-day, Geneva Investment Banking Conference, Head of Analysts Department Henry Jacques advised him his mission was two-fold. Firstly, composing and staging a paper entitled 'Advanced Market Forecasting Algorithms' for the hedge fund futures powwow; really boring, tedious stuff but axiomatic in terms of understanding the forces in play, largely arbitrating futures' investments. An altogether more congenial undertaking, his supplemental responsibility centred on schmoozing potential clients, networking for new business opportunities, and trying to get a feel for market trends and investor expectations.

Additional to the intrepid stock analyst, Trading Floor Sales Manager, Ricky Henshaw and Susan Simpson, The Firm's London headquarters publicity manager, were also commanded to duty.

Along with a multitude of preeminent blue-chip investors, their objective to evaluate players to manage their assets, all the top-tier investment houses from across the globe signed up for the colloquium. Ostensibly a vanilla show, encompassing anything from de-risking fixed income agents to managing equity securities filling the speakers' agenda, Geneva always promised to be a rich environment for those seeking enlightenment in the silky and often sinister world of investment banking.

Over the seasons, the Geneva conclaves had accrued some very good business opportunities for The Firm, especially since the advent of financial services deregulation. Nevertheless, sequent to the Lehman Brothers catastrophe, investors were much more careful about investment house selection, and the SEC's ever-tightening grip had heightened financial instruments governance for those offering investment services. Hence, Geneva became both a fortuity forum and a vehicle for substantiating investment houses' true healthiness from a generic market perspective. Illumination not necessarily available in the public domain apropos investment house consummation extraneously skidded around the assembly, exposing possible shortcomings to prospective investors. Accordingly, The Firm knew it had to preserve a customer-facing image of unadulterated integrity and trustworthiness at Geneva.

Undeterred by the caution hovering over the congress, Geneva still delineated a medium for pioneering ideas and breakthrough innovations, proliferated by some of the most brilliant intellects in the industry. Traditionally, it also threw up some nonsensical, foot-in-mouth, even incongruous and psychotic mavens, their actions and routines though problematical and often beyond event management constraint, permanently residing in the annals of investment banking folklore. Often, Fraser theorised the Ayatollah and Top Cat took some beating in terms of macabre tendencies, but compared to many of the menacing delegates he had met at Geneva conventions, they seemed quite regular and normal.

~ * ~

During registration at the Four Seasons Hotel des Bergues, overlooking fabulous Lake Geneva, Fraser felt a tap on his midriff. Swinging around, Antoinette Parker, a hedge fund manager he used to work with at Merrill Lynch confronted him.

"Well, well, well," Antoinette drawled, "Roger Fraser," enunciating his name consonant to Alfred Hitchcock re-discovering a long-lost mysterious character for one of his suspense movies.

"Ohh…Antoinette," Fraser reservedly proclaimed, his comprehension surging with unsettling memories from yesteryear. "Hello."

Paralleling a farmer about to invest in livestock, she walked around Fraser auditing him.

"So, how's life at The Firm, Roger?" she enquired, her deportment teasing.

"Fine," he confirmed, his reticence growing. "And yourself?"

Anyone overhearing the re-encounter probably detected Fraser's reservation to the brink of being cold with Antoinette. When the pair worked at Merrill Lynch, as per many analysts, he had run-ins with her. Everyone in investment banking goes out on a limb, intent on finding success in their chosen vocation, but some of Antoinette's dubious and extremely risky adventures in the hedge fund arena raised forebodings from her colleagues all the way up to board grade. Persuading pension fund, university endowment and foundation managers on top of astronomical net worth individuals into coughing up readies for plausibly explosive returns, persisted as a constant challenge to all hedge fund managers, but she used underhand and illegal methods to accomplish debatable deals, some, borderline SEC investigation territory. Consequently, Antoinette Parker became condemned as toxic by analysts, but lauded as a risk-taking, ballsy go-getter by fellow hedge fund managers and her boss.

"As you can see from my name badge," she answered, "I'm with Charles Schwab & Co." Still weighing up Fraser, she gently rocked on her high heels and played with her sexy, secretary-style spectacles with her hand. "How longs it been, Roger?" she drilled, continuing the tease by toying with a spectacle arm and provocatively pushing it into her pouting mouth.

"How longs what been?" he snappily imparted. Then recognising his reply could be misconstrued, his steadfast expression mutated into sudden surprise.

Sparkling as if interpreting his petition as sexual innuendo, she didn't respond immediately.

Why did I say that, Fraser considered? *Freudian slip. Holy crap, I don't even care for Antoinette, but she is attractive.*

"How long has it been since we worked together at Merrill Lynch?" she rephrased

"Fifteen years," he recounted, then over-compensating for his blooper, curtly augmented, "long enough to almost remember you fondly."

"Now, Roger," she scolded in her put-on, sexually goading way, "no need to be crotchety about occurrences from way back in the midst of both our careers."

"*Antoinette*," he pealed, his voice segueing into an authoritative resonance, "you sailed dangerously close to getting a pull from the SEC and linking other people by subsidiary association…like me. You could have lost your trading license and severely limited the careers of others unwittingly caught in your spiders' web…like me."

"Relax, Roger," she solicited, almost purring the words. "It happened long ago when I was very young and establishing a beachhead in your male-dominated world." Putting on a butter-wouldn't-melt countenance, she informed, "I don't do those things anymore." Swaying about her hips, she implored, "come on, lighten-up. You were always known to be a fun-time boy, so cut me some slack. Let's be friends."

Relaxing his vilifying stance, he warned, "just so long as you never come anywhere near The Firm."

"It's a bargain," Antoinette approved. "Besides, I'm doing very well at Schwab."

Breaking into a playful smile, she placed her hands behind her derriere and swivelled about the soles of her high heels, essaying for innocence, but only managing to effect more sexual provocation, her glossy aura emanating magnetism. Perennially a pretty girl, since Fraser last saw her, she'd become even more attractive, the late teenage girliness still hanging around in her early twenties replaced by sophistication, elegance and style. She wore it very well.

"Okay, Antoinette," he conceded, "You're on probation."

Her alluring smile broadened. "Roger Fraser," she smoothly crooned, inspecting him in more detail. "Dreamy eyes, tight ass."

"*What?*"

"It's what the Merrill Lynch secretaries used to say about you."

"Now you're embarrassing me."

"They were your redeeming features, Roger," she complimented. "Still might be. Even the burgeoning grey suits you."

Fuming, he blurted, "the male of the species is meant to indulge in sexual innuendo, not his counterpart."

"Oh, Roger," she chided. "That's such an *old*, provincial phrase. It's been called sexism for decades."

"I know," he assured her. "But I don't choose to use the term. It's from somebody else's dictionary I don't subscribe to."

"My, you have grown up since our Merrill Lynch days," she exalted, flashing her perfect gnashers, the vim adding a touch of vitriol to the trick sarcastic praise. Sensing they were getting into feud territory again, Antoinette changed the subject. "I see you are on the spokesmen list."

"Yes," Fraser corroborated, suspecting more baiting. "Tomorrows hedge fund futures congress."

"By the way, where are you staying?"

"Here at the Four Seasons."

"I'm at the Mandarin Oriental with the other Schwab contingent."

"I see."

"Well, do keep in contact, Roger," she cordially requested. "Maybe there will be a possibility for us to work together again in the future," she attached, fluttering her eyelids, the playful come-on barely disguised.

"I'm a happily married man, Antoinette," he upheld, "with three children and a rugby club to absorb all my waking hours, when I am not at The Firm."

Nodding dismissively, she threw a disdainful glower at him then took a step forward. "Oh, Roger," she censured, "you're so old fashioned that it's almost quaint." Radiating, she extended, "see you later."

Emitting a toothy grin, she strode off, the click, click of her stilettos on the marble floor attracting male attention from every quarter.

Sneaking up behind him, Keith Foster, a Warner Quinnell pension fund manager taunted, "lucky dog."

"What?"

"I said, lucky dog, Roger. She's a real fox."

"What…*no*…you don't understand, Keith."

"While the cat's away, hey?" he badgered, dabbing his beak to indicate Fraser's secret abided safe.

"It's not what you think, "Fraser pleaded. "We used to work together. That's all. There's nothing going on."

"Oh, Roger," Foster bayed. "You're *so* old fashioned."

~ * ~

On the second day, Fraser made final preparations for the hedge fund futures council with other orators, counting long-term friend Alfredo Bachelli, a celebrated if not difficult to control in investment banking circles analyst from UniCredit Spa. Gaining a reputation for being a spiky and often intolerant crackerjack, Bachelli did not readily brook fools and reprimanded those he perceived to have been discourteous about his endeavours. Notwithstanding, socially, the variable Italian became transformed into an utterly charming soulmate, his classic Roman heritage coupled with his equally agreeable wife Maria, made visits to the Bachelli's Rome household a pleasurable practice for Charlotte and Roger. Hospitable an understatement, he had also invited the Frasers to the Bachelli ancestral home in Sorrento. Reciprocating, the Bachellis were bid to drop anchor in Hazelwood whenever Alfredo undertook UK business for his employers.

Marking the Italian still wore his coat around his shoulders, El Supremo style, Fraser wondered if his pal had developed a General Franco or a Mussolini fixation, Bachelli illuminating he'd recently reverted to the proclivity, when a chum from university reminded him, he used to show up to lectures in the same literary mode.

Chatting about nothing specific whilst waiting for the session moderator, the pair segued into reminiscence about the instances they had spent together.

On the introductory occasion they met, Bachelli picked up Fraser from Rome's Leonardo Di Vinci airport in his Alfa Romeo sports car.

After firing up the engine, he put on his driving gloves and nonchalantly announced, 'And a now my friend, I teach you how to drive the Italian a way.' Feeling about the passenger seat Fraser squealed, 'what, no seat belts?' Replying in true Italian alpha male vogue, Bachelli insisted, 'seata belts are for sissies.' Successive to the denouncement, he grabbed the rear-view mirror, flung it into the rear seat, floored the accelerator pedal, and they were off on one of the most heart-stopping, white knuckle car rides Fraser ever underwent. Having gone through every red light as if they were green for go, when they reached the UniCredit HQ, he'd become as white as a ghost and had lost at least half a stone in weight through out-of-control perspiration.

Laughing at the stupefying episode, Fraser probed, "what are you driving these days, Alfredo?"

Since the Alfa, Bachelli had owned a succession of ritzy Italian cars, all treated with as much irreverence as his Alfa Romeo.

"Er, atta the momenta, a, er, Maserati GranCabrio Sport. Maria still has the, er Lancia Voyager, the, er, family er car."

"Not been tempted by the Porsche Cayman R or the Jaguar XK?"

Withdrawing, as if astounded by his friend's suggestions, the Italian doomed, "the er, the er, Cayman is er, olda a coffee a pot. It er, it er, makea a lotta steamer, but er—" He smiled. "Yes, I er, likea the Jaguar."

"Old coffee pot," Fraser parodied.

"Er, yeser, Roger, olda coffee a pot," he avouched.

"What makes you use the comparison?"

"Is er, is er, ancient a technology, likea steama engine."

Giggling at the analogy, Fraser congratulated, "very funny, Alfredo, but Porsche is leading edge."

"*No*…no, no. Porsche is olda a coffee a pot," he swore. "Make a, er swoosh, er likea, likea a boiling a water."

Having fathomed from quondam exposure, once Bachelli had made his mind up he became intractable on all counter appraisals, Roger yielded. "Yes, you're right. It is an old coffee pot."

"Of a coursa, I am always a righta," he venerated without a hint of modesty. Then peeking to the heavens, as if expecting imminent beatification, he appended with monastic homage, "I am Bachelli."

About 260 emissaries attended the caucus from investment institutions, blue chip investment companies, private banks and of course the financial press, all awaiting cogent elucidation from what they espied to be the hedge fund gurus, Fraser fourth out of six presenters scheduled to address the gathering.

As had long become the *de facto* goal for such prestigious happenings, the crucial objective for the speaker endured as being memorised by prospective customers, so they'd contact him afterwards to talk about their business issues. Forming the basis of paper dissertations, the residue of the forum centred on an 'aren't we a clever set of bastards' theme, material handed out to proxies to sustain kudos, thought and thereby market leadership and most essentially, positive client perception.

To get noticed, spielers invariably went for the humorous angle, mixing jokes and displaying lewd pictures with the core article.

First up to the rostrum, Aberdeen Asset Management's Nathan Juke commenced with, 'a funny thing happened to me on the way to the amphitheatre,' type jape to get the throng loosened up. Accommodating him, they played the game, both the congregation and his associate rabble-rousers occupying the front row seats, chuckling and mildly applauding at the appropriate crossroads. Just as the terminal strains of merriment faded, a very loud guffawing yawp originated from somewhere towards the stern of the meeting room. Because the lights were down to help onlookers see Juke's PowerPoint slides on a back-lit projector, at the front, necks were craned around by their curious owners, but they flunked pinpointing the source of the penny had just dropped laughter.

Clearing his throat, Juke then smiled, made some remark about there always being a laggard at these events and carried on. Concurrent with slide four, he made another joke drawing measured amusement from the audience, but once again as laughter decayed, the straggler came in with a real snorter. More heads twirled, but it remained gruelling to identify the culprit. Like clockwork, the same call and retarded response drama happened again and again throughout Juke's exposition. From their front row stations, his fellow tub-thumpers witnessed his disconcertion multiplying, causing him to occasionally lose his thread before thankfully, from his viewpoint, concluding the ponderous task.

Climbing down from the stage, flustered and mopping his forehead, Juke exclaimed, "*Good god*! I've never experienced anything so off-putting before. Who the hell is that guy?"

Aberdeen's emissary received noggin shakes and non-committal noises in response, every speaker secretly ruminating security needed to be called in to shoot the phantom laugher.

Next up for lectern duty, albeit still to arrive, Garrett Hartley from Charles Schwab, one of Antoinette's consorts, would be the succeeding recipient of the prankster's belated guffawing.

With an impish lour splashed across his lineaments, Fraser jested, "Hartley is going to get a formidable floorer, when he turns up."

"Yes," Schroders envoy Callum Tudor accorded. "Glad I'm not going next."

During the short break between talks, the others joined in, all thanking their lucky stars they were not next in line for spiel duty, and maybe with Hartley droning on, laughing boy would doze off or better still scram from the meeting.

Acting as session moderator, Sebastian Paynter, the commodity derivatives VP from BNP Paribas beckoned Fraser to come over to talk to him. Previously meeting Paynter, he had rated him to be a good egg and a straight talker, feasibly incapable of pulling the wool. Uncommon for someone in financial services.

"Hello, Sebastian," he joviality greeted. "That infuriating prankster is going to give Garrett Hartley an unpredicted bombshell."

"Ah, yes," Paynter assented in a rattled voice. "That's what I want to talk to you about, Roger."

"Don't tell me," the breezy stock analyst kidded. "You want me to take a dragoon of Swiss guards and eject him from the colloquium?"

"No, not exactly," the ill-at-ease Paynter differed. "But there is a favour we want from you."

Scanning the sea of delegates attempting to decipher which one was laughing boy, Fraser gabbled, "oh yeah, what?"

"We want you to go on next, Roger."

Fraser's cheery demeanour soured. He swore he had just heard Paynter say, 'We want you to go on next.'

"What!" he jabbered, "but I'm on fourth. Hartley is next."

"Well, yes, Roger," Paynter accepted, furrowing his brow with regret. "But erm—" Ceasing, he chortled as if travailing to lessen the blow. "We've had a message to say, Hartley has been delayed."

"And so?"

Meshing into sell-mode, he commended, "well, you are the most senior of all the representatives, so we resolved you'd be best suited to go next."

As the blood drained from his phiz, Fraser became ashen. "How do you make me out to be the most senior?" he bleated.

"You've er, you've been around for longer than the other spokesmen," Paynter argued.

"What about Aaron Maguire or Teddy Briscoe," Fraser fired off. "Hell, they must have ten years on me."

"True," he ratified, "but Maguire has had to make an unplanned call home and Briscoe has gone off to the gents to be sick. Allegedly, he gets stage fright, so the prospect of facing—" Halting again, he wrinkled his nose. "What did you call him?"

"Laughing boy."

"Yes, laughing boy, has brought him out in hives and a cold sweat, so I'm afraid, Roger, you're it."

"What about Bachelli? He's got five years on me."

Grimacing, Paynter sucked in air. "I don't really fancy Alfredo is quite the right person for this sensitive commission. Do you?"

Staring blankly at the session moderator and knowing the makeup of the Roman beast, Fraser resigned himself to the inevitable.

After Paynter introduced The Firm's ambassador, the lights went down, Fraser standing at the stage lectern, peering out into the auditorium labouring in vain to identify laughing boy. About to launch his overture, he goggled up to see Garrett Hartley scurrying into the meeting room, making his apologies to Sebastian Paynter and taking his place in the front row.

Leaving Fraser fuming, he murmured, "bastard."

Consistent with for his predecessor, the cachinnation king dawdled several bars behind the patrons' laughter orchestra in response to Fraser's jocular primary anecdote.

"Perhaps if the gentleman seated towards the rear of the room, could please synchronise his laughter symbiotic to everyone else's," he appealed, "we might evacuate to the bar early before lunch."

Appreciating Fraser's invocation, the attendees reacted with complementary chuckles, but just about to re-engage on his theme, he heard laughing boy suddenly burst into a full raucous bark.

Deciding to seize the bull by the horns and carry on insensible to the clown's antics, he manfully strode through his material, congeneric to a tank commander in Montgomery's Eighth Army taking down Rommel at El Alamein. Only stopping to field sporadic queries from intransigent plenipotentiaries, he spooned more one-liner quips to keep the spectators glued to his treatise.

In rebutting one question about how some forecasting algorithms had harvested egg-on-face type outcomes for hedge fund futures predictions, he finalised his reply saying, "it's akin to the TV basketball pundit who ragged, 'He dribbles a lot, and the opposition doesn't like it. In fact, you can see it all over their faces.'"

Waves of mirth flooded forth from the enrollees, Fraser leaning forward and nudging his left ear ahead of and in elevated anticipation of laughing boy's lucid tones. Duly coming on cue a good five seconds after the foremost hilarity died down, he quipped, "must be an echo in here."

Unflagging, the theatre, or more accurately, the farce, lasted, Fraser making less humorous remarks to meet his allotted time limit. About midway through his conferral, he tallied three security officers adroitly extracting someone from row z of the lecture hall. Slightly putting him off his stroke when a kafuffle resulted, howbeit, at the next juncture he cracked a funny, no ancillary guffawing leaked behind the main chorus. Inwardly, he smiled, surmising his tormentor must have been the security guard's target. Peeping at Sebastian Paynter in the front row, the session moderator nodded, implying Fraser's discomfort had been relieved by his intervention.

Designated to be next up after Fraser's palaver, before Alfredo Bachelli took to the lectern, Paynter reminded the touchy Italian he had a maximum of twenty minutes to deliver his message, Bachelli's reputation for substantially exceeding stint slots going before him.

"Butta whatta you meana?" Bachelli bellowed, either genuinely thunderstruck by Paynter's hint, or just faking it.

Going for what he adjudged to be an adept riposte, he set forth, "well, Alfredo, your, er, your reputation for over-running allocated slots, is, er, a matter of record. I just wanted to make sure you understood the constraint."

Aggrieved, and on the verge of self-control, Bachelli justified, "I take a, as longa as a necessary, and a no er longer." He eyed Paynter forcefully. "*Capiche!*"

"Erm," the unnerved session moderator gibbered, feeling the Italian's heat. "What?"

"I saida *capiche*."

"Oh, yes, I *capiche*."

"*Good*," Bachelli boomed, patting Paynter on his upper-arm. "Then er, we have er, no problermo."

Not wanting to argue further and resigned to the man from UniCredit Spa getting his way, Paynter shrunk into acquiescence. "No, of course a not," he spluttered, "I mean, of course not."

"Good. You er wanta me to starta?"

"Oh yes," Paynter encouraged, rationalising the sooner he begins, the sooner he'll finish, and hoping it'd be on the autumn side of Christmas. "I'll make the introduction."

After ten minutes, Bachelli had processed just three of twenty slides, all humour free. Becoming strung out, session moderator Paynter coughed to attract his regard then tapped his watch but to no avail. Now in full-swing, the Italian became totally impervious to outside stimuli. Italy could be winning the World Cup, but such joy would not deflect his concentration. Fixing his gaze only on his slides and the audience, he lingered oblivious to supplementary gestures from Paynter.

By the twenty-minute mark, he had barely moved on. Upping the ante, Paynter tried to attract his alertness with exaggerated coughs, then by waving his hands in an emulated propeller action, making him look moronic. Fully-seized by his toil, Bachelli stayed transparent to the session moderator's desperate sign language. At the thirty-minute mark, listeners became fidgety, shuffling around in their seats and whispering to each other. Then someone got to their feet and started to exit the meeting.

Logging what he sentenced to be impertinent behaviour from a disrespectful miscreant on the move, Bachelli petitioned in a sharpened Italian accent, "er, *mi scusi*."

Whoops, Fraser cogitated, *not good*. He'd seen people try to abscond from Bachelli's dissertations in the past, only to end up cowering under his vicious tongue.

The man acknowledged the orator, but kept moving.

Affronted, Bachelli menacingly interrogated, "er, where you go?"

Stopping, the man smiled. "Oh, I have to go to another seminar."

Dramatically raising his hands up to his cheekbones to emphasise the intensity of the effrontery, Bachelli glared then snorted, "you wanta to *insulta* me?"

Confounded by the Italian's ticking off, the man lamely mouthed, "erm…no."

"Then sitta downa…you mighta learna something."

Gesticulating, Bachelli motioned for the offender to return to his seat.

Duly obliging, he skulked down in a schoolboy-about-to-receive-six-of-the-best posture, as he made for his former station.

Gaping at Sebastian Paynter, Fraser saw he had placed a wrist across his snoopers and slowly shook his head. "God damn Italian," he mumbled.

Indifferent to the embarrassment he'd caused, Bachelli studied his prompters then catechized, "nowa, wherea was I."

With exasperated talkers queuing up to execute their own patter, eventually the UniCredit Spa man drew his discourse to a conclusion on the hour mark, much to the relief of session moderator Paynter.

Agitated and wronged, Bachelli walked over to Fraser. "I really needa ninety a minutes for my a briefing, Roger," he implored. "One hour is nota enough."

"But Alfredo," Fraser contradicted, "all speakers were allocated twenty-minutes max!"

Gawking at his English friend in astonishment, as if Fraser had just honked all over the Pope, he claimed, "twenty a minutes, huh…I need a twenty a minutes just to warma up. Anything less, they insulta me."

Sitting down, Bachelli browsed the conference-roster then consulted his timepiece. Sincerely, he revealed, "I hope a, they'er quick." Fretfully glancing at Fraser, he conferred, "I hava another a lecture to a go to."

Flabbergasted, Fraser's mouth breached involuntarily.

~ * ~

After the tricky day, Fraser met up with Ricky Henshaw and Susan Simpson for cocktails before dinner.

"How did your hedge fund hearings go, Roger?" Ricky audited.

"Eventful is the most fitting word, with a few unusual surprises."

"Any business leads?"

"Yes. A couple of guys came up to me afterwards to talk about investments. One from Capel Scotney who want to invest in hedge fund futures, the other from the Hanson Group, also contemplating hedge funds along with pension and mutual funds. Then some others caught me over lunch and during the afternoon period." Diving into his jacket inside pocket, he pulled out a bunch of business cards. "Here," he said, handing them to Henshaw. "I've written what type of investment they're seeking on the backs, and said you'd give them a call while they're still in Geneva."

"Will do," Henshaw agreed. "Thanks, Roger."

"Did you have a good day, Susan," Fraser scouted.

"Well, after announcing The Firm's latest press releases, I got interviewed by the *Financial Times*, *MoneyWeek* and *Financial Services Review*. They all wanted to know about our Silverman Greco and JMS agreements, and…those Guatemalan precious metals transactions you brokered with Villa Nueva and Santa Sofia."

"*Really*. I'm stunned," refuted the modest stock analyst. "Neither of those Guatemalan contracts could be categorised as capacious, certainly not compared to Silverman Greco." Apprehensively he drilled, "by the way, Ricky, who'll be servicing Silverman Greco on your team?"

"Odd-job," the trading floor sales manager confirmed.

Justin Knightly, named Odd-Job, not because he resembled Goldfinger's famous chauffeur-handyman come enforcer, but because he took on complex accounts needing a grade of subtlety, wit and inventiveness often beguiling lesser souls, had achieved mythic credentials. One of the more erudite and intellectual bullpen players, with outside interests beyond Porsche 911s and Dom Perignon excesses, he had been reading books without pictures since age twenty-five, quite a feat by modern day trader standards.

Coming to The Firm on recommendation from his auntie, Roslyn Joyce, the London setup's head investment assessor helping Fraser with the Western Goodricke enterprise, The Firm rightly crowned if Knightly possessed the same chromosomes as Roslyn, he'd prove to be an efficacious asset. Though evidently a gifted salesman with a good conk for business and an off-the-scale IQ, nevertheless, Knightly's early exposure to the hoary old world of investment banking tested his sensibilities, Henshaw allocating a particularly onerous private investor portfolio to him, and saying he had a better chance of extracting blood from a stone than getting the solitaire concerned to part with readies, even for a cast iron certainty.

Self-made multi-millionaire, Cedric Mcstuckey, the private

investor at issue, had accumulated a personal wealth in excess of £50m from his ownership of a variety of diverse businesses. Exhibiting poor communication skills and even less empathy with his fellow man, in the bullpen, he became known as the 'Duncan Bannatyne wannabe', after the charmless Celtic nerk destroying manque entrepreneurs on *Dragon's Den*. Also, a hard-to-be-understood Glaswegian, Mcstuckey had a broad, gravelly accent few could interpret, two-way conversation debateable to say the least. Naturally, the incidence of misinterpreting Mcstuckey's edicts erred on the soaring side, dealers mishearing his instructions due to their Celtic to English speech decoder limitations, typified by when The Firm put his investment into salmon anti-poacher schemes, rather than Samuel Pocket makeover themes he premeditated, furious outbursts resulting from the unjovial Jock.

Another opening conduced mayhem when he wanted to invest in Scottish Power, but his instruction came across as 'Scottish poor.' Pumping if he really wanted to contribute to a Scottish charity for the poor and thereby matriculate for tax credits, the assigned muggins received a hail of abuse along the lines of Mcstuckey classified himself as a poor man, and as a matter of principle, he didn't support down and outs.

When Odd-job inherited the account, it had already passed through most hands in the bullpen. On every occasion, the account's unlucky owner receded away from the unidirectional 1-0-1, scorched and brow beaten. However, in spite of him knowing it could be career limiting and usually the broker's graveyard, Odd-job grasped the opportunity with both hands to have a crack at the Mcstuckey account.

Before making his inaugural call to the Celtic terror, smart Odd-job surveyed the account's foregoing owners to dig the pretexts behind their failings. Instantly comprehending miscommunication had become their downfall, he managed to get his hands on an English to Celtic dictionary, and went to the trouble of attending a night class course entitled, 'How to communicate with Jocks.' By the time he called Mcstuckey, he had become fully conversant in Jock terminology and the unsubtle nuances of Celtic phrases, his introductory colloquy with

Mcstuckey a revelation to the Scot. At last, he'd found a London Sassenach who could understand him.

Since, Justin Knightly had been allocated other exigent accounts to manage, as well as some exceptionally toilsome corporate players. Hence the name, Odd-Job.

"Oh, good," Fraser fervidly propped. "I take it Silverman Greco is going to be an intricate account then?"

"Indeed," Henshaw affirmed. "Their hands-on practices and contractual terms and conditions are formidable, way beyond industry benchmarks. Realistically, I couldn't assign one of the Essex faction. Their acerbic disposition would spark gargantuan waves at Silverman Greco within hours breeding pandemonium. No, Odd-job can handle it. He's already mastering how to bend to the Silverman Greco way of doing things."

"Biting his lip while focusing on the money then?"

"Yes, it's the only measure of success."

As their three-way dialogue persisted along the line of business-related texts, Roger felt a vibration in his pocket foreshadowing his lately acquired Blackberry had summoned his application. Inspection exposed he had an email from Gordon Anderson containing a joke based on a topical EU situation, Fraser tittering in reaction.

"Well share the funny with us, Roger," Susan coveted.

"What?" He looked up. "Oh yes, I will." Glimpsing at the Blackberry again he relayed on, "this is from a rugby pal of mine. He sends me yarns based on current affairs. It's about Cameron's veto of the EU's latest attempt to con the English into bailing out the Euro."

"Go on."

"After an EU summit in Rome, due to a strike by Swiss air traffic controllers, various European leaders were forced to take the train. Sitting together in the same compartment travelling through the Swiss Alps were Sarkozy, Cameron, Merkel and the young, very attractive female Danish foreign minister. The train goes into a dark tunnel. A few seconds later, there's the crack of a loud slap. When the train emerges from the tunnel, Sarkozy has a bright red handprint on his cheek. No one speaks, everyone markedly appalled or embarrassed. Angela Merkel deduces, 'not able to help himself, Sarkozy must have groped the Danish girl in the dark, and she slapped his cheek.' Conversely, the Danish girl guesses, 'Sarkozy must have tried to grope me in the dark, but missed and fondled Merkel and she slapped his cheek.' Sarkozy thinks 'why me? Perfidious Cameron must have groped the Danish girl in the dark, cognizant I'd get the blame for it, and she slapped me...the English bastard.' And Cameron relishes, 'I can't wait for another tunnel, so I can smack that little French twat again.'"

Bursting into laughter, Fraser's compatriots agreed Sarkozy got his just desserts. Discerning the bullpen would be enthralled by the gibe, Henshaw craved him to forward-on the email for general distribution.

Continuing to chat about the next day's concourse activities, The Firm's quadrille was interrupted by a waiter wanting to show them to their dining table. Grabbing their cocktails, they made their way over and had just about settled down when Antoinette Parker and Garrett Hartley from Charles Schwab loomed large into Susan's view.

"Roger, there's a woman over there trying to catch your absorption," she acquainted.

Peeking up from his Long Island Iced Tea, Fraser saw Antoinette waving. Out of courtesy, he fluttered a rejoinder back, Antoinette taking it as a signal for her and Hartley to join them. Not what Fraser intended!

Obviously pleased with themselves, the Charles Schwab pair sauntered over, Antoinette explicitly contented, Hartley less euphoric, but still emanating enough vibe to suggest a keenness to talk to The Firm's proxies.

"Good evening, Roger," Antoinette enunciated, her intention to engender a considerate response. "Do you mind if Garrett and I join your party for dinner?"

Being a habitual wolf and between wives, instantaneously Henshaw picked up on the feminine seduction oozing from Fraser's ex-Merrill Lynch playmate. Logging his dripping tongue, Antoinette beamed her most enticing smile, her teeth scintillating with a glint, echoing the Signal toothpaste advert.

Conscious it'd be ungracious to say no, Fraser okayed the request. "Yes, it's fine. Let me make some introductions."

After the flesh had been pressed all round, the Charles Schwab pair sat down at The Firm's table, Hartley revisiting the hedge fund futures session PDQ and profusely thanking Fraser for taking the next slot in the schedule in his absence.

"I heard the chap with the uncontrollable laugh wasn't even an envoy," he confided. "Somehow he managed to get into the conference on a forged name badge."

"It explains why laughing boy seemed so out of place in the normally ultra-conservative and reverential financial services audience," Fraser remarked.

"Yes. Sebastian Paynter told me the hotel security put him in a taxi to whatever mental hospital he'd escaped from."

"What's all this then, Roger?" Henshaw explored, keen to get the SP.

Positioning the violation, Fraser responded with a potted account of the laughing boy occurrence, Hartley complementing with his own obtuse brand of humour on the clash, his earlier sheepishness regarding his late entry apparently spent.

Meanwhile, Antoinette cosied up to Ricky, her body language playful and heady, Fraser speculating, *what little game is going on there?* knowing from old she never did anything without prior deliberation. Surviving in the hedge fund management market for over fifteen years, he calculated she must have cultivated some tricks of the trade to supplement her innate feminine guile. Was she endeavouring to get Ricky between the sheets, so he'd succumb to her abundant charms, spilling The Firm's most intimate secrets? She'd get a shock there. Well known for his cocksmanship, Ricky had the ability to do the business all night long. *She could end up telling him Schwab's deepest secrets*, Fraser envisioned.

Still going through the possible Antoinette-Ricky permutations, out of the corner of his eye, he saw the familiar personage of Emmanuel Goldberg from Solomon Brothers, aka Piranha Brothers, an investment house with a reputation for ruthlessness in the marketplace, hence the moniker. Holding up his hand, Goldberg shined at The Firm's stock analyst.

"Excuse me" Fraser beseeched, "I must have a few words with an old friend."

Moving towards him, Fraser spotted he manifested his usual well-groomed and charismatic self, dressed in a made-to-measure Savile Row suit, Jermyn Street tailored shirt, Bally brogue shoes and sported a City of London Club tie. Every inch the archetypal city gent, his attire projected an aura of solidity, soundness and trust, key prerequisites for attracting potential clients. Old school, honed in the ways of tradition, ritual and custom, Goldberg represented institutional bedrock at its finest.

"Roger, I ascribed it might be you in the distance," he consigned. "My optics are not what they used to be."

"Manny," Fraser reciprocated, shaking hands firmly with the Piranha Brothers man. "How the devil are you?"

One of London's earliest investment houses with a heritage formerly harking from Lord Nelson's era, Solomon Brothers always preferred to be known as 'merchant bankers.' According to their executive board, they attributed the title to have a more exclusive intonation and superior kudos than the newer 'investment bankers.' In the late nineteenth century, Solomon Brothers' forefathers had rubbed shoulders with Nathan Mayer Rothschild, Thomas Mellon, John D Rockefeller and Andrew Carnegie during business trips to Paris, Berlin and New York, the linkages fostering bi-lateral business between London, the Continent and North America, resulting in brokerage underpinning the future of their international organisation. At the heart of the old square mile, Solomon Brothers' headquarters used to be in Finsbury Avenue Square. Every day, they sent out for a supply of bagels and other kosher blisses from nearby Brick Lane, the epicentre for Jewish breakfast cuisine, but when the business moved to the Broadgate Centre in Bishopsgate at the turn of the nineties, regrettably, the traditional breakfast praxis ended.

Taken on as an office junior, Emmanuel Goldberg had been with

Piranha Brothers all his working life, rising through the ranks by carrying out an assortment of investment house functions, culminating in promotion to director of mutual and hedge funds and executive board membership. Now in his early sixties and lasting sprightly, he still pitched with the best of them.

"I'm fine, Roger," he corresponded with a gregarious smile. Feeling Fraser's lapel, he quipped, "hhmm, nice bit of schmutter. If I didn't know better, I'd swear you're using a Jewish tailor."

"Hah."

"And how are your wife and young family?"

"Charlotte is well, and the children are not so young anymore. Wendy is doing her A-levels, James is now a teenager, and our youngest Heather, gets more grown up with every passing day."

"I'm glad for you, Roger," Goldberg enthused. "A man should have a family around him."

"And yourself, Manny?"

"Oh, I'm well ahead of you in that domain. I now have six grandchildren to add to my three children, and my wife Leah still wants more."

"I presume you mean, more grandchildren?"

"Oh yes, we are long past procreation, and I'd need enough Viagra to stimulate a stallion these days to even contemplate matrimonial relations."

"Very funny, Manny. You've always had a strong sense of ironic humour."

"It goes with being Jewish, my boy. We have to see the funny side in everything. *Oy vey*."

Breaking into more laughter at Goldberg's self-deprecating wit, the older man basked in the younger man's felicity.

Running his eye over Fraser, before making an enquiry he knew beforehand would not eventuate in a cogent reply, the Piranha Brothers exec entreated, "tell me, Roger, is business good at The Firm?"

"No…it's not good," Fraser teasingly replied. "I'd say, in spite of the unending worldwide financial crisis, we are doing exceedingly well."

Gleaming, he annexed, "but you know I can't give you any specifics."

"Heavens, always the salesman, hey Roger?" Goldberg acclaimed, scrutinising him admiringly. "Always the loyal Firm employee."

"Jeez," Fraser burst out smirking. "I'm just doing my job."

"I hear you have a new mandate. Is it true?"

"Well I won't be betraying a confidence, if I ratified ancillary to my stock analyst job, I now have a trouble-shooter responsibility." Raising his eyebrows, he appended, "it's fairly common knowledge."

"So," Goldberg ventured, his dial modulating into the inscrutable, "you go around the globe, settling disputes and overcoming business bottlenecks?"

"Something like that."

"Mmmm." Ruminating, he rubbed his chin, his peepers narrowing. "Why don't you ditch that lacklustre investment house, they call The Firm, and come and work for Solomon Brothers?"

"But Manny, I'm not Jewish."

Taking Fraser's arm and propelling him to a couple of easy chairs, the dapper gent propositioned, "for you Roger, we make an exception."

"Ha, ha, ha," Fraser chortled. "You'd say anything to get your way, but you know I'm wedded to The Firm. I couldn't abandon them, above all, now they've given me this glamorous trouble-shooter role."

"*Trouble-shooter role*," he repeated in a demeaning tenor. "Roger, Solomon Brothers could give you a much more exciting and rewarding post."

"Now who's in sell mode?"

"Well, no harm in giving it a try," he cajoled, evincing a resigned but mannerly visage. "It's in the nature of my people to try for the unobtainable. We've been doing it for thousands of years."

"Yes, I know."

"Hey," he suddenly rasped in an upbeat voice, "what's the difference between a Jewish mother and a Rottweiler?"

Fortuitous meetings with Goldberg were not the same, unless he cracked at least one Jewish joke.

"Go on, enlighten me."

Simpering gratuitously, he educated, "eventually the Rottweiler lets go."

"Ohh, Manny, yet another good one. I'll have to tell it to Charlotte."

That's the thing about Jewish people, Fraser meditated, *they're confident enough about their standing in the nation to relentlessly rib their own culture, belief structures and foibles.*

Always admiring self-effacing and unassuming people, Emanuel Goldberg and other Jewish people Fraser had met inexorably fell into the category, whereas others with massive inferiority complexes and the claim for a singular allowance, forced laws to be made to prohibit even the mildest Mickey-take of them. A diffident trait much venerated in rugby circles, it also gained the likes of Goldberg ample esteem in the mainstream of English society and the financial services industry at large.

Consonant with most English people, Fraser believed respect had to be earned. It could not be demanded, and unconditionally not legislated for under duress. Having the inverse effect, those nagging for the special holy cow, untouchable treatment became even more slighted and universally despised.

Prying to where Fraser's companions were talking and sipping cocktails, Goldberg probed, "who's the *shiksa*?"

Facing the table, where Antoinette still absorbed Henshaw, and Susan, also God's recipient in the generous beauty stakes, talked to Hartley, he broached, "which one?"

"The one with fire in her eyes."

"Ahh...Antoinette Parker," he clarified, recognising the apt description. "I used to work with her at Merrill Lynch. She's with Charles Schwab now."

"*Aah*, one of the roundhead brothers," he certified. "They run a *shiksa* farm. I wonder if Charles will hire this one out?"

"Roundhead?" Fraser echoed.

"Foreskin-less," he point-blank elucidated.

"Oh, I see. Well, I'm afraid Antoinette is a bit on the uppity side,

Manny. She'd give you a lot of grief. If not for the ice on her tongue, she'd spit acid when she speaks, though I must admit, she now adopts a much more judicious approach than in her Merrill Lynch days."

"*Oy vey!*" Goldberg exclaimed. "Give me a plain obedient *shiksa* over a beauteous fireball every day. Beautiful but volcanic sirens, I can do without."

"My turn to ask you a question now," Fraser begged.

"Go ahead. If it's within my remit, and I am permitted, I will comment."

"Tell me," he inaugurated, his frontage a mass of inquisitiveness. "Is it true, that all Jewish-owned investment houses, such as Piranha, er Solomon Brothers, really do have *shiksa* farms?"

Recoiling as if Fraser had confessed to partaking of food on Passover, the playful Jewish gent murmured, "Roger, if you want to know, then take me up on the offer I made to you earlier." Pausing, he tapped Fraser on the arm. "Then you can find out for yourself."

"*Oy vey,*" Fraser yawped.

Chapter 12: Supermarket Blues

Like the advent of a daunting black cloud, the appointed hour for the weekly excursion to the supermarket descended on the Fraser household. Usually, Roger tried to avoid participation in the burdensome task by either feigning illness fired by a rare tropical disease, tabling his conscience had become plagued by some long, outstanding gardening commitment needing his engrossment, or more tenuously, inventing an urgent meeting he perchance had to attend, for instance, the Kappa Corinthians 1932 Committee.

An august, some might say regal body of men, the Kappa Corinthians 1932 Committee composed of seasoned, indomitable rugby players, generously giving their resource free-of-charge to pass judgment on and sentence those guilty of club rules transgressions. Fraser had been elected into their exalted ranks after displaying sufficient statesmanship in consideration of rugby standpoints to guarantee his elevated status unopposed. Celebrating the prestigious calling in the traditional way, he let off steam and got blind drunk with Steve Hunt, Gordon Anderson and other Corinthian stalwarts, the festivity originating yet another night spent in the doghouse when he got home, Charlotte applying her own judgement and punishment to her delinquent husband.

More controversially, when supermarket day beckoned Roger had been known to claim he had been summoned for an emergency meeting of the Hazelwood & District Gentlemen's Club, the dippy get-out excuse tricky to get through Charlotte because the association was a thinly disguised name for the good ol' boys drinking union, comprising Steve, Gordon, Roger and fellow long-time friend, Charlie Farley.

Seldom tried and invariably vetoed by Charlotte as a credible excuse, Roger had given up playing the card. One Easter Saturday, she sanctioned the alibi only to employ a double-bluff and caught the drinking club in action at a nearby watering hole The Cricketers, effectively curtailing the option as a valid excuse to be relieved from supermarket duty.

On this particular Saturday, Roger had no justifications, tangible or otherwise, to con Charlotte into approving he'd not be free for the arduous expedition.

Waitrose in South Bromley catered for the Fraser's groceries and fresh food requirements, chiefly because the top-of-the-pile retail outlet had an excellent wine and cheese selection. However, it happened to be the weekend they did the monthly shop at another well-known supermarket chain's Orpington branch, for the kind of bulk frozen consumables Waitrose did not stock. Objectionable in the extreme, often Roger recounted these torturous jaunts to family and friends, in-laws and outlaws alike, prefacing the tale of abject woe with, 'I won't divulge the name of the supermarket, but from what I'm about to share with you, I'm sure you can guess.'

Fussing around the house, he desperately tried to find something, anything, to empower him with a solid, unchallengeable reason as to why he'd be unavailable to go supermarket shopping.

Aware Wendy and James were in the study rapt in homework assignments, he slapped his hands together and glided in, deliberating, *here comes my get-out clause.*

"Wendy," he brightly initiated, "do you need any help with your maths homework?"

"No thanks, Dad," she allotted. "Anyway, I'm sure you've forgotten how to resolve Laplace transforms long ago."

"*Huh!*"

"See."

Protracting his optimism, Roger moved on to his son enquiring, "how about you, James?"

"Do you know anything about the succession of the Tudors?"

190

"Well," his father boasted with conviction, "I'm sure I can name all of Henry VIII's seven wives."

"Six," James corrected.

"What?"

"Henry VIII had six wives, Dad."

"Well, only one out is not bad."

Behind Roger, the study door opened, and in came Charlotte with Heather. For some incomprehensible rationale, over the past few months the youngest Fraser daughter had developed an affinity for going to the supermarket. On the other hand, echoing her 'want nowhere near the damned place' husband, Charlotte did not relish the prospect of tripping to Orpington. Always putting her in an antagonistic mood, anything happening during the cursed chore to annoy her, she took out on Roger. Not enamoured with the notion of spending what amounted to a good two hours expediting the end-to-end operation, as she crossed the study *tout de suite,* he fingered her reticence.

"Do come along, Roger," Charlotte chimed.

"I'm just—" Mindful he'd lay himself open to a tongue-lashing, he decided against completing the sentence.

"Just what?" his wife grilled. In Superman mode, she glared at him with her X-ray vision mince pies, daring him to make some weak, feeble excuse as to why he couldn't go supermarket shopping.

"Er, isn't it about time we went, darling?" Roger plumbed in his best genial voice.

"Yes," she crabbily endorsed. "Why do you think I said, *do* come along?"

"Yes, come on, Daddy," Heather encouraged. "We've got lots to do."

"Oh, have we," her father rejoindered, still perplexed by her supermarket enthusiasm.

"Enjoy yourself, Dad," Wendy purred, a touch of irony billowing in her speech.

"Oh, Dad, I nearly forgot," James prompted.

Here comes my get out clause, Roger deemed, late, but still very welcome.

"Yes, James," he acknowledged, developing an affable smile.

"While you're at the supermarket, can you get me *The Inbetweeners Movie* DVD? You can take the cost out of my pocket money."

"*The Inbetweeners Movie* DVD," Roger replicated, his mien changing into a grimace.

"Yes."

Folding his arms about his chest resembling a waiter taking an order from a snooty diner, he mordantly quizzed, "is there *anything* else you want? Perhaps the latest edition of FHM or Maxim magazine?"

"Well, if you're offering?"

Glaring, he snorted, "I was being sarcastic, James."

"Oh, do come along, Roger," Charlotte scolded again. "No more delaying tactics, please."

Thundering out of the study with Heather in tow, she left her husband open-mouthed.

"But I wasn't," he croaked, leaving Wendy and James sniggering, knowing how much their father hated supermarket shopping.

"*Roger*," Charlotte reproduced in a louder voice, as she released the front door catch and made her way towards the MPV.

"Yes, yes, I'm coming, I'm coming," he shouted.

"You're not even breathing hard," she uttered under her breath.

Incensed, Roger frothed at the mouth. "Oooohhh, mollusques!"

~ * ~

Sensing from Charlotte's erratic driving she still seethed at the cerebration of supermarket shopping, for Roger the short trip to Orpington became a juncture to mentally prepare for any eventuality. In the course of most former outings, somehow, he'd inadvertently managed to incur either a supermarket officials' or a shoppers' wrath, checkmating in the Frasers nearly getting thrown out by security guards and heightening his wife's mortification.

Her indignation surging into the red, Charlotte flung the MPV around corners, Roger reflecting one of the chief drivers for investing in a Mercedes Viano centred on the crux it could take a lot of stick without complaint. Regardless of her multiple abuses, the Merc never threw a wobbler and had never let them down. Of course, Roger categorically refrained from permitting her anywhere near the driving seat of his beloved beamer, the dread of her abusing his baby, just too excruciating a notion to allow. She surmised BMW stood for 'big man's willy', the M3 acting as his dick extension. Fortunately, penis envy had not penetrated the pantheon of her hang-ups, so under no contexts did she ever express the slightest desire to test out his pride and joy.

"Daddy," Heather commenced, "you will behave yourself today, won't you?"

"I'll do my very best, darling," he solemnly averred.

Shooting an abrasive gloom at him, Charlotte whined, "some hope," tutting and tossing her napper back in disbelief.

"What?" Roger refuted in all innocence.

"You probably theorised no long-standing significance, but on your prior jaunt to the supermarket, the manager took great exception when you disputed the integrity of the wine pricing policy."

"Well, *really*," he protested. "How gullible does he presuppose his customers are? I mean, half price *Gisborne Chardonnay* for £5.99." Mimicking Charlotte, he tutted and cocked his head back. "As if anyone with even half a brain cell accepted the recommended retail price is two pence short of £12."

"Whatever, Roger," his wife retaliated. "I found it most embarrassing."

"In financial services," he castigated, "we are indefatigably accused of conning the public, whereas they cue up like lambs to the slaughter when it comes to retail outlets fleecing them every day."

"If you're going to be disingenuous, we're going straight home."

Lead me on wifey, darling, Roger delighted, *I can't wait.*

In usage, Charlotte's idle threat passed, the MPV moving ever nearer the scene of her husband's last crime against the retail trade.

Still perplexed by his youngest daughter's observable appetite for the human zoo, her father pleaded, "tell me, Heather, why is it you enjoy going to the supermarket so much these days?"

"It gives me new ideas for being a game show host when I grow up," she squarely briefed him.

"How do you mean?" he investigated; puzzlement embossed into his lineaments.

"I've run out of plots for stuffed animal contestants."

"So, you're giving Papa Smurf, Miss Piggy, Kermit and the rest of the menagerie a rest from an Ann Robinson-like caustic tongue?"

"I'm not sure what caustic means, but if you mean, will I be stopping telling them off for getting answers wrong on *The Weakest Link*, then yes."

"Oh, why?"

"Because now I use real life rivals from school," she explained, "like Adelaide Perrett and Zoey Harvey."

"I see, but how does going to the supermarket help?"

"Daddy," she admonished, "isn't it obvious even to you?"

"What?"

"I make up games based on what I see."

"You mean, the people shopping?" he interpreted.

"*Yes*," she affirmed, as if he'd been slow to twig. "I have a game based on me telling Adelaide and Zoey about someone I have seen at the supermarket, and they have to mimic...is that the right word?"

"Yes."

"They have to mimic the person I describe. Then I award points for how they perform. Then Adelaide will describe somebody then Zoey, for someone else to mimic."

"I see, and where do Adelaide and Zoey get their people from to impersonate?"

"We started off copying our parents, brothers and sisters, and...school teachers. But when we ran out of people we know, I said we needed to get them from somewhere else."

"Hence the supermarket."

"Yes, Daddy. But we also copy our parents at the supermarket, such as when you had that argument with the manager about wine prices."

"You mean—" Discomposed, he developed an incongruous gleam. "You told Adelaide and Zoey about it, and they parodied me?"

"Of course," she snappily defended, her governess-matching intolerance of his incapability to comprehend the game generating more criticism. "Sometimes, you are really slow understanding what I say, Daddy."

Grinning, Charlotte joined in the, 'let's make Roger feel really uncomfortable' wind up. "They even made a painting of you being escorted out of the supermarket by security guards."

"But it didn't happen," he grouched. "They just cautioned me."

"Put it down to poetic license," Charlotte interjected. "When we next go to Heather's school for a parent-teacher meeting, you'll be able to see yourself in a painting hung up on the classroom wall."

"A-ha," Roger chided, imagining he'd still be safe from ridicule. "No one will know it's me."

"Oh yes, they will," Charlotte promised. "Zoey entitled it, 'Mister Fraser being arrested for arguing with the supermarket manager.'"

"*What!*"

"It's true," his wife reinforced, basking in her husband's discomfort and temporarily forgetting the onerous travail ahead of them. "All the kudos you've generated at Chelsfield Grammar School for Girls with your business studies evening classes is in danger of crashing down, when the same parents see, shall we call it—" She discontinued for effect. "Your dark side."

"*What!*"

"Stop saying what, Roger," Charlotte droned. "You've taken in what I mean."

Engaging Heather, he urged, "I trust you'll not be taking notes on any unforeseen circumstances I might involuntary find myself in today."

"I'm not sure what you said means, Daddy, but it's too late anyway. I began memorising things when you were trying to get out of shopping by wanting to help out Wendy and James with their homework."

Stupendous isn't it, Roger adjudged. *I'm a figure of fun at the junior school, and all those business study girls and their parents prizing me so reverentially will now condemn me as a monumental berk*!

Arriving at the supermarket car park, Charlotte had to fight for a parking space. With the MPV being longer than most cars there were only so many parking slots large enough to accommodate the vehicle. Parading around the car park with other MPVs and Chelsea tractors, she tried to find someone about to set off. As the merry-go-round continued, each driver ogled their space-competitors surreptitiously, some making threatening gestures and mouthing 'stay off the grass' parallel words. Arbitrating by her reactions, Charlotte intuitively understood the didactic phrases, but they tarried beyond her husband's inference decoder, Roger's cognition persevering set on the ghastly deadweight before them.

Suddenly, 'Stirling Moss' Charlotte saw a Ford Galaxy moving out. Smartly accelerating, she then pulled up ready to reverse into the spot as soon as the Galaxy cleared. Unfortunately, another parking space marauder in a Land Rover Discovery also saw the opportunity, driving straight into the vacant space, front first. Grimacing, Roger recalled how badly Charlotte reacted to the 2012 Olympic Games demonstrators in Greenwich Park a few months earlier, ending up with him being poleaxed by a right hook from his wife's female adversary, intended for her. Now she had the same shine of Vesuvius about to erupt expression.

"*Aaaggghhhhh,*" Charlotte screamed.

"Now, darling, no need to get upset, we can find another parking spot," Roger caveated.

Not even bothering to debate with him, she leapt from the MPV and strode over to the Discovery owner, another female, locking her vehicle. *Its decision time,* he perceived. *Do I intervene, play UN Secretary General peacekeeper and possibly get another right hook, or do I remain in the MPV and wait for the inevitable explosion from Charlotte?* Feeling his chin and remembering the bruise he had incurred on the previous occasion, he decided discretion endured as the better part of valour.

"Is Mummy going to bash that woman, Daddy?" Heather tested.

"Depends," he qualified, "if the woman can digest she is up against insurmountable odds."

"What do you mean?"

"I mean, if she is smart, she will let Mummy have the parking space."

"Are the police going to be called again, like at Greenwich Park?"

"No," her father bonded. "Mummy can handle this without breaking the law…just so long as the woman doesn't call her stupid."

Whatever Roger's darling wife chitchatted about to Missus Discovery, it worked. Clambering inside her vehicle, she withdrew within seconds, Charlotte retracing her steps to the MPV flaunting a very satisfied sparkle.

Curiosity got the better of Roger. "What did you say to her?"

"You're too sensitive to hear what I said," Charlotte dissuaded.

"Estimating by the speed she departed, it must have been impactful."

"I did say in no uncertain terms the space is mine."

"Well, you'd better get into it quickly."

"Why?" she disputed, still putting on her seatbelt.

Denoting backwards, Roger advised, "there's another car coming up fast, and it's heading for your parking spot."

Craning her noggin around, Charlotte gawked and her mouth unlocked. "*Aaaggghhhhh.*"

Covering up Heather's ears, Roger protected his daughter from the ensuing verbal bombast.

~ * ~

At long last the Fraser cadre made it into the supermarket, Charlotte exhibiting a determined, 'mess with me at your own peril' phizog, Roger scouting around for other possible sources of consumer conflict, Heather mentally noting his every stirring for her next emulation game.

If there's just one trolley in a stack of 5,000 having a wobbly wheel making it clank along annoyingly, Roger contemplated, *you can bet I will be the poor sucker it's handed to.*

And yes, such an embarrassing conveyance became allocated to him by a Coco the Clown ringer, supermarket trolley flunkey, bidding him, "have a good day, sir".

Pushing the insufferable noise generator along, whilst muttering incomprehensible words about wanting to seize the menial and shove him into a herd of crocodiles to play with, everyone stared at Roger thinking, what an idiot.

Well-versed in the loathed assignment, before she went off to the fresh bread counter, Charlotte detailed her husband for vegetable needs. Convinced the only way to open the tiny, vacuum-sealed plastic bags, shoppers were somehow expected to place sprouts or cauliflower inside involved a power drill, historically he had wrestled with the burden to the point of despair. Always presenting him with a portentous obstacle to overcome, as usual, no one else had the problem. Confounded, he goggled in awe as anyone between eight and eighty opened what he termed 'temper traps' with authoritative dexterity. Of course, when it came to his stroke, he grabbed at the bags hoping to extract just one, but predictably came away with at least twenty. After doggedly separating them, he tried to find the edge of one bag to place leeks into. Could he find it, could he fuck! During a bout of blooming frustration, he pulled at every possible separation flap rendering the bag torn and thereby useless. Grumbling, he threw the damn thing into the veg.

Monitoring her father's ineptitude, Heather took pity on him.

"Do you want me to open a bag for you, Daddy?" she volunteered.

Radiating gratefully, he articulated, "could you, darling?"

Adroitly extracting a single plastic bag from its container, in an instant she had it ajar and piled leeks inside.

Screwing up his mush in astonishment, Roger bewailed, "how did you do that?"

"It's easy, Daddy. You carefully grasp the bag you want from the container, rub the opening, then part the sides."

"Oh, I see…rub the opening, hey?"

"Yes, you have a go for the carrots."

Spliced with confidence, he managed to extract a single bag from its container, triumphantly blurting, "ah-ha!" Alan Partridge fashion. Undertaking to execute Heather's prescribed method, he attempted to break the bag entrance, but it didn't want to work for him. After several attempts to coax the bag into slitting via the magic of rubbing without success, he lost patience again, ending up pulling the wretched thing apart, much to the consternation of other root vegetable buyers.

Evaluating from their dismissive kissers they took him to be the local village idiot, he cringed with vexation.

"Oh, Daddy, you're hopeless."

She sounds more like her mother every day, he subliminally credited.

Further into the depths of the purchasers' jungle, Roger noted his slim-line Louis Cartier chronometer showed 10:30. Nearly an hour had passed since setting out from Hazelwood, and they had barely begun to expedite Charlotte's long list of items to be acquired. Gazing at the dust-proof, water-proof, shag-proof and shit-proof wristwatch again, guaranteed to withstand pressures of up to two Bar, just over two tons per square foot in real pressure units, he speculated if it would survive the pressure-cooker cauldron of the supermarket. More to the point, would he?

Damning it to be very kitsch on men, even chavish, Roger had never gone in for ostentatious jewellery, sentencing it to be effeminate to be mantled in bling from noodle to toe. Even worse, in his opinion, tattoos really hit the bottom of the degenerate pit. Apart from his twenty-four-carat gold wedding ring, the Louis Cartier had long been the only other item of jewellery to adorn his body.

Brooding James had come home one day accompanied by his mates Billy 'the Mountain' Swan and Neville Matthews, each with six pieces of flashy, glittering rubbish, picked up for the stately sum of £10 from some Dartford dive, he glowered at the remembrance. The halfwits had also invested in bump and grind pimp attire, making them resemble total dorks and thereby candidates for his abrasive derision. 'Wear that lot in downtown Brixton, and you'll be mistaken for brassy Alabama Slims' he warned them. Thankfully, it became an ephemeral passing fancy. Within hours, the James gang ditched the Johnny Go-lightly attire, reverting to more manly pursuits, meaning girl-gawping and imitating the more strident blockheads from *The Inbetweeners*.

Glimpsing at the timepiece again and knowing at least a further hour lay ahead to finalise the shop, Roger winced at the notion of battling through the FMCG war-zone.

Being a Saturday morning, the jam-packed supermarket resembled a drove of asinine zombies caught in a bloodsucker's paradise milling around without direction or purpose. More exasperating than Tower Bridge at rush hour on a Monday morning, not that the option had been his since Red Ken brought in his infernal congestion charging, Roger's spirit sunk. Battling to maximise shelf-space, all supermarkets minimised aisle access, apparently believing to optimise the trolley traffic, shoppers adopted an orderly procession based on the rules of the road. In practice, the Hans Christian Anderson analogous hope against hope hadn't an earthly of functioning, those unacquainted with the highway code, and even shoppers with their own wheels ditched road etiquette sensibilities once they crossed the supermarket threshold. Gauging by the way they parked their trolleys across aisles, stopped to jabber endlessly with people they bumped into, and ignored the right-hand drive, larboard side of the aisle convention, Roger counted them as astronomically bad motorists.

Returning to the vegetable area with her bread batch, the Fraser threesome then made their way along a frozen foods aisle, Roger shoving the trolley, Charlotte and Heather gathering the goods. All went spiffingly well until a very large woman pulled her trolley sideways to his front, blocking the aisle while she inspected the frozen meat offerings. In the distance, he saw a queue building up beyond her, and glancing behind, the build-up was just as bad. After an interminable spell, the large lady still, 'faffed around like a tit in a trance', as Steve Hunt regularly said.

"Excuse me," Roger petitioned, his call designed to solicit attention without seeming overly critical.

Dragging her enormous cranium out of the freezer cubicle, she stared at him as if being affronted by a totally new species to her experience; human and with good manners.

"Wot?" the woman cross-examined.

In a jiffy he witted the softly, softly approach did not register, and a more direct line of communication needed to be embraced to let fatso know, her quest for frozen meat had instigated a major shopper jam.

"If you'd care to move your trolley another six inches to the right," he sarcastically nominated, "you'll block the aisle entirely."

Fatso lingered wooden-faced.

"Wot?" she burbled again.

"I *said*," Roger replicated, "if you move your trolley another six inches to the right, you'll block the aisle entirely."

"*Roger*!" Charlotte reprimanded. "Stop it."

Blazing, the oversized woman stood to her full height, and *ooohh-ee* Roger heeded, *she's a mountainous one, much bigger than me, a real lard-arse as they say in New York, Giant Haystacks in build and just as ugly*, but he refrained from asking if she used to wrestle Big Daddy on Grandstand, with Kent Walton commentating. *Have I bitten off more than I can chew*, he pondered? Concluding maybe, he decided with the Fraser name at stake to brass her out *mono-e-mono* gladiatorial style. Issuing him a dismissive sulk, resembling Minotaur about to swat a fly with her gigantic hand, it mutated into a disparaging lour, her nostrils flaring. *Soon, she'll kick fictional dust on the floor, ala an enraged bull about to storm forward*, he imagined. Then all of a sudden, she became aware of the traffic jam developing around her. Gaping behind and to her front, she saw miffed shoppers in both queues wanting a swift resolution to their inconvenience.

Hissing, she scowled at her adversary and grunted, "al-*right*," in a rougher than rough voice, having ex-East-End Dockers running for cover, if any were in earshot. Swinging her overloaded trolley in line with the freezer cabinets, she growled at Roger before moving off, the traffic blockage at last released.

When the Frasers got to the end of the aisle, Charlotte beseeched, "Roger, you must learn to be more tolerant of other people."

"But, but, but," he objected, "I did everyone a favour." Peeved, his veneer clouding up with incredulity, he remonstrated, "anyway, you have no room to talk after you despatched that woman toiling to steal your parking space."

"That's different," she argued, paralysing him with one of her Medusa-doubling stares. She forged ahead with Heather, leaving her husband to struggle with the gaping trolley already piled to the top with goods. "Come on," she called, "or we'll never get out of here."

Facing a barrage of on-coming shoppers, Roger felt like Michael Caine in *Zulu,* confronted by 5,000 rampant Zulu warriors at Rorke's Drift with only a peashooter to defend him. Carefully negotiating his top-heavy conveyance through the throng, his Caine incarnation transmuted into Tippi Hedren in Hitchcock's *The Birds*, a multitude of human crows and gulls flapping their wings and fluttering in his puss, their veracious beaks intent on pecking out his spiers.

As the female Giant Haystacks faded into distant memory, his wit became overloaded with more graphic film images. Reminding Roger of the runaway ship in *Speed 2: Cruise Control* mowing down harbour vessels as it relentlessly moved towards the quayside, one peculiarly inarticulate shopper, a man nearly as herculean in build as her, came crashing down the aisle bumping into everyone going in the opposite direction, including him.

"*Trolley hog*," Roger trumpeted as he swept past, his remonstration drowned out in the maelstrom noise created by shoppers, *ad modem* to hungry locusts devouring the contents of shelves. Steadfastly surging through the melee like a frenzied JCB driver on ecstasy tablets, the culprit barely recorded his complaint.

Stopping to pick up Jacobs cheese biscuits, Roger accidentally knocked over a stack of cheese-stick boxes. As he busily picked them up, inwardly cursing with every box replaced on the shelf, yet another porker-sized woman nearly took his bonce off with her trolley as she rushed past, before stopping at the crisps shelf and picking up six ginormous-sized packets of Walkers.

Cracking with visions of wolfing down the entire purchase, she quipped to him, "you have to treat yourself once a day, don't you?"

Amazed, he muttered, "looks like you've taken a whole year's supply of treats in one day."

"What?" she delved.

"I said—" About to recapitulate what he'd whimpered in revenge for the woman coming perilously close to decapitating him, he thought better of it. Not wanting another showdown with the supermarket security guards, as had happened beforehand when he squared up to someone incurring his outrage, he forced a smile and croaked, "lovely day for shopping, isn't it?"

Going on for what seemed to be centuries in Roger's fragile mind, only fifty excruciating minutes of sheer unadulterated, grade-A, asylum circus hell had elapsed since the Frasers stepped inside the supermarket. With items meticulously ticked off on Charlotte's exhaustive bucket list, his wife and daughter piled more and more goods into the trolley, Roger scarcely able to see over the ever-growing mountain filling the noise-making conveyance, let alone push it. As the soul-destroying campaign continued, his enforced harnessing to the yoke of drudgery loomed endless without respite for good behaviour. Deliberating if he'd ever see daylight again, he had visions of being permanently entrapped in the pandemonium's vortex, never returning to The Firm or playing for his prized Kappa Corinthians again.

After Charlotte and Heather went in search of ladies' toiletries, burdening him to pick up scores of canned foods, fortuitously Roger saw a friendly face in the distance. Coalescing into the recognisable features of Allan Mallory, another innocent victim of death by supermarket, accompanied by his lovely wife Francine, Roger twinned a drowning man seeing a life raft on the horizon. Grabbing the weighed down, difficult-to-control trolley with renewed grit, he drove on banging into other trolleys comparable to a pin-ball bouncing off the machine's buffers. After several stop-go interludes with more kamikaze shoppers in his path, he got within hailing distance of his friends.

"*Alan…Francine*," he cried out.

"You look like a man needing a stiff drink," Francine observed as he neared the finishing line.

"Hello Francine, hello Alan," Roger sighed. "Which way is sanity and civilisation?"

"Unendingly bad, is it?" Alan debated.

"I've been in some nasty London traffic jams," the irate shopper recollected, "and seen some horrific crashes in the traders' bullpen, but this…this is sheer bedlam populated by the Devil's offspring."

Chortling, Francine posed, "not enjoying your shopping expedition then?"

"I've run out of life-support rations to help me make it to the check-out," he lamented, "and I'm not far off surrendering, lying down and just letting my toes turn up."

"You're *not* by yourself, are you?" Alan queried, anxious for his friend's safety.

"No," he endorsed, panting. "Charlotte and Heather are somewhere out there in the chemist's dispensary." Betokening the waves of greedy, gung-ho, rapacious, voracious, avaricious, credit card toting, frothing desperados in front of them, he notified, "they're getting some small toiletry items."

Bartering more comments on the reptilian-inhabited zoo, the friends mutually consented Saturday supermarket shopping corresponded to the human condition at its worst. When Charlotte and Heather joined them, the group inaugurated a general discussion about the vagaries of supermarket shopping, and they should really use the delivery service a lot more, rather than losing their rationality doing battle with the philistine masses. After the salutary conclusion, Alan and Francine made their farewells, and the Fraser party headed to the no-man's territory known as check-out central, the penultimate leg of the exigent marathon.

~ * ~

Ahead, they saw huge queues at the normally 'womaned', to use a Roger non-word, albeit sometimes manned, check-outs. Implicitly, Saturday mornings represented the apex period for consumer buying, yet of the 3,000 check-outs vanishing in the distance to infinity, only a handful were operational. Long considering those in charge reckoned their clientele were brainless, because scores of lackeys constantly on the move in advance of the check-outs, directed customers to the check-out queue of their choosing, Roger shook his noggin in disbelief.

"They really do specialise in *peeing-off* the client, don't they?" he spat. "What's the point in all these check-outs, if they remain abandoned even when the supermarket is bursting at the seams with shoppers?"

"Yes, alright, I'll give you that one," Charlotte conceded. "It is a waste of capital investment when the queues clog up the shopping areas."

"Quite. Any of the business studies students in Wendy's A-level class will tell you, minimising running costs by only having a few check-outs 'womaned', is a false economy, because disgruntled purchasers will go elsewhere."

Drawing up beside Charlotte, one of the totally useless floorwalker functionaries squeaked, "number six will be coming free shortly."

Before Charlotte could reply, quicker to the draw for once, her husband bawled, "*really*! You wouldn't think God had given us optics to see with and brains to make a finding, would you?"

"*Roger*!" Charlotte blurted before smiling serenely at the put-out minion.

Without retort, she evaporated to find more mentally handicapped punters, supposedly incapacitated to make the most elementary decisions.

"Well," he rasped. "For goodness sake. What *do* they presume we all are, morons?"

"She's only doing her job," Charlotte defended.

"She'd be better off manning, or 'womaning' to use my non-word, those thousands of vacant check-outs, along with the other airy-fairy, fingers-up-their-rectums meditating floorwalkers, rather than giving inane advice as to the shortest queue to stand in. We're all gifted to work out that conundrum, Charlotte."

"What's a rectum, Daddy?" Heather canvassed.

"Well, there are plenty of examples of the walking, talking variety swanning around this check-out area," informed her infuriated father.

"*Roger*," Charlotte admonished, jabbing him in the ribs with a French stick.

"Well," he groaned, shrugging his shoulders.

Not shortly, as the floorwalker promised, but twenty-five minutes later the Frasers breached the check-out threshold. To their front, a punter answered a thousand and one security questions, incorporating verification of his inside leg measurement and reciting the third verse of *God Save the Queen*, not the Sex Pistols rendition, but Thomas Arne's traditional version, before being allowed to complete his credit card transaction. Witnessing the turgid proceeding, Roger derived London Stock Exchange multi-million-pound trades done every moment of the working day were child's play compared to paying £51.76 for supermarket groceries.

Finally, the Frasers made the payment zone. Under starter's orders, ready to unload the mega contents of their trolley and erect a FMCG mountain on the check-out inbound conveyor belt, they awaited the check-out girl's okay to begin the gargantuan logistics onslaught.

Given the go signal, they began, Charlotte and Heather methodically arranging the goods to maximise use of the space available, Roger throwing them anywhere and everywhere. Obscured from their view by the craggy, irregular peak they created, the check-out girl became blanked out. Moving onwards to finalise the mammoth enterprise, they got their germinal sighting of her.

First hand, she paralleled a cross between one of Long John Silver's motley crew and a refugee from a punk-Goth waxworks museum, her blinkers nearly blotted out with eyeliner, her bedraggled hair serving as a hive for a wacky assortment of ribbons and hair grips, and her sallow skin irrevocably marked with tattoos, proclaiming her admiration for Johnny Depp and Millwall FC. Tempted to ask if she had played an extra in *Pirates of the Caribbean*, instead Roger dropped into the sympathetic, deeming, *Jesus, some poor sod has to go home to that every night.*

"Hello," she welcomed in a dead-pan voice between chewing gum. "Need any help with your packing?" she augmented, as if they seriously conjectured she was capable of multi-tasking.

"No, it's quite alright," Charlotte replied. "We'll take care of it."

Much to his wife's amusement, when Roger pitched in to help put their purchases into flimsy, under-sized shopping bags, he had the same bother as in the vegetable area, slitting the damn things open. By the time he conclusively got one to behave, his wife and daughter had seemingly unsealed millions and piled in their goods, the wonky-wheeled trolley once again full to the brink of capsizing, leaving Roger to pay the slovenly, juvenile check-out girl, still relentlessly chewing on her gum.

Whilst theorizing if she used the same supplier as Sir Alec Ferguson, also having a piece permanently stowed in his north and south, he perused the girl, determining she resembled a typical, gormless, failed antagonist from *Big Brother*, a yawn-drawing reality show drooled over by delinquent chavs, and those ranking *Shameless* to be exalted culture.

"The total is £172.39," she announced between chews.

"Right," Roger accepted.

"Do you have a loyalty card?"

He rubbernecked Charlotte. "Do we have a loyalty card?"

Opening her mid-sized handbag, she fiddled around in its inner compartments pulling out a knuckle-duster, the deterrent used as a final resort when motorists refused to agree a given parking spot belonged to her, scrunched up bills, hand-written notes and other assorted paper items before discarding them, Roger thinking, *good job she doesn't use a large handbag, or she'd be discarding uncut volumes of receipts and notes.* Then after rifling through at least a score of different credit cards and store cards, she produced the requested loyalty card, Roger handing it over to Miss Congeniality.

"Do you have any offers you want to use?" the girl mechanically drawled.

Reasoning, *getting repetitive isn't it*, he trained his pout on Charlotte again mimicking the girl's android cloned voice. "Do-we-have-any-offers-we-want-to-use?"

Out came the handbag again, his wife diving into a different compartment and producing a wad of offer slips. Briskly flicking through them, Maverick shuffling playing cards fashion, she gave her husband five offer slips all bearing the supermarket's moniker which he handed over to the check-out girl.

Executing a calculation with her point-of-sale till, she then specified, "the revised cost will be £170.29."

Peering at Charlotte, Roger blustered, "all that, just to save £2.10 on a £172.39 purchase. *God preserve us!*"

"Roger!" his wife reproved; her familiar annihilating bore blossoming.

"How'd you like to pay?" the girl polled.

How about in used bottle tops and refunded Tizer bottles? Roger contemplated suggesting.

"American Express," he crisply denoted.

"I'll need to take some personal details for using American Express. What is your full name?"

Pressing his lips together, Roger complained, "we don't have this problem at Waitrose."

"Roger," admonished Charlotte yet again, even more forcefully.

Frowning, the girl tutted then instructed, "I need your full name."

"Tell her, Roger." mandated his ever-so-tolerant wife, though he knew she faked the cooperation stance.

"Roger Archibald Cedric Hubert Fraser, the third."

"*No, it's not*," Charlotte chastised. "Tell her your real name."

"Roger Jon Fraser."

"Your billing address?" the girl catechized.

He told her.

"Your date of birth?"

He told her, then attached, "Thirty-six inches and blood red," before whispering under his breath, "preferably check-out girl blood red."

"What?" she quizzed.

"They're my inside leg measurement and colour of choice."

Developing a, 'well I didn't visualise it's the length of your dick' sneer, the girl tutted.

"Roger," Charlotte exclaimed for the nth time.

"*Well,*" he exploded, his frustration boiling over. "Next, she'll want to know what I had for breakfast this morning, and what club I think is going to win the FA Cup."

Curling her upper lip at him as if to say, cheeky bastard, Miss Congeniality then hit a few buttons on her till, and hey presto, after over two and a half hours of sheer, unmitigated hell, the Frasers had a perfected transaction.

Walking to the MPV, Heather applauded, "thank you, Daddy."

"Thank you. Thank you for what?"

"You've given me lots of choices for my person identity game."

"I'm so glad there is an upside to this venture," he jeered as he struggled to push the trolly.

"Do come along, Roger," Charlotte harried.

Now for the journey home, he pondered. *I bet someone has blocked in the MPV and Charlotte has to get the supermarket to broadcast the culprit's number plate over the tannoy system. Whoever it is will be slow off the mark and there could be another Greenwich Park cognate calamity.*

Staring to the skies, hoping the great deity granted him relief, he uttered, "I'd rather go *mano a mano* with Dwight Armstrong again than suffer the slings and arrows of another supermarket misfortune."

Chapter 13: Czech Mate

During a typical day at The Firm, Fraser became bombarded with petitions for heavy-duty, revenue generating leads from brokers desperate to make their quotas, directives from Toby Chalcroft *vis-à-vis* equities and futures ingenuities, and the usual cut and thrust of market analysis engendering debate with his fellow analysts, apropos The Firm's best investment options.

Topping the free-for-all, he also took a meeting with Dewey Osborne, Investment Director for Chadwick Meechan, a holding company for a bunch of potent, risk-averse private investors. Fearing another imminent Lehman Brothers type cataclysm, they kept on calling him about their mutual fund investments. Assuring Osborne that Chadwick Meechan's investments with The Firm were sound, and no evidence or data hinted at a Lehman's scale meltdown swooping on the world of investment banking, Fraser convinced him his investors fretted unnecessarily. Admitting he too could see no wrecking balls on the horizon, Osborne confessed his company had been overtaken by imagined dark forces. Empathising, Fraser said investors often became inhibited by over-active thoughts of negativity and disaster. Tongue-in-cheek, he prescribed several sessions on the psychoanalysts' couch for those exhibiting the worst paranoia. Self-consciously, Osborne whined profuse words of apology for wasting the stock analyst's time, making Fraser feel akin to a benevolent social worker administering to the hyperactive needs of the hypersensitive, hyper-rich, rather than a hard-nosed businessman.

With the fray reducing at London Stock Exchange trading

termination, Henry Jacques came into Fraser's den to talk about a prospect The Firm might take a peek at in the Czech Republic. Attired in an even more eccentric outfit than usual, he immediately transfixed Fraser's gaze. Forever on the verge of being mistaken for an Oxbridge don, his sophisticated style had been added to with a bowtie approximating the size of a large butterfly with a paisley dayglow pattern, and the monocle Fraser conjured up would suit Jacques at the Bembridge Cheyne Walk shindig in the summer, had become actuality, the combination amplifying the perception he had stepped straight out of the cast of *Call My Bluff* as a Frank Muir tribute act.

Handing him the business card of a contact Dennis Passmore had happened upon whilst attending a trade delegation symposium at the Czech Republic Embassy, Fraser scanned the card details. Mentally reading, B.A T'sor - First Secretary, Commercial and Investment Division, he flunked figuring out how to phonate the contact's name.

"Henry, how is this guy's surname pronounced?"

"According to Dennis, T'sor is pronounced, 'Tosser.'"

Smiling, he rebutted, "Dennis is having you on."

"No, I double-checked," the erudite head of market analysis affixed. "It is definitely pronounced, 'Tosser.'"

Studying the card again, Fraser vocalised, "B.A T'sor," then repeated it with an alternative but significant subsidiary meaning. "Be a tosser!" Smirking, he proclaimed, "surely the name's owner has seen the double entendre in the making?"

"Yes, I wondered if the Czechs understand the significance of both the name and the phrase in English."

"My notion exactly. It's nearly as bad as Otto Wanka pronounced with a V, from our Frankfurt office. Those undiplomatic Essex boy traders call him Otto Wanker!"

"Quite. Anyway, explicitly," he authenticated, "in the Czech language, letters normally occurring in English words are not always used. Some words or even names are more like clues, having to be decoded from the evident shortened written form into the fitting verbalisation."

"So," Fraser inducted, summoning up all kinds of exceptionally contentious possibilities in his mind, "how did Dennis address this Mister 'Tosser'?"

"From what I can gather, he didn't. Once the gentleman had guided how to pronounce his surname using the Czech convention, my impression is Dennis skilfully skirted around using his surname."

"Typical Dennis," Fraser extolled. "Next to you, he is The Firm's best diplomat when it comes to foreigners' disingenuous names, and, their often-strange habits."

"For sure," Jacques accorded. "Such a skill…I'm not sure if it's a talent, but more of a quick reactive response, based on finely honed interpersonal skills, is what makes Dennis an immense loss to the Civil Service in general, and the Foreign Office in particular."

Ancillary to investment banking, Dennis Passmore had a penchant for cricket. A carved-in-stone member of MCC and a fervent proponent of cavalier cricket commentators, his supreme god endured as the late Brian Johnson, famous for some classic double entendres himself, Passmore's pick being, 'The bowler's Holding, the batsman's Willey', a positional reference to West Indian bowler Michael Holding and England batsman Peter Willy. When not immersed in professional or domestic activities with his wife Georgina, invariably he could be found at Lords Cricket Ground, his fellowship of harmonious willow-on-leather aficionados comprising many of The Firm's client appointees, and others from the world of financial services. Accordingly, able to pull the old boys routine when The Firm needed to know the inside track about goings-on in their client base, not necessarily surfacing during nine to five-thirty business hours, Passmore had become a kind of latter day intelligence facilitator.

Also acting as chief entertainments officer to those The Firm wished to cultivate having a cricket interest, he set up members' enclosure tickets for private investors and blue-chip corporate consuls, escorting them around the beloved halls of Lords, the glorious baptism supplementing The Firm's kudos and differentiating it from other investment houses.

Erstwhile, Fraser had introduced his cousin Barry to Passmore. Impressed by Barry's cricketing credentials, he arranged members' enclosure tickets for Barry and Roger to see Middlesex take on Yorkshire. Sending Barry into raptures of elation, he reprised the once-in-a-lifespan happening to fellow Yorkshire League players to the brink of tedium. A typical reaction, it echoed the impact a visit to the Lords inner sanctum had on even a mature cricketer such as Fraser's cousin.

"I've always gauged Dennis to be a natural for the UN," Fraser complimented. "People get attracted to him by the sheer force of his makeup, and more importantly he's such a terrific communicator. Bembridge ought to have elected Dennis for the trouble-shooter job…not me."

"Hhmm," Jacques murmured. "Notwithstanding Dennis having many admirable peculiarities, he hasn't got your impetus to succeed under complex climates or innovative skills to meditate outside the box."

"Ooohh," Fraser gushed. "Thank you, boss. I'll take any praise going, especially when it's from you."

"Right, well, before we suck each other's dicks anymore." Nonplussed, he stopped abruptly. "*Golly*, I'm not sure where I picked up that phrase."

"Probably from the bullpen. I'm always subconsciously regurgitating guttural and sub-cultural phrases, percolating into my psyche from overexposure to the Essex boys."

"Yes, might explain it, but, er—" He lowered his head. "Without thirsting to come across as superior or snobby, it's hardly in-keeping with the aura I usually project."

"Quite."

"Roger, if you hear me lapsing into Essex boy lingo in the future," he requisitioned, "please cough, or cut me off, anything to avoid others witnessing my drop into banality."

"My pleasure, Henry, my pleasure."

"Anyway, Czech Republic energy conglomerate CEZ Group is seeking foreign investment. They need someone from The Firm to meet with Mister T'sor, to give him his precise name, to discuss the possibilities."

Gleaming, Roger opined, "and I'm to be the chosen analyst, am I?"

"Yes. You can use your know-how in the energy investor sector to evaluate the CEZ Group requirement."

"I see. Now…my other transient excursions into the ex-Eastern Soviet bloc intimate that, on launch meetings, their representatives count on some formality."

"Indubitably, if it involves government people."

"Well, due to the distinct possibility to offend," Fraser reviewed, "on this occasion, I will be addressing Mister B.A. 'Tosser' by his Christian name from the off."

"Very wise," Jacques concurred.

~ * ~

To avoid any embarrassment pertaining to the Czech's unfortunate surname pronunciation, Fraser called in a favour from an acquaintance at the Foreign Office, establishing the diplomat's full name to be Bedrich Ambroz T'sor. Resident at the Czech Embassy, 26 Kensington Palace Gardens, Fraser telephoned arranging to meet him for lunch at Wheelers in Saint James's Street, not far from the embassy, T'sor making the reservation. During the phone conversation, in preparation for the lunch meeting, Fraser qualified the CEZ Group business opportunity and positioned The Firm's expertise in the energy vertical.

For the day of the meeting, he pre-ordered a taxi to take him from Canary Wharf to Saint James's Street. However, his travel plan became compromised. Keeping a roving eye on the capital's traffic flows on her desk top computer, April Harrington, the analysts department PA, designated a demonstration occurring around the Trafalgar Square and Whitehall area impacting his travel intentions. With some roads cordoned off by the police, and traffic jams building up around all the peripheral roads converging on central Westminster, she recommended him to take the Tube.

"Oh no," Fraser bleated, "I was hoping not to use the troglodyte transport system for once."

"*The what*?" April trilled.

"London Underground."

"Oh, Roger, you do have a capacity for graphic description. The troglodyte transport system…really!"

"If you'd had as many maulings on the Tube as I have, my girl, you'd not relish the thought of using it."

Grinning, April advised he could jump on the Jubilee Line at Canary Wharf taking him directly to Green Park, and from there he could waltz into Wheelers. What on Earth could go wrong?

Past bitter experience of using London Underground for business had taught Fraser that being flabbergasted by the unexpected was a regular juncture. Formally, en route to the Landmark Hotel on Marylebone Road for a very influential meeting, due to seized braking apparatus, the train Jacques and he were on came to a juddering halt midway between stations. On another uniformly dispiriting journey, Ricky Henshaw and Fraser were travelling to The Firm on the eastbound District Line after a South Kensington based private investor meeting, when the service became stopped at Blackfriars due to 'unforeseen signalling dilemmas' as the Tannoy emcee described them. Unable to get a taxi, they walked over Southwark Bridge to the south side of the river, catching the Jubilee Line at London Bridge to finalise the journey.

Nevertheless, the most bizarre episode transpired changing trains from the Bakerloo to the District Line at Embankment, after a meeting with Maida Vale based venture capitalists Knappett & Timmins. Minding his own business, Fraser awaited the eastbound District Line train on a crowded platform when a couple of Rastafarians, he supposed Rastafarians from their Ethiopian flag coloured shawls and colossal, head-warming tea cosies, parked themselves next to him. Soon it became clear from their heated wrangle, mainly embodying a stream of unfathomable sentences delivered at breakneck speed and consistently ending with, 'motherfucker', that the pair didn't see toe to toe.

Eventually, one of them spouted a vaguely insulting dirge, inevitably terminating in 'motherfucker', bringing the squabble to a close, then walked off.

Goggling at Fraser, the other one moaned, 'Motherfucker says this. Motherfucker says that. Motherfucker says everything. Motherfucker,' the bewildered stock analyst left short on a cogent rejoinder, and only able to utter, 'Well, I guess that's motherfuckers for you,' in response.

Beyond the unforeseen and congeneric with making fitful road journeys on the M25, everyday Tube hold-ups and cancellations plus station closures decimated journey plans, thereby slowing business.

Asking a Department of Transport statistician about the glitch, when they met at one of Charlotte's friends' parties for the arts and crafts crowd, he cited to Roger it came down to out-of-control magnitudes of road users, typically foreign juggernauts on the M25. The Ministry man went on to explain, as London's population ballooned unbridled, similarly the Tube became swamped to breaking point in the early part of the millennium, impacting rolling stock and track scheduled maintenance, thereby inciting facility disruptions.

"Just as a society has an upper population limit, in terms of a peak permissible numeric beyond which bedlam sets in and meltdown results, any transport framework has its zenith limits," he told Fraser. "The sheer volume of road traffic on the M25 and a saturated London Underground means the probability of accidents and failures causing widespread disruption have reached epidemic proportions."

"You mean, we're bordering on chaos?"

"*Holy smoke*," the statistician bellowed, "the critical boundary passed in 2000, but it had been on the cards for a long time."

"How long?"

"Since the late nineteen-seventies, when the double-digit trend in overpopulation really started to show itself."

"But I don't see these transport complications in other European capitals or in USA cities," Fraser noted.

"Quite right," the statistician sanctioned, "but they're not suffering England's chronic overpopulation. It all comes down to population density. England has been the most densely packed country in the world for at least a decade, and it's snowballing."

"So, are you saying a limit needed to be set for maximum population size, especially in the dense urban areas?"

"Yes."

"What's the number?"

Recoiling the statistician divulged, "can't say. It's political dynamite."

"But you do know?" Fraser persisted.

"Of course. Just let's say, we breached the ceiling in the middle nineteen-eighties, and at the prevailing population growth rate, it will be twice the figure by 2015."

"You mean, the politicians are defending the indefensible for ulterior political pretexts?"

Simpering, the statistician enunciated, "it's what modern politics is all about, from staying in the EU, to allowing unrestrained inward immigration. It's all smoke and mirrors, pulling the wool, pretending everything is alright and keeping the truth out of the public gaze. It's also unjustifiable and totally unsupported by society in general."

Assimilating Charlotte's arts and crafts cabal he uttered, "hhmm, I'd keep the bombshell to yourself in this company."

"But why?"

"Because they've all been hit with a solid dose of political correctness. If you open the overpopulation can of worms, you could find yourself dobbed-in to the PC thought police, the effect limiting your career prospects at the ministry."

"Ahh, I see."

"I know this must be an imposition going against all the tenets of free-speech and even acting responsibly, but to me such mentality equates with the general state of play in some sections of modern society."

"Right, enough said," he acknowledged, pulling an imaginary zip across his mouth.

Finishing the repartee, Fraser whooped, "I'll put you in touch with my mother in-law. You've just articulated in fact, what she has been assuming in theory for years."

~ * ~

Remaining distrustful of London Underground, with an hour to spare, Fraser exited The Firm for Canary Wharf Tube station cerebrating what little tragedies awaited during his journey to Green Park.

Everything went according to plan until Waterloo, where the Jubilee Line service terminated due to a safety pickle at Westminster. Probably demonstrators pulling faces at London Underground staff, Fraser decided. Ludicrously applying the Terrorism Act 2006, it took as little as that for them to call a security alert, the same law misused by local councils to pursue and persecute hacked-off council tax payers, residing dissatisfied by their council's piss-poor track record and refusing to fund their fact-finding trips to the Bahamas by stopping their council tax payments. With no end to reducing freedoms and true democracy by the shameful, power-crazed vultures fearing rebellion from within, such *Nineteen Eighty-Four* shaped abuses of authority appalled Fraser.

Still optimistic of completing his journey in one piece, Fraser jumped on a northbound Bakerloo Line train, alighting at Embankment to await either the westbound Circle Line, or God willing not, the District Line train.

Based on misfortunes to date, Fraser compared riding the District Line, particularly from west to east, though it could be as equally testing going in the opposite direction, to climbing out of *Doctor Who's* Tardis and surmising you've put down in either the middle of a combat zone on Planet Zog, or have joined the queue for the freaks, androids and dropouts asylum. Worse, he allegorised some of the creatures skulking in the train carriages to be zoo exhibit refugees, difficult to certify if they were human, or some form of intergalactic space breed, cascading through the stratospheres driven on by the, 'All weirdo's welcome beacon' synonymous with the District Line, and had somehow ended up travelling from Upminster to Ealing Broadway and reversing, continuously.

Categorical some of the troglodyte doubles had made the District Line their permanent home, he never ceased to be amazed at the incomprehensible curiosities to be seen lurking in corners or hunched up under anoraks. A magnet for druggies, pimps, arse-bandits, dropouts, greens, political activists, protesters, anarchists, hooligans, hoodies, crims, failed asylum seekers, busted politicians, and the so-called educationally, socially and economically disadvantaged, whatever the hell that meant in sociology babble, it became John Cooper Clark's *Beasley Street* brought to life in a series of worm-like, dynamic conveyances, scurrying beneath the surface, station to station, from five o'clock in the morning to gone midnight. Travis Bickle's skunk pussies from *Taxi Driver* would have a ball down in the Tube's depths, indisputably Bickle feeling the urge to 'wash the scum off the streets.' Holy kamoley, Fraser had often debated, Duke Ellington's ultra-classy *Take the A-Train* never invoked such harrowing visions.

Howbeit the wonderments could be jarring, the most knock-out aspect of the District Line manifested itself as carriage smells. Every night after the network shut down, a huge team of cleaners dressed in the same NCB uniforms worn at Porton Down, attempted to disinfect the District Line carriages. Whatever solvents they put down became absorbed and destroyed by the gut-wrenching toxic waste ingrained deep into the very fabric of the carriages, not just the seats, but the woodwork, the plastic, and even the metal.

Fraser had observed what could only be described as normal Tube clientele holding cyclist air filter masks to their mouths and nostrils in an effort not to pass out through fume inhalation. More hazardous than waking up and finding speech impediment queen Jannette Spliff Snorter next to him, his most daunting nightmare became being stranded on the District Line. Before expiring of dog-breath inhalation, he'd scribble a final letter to Charlotte, telling his wife he loved her and to care for the children, before the grim reaper came for him.

One time, like a holy man dispensing the word, he'd seen a ferret-resembling creature with a scrappy, nerve jangling voice, moving among the underground viperous underclass brethren. Turning out to be Ken Livingstone vote snaring, he'd also witnessed Diane Abbot and 'Doris' Johnson performing the same self-humiliating and degrading act, their schnozzles and tongues stuffed so far up rectums intent on safeguarding votes, it necessitated their sycophant helpers to recurrently wipe their dials with toilet paper.

Petrified by the recollections, he gurgled prayers to God, promising all kinds of undeliverable good deeds and penances, in exchange for a Circle Line train being posted coming into the station. Unfortunately, God rested on his lunch break, or listened to some other poor sod. Glinting at the annunciator sign, he clocked it displayed, 'Wimbledon two minutes', meaning an imminent District Line train arrival. Surveying his timepiece, he calculated if he didn't take the District Line train and change to the Victoria Line at Victoria to head north to Green Park, he'd be late for his luncheon with Mister Tosser.

Whilst mulling over the quandary, the District Line train came to a stop.

"What the hell," he mouthed. Taking as capacious a breath as his lungs could hold, he stepped onto the train, the doors slamming shut, but no train movement occurring. Figuring some alien had let its tail stray between the sliding doors inhibiting the electric drive, the macabre belief made him reflect Lizard King Luther Bembridge would be top of the pile down here, his scaly tail majestically sweeping other aliens aside, The Firm's VP Investment Banking ruling the zoo roost, unopposed. The doors skated open again, then shut. Whoever's tail had been trapped, must have whisked it inside. As the train pulled off, Fraser stood in the corner of a carriage next to the sliding doors exit, ready for a quick getaway at Victoria. Conspicuous with his smart, clean shaven presentation and pristine Armani suit, amongst the legions of unshaven mugs, and that just depicted females, with their moth-eaten trainers, fatigues, grubby boots, split jeans and chinos, to quote his Jewish friend Manny Goldberg, he felt like a bacon butty at a *bar mitzvah*.

Grunting and snickering, the alien hordes ravenously licked their lips at the sight of him as if preparing for an early lunch. If it hadn't been for a London Underground official going through the carriages examining for free-riders, Fraser abided sure they'd have torn him limb from limb and eaten him like in one of those day-of-the-living-dead type zombie films James treasured so much. In the end, he could hold his breath no longer. He breathed out, intrinsically breathing in, the motion climaxing in nausea overtaking him. Tougher still, the baking carriage had fried-up effluence odours, drifting around as an invisible lethal cloud in the not far from vacuum-sealed atmosphere. Buckling under the intoxication, he anticipated liquifying into a runny mess and being hosed out of the carriage at termination of the facility.

Then miraculously, Westminster station came into view, the train grinding to a halt, the doors slithering open, Fraser gulping a breath of relatively fresh air. Glimpsing about for marauding demonstrators attacking Tube staff, the platform endured calm apart from the rush of commuters. Either they had moved on, or London Underground had overreacted to an illusory threat never happening!

Predictably, the unnerving process became replicated at St. James, before the plucky stock analyst alighted at Victoria, made for the Victoria Line and within a jiffy, headed up the escalator at Green Park into daylight and the fresher air of Piccadilly. Making it and still in one piece, he felt like Mel Gibson in the *Mad Max* series, after the light-on-words Aussie avoided being eaten alive by the semi-human remnants from a make-believe worldwide nuclear holocaust.

Composing himself, Fraser briskly walked off to Wheelers.

~ * ~

Feeling a whole lot better post his Tube stress test, The Firm's stock analyst checked in with the restaurant's maître' d.

"Good afternoon, I'm Roger Fraser, Mister T'sor's dining companion."

"Good afternoon, sir." Picking off names on his reservation list, the maître' d confided, "I can't find a Mister T'sor, sir."

"Ah, he's First Secretary, Commercial and Investment Division at the Czech Embassy. Maybe the reservation has been made in the embassy's name."

Inspecting again, he shook his napper then glanced up at Fraser. "I'm sorry, sir, we don't have a reservation either in the name of T'sor or the Czech Embassy."

Ruminating fast on his feet, Fraser discretely whispered to the maître' d, "try Mister Tosser, Mister B. A. Tosser."

"Ah, yes," he recalled. "The name does ring a bell from when the gentleman made the reservation." Bending forward so as not to be overheard he validated, "we do have a reservation for a Mister Tosser."

"T'sor," Fraser amended.

"Quite. If you'd care to follow me, sir."

Escorting Fraser through the restaurant, the maître' d indicated to where his luncheon partner awaited.

"Mister Tosser, er Mister T'sor?" Fraser instantly rectified.

"Yes, I am T'sor," the reply came from the seated gent.

"Hello, Mister T'sor. I'm Roger Fraser with The Firm."

Radiating at Fraser, T'sor rose to shake hands.

Appearing to be the archetypal Eastern European of folklore, not quite Vlad the Impaler, but conclusively possessing the earmarks of Christopher Lee at his dastardly Dracula best, tall and on the slim side, with sunken cheeks and brushed-back black hair, Fraser estimated his counterpart to be in his late thirties.

"Please, Mister Fraser, take a seat," T'sor invited.

"Thank you," he warmly voiced. "On account of our introductory telecom, can we dispense with formality?"

"Of course…please call me Bedrich."

Thank God for small mercies Fraser blessed.

Present-day Wheelers of St. James had evolved through a collaboration between Marco Pierre White and Sir Rocco Forte reviving the world's oldest and finest fish restaurant in the heart of London's most distinguished location. On the site of Madame Prunier's fish restaurant, one of the capital's most fashionable eateries in part one of the twentieth century, by the nineteen-nineties it had fallen into a shabby fettle. After a stunning makeover, the restaurant's glamorous dining room, private room and bars, supplemented by a refurbished traditional exterior made it a popular fine-dining destination for business people, tourists and locals alike.

Roger and Charlotte had taken his brother Colin and his wife Louise to the famous fish restaurant the previous year, and they had swooned at the venue's ambience and the mouthwatering menu, the acquired positive proficiencies planting the foremost justification why Fraser tabled Wheelers to the Czech.

Sipping on Perrier water with ice and lemon, the businessmen browsed the menu.

"I've not been to Wheelers before," T'sor acquainted. "We tend to use the restaurants in Kensington and Holland Park, but this place…" Reconnoitering around the ornate restaurant interior, his features filled with admiration. "…is a cut above Launceston Place and L'Etranger. It's very similar to the Belvedere, only better."

"Ah, yes, the Belvedere is an old-style Marco Pierre White restaurant," Fraser explained. "He also had a substantial contribution to the refurbishment of Wheelers. For my part, I prefer the Belvedere, but Wheelers is easier to get to for both of us."

"You seem to know this part of London well," the Czech commended.

"In my younger days, my future wife and I frequented Bill Wyman's Sticky Fingers restaurant in Phillimore Gardens off Kensington High Street."

"Ah, I know it well," T'sor interjected. "I'm a mammoth Rolling Stones fan."

"Oh, so am I."

"Sorry, I interrupted you."

"Quite alright," he permitted, developing rapport with the Czech. "Then, we'd go to Sticky Fingers just for fun, and in the hope of seeing Bill."

"Did you ever meet him?"

Beaming with due deference for the Stone's ex-bass man, Fraser shared, "we must have been in Sticky Fingers at least ten times, but Bill never showed up once."

"Pity," T'sor empathised. "Where else did you used to go in Kensington?"

"Well, I play rugby, and in the late eighties we'd go to The Roof Gardens at 99 Kensington High Street to celebrate or to drown our sorrows after matches. A real bear pit, blaring out music so loud, you had to shout your order to the waiter. It's relatively expensive, but very chic amongst the yuppie and Chelsea tractor set."

"I know the venue."

"*Really.*"

"Yes, it's still called The Roof Gardens, but the management has attached Babylon, a seventh floor terrace, al fresco dining room overlooking West London, and The Club, a kind of dance venue I suspect formed the foundation of The Roof Gardens when you knew it."

Protracting their talk about the Kensington locale, Fraser and T'sor covered off more recreation venues until a waiter discretely sidled up beside them, enquiring if they were ready to order. On Fraser's recommendation, the Czech went for half a dozen rock oysters, to be followed by white *halibut à la Grenobloise* with shrimps, spinach and creamed potatoes. Correspondingly, he opted for the *Carpaccio* of tuna, succeeded by *Dover sole à la Sicilienne* with lemon, braised red cabbage and new potatoes. Perusing the wine list, they mutually decided to share a bottle of *Chablis Mont de Milieu* to wash down their luncheon feast.

Having loosened up his opposite number, Fraser segued into the commerce of the day. "Could we touch on our bilateral business?"

"Certainly. You've probably done a company's search on the CEZ Group already, so I will not reiterate old ground. Substantively, you want to know more about their financing requirement, the risks, the ROI timescales, and the constitution of the energy investment."

"Just about describes my chore perfectly."

Over lunch, T'sor dispensed the lowdown on the CEZ Group's business in renewable, solar and nuclear energy, sketching the bandwidth of the company's networks, his purport also implying stability, thereby mitigating investor risk to some extent.

"Venture capital is needed for oil and gas deposits exploration in Moravia, a region in the south-east of the Czech Republic bordering on Slovakia," he established. "The deposits are not large in global terms, but significant in self-sufficiency provisions and, proffer foreign earnings potency."

"I see." Rubbing his chin, Fraser assayed the data. "Petro-carbons can be a very risky business for investors. They tend to attract private investment individuals or groups setting aside venture capital on the basis of explosive returns, rather than ultra-low risks."

"Very true."

"Can you give some initial prognostication as to the probable product yields?"

Obliging, T'sor outlined projections, Fraser noting down the paramount factors determining risk. His brokerage of other energy deals had empowered him with an orientation of what to steer away from, and what resembled a judicious bet. From the Czech diplomat's description, the CEZ Group trade risk didn't seem on the button either way. Consummately, it bore the hallmarks of mercantile interest, but before discussing any terms of investment The Firm needed to see independent geologist reports regarding potential oil and gas yields.

"What level of investment is the CEZ Group seeking?" Fraser balloted.

"Something in the region of £250m over three years. The envisaged ROI in terms of selling the realised oil and gas commodities internally in the Czech Republic, primarily to petrol refiners and gas distributors will last at least ten years."

"I see," Fraser logged, mulling over the prediction. "Rate of capital return really adjudicates the risk, in itself the function is dependent on how speedily the deposits can be sold."

"I agree. CEZ are currently forecasting the embryonic assets to be in production within two years of exploration commencement."

"An equitable timescale, but the investment will hinge on the geologist reports before The Firm applies interest digits to the capital, much less take the initiative to the next stage."

Au fait with the protocol, T'sor tattled, "yes, I divined you'd table such a caveat."

Concluding their meeting, T'sor took an action to set up a three-way meeting encompassing CEZ in the next stage of the business assessment, and to have them send The Firm the geologist reports. Complementing, Fraser agreed to develop an interim investment prospectus for CEZ, and feel out some plausible investors.

Vigorously shaking hands on the steps of Wheelers, both men chipper about the enterprise they parted, the Czech by taxi to the embassy, Fraser in two minds whether to go for an elongated taxi journey to the ranch, or risk the Tube again. Feeling good about the meeting, after due consideration and not wanting to fall foul of the District Line again, he chose the taxi option.

~ * ~

After scrutinising geologist reports the Czech had couriered over to Canary Wharf, Fraser had several telecoms with him further qualifying the investment scope. Hosted by T'sor, he also met CEZ commissaries at the Czech Embassy to discuss the investment in fine detail. Able to subsequently tick all the right boxes, and coupled with a heartening response from the investors Fraser had propositioned, in all probability, The Firm would soon be doing business with CEZ.

Belting and bracing the endeavour, Fraser and Jacques then discussed the negotiation details with Toby Chalcroft and Ricky Henshaw, both lending their advocacy to the investment contingent on the geologist reports being impartially verified for accuracy, and CEZ accepting The Firm's standard terms and conditions in principle.

Ensconced in Jacques's office, he and Fraser extensively parsed the various components and personalities in the investment.

"I scent you have become quite pally with Bedrich Ambroz T'sor," Jacques claimed.

"Yes, the more I get to know him, the more I find we have in common, more than just being Rolling Stones aficionados. He is also married with three children and he plays rugby."

"Mmmm, a meeting of the Brains Trust then?" Jacques teased. "It could be the beginning of a beautiful friendship," he annexed with a touch of tongue-in-cheek irony.

"I credit you're not going to make a droll attempt at a pun," Fraser contested, "by suggesting he is my Czech-mate?"

"Ha, ha, very good, Roger. No, I merely made an observation. It always smooths the rough edges of any transaction if the principals involved get on."

Grimacing, Fraser cross-examined, "do you foresee any rough edges with the CEZ settlement?"

"Well, let's wait until we get self-supporting verification of the geologist's reports before breaking out the champagne."

"Actually," Fraser cautioned, "for the past few days, I've been conjecturing this is going far too well. Usually, an irritant crops up from the depths of hell to put a spanner in the works, noticeably in the energy sector, but—"

"But nothing has and it seems a little too good to be true?"

Scowling with solicitude, he admitted, "it does. It's like if you stare at a mind-blowing woman for long enough, you begin to see the minor blemishes. Nothing is perfect and when perfection is artificially rendered, for instance in art, it lacks authenticity, ultimately becoming boring because there isn't even a third order flaw. Defects form attention getters. Even Marilyn Monroe had a beauty spot."

"Hhmm, very poetic. Well, it's still early days, Roger. If history is a reliable signpost, and it usually is, an abnormality will come into play. It's the litmus test to gauge whatever is going on in the city, and is much better in reliability provisos than the FTSE barometer."

"I'll ask Ricky to have a one-to-one with CEZ, just to make sure I didn't miss anything. Often he can ferret out issues otherwise tarrying hidden."

"Sensible thinking."

"I suppose it's the nature of investment banking in general and The Firm in particular."

"How do you mean?"

"Even when we've sliced and diced a contract to the nth degree, we can never quite believe it is free from warts."

"No, it goes with the risk-averse standpoint of the money markets, but I must say, I can't detect an elephant in the corner waiting to trample over the deal."

"All the same, I'll invite T'sor over for dinner at Hazelwood for a definitive scrutiny." Gleaming, he moderated, "let's see just how much of a Czech-mate he is."

"Good idea."

"My only reservation is, one of the kids, probably James, and he will do it on purpose, will get Bedrich's name wrong and address him as 'Mister Tosser'!"

Chapter 14: Candidates for Room 101

Sporadically, meaning once in a blue moon, and as a reward for carrying out Charlotte's explicit instructions to the letter, she rewarded Roger with what he called an 'open pass out.' Such precious certificates had no time constraints and irrespective of what he got up to, the terms of the pass made him fire-proof to any remonstrations from his wife's tongue and thereby penance in the doghouse.

During such rare and joyous milestones, Roger slinked off with his mates from the Hazelwood & District Gentlemen's Club to some retreat where they put the world to rights, reminisced about lost opportunities, notably on the rugby field, and tackled manly pursuits. Invariably, the blowout embraced eating the entire stock of rump steaks and devouring the wine cellar of a swanky, upper-crust restaurant, before retiring to an anteroom to nurse numerous glasses of vintage brandy.

~ * ~

For this conclave, Charlie Farley booked a private room for Steve, Gordon, Roger and himself at

Chapter One, a Michelin-starred restaurant at Farnborough Common, not far from Hazelwood. Using the eatery for strictly alpha male conferences in the past, they had never been disappointed with the food, the beverages, or the friendly service. Essentially, it catered for smart casual attire, a regime stringently verboten without compromise at the full formal dress code expectation of West London *cordon bleu* restaurants in Mayfair and Kensington.

After ravaging plentiful helpings of fricassee of wild rabbit, treacle cured Loch Duart salmon, roast quail with pancetta, Gloucester Old Spot pork and hot Valrhona chocolate fondant washed down with *Carignan Cotes Catalanes*, the luncheon set retired to easy chairs in the private room Charlie had booked to gorge themselves silly on a selection of English and continental cheeses lubricated with *Barros Vintage 1997*.

All chilled out, knowing within their binding friendship anything expressed never saw the light of day beyond their company, the four comrades talked about unfulfilled ambitions and lost horizons.

During Roger's eulogy about misgivings and regrets, he submitted, "I don't reckon I'll ever become a Fast Eddie Felson. I'll always be a Vincent Lauria."

"As in *The Color of Money*?" Charlie broached.

"Yep."

Not quite perceiving the connection, Gordon besought, "how do you mean, Roger?"

"To some extent, the juvenile Vincent Lauria character represented me when I saw the film at age nineteen, whereas in his forties, Fast Eddie Felson had acquired a gravitas I yearned came my way later in life."

"But what are you actually driving at?" Steve expedited.

"I'm converging on my mid-forties, and in many ways I'm still a Vincent Lauria. I also perceive the kudos of a Fast Eddie Felson is never going to come my way."

"But, you're successful in your home life and your profession," Gordon extolled. "How many other trouble-shooters are there in the financial services industry? To be awarded such a special job, you must be immensely regarded at The Firm."

"True, but somehow, I can't ever see myself making the transition from Lauria to Felson, or more accurately, people acknowledging the shift from junior high school prick to elder hallowed statesman, no matter how old I get."

"You're being too hard on yourself," Charlie asserted. "Just because your natural constituency is carefree fun and games like the rest of us —" Breaking off, he waved an encompassing arm around his playmates. "It doesn't mean you have no cachet and standing in the wider world."

Embarrassed he'd raised the concern, Roger confided, "I could be applying too much self-psycho-babble to a phoney stumper, but dissimilar to my father and my elder brother Colin, both oozing aesthetic distinction, I can't see myself being seen as an accredited and recognised person of soaring esteem."

"Charlie is right," Steve buttressed. "You're agonising about a suspicion not founded in fact, but fancy. People do get recognition based on their repute and accomplishments, but it's somewhat intangible. There's no structure whereby if you stack up a certain amount of brownie points, you then become honoured with some form of societal deification."

"Rather than a physical entity," Gordon argued, "it's largely a gauge of perception anyway."

"So," Roger sheepishly polled, "you all appraise I'm being ridiculous?"

"*Yes*," his three chums forcefully bayed in unison.

"Now," Steve insistently budded, "can we discuss some less elevated themes other than young Fraser's psycho hang-ups."

"Damn right," Charlie vaunted. "Let's get back to good-old, superannuated, alpha male bullshit stories, and relentlessly lambasting and lampooning modern society."

"Absolutely, Charlie," Roger endorsed. "Say, have any of you heard from Dwayne Daugherty lately?"

"Ahh, the ex-Kappa Corinthian who is confidante to yesteryears' rugby stars and purports to have clandestine knowledge of every adorable gal on this side of the Atlantic," Gordon positioned. "What about him?"

"Charlotte bumped into him while shopping in Regent's Street last week. He told her he had quit chasing the ladies, settled down, and had got married."

"*No*," Steve boomed. "I don't believe it. Dwayne's a natural bachelor."

"That was my reaction, but he showed Charlotte a photo of his wife and he donned a wedding ring."

"Good god," Gordon groaned. "Who'd have thought it. So, the last of the distinguished shag-*meisters* has hung up his girl-hunting boots."

"Appears to be so."

"It's the end of an era," Steve lamented. "There was a time when he had a different filly on his arm for every mixed-sex rugby social."

"Just goes to show," Roger mourned, "even the best of them eventually get snared."

As a mark of profound respect, the pals saluted Daugherty with a one-minute silence, then toasted their fallen ex-comrade, a tear forming in Steve's, usually unmoved by any catastrophe, eye.

"Hey," Charlie hailed, drawing them out of gloom. "Are you guys tuning into tomorrow's Abu Dhabi Grand Prix?"

"I will be," Gordon piped up.

"Me too," Steve affirmed.

"What about you, Roger?" Charlie grilled.

"Improbable," Roger professed. "Charlotte will not extend my pass out to include Sunday. She'll have all sorts for me to do, and if I try to weasel out of them, I'll be in the doghouse again. Besides, I don't really trace Formula 1 anymore."

"Oh, why?" Gordon interceded.

"It's no longer a test of driving skills. The driver has become the on-board technician, communicating with his race mechanics to optimise car performance. As always, all drivers are capable of winning, but whoever is in the best car wins, unlike in the newsreel you see of Fangio in the fifties, wrestling his Alfa to outfox Stirling Moss and Giuseppe Farina."

"You might be right," he allowed. "Indisputably it's lost all its charisma since the BBC jettisoned magnificent Murray Walker."

"True," Steve mournfully waived. "And, it has become yet another vehicle, if you'll forgive the pun, for the state broadcaster to browbeat the nation with its PC indoctrination roster."

"Yes," Gordon sealed. "It's now the Lewis Hamilton appreciation society show, and it hasn't gone unnoticed Jordan and Coulthard lick his rear end like it dripped honey."

"But they don't do the same for Jenson Button," Charlie complained. "Hardly equitable, is it?"

"No, but I'll tell you what I do watch almost religiously," Roger assigned. "Moto GP. Extremely exciting, and commentators Charlie Cox and Steve Parrish are such sparky and funny dab hands."

"I agree," Gordon concurred. "Whereas Formula 1 has become prosaic, bordering on the boring, Moto GP is electrifying."

"The early years saw the golden age of Formula 1," Charlie conceded. "It really went off the boil in the late seventies."

"Affirmative," Roger backed. "Those newsreels of Jim Clark, Graham Hill and Jackie Stewart careering around tracks in BRMs and Lotus's are much more exciting and stirring, just the same as today's Moto GP." Stopping, as if caught in distant memory, a wide-eyed goggle matured on his clock.

"Ay, ay, the cogs are revolving," Gordon remarked. "Out will pop some fond remembrance at any moment."

"Cheeky bastard," Roger scorned. "As it happens, I did get briefly transported to an early experience."

"Go on," Steve motivated, "let's have all our yesterdays, Fraser *à la mode*."

"Another cheeky bastard," Roger blasted. "*Jesus*, I'm caricaturing our eminent Antipodean friend, Dusty Maltman."

"Just get on with it, Fraser," Charlie pushed.

"Colin and my father tuned into the televised 1970 Monaco Grand Prix, saying to me, 'Come and take a gander.' Taking plaudits from the media and waving to the adoring crowds like a fifth Beatle candidate in the making, I saw Jackie Stewart walking around the paddock area with his lovely wife. He came over as so cool and composed, his long hair flying about and his dark shades giving him a schooled, studied and sophisticated vibe. I've been a Jackie Stewart fan since."

"And don't let us forget John Surtees achieved a unique double," Gordon reminded them. "Crowned 1964 F1 champion, he'd also attained motorbike world champion status with MV Agusta multiple times."

"I must say," Steve declared, "my enthusiasm for F1 has waned since the days of Nigel Mansell and Damon Hill winning the title."

"Difficult to see young kids being comparably enthused today," Charlie put forward.

"For sure," Roger corroborated. "The last F1 GP I caught sent me to sleep." Pausing, he then volunteered, "let me tell you a funny story about F1."

"Go ahead," Steve urged.

"When I was with J P Morgan, Roberto D'Ascenzi, an Italian on secondment from Milan, joined the corporate investment team. One day, Investment Evaluator Dave Voller and I were talking about Formula 1. Roberto came up to us and said, 'You're a talking abouta the granda pricks?' Dave redressed him saying, 'Roberto, it's not pricks, its *prix*.'"

Relishing the impropriety, his buddies laughed at the plot twist.

"Sneering at Dave, Roberto gabbled, *'Mi scusi.'* Iterating the alteration, Dave crowed, 'Its prix, not pricks.' Having none of it and towering over the shorter Dave, Roberto badgered, 'It's a pricks.' 'No, no, no,' Dave bleated, 'it's prix.' Leaning on Dave, Roberto holds, 'It's a pricks.' Fearing he is going to get eased Italian style, Dave echoes, 'pricks.' *'Se'*, Roberto authenticated, 'a granda pricks.' Giving Dave a curious ogle he enquired, 'What a meana pricks in English?' Dave muttered, 'tool.' 'What?' Roberto yawped. 'Tool,' Dave recapitulated fingering his groin, Roberto not seeing the indication."

Reacting, Charlie, Steve and Gordon guffawed, their physiognomy approximating crazed chimps.

"Wait, that's not the end to it," Roger begged. "Roberto gaped at Dave. 'Pricks a meana tool?' 'Yes,' Dave nervously validated. 'So,' Roberto proposed, 'when I a goer to a hardaware a shop, insteada of a asking for a tools, I shoulda saya, wherea are the pricks?' Coming over all vacant, Dave mumbled, 'yeah.' Roberto smiled, whispered, *'ciao'*, and walked off. I joked to Dave, 'I hope for your sake, he never has to buy tools in England,' Dave nodding apprehensively. Then I gibed, 'Di Achenzi, it's a strange Italian surname. It can't have any equivalent in English.' Dave contended, 'it can.' 'What?' I catechized. '*Twat*,' became the response."

Wholly losing it, Roger's pals chortled again, this time homologous to demented pixies.

"Some story, Roger," Steve opined, "and for once quite believable."

"What! *All* my stories are believable." Caught up in the frivolity of the interlude, he laughed then persisted, "I'll tell you another one about the celebrated Dave Voller."

"Oh yeah," Steve reacted. "Better be funny."

"It is, and much funnier than any of your puerile efforts from the world of delinquent solicitors."

"Go on," Charlie sanctioned.

"Guzzling my packed lunch and reading Private Eye one day at my desk, Dave sauntered up to me with a huge cigar hanging from his mouth and looking all superior...him by the way, not the cigar. Plonking himself down on the edge of my desk, he took a massive draw on the cigar then slowly blew it out with supreme satisfaction. Quizzing, 'What are you doing with that weed?' Dave castigated, 'It's not a weed, it's a cigar.' I jeered, 'I'm talking to the cigar.'"

Glad Fraser told the yarn, more chuckling burst forth from the listeners.

"One more," Roger beseeched, "then I'll stop."

"Oohh," Gordon jabbered, auditing Steve and Charlie. "If you must."

"This is a Roberto tale," Roger established. "J P Morgan dealer Ralph Barker owed me £5 for a bet I'd won but lingered deficient with prompt payment. One day Ralph passed my desk and I griped, "Hey Ralphy baby, any news on the fiver you owe me?" He gave me the finger and blared, 'In your dreams, Fraser.' Roberto just happened to be hovering around the area and overheard the conversation. When Barker decamped, he came up to me and queried, 'Heya, Roger, does a thata guy owe you a money?' 'Yes,' I allotted, 'I won £5 fairly and squarely, but Ralph is holding out on me.' 'Ahh,' he replied, 'a debt of honour.' 'Yes,' I approved. 'Leave it a with me, Roger,' Roberto implored, 'wherea I a come a from, we have a ways of a making a sure debtors pay.' Gesturing to the little stiletto knife he kept in his sock that he told me he only used for emergencies, he then strode off to find Ralphy baby. Brooding fat chance, I shook my head. Then to my absolute surprise, shortly after, Roberto drew up beside my desk again, brimming with pride. 'Heya, Roger,' he said, 'I hava your a fiver pounds.' 'Wonderful' I blathered. Smiling, he fanned out five crisp oncers in his hands. Then he yammered, 'One a for you,' and thrusts a pound note into my hand, 'and a one for me, one for you, and a one for me, and one final one for you.' 'But Roberto', I protested, 'I'm two pounds down on the deal.' Eyeing me sternly, he tapped the stiletto and defended, 'is er overheads and a finders a fee I take a.'"

"So, Fraser got ambushed," Steve mouthed off. "That's even funnier than your tale."

"Definitely," Gordon supplemented. "The financial whiz kid got mugged."

Tickled by the sentiment, they broke into raucous laughter.

"Haa, bloody haa," Roger whined. "I told you the anecdote to make you laugh, not to ridicule my extortion by the Mafia."

"Oh, Roger," Charlie bewailed, "it could only happen to you. I didn't envision investment bankers bought into negative equity."

"It's the funniest thing Fraser has ever told us," Steve enthused.

"*Enough*," Roger vehemently demanded.

~ * ~

After ripping into Roger, the friends segued into their usual topics. Who's been shagging who, intense debate regarding the off-side rule in rugby rucks and mauls, who got caught having sex with a lama, why most modern politicians are traitors and should be hung, drawn and quartered repeatedly, who's been shagging who, why the cricket lbw laws should be updated in favour of the batsman, why Jeremy Clarkson should be made Minister of Justice, and of course, who's been shagging who.

Revisiting further tales of social mayhem, the four caballeros wrangled everything from delinquent foreign motorists eternally clogging up motorway outside lanes, to cyclists failing to stop at red lights, causing accidents. Overpaid civil servants making their already large houses into grotesque, hotel-sized edifices certified by ultra-weak council officials and the need to cull special constables, the most ineffectual and useless set of prostrate wooden-tops yet to be foisted on the public masquerading as policemen, also reproached and reprimanded. Aggrandising on their grievances, given the limitless mandate, they discussed who or what ought to be put into Room 101.

"For me," Steve announced, "apart from delinquent ambulance chasing and human rights solicitors giving my profession a bad name, I'd nominate fatuous TV reality shows and gormless soap operas, or those idiots depositing charity bags through my letterbox nearly every day, surmising they will be filled to the brim."

"I get your television examples," Gordon vouched, "but please enlighten us as to why charity bags have incurred your animosity."

"When Colette, the kids and I moved into our present house, we used to get charity bags shoved through the letterbox about once a quarter. Fast-forward to the latest years, charity shops are the only growth industry on the high street, and we get one of their infernal bags stuffed through the letterbox every other day." Glowering, he advanced, "what do they presume we do? Go out and buy a new set of back warmers for the entire family, and a few days later, put the sum total in a charity bag?" Ceasing, he let his assertion sink in before recommencing his diatribe. "Latterly, we had a bag through the letterbox from one charity with a note saying, 'We need your old furniture.' Mystified by the request, I actually made contact, informing them we did have some redundant furniture and when could they collect it? To my astoundment, the silly cow I spoke to almost nonchalantly told me I'd need to hire transportation to bring the furniture down to their shop myself. After entreating, 'who pays?' she impudently enounced, 'Oh, you do.' Incredible!"

"What did you tell her?" Charlie probed.

Rearranging himself in his comfy chair as if preparing for an assault, he ratified, "I told her in no uncertain terms, she could get stuffed."

"Startled by your response, was she?" Gordon quizzed.

"Oh, yes. She got all moralistic and uppity, gave me a right bashing of the inner ear for having the audacity to contest her sensibilities and perspicacity for moral rectitude."

"I begin to see your gist," Roger yielded. "Now you mention it, our hallway table is always stacked with those charity bags."

"Some of them are illegal," Charlie testified. "Last week, I read of a case in the *Telegraph* of some Romanian economic migrants being jailed for bogus charity collections. Transpired they were actually picking up the donated goods, then selling them in Romania."

"Okay, Steve, what's for Room 101?" Gordon egged-on. "TV reality shows and soap operas, or bogus charity bag cheats."

"*Both*!" he spat out. "But only having one choice, it has to be the former, because reality shows' and soap operas have become so ubiquitous that Colette and I seldom switch the box on these days."

Pulling an imaginary lever, Gordon sent the TV trivia programmes to oblivion. "What about you, Charlie?" he interrogated.

"Mmmm, there are so many candidates embodying our local MP—"

"Here, here," Roger interrupted for the motion.

"And," Charlie appended, "grasping GPs working about six hours a day and not at the weekends. They never want to make house-calls, never want to touch you, let alone examine you, and get paid on average about £300,000 a year."

"Here, here," Steve and Gordon chimed in unison.

"I'd also designate *The Simpsons* and *American Dad!*" Charlie attached.

"Yeah," Steve propped, "I've always pigeonholed Homer Simpson as a complete tit, and BBC 3 screening tripe like *American Dad!*

really is the pits when it comes to dumbing down television broadcasts."

"Quite," Charlie agreed. "However, I'm going to specify political correctness and the University of East Anglia."

"Why the University of East Anglia?" Steve butted in, grinning at the unforeseen selection.

"Because, they were the silly bastards responsible for the climate change scandal," he affirmed.

"Oh, yes," Gordon responded. "I'd forgotten about that conspicuous episode. They rigged the results of test measurements, didn't they?"

"They did." Rising to his feet, Charlie proclaimed, "once, an epoch existed when scientists were honoured to be independent of political pressures, but it became obvious these charlatans in the Climatic Research Unit didn't need any persuasion from Gordon Brown and the tree-huggers lobby to falsify the data. Fully paid up members of the Green Party, undeniably they had a political agenda to accomplish. They even made out the glaciers on Everest were melting, provoking the Ganges to flood, until the Indian Government made a statement equating it with comprehensive bollocks."

"I see what you're driving at," Steve permitted. "But what's your specific beef? Why should the University of East Anglia go into Room 101?"

"Because, my dear Steve," he justified, "their scurrilous manoeuvres have brought the entire scientific community into disrepute. It's an unforgivable contrivance. Credible scientists from other disciplines have been undeservedly tarnished with the same brush. Eminently valid data and scientific strategies are being disputed, and those irresponsible, politically impelled antics from the University of East Anglia are to blame."

"Harsh but very fair," Roger adjudged. "And your rationale for political correctness?"

"*Holy moly*," Charlie exhorted. "How much time have you got?"

"Yes, I fancy we could all finger political correctness," Gordon avowed, "torn it apart for days, and still have only scratched the surface."

"I'll give you the shortened version, though I doubt anything I say will be news to any of you." Narrowing his peepers, as if about to talk on an oppressive topic making his blood boil, he argued, "over the past quarter century, political correctness in all its many forms and far-reaching manifestations has become the cancer ruining, if not destroying, much of England and her traditions, constitutions and culture. From positive discrimination through to special consideration for immigrants, laws exclusively designed to benefit so-called minorities to the near eradication of free-speech, the dictats of the federalist EU to the creation of sacred cows given cart blanche by liberal elitists to ride rough shod over the rest of us, these are the wrecking elements irretrievably weakening England and making us ripe for an unrestricted takeover by foreign interlopers." Halting, he curled his top lip. "There are no great men today, only shades of mediocrity. There is no truth anymore, only degrees of political correctness."

"Finished?" Roger cautiously submitted.

"I could go on," Charlie rejoindered.

Gordon held up a hand. "No need, Charlie. We're not going to disagree with any of your opinions and findings on this subject, practiced daily by traitors from the political and media classes."

"Well," Steve buttonholed, "which of your two options are you going to confine to Room 101 forever?"

"It has to be political correctness," Charlie stipulated, "because it's the catch-all for every other PC issue fucking us silly, counting the University of East Anglia."

"Right, stout thinking. In it goes," Steve blithely articulated. "Zzzzzzziiippp. There, gone forever. It will never distress you again."

"If only we could really do that," Charlie wished.

"*Yes*," his friends resolutely warranted.

"What about you, Roger," Gordon drilled.

"Oh, you go next. I'm still weighing the contenders."

"Right. I nominate the BBC and Rowan Williams."

"What, the Archbishop of Canterbury?" Steve specified.

"The very same."

"What's he done to incur your antipathy?" Roger cajoled, anticipating a lucid retort.

"Apart from being a bolshie Welsh druid pandering to pinko causes and denigrating the Church of England with his trendy PC bullshit—" Abruptly breaking off, Gordon glared intensely. "Did you know, while the bombs were going off in London on 7-7, Williams cosied up to Muslims, as did Charles Kennedy; the drunken, ginger tosser who used to run the Lib Dems? I don't trust him."

"What the Archbishop or the ginger tosser?" Steve posed.

"Both, but uppermost, I don't have any faith in Establishment grey beards."

Twinkling at Gordon's eye-opening demarcation, Charlie tested, "why?"

"I have an inherent wariness of men, and women, with elephantine grey beards and receding hairlines. The overgrown facial fuzz can hide a plethora of sins, and disguise true body language masking-off all kinds of skulduggery."

"Wow," Roger drawled, "I never realised you were anti-beard. It will get you a commendation from Jeremy Clarkson."

"I'm not anti-beard *per se*," Gordon clarified. "I've always been a fan of Frank Zappa's full set, but Frank fielded a dark hue. It's the grey beards that foster dubiety."

"A little contentious," Steve criticised. Glancing at Charlie and Roger, he granted, "but we'll let it pass. What about the BBC? Give us your grounds for consigning the most zealous institution in Christendom to Room 101."

"I used to be a BBC proponent, acknowledging it as a valuable and prestigious jewel in the crown, delineating English tradition, culture, history and values." His bent modulating into sullen, he updated, "but alas, as per every other key English seminary, the BBC has become riddled with what Charlie calls the PC cancer. Instead of informing, the holier-than-thou BBC indoctrinates us daily with its own branded PC syllabus and with a breathtaking scale of arrogance, and—" He frowned. "At the taxpayers and licence fee payer's expense."

"Traitorous bastards, aren't they?" Steve chastised.

"*Yes*," came the replies all round.

"A once venerated, even loved corporation," Gordon grumbled, "has become a vehicle for PC talking shops, a club where the liberal elite blow off hot air venting their consciences of whatever they pronounce to be politically incorrect. They tell us who we must like, who we mustn't like, what to say and what not to say, how we must act and what we shouldn't ponder. The sacred cow paradigm extends into children's broadcasts, so as to indoctrinate them with the PC propaganda right from the cradle. Even with Chris Patten running the BBC Trust, nothing has regenerated at the BBC. It is still a PC zealot's paradise for disseminating their perfidious doctrine."

"Don't sugar-coat it, Gordon," Roger taunted. "Tell us what you really think."

Fathoming the send up, his pal smiled at him.

"Okay," Charlie pealed, mimicking Paxman's 'I'm in charge of the world' manner, as the half-paid-up member of the PC fraternity does on *Newsnight* and *University Challenge*. He even resembled Paxman with his curly hair, gaunt kisser and tall, dominating stature. "What's it going to be for Room 101, the Archbishop or the BBC?"

"It has to be the BBC," Gordon named. "Rowan Williams is a symptom of PC mentality. A weak, sniffling little prick, who should know better than to pander to the PC brigade, but someday he will be replaced, god willing by a George Carey type. Comparatively, the BBC is an overarching guild, with the infernal clout of radio and worst still television behind them to spread their deceitful dogma. So, it must be the sanctimonious, self-righteous, smug, priggish and pious BBC for the drop."

"Right, allow me." Charlie motioned, pulling a make-believe lever then snarled, "in you go, replete with Jonathan Woss, Graham Norton, David Dimbleby, chavy actors and conceited news readers, all consigned to the fiery hell of Room 101 forever."

"As a matter of purely academic interest," Roger examined, "you'd replace the BBC with what?"

"That's easy," Gordon insisted. "Kappa Corinthians broadcasting services with me as director general. I'd give the body politic what it really wants. News free from lying PC bias, chavy soap operas sold to ITV, no more PC investigation telecasts, and a restoration to broadcasting live test match cricket and screening blue-ribbon films again."

A deafening cheer went up from Gordon's compatriots with shouts of, "here, here".

"Right, we're only to hear Fraser's nominees," Steve enunciated. "What's it going to be?"

Glinting impishly, he promoted tongue-in-cheek, "well, I could say Cranbrook Crusaders." Knowing the significance behind the nomination, his companions licensed themselves a touch of mirth. "But after careful study I propose whinging, whining footballers or, Doris Johnson."

"Both good candidates," Gordon applauded. "So come on, give us your proof."

"Since the Premier League launch, we've seen the rise of club foreign ownership, foreign managers and far too many damned foreign players."

"Incontrovertibly," Charlie countersigned. "Less than four per cent of players in all four English professional leagues are indigenous English."

"True," Roger declared. "And it's deplorable."

"At this rate, by 2025 there will be no Englishmen in the game we invented and gave to the world," Charlie enumerated. "Isn't that what PC people call, 'ethnic cleansing'?"

"Categorically," he verified. "It's a tragedy of Shakespearian proportions, and an indictment of how politicians and the PC freaks have treacherously sold out England, but what I'm driving at is the lack of moral fibre, the on-field theatrics, the moaning about what one player barked to another in the heat of the moment, and the general woe is me, I haven't been picked to play today, and I'm only earning £100,000 a week bombast."

"Quite right, Roger, it's dreadful," Steve backed. "The bastards don't know their born. They're pampered and preened more than prima donnas. Huh, poor excuses for real men."

"There was an era," Roger extolled, "when football legends exemplified by Stanley Matthews, Tom Finney, Bobby Charlton and Bobby Moore were bastions of the realm. Much respected men, having no ego drive, and playing the game in the spirit its founders intended. They didn't get involved in night club and drugs scandals, using and abusing women, crashing expensive cars, stupid, idiotic and childish dances to celebrate goals, throwing tantrums and sulking if they were substituted. They were genuine gentlemen, playing the game because they loved it, and they didn't get paid a king's ransom every Saturday for kicking a pig's bladder around a muddy park."

"Contrast that idyllic setting with today's greedy, gluttonous, disloyal foreign mercenaries," Gordon cited, "deeming they are doing a club a humongous favour by strapping on their colours and strolling around the pitch like pregnant, posing faeries."

"Do you know," Steve spouted, "Yaya Toure at City gets a basic of £200,000 per week summing to £10.4m a year, and with bonuses, the total is £24m a year minimum, guaranteed. And, there's about eighty foreign footballers on an average of £100,000 a week, equating to £416m a year flooding out of England's economy, most of it untaxed in the UK." Dwelling, he became agitated. "So why don't the media and the politicians make an expansive noise about the travesty, particularly when unemployment is rising, economic growth is flat, and the national debt increases every year?"

"Oh, that's easy," Gordon offered. "It'd be politically incorrect!"

"Incontestably," Roger evinced. "And without aspiring to justify the salary excesses of my industry, £10.4m per year is in the region of what banking CEOs receive with bonuses. We get vilified for greed, yet these foreign footballers are not tarnished with the same greed brush." Terminating, he furrowed his brow. "Anyway, we've drifted from the resolve of the Room 101 game. Under the whinging, complaining, moaning banner, I'm nominating modern footballers for Room 101, with the exception of Steven Gerrard, Michael Owen, Frank Lampard, John Terry and most of what little remains of the English phalanx."

"What about Doris?" Charlie reminded him.

"Oh yes, Doris," Roger recapped. "I have little piety for most modern-day politicians, but I have grown to loathe Doris Johnson with his vote buying by ploughing council tax into gay pride marches and every other so-called minority group and, his constant sucking up to them. He's an even worse sycophant than Red Ken."

"And the basis for being condemned to Room 101?" Gordon prodded.

"Because he's a blithering idiot, a buffoon comic whacko putting his foot in more things than Frank Spencer. And—" Roger's snoopers bulged. "The bastard wants to construct an airport in my back garden, well…on the Isle of Grain or in the Thames estuary. But it amounts to the same thing in terms of social impact. Worst of all, this *fool* on gherkin hill aspires to be PM!" Grimacing, the notion understandably incongruous to him, he postulated, "can you imagine what a laughing stock it'd make of England on the international stage? I've grown to see Cameron's severe limitations, but at least he has a little gravitas and is acclaimed amongst the world's trailblazers. Those same skilled politicians would take the gullible Doris to the cleaners, and he'd sign us up for even more tax payer funded international aid and inward migration, and unqualifiedly surrender our sovereignty to the Nazi-style tyrants running the EU."

"I have to admit," Charlie sanctioned, "he's not what I conceive for a Mayor of London, and I can't see any differences in his social policies to those of Red Ken. When Doris moved into his ivory tower, business resumed as usual for the excesses of the PC crowd to waste council tax payers hard earned money on their self-centred agendas."

"So," Steve submitted, "its Doris Johnson versus whinging footballers for the drop."

"Tricky choice," Roger proposed. "Much as I loathe Doris, using Charlie's rag-bag for political correctness, I'd have to plump for whinging footballers because most of them don't pay taxes in England."

"Goodbye whinging footballers," Charlie fixed, pulling a fictional lever jettisoning them into Room 101."

"Cor," Steve tendered, "did you hear their scuzzy screams?"

"Yeah," Gordon verbalised. "If only it transpired as that simple in practice."

Philosophically Roger stipulated, "you know, it occurs to me we have all become borderline anarchists."

"In what way?" Gordon scrutinised.

"Well, none of us really has faith in the political fabric anymore. Collectively, we're dismissive about all the major parties, and there is little prospect of either the English Nationalists or UKIP coming to power, because pure bred English people are an ever-reducing minority. Whether we care to admit it or not, we've become renegade outsiders, participating in the colossal charade under duress and out of commitment to our families."

"I've been of the same opinion for eons," Steve acceded. "And, we're not alone. Millions of disenfranchised English people have also given up on the order, because it has been loaded for the advantage of others, and we have no redress whatsoever to swing the pendulum to where it should belong."

"True," Gordon attested, "I haven't voted in any local or general elections for years. It seems to be a totally futile act because nothing ever changes. The nation's burdens continue to be thrust onto people like us to bear without any consultation, or our approval. Have you three voted in recent times?"

Steve, Charlie and Roger peeked at each other.

"I certainly haven't," Charlie propounded. "I gave up on the system long ago."

"Me to," Steve added.

They all gawped at Roger.

"Charlotte upholds we must vote because we live in a democracy," he confided, "I argue democracy has become cosmetic and elections modify nothing in England, meaning the will of the majority has become watered down to the degree whereby in reality, our framework is a benign dictatorship led by the cross-party liberal elite. So, unless you happen to concur with the prospectus, what's the benefit in voting?"

"But you still vote?" Charlie bickered.

"No. I go along to the polling station with Charlotte, but then soil the voting slip by scrawling on it 'None worthy of receiving my vote'. She doesn't know, so still guesses I vote."

"We sound like revolutionaries, don't we?" Steve tabled.

"Yes, it's an update on the igniters behind the American War of Independence," Charlie particularized.

"How do you mean?" Gordon queried.

"That war hinged on no taxation without representation. Ours should be no taxation or voting, without *effective* representation. Effective is the axiomatic word, meaning the will of the majority must be made law and their covets carried out in Parliament, as opposed to the prevalent mechanism conning us into choosing politicians, who then ignore us."

"Yep," Roger assented, "but it's never going to happen. They cast the die at least twenty years ago, and all the prime parties have bought into it. I distrust the Conservatives just as much as New Labour."

"All we can do," Gordon advised, "is work for our families to make sure they are safe and secure, and, appear to be playing the underlying societal game demanded by the political and media classes."

"But it doesn't mean they will own our hearts and minds," Charlie maintained. "Freedom is a state of consciousness, and so long as the thought police don't snatch and imprison us for our anti-PC rhetoric, we can pursue criticising and disparaging those betraying us, and relentlessly rip into the absurdities of modernity."

"Yes, no one can take that away from us," Steve avowed.

"So," Roger said, consulting his Louis Cartier, "it's just coming up to five pm. If we start the revolution now, we should have Westminster under our control by six, and be home for tea, muffins and medals by seven."

Chapter 15: The Hay Wain

Keen antiques collectors, the Fraser clan headed off to the Kent Showground at Detling to attend the twice annual antiques fair, the pageant providing many of the bone china, porcelain and glassware artifacts furnishing their Hazelwood home. Howbeit Victorian and Edwardian cheese dishes were Roger's whim, he also had a penchant for Royal Worcester figurines and Edinburgh crystal. Complementing his desires, Charlotte's predilection incorporated Coalport porcelain and bone China figurines, plus anything in Royal Doulton or Crown Derby. If she had her way, their treasure trove would litter every room in the house, even the en suites and cloakrooms festooned with riches from yesteryear.

During one Detling sojourn, they had seen TV personality David Dickenson. A vision of gleaming ginger in his brown suit and orange tinted face makeup, Roger became tempted to ask him, as well as being an antiques guru, did he also double as a mobile Belisha beacon.

During the journey along the M20, the Frasers talked about their preceding tours to antique fairs and some of the unforeseen and ultimately challenging brushes various family members had to reconcile, chiefly Roger.

"Of course, my pick," James chirpily remembered, "endures as when Dad mistook a woman for a man at the Royal Horticultural Hall Antique Fair in Greycoat Street."

On the day under review, Roger had spent over an hour toiling to find somewhere to park the MPV off Horseferry Road in Victoria, Charlotte telling him he simply did not have her technique for nosing out parking spots. When he did find one, he let some other Herbert beat him to the draw, further exacerbating her scolding. Underlining he had to be more ruthless, brook no interlopers and just go for it, she drove home his parking inadequacies. Eventually, they wound up in the Rochester Street NCP multi-storey. Remarkably, spaces had become available, whereas on the previous five happenings they toured past its entrance, the car park sign illuminated, FULL. Still feeling the burn from Charlotte's destruction job, after they'd walked the short distance to the Royal Agricultural Hall, Roger's temper resided non-conducive.

Similar to the Charlie Kelcher gender recognition conundrum at Zicon General, on this occasion Roger really did take the person under deliberation to be a man. Albeit veritable, the gender boo-boo only served to heighten his discontent.

Laughing at the remembrance, Charlotte reprimanded, "how on Earth did you blunder into such a monumental error, Roger? I mean, there's no doubt it was a woman."

"Well," he averred, trying for self-justification, "anyone could make the same slip."

"I knew you were in for a beating, Dad," Wendy chirped up.

"Yes, thank you, Wendy," he bluntly acknowledged. "No doubt we all retain it in memory."

Clustering around Peregrine's Antiques stall, the Fraser family had audited Victorian and Edwardian cheese dishes amongst other bone china kitchen and tableware. Seeing an unusually attractive Victorian cheese dish and cover, Roger discerned it'd make a valuable addition to his already large accumulation. Opening a powwow with the seller, initially he found the person unwilling to reduce the £199 price tag, but in the end Roger's ultra-smooth negotiating skills reduced the selling price down to £145. During the bartering, Roger really thought he spoke to a man. Undividedly, he looked like a man, voiced like a man, and even dressed like a man. Having grudgingly reduced the price of the item for sale, the seller tarried as in no mood for insults, causeless or otherwise. When Roger delved, should he make the cheque out to Mister Peregrine, the seller turned nasty, doubtful about Roger's eyesight, before picking up a walking stick and waving it at him, while remonstrating the cheque should be made to Miss Georgina Peregrine. Matters irretrievably deteriorated when Roger babbled, 'All right, all right, George, no need to throw a wobbler,' the woman angrily replying, 'It's *not* George, its Georgina.'

"Honestly, Roger," Charlotte berated, the nostalgia still making her laugh at the goof. "You've put me in some embarrassing positions over the years with your daily dose of gaffe dumps, but that one takes the biscuit. Fancy adding insult to injury by calling the woman George, when she'd told you her name was Georgina."

"I just tried to bring a touch of levity to the exchange," he justified. "Anyway, if it really was a woman, how come it mirrored and talked so like a man?"

Associating the discussion they had at Aunt Jemina's, after their visit to the Summer Exhibition at the Royal Academy, James nominated, "perhaps you engaged in social intercourse with a tranny, like Grayson Perry."

"*James*," his mother scolded. "I've told you before, Grayson is not a tranny as you so indelicately put it. That's his alter ego, Claire. And don't be so vulgar with your assimiles."

"But social intercourse is a perfectly valid phrase."

"Maybe so, but in your vocalisation, like your father's, it decidedly sounds indecent."

"Mummy," Heather began.

"You're not going to ask what a transvestite is again, are you?" Charlotte guardedly broached.

"No, after you explained at Daddy's Aunt Jemina's, I know what one of them is now, and I'd recognise one if I saw them."

"What is it then, darling?"

"I wanted to ask if Daddy will be mistaking any women for men at today's antiques fair?"

Furrowing her brow at Roger, Charlotte elucidated, "put it this way, if he does, it's a long walk home from Detling to Hazelwood."

"Hah, hah," Roger guffawed in as sarcastic an infliction as he dared to generate, without being sent from the MPV there and then.

"There's the other time," Wendy zealously put forward, "when Dad destroyed a whole pack of national treasures."

"I did *not* destroy a whole pack of national treasures," her father protested. "If it's the same circumstance I assume you are on about, it merely occurred as an unfortunate accident."

Wendy referred to a trip they had taken to the Dorking Halls antiques fair, her father inadvertently breaking some Josiah Spode II plates when swinging around to signify an early Moorcroft jar he wanted to draw his wife's appreciation to.

"Yes, Roger," Charlotte interjected. "Your mishap cost us a fortune."

"I did not destroy them on purpose...they moved," he griped. "Besides, a huge devil dog biting at my ankles led to the sudden movement."

"*Devil dog!*" she repeated.

"Yes, Mum," James confirmed. "You must call to mind the daxon nibbling at Dad's shoe laces."

"Daxon," she squealed. "Hardly a devil dog, was it?"

"*Weeeeell*, that's what it equated to for me," complained her put-out and incrementally agitated husband. "Anyway, enough Roger baiting. You'll all be giving me a complex. I won't be able to go into the Detling antiques fair without feeling the need to keep my mouth shut and my hands permanently behind my back."

"Now there's a good idea," Charlotte credited.

~ * ~

Very different to Victoria, Roger managed to evade parking difficulties at Detling. Quickly finding a spot for the MPV, the antique hunters then set forth.

Out on the slopes of the North Downs, the Frasers found the Kent countryside air bracing, a portent winter evidently fast approached on the heels of autumn. Largely untouched by modernity for hundreds of years, like Elysian Fields, the ancient, arcadian landscape lingered rugged and uncompromising to change. Intrinsically blooming with a rustic charm, it perpetually reminded the observer of a Constable scene, replete with towering oaks, farming implements conceived in the industrial revolution and church spires in the distance.

Beaming to herself as she surveyed the inspirational vista ahead, Charlotte instructed her husband, "you should enjoy the Downs countryside, Roger. It's good for the spirit and the soul."

Verging on the sardonic, he expressed, "well, I'm very bucolic, and I'm all in favour of pastoral care."

Not catching on to her husband's mordant wit, she propositioned, "mmmm, it really does make you want to explore nature and find your ethereal side, doesn't it?"

"Oh, yes," he accredited, artificially hanging on to her every word, but developing a detracting wince.

"Come on," she implored, "let's bask in the hinterlands of this marvellous setting."

"I'll follow you anywhere, my leader," he promised with a hint of derision.

Clicking his heels together, the dark humour made James smile.

Suddenly attuned to his light mocking, Charlotte chided, "less of the sarcasm, please." Avalanching into strict governess mode, her idyllic expression faded. "You're not out on one of your rugby club junkets."

"Yes, dear," he affirmed, deciding to ditch satire, at least provisionally, and go for a submissive deportment.

Often at these events, sale items approximated booty or plunder from Captain Blackbeard's gem chest, rather than refined riches created by jewellery artisans and ceramics craftsmen. Sometimes, Roger presumed he handled pillage from a ransacked Kent manor, or some *nouveau riche* stockpile amassed by thieves and ne'er do wells out for a quick bit of trade. Ready to pounce on those holding them, he'd also pondered if undercover rozzers cruised around antiques fairs probing for stolen items.

On one quondam outing, he had picked up an early nineteenth

century Wedgwood Jasperware teapot, priced £240. Cognizant it should really have been set at around £450, he mused one hell of a bargain then became rapt in intuitions of it being just too good to be true. Post-haste, he ordained the Jasperware must have been purloined, and cops were observing him from the wings, waiting to handcuff him for buying stolen goods. Telling Charlotte about the premonition, she tutted, superciliously raised her eyebrows and called it chronic paranoia.

Detling contained four very large, old, farm buildings used to display items for sale, also acting as venues for antiques experts like David Dickenson to give buying do's and don'ts lectures to enthralled audiences. Invariably, they were more mesmerised by his noodle to foot, shimmering, carroty trademark identity rather than his advocate's content. Additionally, marquees were temporarily erected to house stalls, and the pathways winding from the car parks and those interconnecting the farm premises were laced with outdoor stalls, their owners endeavouring to entice passers-by to stop and browse the cachet of cherished items they sought to sell.

No sooner had the Frasers glided into the largest of the farm properties, actor Ian McShane came into view, conducting an impromptu press conference with the antiques collector's press.

"Heavens," Roger cried, "it's Lovejoy."

"Hhmm, what?" Charlotte brayed, already attracted by an exhibit of early twentieth century Moorcroft.

Signalling onwards, he replicated, "I said, it's Lovejoy."

"Oh, yes," she acknowledged, swiveling in the given direction then laying a hand on her husband's arm. "Now don't embarrass me by acting like a docile teenager and ask for his autograph." Scintillating one of her 'I'm immovable on this issue' goggles at him, ramming home the request she appended, "you read me?"

"*Yeesss*," he reluctantly acceded.

Staring at McShane, Roger recalled one *Lovejoy* episode in which the lucky, lucky, lucky bastard got to go sailing with the delightful and yummy Joanna Lumley. If not for Charlotte, he couldn't picture anything more delicious than a day at sea with Joanna.

Registering him cogitating, his wife importuned, "stop daydreaming about Joanna Lumley."

"What?"

"I know you're mulling over the *Lovejoy* episode which starred Joanna Lumley."

"How could you possibly know that?"

"I know everything."

"Of course—" Floutingly, he slapped his forehead. "You're a woman. Whatever was I thinking?"

Ignoring his contempt, she shook her head. "She must be over twenty years older than you, Roger."

"Yes, I know," he substantiated. "But at James's age, I had the most enormous crush on her, and it lasted until you came into my life, my darling."

"You were doing the same thing at the Carriage Works, when your cousin Barry took us to see *Whitehall Farce*. As soon as I mentioned Joanna Lumley had performed in the film version of the stage play, I knew you'd be sighing internally."

"Don't know what you are talking about?" he refuted, secretly discriminating his wife to be absolutely right.

Intentionally changing the subject to avoid further admonishment, Roger informed, "*Lovejoy's* the reason I really got into antiques."

"Yes, me as well," she admitted.

Nodding towards McShane still holding court, Roger observed, "he looks just the same as he did twenty-five years ago. Do you suspect he colours his hair?"

"Possibly," she fancied, gawking at the columbine and his adoring admirers. "He's shorter than I imagined."

"Yes, it's often the case. When you see someone from film or television in real life, it's their height, or lack of it that surprises you the most, namely, as when we saw Bob Dylan at Hyde Park in 1996?"

"Oh yes, with the Who and Eric Clapton."

"Only when I saw the Zim standing next to his band members,

did I suss he's far shorter than I postulated. And it's the same with Ian McShane. Conversely, I had the exact opposite, when we saw Jeff Beck at Ronnie Scott's a few years ago, his height as I'd always imagined it to be." Resting, a huge grin built around his phizog. "Do you remember Jimmy Page and Robert Plant were in attendance?"

"I do. It became another occurrence when I had to stop you running over to them like a gormless, moonstruck, adolescent schoolboy begging for their autographs."

"Yes, *you did*, didn't you," he rebuked. Pinpointing the Fraser siblings, he drilled, "now children, listen to and hear your father well. There are legendary guitarists…Hendrix, Page, Clapton and Peter Green for example. Then there is—" Breaking off, he put on a deep Jeremy Clarkson voice. "Jeff Beck."

"Hhmm, I recall you virtually wet yourself, every time Jeff hit a note," Charlotte vented.

"Yes, it's true," the Beck devotee warranted. "Spellbound by the extraordinary reverberations he made, I kind of swooned. We could see every motion of his fingers on the fretboard, every expressive facial reaction as he churned out terrific anthems, and his band…well, they were amazing."

"When you two have finished reminiscing about the monsters of rock," James scornfully mocked, "can we get on?"

Glistening at the amusing rebuke, his father ascribed, "quite a good phrase for you, son. I can see you're developing my sense of subtle humour."

"*Subtle humour*!" Charlotte blurted. "Your humour has always used sarcasm as its baseline and incessantly borders on the banal." Slinging a disparaging scowl at her son, she ordered, "James, I forbid you to take after your father."

~ * ~

Sub-ten-year olds are eminently ingenious, Heather Fraser more than most. Contiguous to Alton Towers and the Royal Academy Summer

Exhibition, antiques shows typified a paradise for fun and adventure for the youngest Fraser, her curiosity for the unfamiliar and her urge to test the ruggedness of the most delicate items by climbing over them, just too much a temptation to resist.

After the Lovejoy intermission, the family moved on. Scoping the horizon for something she had not come across before, Heather forged ahead of them, homing in on a presentation of Crown Staffordshire and Burleigh Davenport china, together with a dozen petite to extra-large Qing dynasty vases, each set on a plinth, no more than twelve inches from the floor. However, the pricey bone china had not attracted her. Tinkling in the slight breeze created when someone unfastened the building door to enter or leave, she stared bedazzled at a series of Feng Shui antique metal wind chimes.

Noticing her straining to touch the device, and thereby the potential costly catastrophe in the making, her mother called in an authoritative voice, "Heather." Stopping, the youngest Fraser blithely stared up. "Careful not to break anything on that display."

Coming over all innocent, she defended, "yes, Mummy, but I only want to look at the chimes."

"Just wait for me, darling," Charlotte hailed, "and we'll examine them together."

"Yes, Mummy," she meekly accepted.

Seeing the precious artefacts, Roger proclaimed, "ahh, a possible treasure trove. Let's investigate if there is anything worth acquiring."

Perceiving the Fraser column coming his way, the stall owner smiled and greeted them with a warm, "good morning."

"Good morning," Charlotte parroted. "My, you do have some interesting stuff. Can we take a peek?"

"Of course," he approved. "Feel free to peruse anything you wish."

Clocking a sign behind the vendor reading, 'All breakages must be paid for', Charlotte nudged Roger and motioned at the warning.

"Hhmm," her husband took onboard.

While they inspected several pieces, Wendy and James contented themselves playing I-spy. Meanwhile, Heather eyed the hanging metal wind chimes, their clinking cadence persisting as a fount of fascination to her. Heedful of the demand to behave, she resisted the temptation to pull the chimes to make them peal louder.

Spotting the Qing vases, Roger commended, "you'll prize these."

"Yes, but where would we put them?" Charlotte questioned. "Every space on every surface in the lounge, the dining room, the library and our bedroom is crammed full of ceramic antiques, including numerous vases."

"Yes, and they are very expensive. £650 for the petite vase alone and over £5,000 for the set, but I do adore them."

"We could store some items in the loft to make way for other exhibits," Charlotte proposed, "but, all our existing stuff is either English or German. Chinese Qing dynasty items will be out of place among the Moorcroft, Royal Worcester and Goebel porcelain and ceramics collections."

"You're right."

"On the other hand," she reopened, taking her husband's arm, "I really do care for that Crown Staffordshire vintage tea set. If we put the existing late-nineteen-forties Royal Albert tea set in one of the kitchen cabinets, it could go in the breakfast room's Welsh dresser."

"For sure. Is it vintage or post-Edwardian Crown Staffordshire?"

Picking up a piece, Charlotte adjudicated, "vintage Edwardian. The potter's mark is 1910."

"Hmmm, pre-First World War," he whispered. "It means the stall keeper will want a tidy sum for the complete service." Switching his vigilance to him, he begged, "excuse me, this, er, Crown Staffordshire set."

"A most rare and treasured collection," the seller felicitated.

"It's marked 1910."

"Yes, early Edwardian."

"Does it have some form of provenance?"

"I acquired it from a house clearance sale at Boughton Monchelsea. Alas, any documentation such as a sales receipt has long gone, but in the attic, I found the real McCoy boxes housing the tea service. They were imprinted with J.W Plaistow & Sons, a bone china retailer in Maidstone for part one of the twentieth century."

"I see. Do you have the boxes?"

"I do. Just give me a minute, and I'll retrieve them from my stash."

After the man evaporated, Charlotte apprised, "each item is priced individually to allow piecemeal sales. He might give a discount if we bought the entire service?"

"How many are we talking about?"

"I did a quick tot-up while you were talking. The entire twenty-three pieces, composing a three-tier cake stand, tea pot and hot water container is around £590." Propitiously, she affixed, "the service looks to have been on display more than it's been used, and I can't see any cracks or chips on any of the pieces."

"You want this set then?"

"Yes."

"Here we are, sir," they heard the vendor say, returning with the boxes.

Browsing them, Charlotte and Roger discovered the packaging indeed bore Crown Staffordshire stamps, with J.W Plaistow & Sons embossed on the bottom of each box.

"Right," Roger cheerfully reacted, readying to go into barter mode. "What price are you asking for the entire service?"

"Well, owing to the early Edwardian provenance and the pristine condition of the set, £585."

"Hhmm, before the economic downturn, I'd have avouched it's a fair price, but in today's climate—" Grimacing at the seller, he bared his teeth, taking a sharp intake of breath, necessary gestures to pre-warn of imminent price negotiation, "I'm speculating more along the lines of £250."

"Ooohh, your offer vastly undervalues the set," the seller countered. "I couldn't let it go for anything less than £500."

"I see." Squinting down the aisle of stalls vanishing into the distance, Roger cordially said, "well, it's been very pleasant talking to you. Thank you."

The Frasers began to walk off.

"Wait," the pedlar entreated. They wheeled about. "I might be able to do you a special price."

Dwelling, Roger then joshed, "you articulate like the bazaar seller in *Casablanca*, labouring to get Ingrid Bergman to buy his lace tableware." Prying over the seller's shoulder, he ribbed, "Humphrey Bogart's not behind you, is he?"

"Er...no," he denied, all at once perplexed by Roger's invention and travailing to retain focus.

"What do you have in mind?" Roger catechized.

Gleaming at the Crown Staffordshire tea set, the peddler appealed, "it'd be a shame to break up a complete service...how about...£480?"

"Make it £380, and we're in business."

"£450."

"£400."

"£420."

Twinkling, Roger sanctioned, "done. Pleasure doing business with you. To whom should I make the cheque out to?"

"*Oh*," the pusher opposed, "I only take cash, sir."

"Thought you might say that."

Coming prepared with cash on the hip, Roger withdrew a thick wad of the folding stuff from his inside jacket pocket, counting out the readies to meet the negotiated trade price.

Whilst the merchant placed the tea set into its original packaging, Heather could no longer resist the temptation to make the hanging metal wind chimes clatter louder. Leaping up she managed to grab at one of the larger tubular objects, a chime in the lower frequency range booming as it crashed against its smaller sister chimes, echoing in sympathy. Numbering the vendor, the sudden burst of cacophony attracted everyone's circumspection. As Heather travelled earthwards, her heel caught the edge of a plinth, sending a petite Qing dynasty vase skywards, everyone ogling in awe as it catapulted upwards, cart-wheeling during its fleeting trajectory before attaining peak height, and beginning the downward journey to terra firma. Unlike NASA space capsules descending through the stratosphere, the delicate Qing vase did not have parachutes and an inflatable dinghy to break its fall. Quick as a flash, Roger dived head-first, consonant to how he used to in his rugby prime, scoring a try for Kappa Corinthians, his outstretched mitt managing to seize the expensive item before it could crash to the floor and explode into a thousand pieces, much to the vendor's relief.

"Clumsy oaf," Charlotte bleated. "You nearly dropped it."

"But, but, but…I saved it, and it wasn't me making it fall anyway!"

~ * ~

After depositing the Edwardian tea service in the MPV, the Frasers resumed their tour of the antiques fair. While foraging in another of the farm premises for more items to add to their Royal Doulton and Moorcroft inventories, Wendy saw a figure in the distance waving at her mother.

"Someone is attempting to attract your attentiveness," she acquainted Charlotte.

Engrossed in checking out a large Moorcroft bowl Roger assured her dated from the late nineteen-forties, though its price tag signified 1919 vintage, she hardly heard her eldest daughter.

"Hhmm," Charlotte responded. "What did you say, Wendy?"

"I said, Mother, darling," Wendy reiterated. "Someone is attempting to attract your attentiveness." Evincing to her right, she directed Charlotte's line of vision.

"*Oh*, it's Hattie Harriman. She's a lecturer on my arts and crafts course."

"Hattie Harriman," Roger mimicked, an abject glower of disbelief written over his boat race. "What kind of a comic book rhythming, half-ass, bleeding name is that?"

"Roger," rebuked his wife at the mild swear word. "Not in front of the children."

"Oh, Mum, that's nothing," James piped up. "You should hear some of the words I hear at school and in the films I watch, and of course *The Inbetweeners* is littered with expletives and blasphemies." Noting his mother had engendered her menacing punishment stance hands on hips, he waffled, "*what*?"

"You'd better stop there, son," his father submitted. "You don't want to offend your mother's sensibilities, do you?"

"Charlotte," Hattie called, advancing on the Frasers. "I thought I recognised you."

Making a quick assessment of the newcomer, Roger appraised her to be ancient, not quite pre-historic but analogous to an ordnance survey map, her heavily lined and gnarled features produced hills and valleys mirroring her entire life experiences. Whether they were sad or delectable, he could only hypothesize. Albeit, beneath her gaunt exterior bordering on frail, she emanated an inner strength that only comes from self-confidence and belief.

"Hello, Hattie," Charlotte welcomed. "How are you today?"

Obviously, my wife has to suck up to this woman, Roger consigned, *or she might fail her on the arts and crafts course.*

"I'm fine, Charlotte. Is this your family?"

"Yes."

Introducing her family members, Hattie dickered a few words with each of them like the Queen swapping courtesies with entertainers backstage at the London Palladium after a Royal Command performance.

"Are you enjoying the antiques fair?" she asked the youngest Fraser.

"Yes. Especially when Daddy nearly smashed up an expensive Chinese vase."

"*Oooh!*" Hattie whooped, fixing Charlotte with a concerned gawk. "Nothing tragic, I hope."

"No," she half-heartedly validated. "My husband managed to grasp the piece before it hit the floor."

Aggrieved before a stranger, Roger coughed then designated, "I can assure you, no damage occurred."

"Oh, good," Hattie replied. "An antiques fair is hardly the place for the gauche and the maladroit, is it?"

"But, but, but," Roger gabbled, before glancing at his family seeking their help.

"Yes, Roger," Charlotte wryly voiced.

"Oh…*nothing*," he whinged.

Knowing her culpability in the near tragedy, nonetheless, Heather feigned unreserved innocence and hustled, "are you in trouble again, Daddy?"

"As usual, Heather—" Dawdling, he sighed. "Daddy's in the doghouse."

"Before I forget, Charlotte," Hattie initiated, "you're friendly with Natasha Belmont, aren't you?"

"I am."

"I'd be grateful if you could have a word with Natasha about the way her daughter Emma dresses for the arts and crafts classes. She seems to have a fixation with both Jane Austen and Mary Shelly. Her lofty, even puritanical attitude, combined with what I'm told is 'goth' garb and facial makeup is very off-putting for the other students, and—"

"You mean," Roger interrupted, "she's a cross between *Mansfield Park* and the bride of *Frankenstein*?"

"Bless me," Hattie blathered, as if shocked Roger could engage in dialogue let alone possess literary expertise. "You are familiar with the works of Jane Austen?"

"Oh yes," he flamboyantly boasted, "I'm an avid Jane Austen reader – *Sense and Sensibility*, *Pride and Prejudice*, Nob and Nob-ability—" the latter falsely fabricated, salacious title flying over Hattie's head, undetected.

"*Roger*," Charlotte barked.

Dry after their bookish impact on contemporary youth exertions, the Frasers went off with Hattie to the refreshment's marquee. Sitting under canvas drinking tea, apart from Heather who asserted for some obscure reason, tea growing affected the Indian elephant's habitat, and any responsible animal lover should boycott Typhoo, the group talked about antediluvian goings-on.

"An antiques fair is such an inspiring environment for those interested in the arts," Hattie tendered, as if she had been elevated to the delirious rank of Surveyor of the Queen's pictures. "They always promise a cornucopia of breathtaking highlights and unexpected climaxes."

Climaxes, Roger psychically duplicated, *such an offbeat word for an old buzzard to use. I wonder if she's ever had any climaxes of a horizontal construct.*

"Oh, I couldn't agree with you more," Charlotte endorsed. "I've always rated antiques fairs to be at the very fault-line of the arts and crafts schism."

Still smarting from his embarrassing interlude in the presence of Hattie, who seemed to enjoy his humiliation, Roger augmented in as mocking intonation he aspired to escape with, "oh yes, indubitably, they're filled with the ambience of bygone eras."

Feeling Charlotte's foot come into contact with his shin, he distinguished he hadn't been subtle enough after all.

"Do you really think so?" Hattie pumped, her inquisitor-comparable blinkers probing Roger for veracity.

"Oh, yes," he pledged.

"Axiomatically, it helps educate the prodigious mass of the people receptive to art," Hattie allotted. "After all, art is the property of everyone. I do so detest those worshipping materialism. Art is what counts, not bourgeoisie paraphernalia. The many shouldn't be putting money into banks. No, they should be hiring eternity for otherworldly and spiritual values."

What the hell does all that mean? Roger contemplated.

Embarking on a hifalutin chin-wag about the Tate, not the airy-fairy one at Bankside, but the real Tate on the 'Chelski' Embankment, Charlotte and Hattie left the others behind. Yearning for a shift of topic and company, Roger and the kids shuffled their feet, either bored with the pompous interchange or essaying to catch forty surreptitious winks.

Really getting into her stride, Hattie lavished, "the Tate has attracted works crediting the most outstanding artists of the past 500 years, constituting pearls from the renaissance all the way through to a sensational cache from an eccentric auxiliary cast of twentieth century renegade artists."

"Yes," Charlotte favoured. "Expressly, the post-impressionism epoch swept across the world of art replete with a radical new style, but it did have limitations."

"I couldn't agree with you more, my dear. Though the advent of Picasso and Matisse heralded an immense plethora of new axioms, predestined to go on for at least a century, the prelude also emerged to be its finale. Since, it has never sustained upward mobility, and in recent times became stricken with a kind of creeping paralysis, in vogue with evolving society but still crumbling apart in slow motion."

With her penchant for post-modernism, what will Charlotte make of that? Roger subliminally contested. *She's bound to go on the defensive.* Irrespective, much to his astonishment, she remained impassive. Lucidly, her panoramas were on gaining top examination marks, not challenging the art connoisseur's sentiments in public.

Elaborating her art appreciation, Hattie affirmed, "the revolutionary period in twentieth century European art still evinces a radical manifesto, joined as if by osmosis to the changing historical landscape it reflected."

Wow, that resounded good, Roger mentally applauded. *This woman might border on the objectionable, as per so many of Charlotte's arts and crafts crowd, but she has one hell of a vocabulary.*

Out of the blue, Hattie milked, "what's your take, Roger?"

Unable to resist the fortune to send up the egghead chatter, he ostentatiously retorted, "oh, it's definitely poetic gorgeousness made flesh."

"Very lyrical, Roger," Charlotte lauded. "Most unlike you."

"Oh, I'm a man of inestimable proficiency in these essays," he artificially bragged.

Radiating, Hattie complimented, "very impressive."

"I was actually aiming to be derisory," he muttered under his breath.

"What did you say?" Charlotte brusquely solicited.

Ever survival prudent, Roger tattled, "I said, hadn't we better continue with the tour?"

~ * ~

Lunchtime came and went with the Frasers gorging on hamburger and sausage baps washed down with weaker than weak tea. Sold at such astronomically inflated prices, Roger offered to take one hawker public on the London Stock Exchange with a winning IPO, breeding a debate about prices in general and how to justify them in particular.

"The price," Roger certified, "is the count it is sold at under prevailing market conditions, the value is whatever it is worth to the seller. Quite often, the two have nothing to do with each other."

"So, what you're saying," Wendy shortened, "is the pricing of goods and services is determined by market coefficients, additional to cost recovery and profit."

"Quite right. All commodities are currency valued depending on whether the market is saturated or hungry. What sold at say £15.50 per share in a rising bull's market, might well sink to as little as £2.50 in a falling bear's market. It's all about perception, confidence and risk."

"That parallels some of the things you taught us in the A-level business studies evening classes," she rendered.

"Exactly, and it's the same with fast food vendors, as we have seen here today. Corner the market with franchise limitations eliminating open competition, congregate the punters into a confined space, and the unit price rises. Put those same pedlars into high streets crammed full of McDonalds and Burger Kings, and watch their prices drop through the floor."

"*Huh*," Charlotte taunted, "isn't that the foundation of capitalist economics?"

"Precisely, my darling, precisely," Roger answered, ignoring her disdainful dismissal.

"Yes…well," she ticketed, "really makes the proposition for State ownership in all things, doesn't it?"

"*Charlotte*, such an incendiary remark is blasphemy," her husband scolded. "Don't let Lady Macbeth hear you saying things like that."

"Well, these people at the tech might have a legitimate perspective with their left of centre teachings, and my mother could be downright wrong."

"Do you want to tell her, or should I?"

"Neither of us," she argued. "Lady Macbeth, as you so indelicately call her, is way past reviewing notions of progressive political ideals, let alone a seed change in the country's economic strategy."

"You might consider your friend Hattie and others of her ilk couldn't lead their denizen lifestyles, enjoying the finer things in life, by way of illustration - art, music, hitchhiking, camping, and insulting those they perceive to be their intellectual inferiors, if not for the sterling efforts of wealth creators, and people in the private sector paying galactic volumes of tax to feather-bed their world and fund their life choices."

Biting her tongue, she spewed, "I *knew* you'd say something like that."

~ * ~

Still in pursuit of more items to add to their inventories, the Frasers moved on to the residue of the antiques fair. Ancillary to Georgian, Victorian and early twentieth century furniture, fine art paintings, sculptures and ceramic craftsmanship, country antique fairs also attracted some of the more bizarre *objet d'art*, counting weird concoctions of supposedly medieval wood carvings, brass and pewter ware, and even inaugural metal farming implements.

Spurred on by their curiosity to ask a merchant about a rustic hoe, an engraved loom, or a brass plate depicting the tragic story of John Barleycorn, Roger and Charlotte could get distracted for an inordinate magnitude of cycles. Rather than the sophistication of hand-painted Moorcroft, exquisitely turned Waterford Crystal and Staffordshire's finest, even the children found more interest in these oddball items.

Attracted by a mixture of traditional antiques and the more rugged examples of English heritage country craft, they stopped by one such enormous stall to pour over a nineteenth century cart, straight out of Hardy's *Far from the Madding Crowd*.

"It's the great Miss Havisham of Wiltshire," the vendor revealed, "still dressed up in its finery, but withdrawn from the world."

"Has it ever been used?"

"No," he confirmed.

"I see. Why?"

"Originally, a country squire bought it, not as a conveyance, but as a leisurely carriage to serenade his intended."

"What happened?"

"Legend has it, his bride-to-be jilted him for another man, the cart eternally stored in a barn and never used, hence the 'Miss Havisham' tag."

"How did you come by it?"

"The squire's current descendants recently sold off a lot of their land for housing and light industrial developments, inclusive of the barn housing this old beauty."

"And you bought it?"

"Yes, at an auction."

Conjuring up visions of hay cart rides through Hazelwood with Charlotte, their children and various friends, and also sauntering to Kappa Corinthians in Farnborough under horse-power, Roger became drawn to the relic.

"What do you think, Charlotte?" he keenly grilled.

"What do I think?" she imitated. "What do I think about what?"

Outlining his vision to her, he painted pictures of the pair of them trotting through Kent's country lanes under a blazing sun, with James functioning as their horse and carriage driver.

"We could loan a horse from Cruella," he enthused. "Er, Brigit Hammond, and—"

Raising a hand, she cut him off. "You must be joking." Stepping forward, she assayed his physiognomy. Recognising his plea to be genuine, she cackled, "you *cannot* be serious."

For a moment, Roger fantasised John McEnroe had addressed him. "The ball hit the line, chalk flew up," he mocked.

"*What*?" she barked, perplexed even more by her husband's sudden excursion into the rustic charms of yesteryear English country life. "Have you lost your marbles, Roger?" Confounded, she shook her head, a sure presage of more denigration to come. "You must have been staring at Constable's *The Hay Wain* for too long, and it's become indelibly stamped on your psyche."

"Please, no psycho-babble today," he pleaded.

"Taking sunlight or even moonlight in Manhattan type trips in a horse and cart is not on my dance card for this season, and presumably you'd have to stack the cart with hay for effect?"

"Of course," he merited, all wide-eyed and innocent, but consummately failing to comprehend his wife's obvious abhorrence of being conveyed around Hazelwood, plough-girl style.

"It's hardly in-keeping with village social aspirations, *is it*?"

"Oh, I'm not so sure," Roger thwarted. "The area is festooned with nags at the weekends. Where's your sense of adventure?" Rubbernecking the kids, he ticketed, "what about it?"

"Hhmm, very romantic," Wendy conceded.

"I thought you'd given Sly the burly heave-ho," her father purported.

"Oh, I'm not envisioning him," she betokened.

"What?" Roger gibbered. "You don't mean you have another beau in mind, do you?"

"Well, I'm scoping someone, or rather he has his scope on me."

Alarmed, Roger canvassed, "he's not at the LSE, is he?"

"Oh, no," Wendy guaranteed.

"Thank god," Roger blathered, relief bursting out of him. "We'll revisit your latest paramour later." Tapping James' upper arm, he requisitioned, "how about it, son?"

"Sounds good to me, Dad. We could play Ben Hur having chariot races, and—"

Roger waved a dismissive hand. "Yes, yes, that's plenty," he interjected, "not quite what I intended." Bending down to scrutinise his youngest daughter, he earnestly supplicated, "what do you think, Heather?"

Gawping up at her father she scouted, "does this mean I can have a horse as a pet?"

"Yes…*no*," Roger quibbled. "It's not what I intended either."

"See what you've done now, Roger," his wife scolded. "You've really put the cat among the pigeons."

Frowning, he insisted, "well it's better than putting the cart before the horse!"

Chapter 16: Monica Lewinsky and the Fatherland

As part of a company-wide initiative to go after the hindmost strands of EU investment in Ireland before the Euro crashed down and disintegrated, VP Worldwide Manufacturing Investments, Milton Crossman, also known as Mad Milton, a mover and shaker from The Firm's New York HQ was coming to London. Reputedly as tough as a rhino's hide, Crossman had a reputation as a bare-knuckle, backstreet, squabble-buster and a Rambo incarnate one-man, killing machine when it came to closing deals in the stock market trading zone. Acclaimed to be a super-badass, he'd been rejected for a role in *The Sopranos*, after commenting everyone from New Jersey played around like pussies compared to those hailing from Brooklyn, and hard man James Gandolfini's portrayal of mobster Tony Soprano resembled Donald Duck playing Donald Trump.

To those in the know, and not in the slightest influenced by rose-tinted politicians' pronouncements, the days of the Euro, a piece of politically constructed expediency without economic foundation, were numbered. Unless German taxpayers could be persuaded to fund the government excesses of most of their co-Euro members, inevitably those countries with toxic sovereign debt would default on their gigantic loans. Before the fatal catastrophe happened, there were still opportunities for investors, Ireland specifically receiving a massive cash injection, principally from the World Bank and the EU, to be channelled to the markets through the banks.

Dan Lebowski recommended to Mad Milton he made Roger Fraser part of the Ireland team, Crossman telephoning the stock analyst while still in the Big Apple on the pretext of discussing the endeavour, but really, he wanted a favour.

"Lebowski gave you a glowing reference after his visit to London a few months ago to size up the global futures forecast," Crossman praised after initial introductions.

"Yes, I got to know Dan quite well."

"We'll talk about my mission in detail when we meet, but er…there is a spectacle I'd appreciate you setting up in advance."

"Oh, what?"

"'I've always wanted to go to your Houses of Parliament, to see the founding father of American democracy in action. Can you get me in?"

"I can get you into a PQT session" Fraser advised.

"*PQT*," Crossman echoed. "Hell, it's the very picture of a woman's complaint!"

"Yes, a lot of people get it mixed up with PMS. Often its impact is much the same."

"So, what is this PQT, Roger?"

"Prime Minister's Question Time. It's the best show in town. Much better than anything in West End theatre, maybe even Broadway. I'm sure you'll be absorbed."

"Wow, some build up. Can't wait for it."

Albeit usually useless to the fringe of chronic ineptitude, remarkably, Fraser arranged for passes through his intellect-limited, everything must be dumbed down to my level, local MP, enabling Milton Crossman to fulfil his Houses of Parliament ambition, with the stock analyst come trouble-shooter acting as his host.

~ * ~

Tasked by Henry Jacques with working out a stratagem for meeting with various business partners and potential clients in Dublin, Fraser screened all the bases. Moreover, Toby Chalcroft declared his individual set of instructions to Fraser, saying in spite of the attractiveness of the investment possibility, caution was needed because, as he put it, 'The bog trotters are very capable of pulling the wool. Don't get fooled by their lilting voices, protestations Ireland is a poor country, and they're babes in the wood when it comes to investment mechanisms.' Having former business tastes of the Emerald Isle, he squarely knew what Top Cat referred to.

Extra to Fraser, Ricky Henshaw formed The Firm's English cohort along with Bradley Purnell, a kind of young gofer from Bembridge's suite, still wet behind the ears and naive to the borderline of wanting to give him a slap. Also the Ayatollah's nephew, any wrangle apropos his inclusion on the team became negated. 'This trip will give Bradley exposure to the mechanics of investment banking,' Bembridge told Henshaw and Fraser, really meaning, he's going with you, so let's have no arguments.

Still rampant in the financial services industry worldwide, notably in the upper-middle management to board executive stratums, nepotism had become the channel for the less naturally gifted to find their way into the ranks of power and responsibility. Never ceasing to surprise Fraser just how many young women, or come to that young men he met during the course of his duties, betided as someone's little darling or son and heir, he had stationed the custom as *de facto* practice. Those with unassailable abilities for making money presupposed the talent to be in the genes and thereby inherited by succeeding generations. Attempting to preserve family kudos and reputation, the self-serving nepotism apparatus came into play as a means to artificially inflate the skills-deficient offspring's position. Often, it eventuated to be a massive fantasy, the family member under survey about as useful as a spare prick at a wedding.

Largely falling into this category, whilst willing, Purnell neither fitted the part for customer facing obligations; to many seasoned campaigners, half the battle, significantly in 1-0-1 meetings, nor possessed the nous to really take in the intricacies and subtleties of investment banking, much less the idiosyncrasies of money markets. Gaining a degree in accountancy from one of the lesser halls of knowledge, cosmetically elevated to university status by President Blair to realise his fifty percent of all young people should go to university codswallop, Purnell materialised at The Firm pumped up for duty.

As Fraser specified to attendees at the A-level business studies supplementary evening classes, a higher education qualification only represented the first rung on a very tall fulfilment ladder. Merely a stepping stone, it enabled those attaining the required grades in examination excellence to be awarded a first degree, and thereby the mandate to join the real world of business. Some made the transition very well, seamlessly blending in and quickly finding their feet. Others faltered, unable to cross the boundary between lecture theatre theory and business convention. Sadly, Purnell fell into this latter group.

Soon finding his inadequate antenna abided insensitive to receiving 'Money never sleeps' feeds to quote Gordon Gekko, some unkind observers declared, 'You can't make a silk purse out of a sow's ear.' Consequently, he fled to his Uncle Luther's office, finding sanctuary in the post of glorified office boy.

Despite all his short-comings, Fraser had a soft spot for him, perceiving Bembridge's sister might have coerced him into giving her son a chance that he probably didn't want anyway, but acquiesced to his mother's desires.

Because the opening held pan-European wide status, The Firm's German organisation in Frankfurt insisted they were part of the Dublin bound team, meaning Obergruppenführer Heinrich Metzer, Director of Manufacturing Investments for the German-speaking parts of Europe, an ex-professor in psychopharmacology at Heidelberg University before joining The Firm in 2002, qualified as one of Fraser's cardinal preoccupations. Not the most discreet of gentlemen, Metzer inclined to bluster without first engaging his brain in delicate involvements, his sensibilities failing to register slippery climates as they developed, or more seriously, he crossed the line causing waves with his, no nonsense, 'we're doing it the German way' approach.

When it came to the undiluted intolerance of anything he attested flew in the face of the approved agenda, and therefore needed irrevocable deletion from the record, Heiny baby could even give Charlotte a run for her money. Though less than fifty, Metzer had an old-school background commencing from the cradle, very old school when it came to hierarchical respect and operational disciplines. Gathering his team together in Frankfurt, the Obergruppenführer invariably veered to the brink of saying, 'Und I vont to hear von click, ven you stand to attention as I enter.'

A terror even by The Firm's New York paradigms, his intolerant reputation bordering on the tyrannical went before him. Discerning even a semi-veiled quail of criticism apposite to his methods, he could give offending subordinates nightmares for weeks on end, ultimately spelling an end to their careers at The Firm. Accordingly, most people were exhaustively careful not to incur his rage. If under bouts of extreme anger, Luther Bembridge possessed the capability to metamorphose into a dangerous lizard, his intent to devour those annoying him, Metzer had evolved into just as hazardous a beast to do battle with, and withdraw unscathed. Many envisaged that beyond the realms of his executive suite in downtown Frankfurt, lay a torture chamber. In their popular imagination, Metzer took tremendous delight in meticulously dissecting those having the misfortune to be selected for rectal scrutiny experiments, resultant from incurring his displeasure.

Some claimed he descended from one of Hitler's elite clique, his forefathers having managed to reinvent themselves and elude detection by British Nazi hunters after World War Two. Convenient folklore, it became an attempt to give rationality to Heiny's vicious nature. In truth, he might have read *Mein Kampf*, and in the darkest recesses of his creepy Bavarian schloss, dressed up as an SS officer replete with the Iron Cross to re-enact scenes from *The Night Porter* and *Cabaret*, but beyond those unproven narcissistic fantasies, his sadistic disposition and often brutal temperament came from within. Vaunting a clinical deportment, he never raised his voice, lost control, or let slip emotion; things he deemed to be weaknesses and thereby strictly avoided. Transfixing people as if by levitation, his menace really came from the way he peered at them, and the subsequent grisly, teeth-grinding tone of whatever he imparted to make his victims quiver into jelly.

Metzer believed in doing it by numbers. Rotate the wheel in the prescribed manner, and out will pop the investment. Stipulating the methodology be adopted by his investment fund team without exchange, since inauguration, unmistakably it had delivered the goods in Metzer's assigned territory, the big cheese at Frankfurt sanctioning dispersal of his method-driven drill to other revenue-bearing departments. Whence, it became rolled out and implemented across all the German-speaking countries, echoing a Panzer division let loose to subdue and quell all resistance.

~ * ~

Arriving in London charged up and ready for combat, Mad Milton wanted to do the Houses of Parliament gig without delay. Dissimilar to ravished and burnt-out after four decades in investment banking Dan Lebowski, for a man in his late fifties Crossman preserved a relatively unblemished outer shell. Not quite fire-proof, he did however have a confident, self-assured comportment about him, only coming from a mammoth amount of prosperity in whatever he had been commissioned to accomplish by The Firm, and his previous employers.

Fetching up his CV on The Firm's intranet channel, Fraser discovered Crossman's achievements were pretty much unsurpassed. Whether he had always verged on the crazy to fulfil his given objectives, hence his Mad Milton tag, or the craziness had developed over eons of flying by the seat of his pants, became hard to figure out.

Meeting him *mano a mano*, Fraser could not divine why the New Yorker had become even remotely tarnished with the 'less than normally sane' brush. Irrefutably, his demeanour bordered on the brusque with those he considered to be his underlings, and he emanated an aura suggesting impenetrable resolution of absolute belief in his capabilities. Howbeit, beyond the bravado he appeared to be a standard issue, Big Apple heavy hitter, not in the slightest Tonto or needing a straight-jacket. Banking he'd see a different side to the beast when competitive circumstances prevailed, Fraser knew under battle conditions bullpen mentality pervaded all on the buy and sell side of investment banking, Crossman no exception.

Responding to his supplication, Fraser had emailed him about the next PQT, the VP crossing the pond the prior day. After doing his fearsome inspection tour of The Firm's London troops the next morning, and in the process infuriating Luther Bembridge to the precipice of having to be checked by Toby Chalcroft from throttling the formidable New Yorker, Crossman and Fraser headed to Westminster.

During their taxi ride, he quizzed Fraser about the frame of mind in the London bullpen.

"Has there been much alteration in dealer attitudes since Dan Lebowski enacted his futures scorched earth policy?"

"Some," Fraser attributed. "After Dan went through them consonant to a dose of salts, I did spot an upturn in centralising behaviours in line with the prescribed sales strategy, coupled to transaction compliance. Unambiguously, the rate of foul-ups has dropped off dramatically, markedly amongst the Essex boy-trader ring."

"Hhmm, it's been the same in the Americas and Asia-Pacific. The sub-prime debt and casino banking easy street outlook has waned. We're regrouping to the bedrock of solid traditional investment banking strategies and tactics."

"MIFID 2 will be the underlying equaliser," Fraser avowed, "because remarkably, some anal traders saw the earlier MIFID 1 edict as the Holy Grail, almost fetishising about financial instruments, as if they were icons of rare antiquity. Never the inclination of the Markets in Financial Instruments Directive, in practice, it's a concrete baseline to ensure regulation compliance, topmost after the Lehman's meltdown, but it should not be used to excuse frailties in innovation."

"Yes, I agree. MIFID has been used by some as a get out clause when they fail to secure agreements, but I don't buy into such lame pretexts. Lebowski's doctrine takes full account of MIFID 1 and 2 in their execution, so there can be no excuses."

"Sometimes I dream up an admiration of the ridiculous is

required to make it in the analysts' profession," Fraser argued. "It's bad enough having to work with Essex boy bullpen drones and zombies, but what gets me most of all is some of them fantasise they are financial geniuses, and god's gift to investment banking. But they know very little, Milton. Most of them still reckon cyberspace is the layer between the atmosphere and outer space."

Breaking into a hearty laugh, Crossman tapped Fraser on the arm. "I must remember that one."

"Sometimes I hear stupefying snapshots of their conversations, as I pass by the bullpen. For instance, 'He's the player in the white shirt with the white stripes', or 'Is he still alive?', the riposte, 'He was the last time I saw him.'" Stopping to let his stinging indictment sink in with the New Yorker, he then mocked, "real brainy, intellectual stuff."

"Yes, we have the same problem with some of the dealers from Queens and the Bronx. Apart from their Seersucker or should it be 'cocksucker' suits, and sculptured haircuts used to impress clients, they have very little between the ears in terms of innate common sense and wit."

"Don't get me wrong," Fraser hedged, "I'm an impassioned advocate of the meritocracy system, the best and most able put into vital stations, as opposed to socially engineered PC quotas culminating in mediocrities running the shop. But talent must be coupled to at least a modicum of traditional empathy for the protocol presumptions of any given institution or industry. Without the prerequisite, those saying there's been a plebification of London's square mile over the past thirty years, might just have a point."

"In the Big Apple, we call it the changing effect in the zeitgeist."

"How do you mean?"

"When I hit Wall Street, if someone had made a blunder, or worst still lied about it and been found out, they invariably admitted their guilt. Today, when say a broker bends the rules and tries to pull the wool, and his manager asks, 'Why did you lie to me?', habitually the response is, 'Because I didn't want you to find out!', meaning they judged they could cut and run with it. This Persian bazaar style of selling is the reason why

MIFID came about. Before regulation, no one reconnoitered for elephant traps because managers had so many time constraints, they couldn't audit every trade for validity and compliance. Automated compliance applications went a long way to pulling shady trades by exception, but they're by no means fool-proof when confronted with a tricky trader, if you take my meaning."

"It's my experience as well, and in all frankness, the executive and board layers have played their parts in creating the present-day mess in financial services. Too much blue-sky thinking and helicopter vision has overridden dependable business principles. I've often tallied it ought to be the other way around, with due observance for sagacity and governance superseding flaky theorems."

"Oh, don't get me going on that bugbear, Roger," Crossman beseeched. "Collegiate policy fostered by bull-brain colonels has been responsible for more screw-ups than any infantile misdemeanours perpetrated by lamebrain brokers. In the US, these paragons of cloistered naivety are deferentially known as The Sons of Baltimore…more like the sons of bitches, as far as I'm concerned."

"Quite."

~ * ~

After making themselves comfortable in the House of Commons public gallery, Crossman and Fraser regarded the chamber below as the members assembled. Making various statements *vis-à-vis* the state of play in the British economy and updating the House on the current Euro-crisis, David Cameron covered the nation's business of the day before the speaker announced Prime Minister's Question Time, and the real tableau got underway.

"Who's the dude speechifying now?" Crossman tabled.

"Ed Miliband, the Leader of the Opposition, also known as Ed Miligeek."

"Emphatically, he has the guise of a geek," he decried, "and sounds like a deranged Muppet."

"Yes. Recently he had surgery on his nose, to make him sound less like a Muppet."

"Hasn't been successful, has it?"

"Apparently not," Fraser conceded.

"And I presume the geek manifestation is permanent?"

"I'm afraid so, unless he has a head transplant."

Leaning over the rail partition to gain an improved angle on the Government benches, Crossman queried, "who's the chubby fop waving his hands around, a few places away from Cameron?"

Focusing in the given direction, Fraser elicited, "Patrick McLoughlin. He's the Chief Whip. Sounds kinky, doesn't it?"

Glinting a jaundiced emission at Fraser, Mad Milton disparaged, "he replicates a crazed cop directing traffic at a downtown baseball game."

"He's actually burdened with marshalling loyalty for the Government from back benchers. It's why it's called the chief whip."

"Mmmm. I'm not sure the folks on Capitol Hill could cut loose with the job title chief whip. Correlates as distinctly dubious and un-American."

"Quite," Fraser shrewdly obliged.

Scanning further around the chamber, Crossman polled, "why are those cleaning ladies sitting amongst the members?"

"What cleaning ladies, where?" Fraser refuted.

"Over there," he replied, betokening the opposition benches, "behind the geek."

"They're not cleaning ladies, they're the latest generation of Labour Party babe MPs."

"*Jesus*, they're dressed the same as Michelle Obama," he observed. "The opposite of her sharp-dressed husband, she dresses like a field hand. New York were shocked when she met your Queen dressed in a cardigan, instead of a smart ladies' suit or dress." Shaking his head, still used-up in disbelief at Michelle's appalling frumpy fashion, he affixed, "besides, I understood your lady members of Parliament all wore chic Missus Thatcher dubbed suits."

"Oh, it's still partially true," Fraser acceded. "If you peruse the Government back benches, you'll see some of the lady members are attired in the Lady Thatcher mode."

Rising in his seat, Crossman spied in the direction indicated. "Oh, yeah, they're Thatcher dolls, aren't they?"

"Ha, ha, ha," Fraser laughed under his voice. "Very good, Milton."

"By the way," he flattered, "I actually like the Irishman."

"Irishman?" Fraser parroted, not catching on.

"Yeah, the Pres. With the name O-bama, he must hail from the Emerald Isle." Scintillating extravagantly, he counselled, "we could use the heritage tag to good effect with the bog trotters we're going to see."

"Ha, ha, very funny again, Milton. You'd go down a gas on *Letterman*. But I agree, I get the affection Obama is very personable, a lot more so than say, Newt Gingridge."

"*Ahh*, Newt's a pussy cat," Crossman argued. "He looks like a pugnacious bulldog with a bug up his ass, even downright ugly, but believe me, behind the scenes, he's as soft as the rest of the pussies on Capitol Hill."

"Hhmm, given the choice, I'd still elect to go for a beer with the Irishman, as you call him."

"Right," Crossman agreed. Studying proceedings below, someone else drew his curiosity. "Who's the guy giving your Prime Minister heat?"

"Dennis Skinner, known as the Beast of Bolsover."

"You don't say." Viewing again, he complimented, "ballsy little bastard, isn't he?"

"Dennis has quirkiness, and like Frank Field, another Labour Party MP veteran, he's one of the few trustworthy members on either side of the chamber."

"These Labour Party MPs seem to appeal to you," Crossman implied. "I rationalised being a man from the city, you'd be a conservative."

"I used to be, but now I don't lend my patronage to any party flag."

"All as bad as each other, eh?"

"Huh, undoubtedly."

"I hope you won't mind me saying this, Roger," Crossman prequalified, "but it's er...it's a lot more aggressive than our House of Representatives and the Senate. Their brethren tend to be more genteel and courteous to each other, at least in formal sessions. Your boys and girls use the House of Commons as a forum for mudslinging."

"Hence why I told you during our telecom, it's the best show in town. You couldn't get better distraction on Shaftesbury Avenue or any of the outlying London theatres. This is pure play drama and comedy, equalling any Oscar Wild satire or J.B Priestley tragedy, and...it's all free of charge."

"Yep, I begin to see what you mean," he approved, tuning into the spectacle.

"It's still mightily Machiavellian though," Fraser clarified. "The cut and thrust of British politics is as bloody and barbarous as any to be found on God's green Earth."

"Yes," Crossman assented, surveying the clowns and jugglers in the chamber vying for deliberation from Mister Speaker. "There's quite a lot of shady characters down there, doubtless they have more fronts than The Joker in *Batman*."

"An astute and very true observation. These days, honour, integrity and loyalty to the people are redundant concepts in British politics. Gone are the glories of Churchill and his vast legacy. It has been replaced by what you colonials, er excuse me, Americans, call carpetbaggers, and we call political opportunists. They are out for themselves, and don't really give a damn about England's future, irrespective of what colour flag they fly."

"I see," he corroborated with a weighty permanence. "It's the same in the States. Arguably, FDR endures as the ultimate president to authentically exemplify traditional American values, and Eleanor Roosevelt the last first-lady we could tag to be American royalty, though Jackie Kennedy also fits very snugly into the same illustrious bag.

Eisenhower tarried as a robust, if unspectacular pair of safe hands to carry the torch, and Kennedy transcribed as really good before he succumbed to the assassin's bullet, but since we've had a series of false prophets and shysters." Seeing more parallels in Washington, Fraser's scathing condemnation of British politics really hit home with Crossman. "Of course," he labelled, "the same as in your political structure, neither Republicans nor Democrats can really count on their own kind. Back stabbing has morphed into a type of normalised and expected weekly event on the steps of Capitol Hill, making Brutus's attack on Caesar seem tame."

"Doesn't jolt me. It's *ad modem* the story of the newly appointed junior minister promoted from the back benches to the front bench. He says to an infinitely more accustomed colleague, 'So that's the enemy', denoting across the chamber. His more practised collaborator replies, 'No, that's the Opposition, the enemy is behind you.'"

"*Holy shit*, Roger," Crossman spat in a raised voice, "our business is babes in the wood territory compared to politics."

"I agree. The tally of rogues and charlatans down there," he chronicled, sighting the chamber, "must account for at least two-thirds of the 650 MPs, and the proportion multiplies at every election."

"Well, over the past twenty years our framework has had its own fair share of con-artists," Crossman confessed with surly gills.

"You must be talking about Clinton," Fraser mooted.

"*Clinton!*" the American repeated in a loud voice.

"Sssshh," he accosted, raising a finger to his mouth. "You'll be giving the Labour Party leadership a heart stopping moment, if they hear his name."

Sure enough, when Fraser stared down into the chamber, he found Ed Miliband, Ed Balls and Harriet 'Harperson' scowling at him.

Lowering his voice, Crossman demanded, "don't mention that draft dodging, womanising, double-dealing, son of a bitch to me. He made the Oval Office into a kind of fraternity house for his liberal elitists. TV made a series about it called *The West Wing*, and…he came down heavy on Wall Street, using us as a scapegoat for his failed fiscal policies, an unforgivable act of leaden betrayal and viperous duplicity. The man is a lying, deceitful, conniving, treacherous *bastard*."

"Mmmm," Fraser propped. "And they are his good points."

"Boy," Mad Milton enthused, "it'd give me a wealth of gratification to take a buggy whip to that philanderer."

"Evidently," he whispered, tongue-in-cheek, "Monica Lewinsky voted Republican after her affair with Clinton, saying the Democrats had left a bad taste in her mouth."

Staring at Fraser perplexed, Crossman suddenly caught on to the joke. "Oh, I get it. Very good, Roger."

"She's a bit of a porker, so I could never see the attraction. On the other hand, Gennifer Flowers is a real fox. Very, very attractive."

"Yeah, but Clinton did it with anything having a heartbeat." Hesitating, he prudently qualified, "I guess we all adore young women, but we also credit the President of the United States to show some Goddamn restraint with his pecker."

"Here's one you'll revel in," Fraser promulgated. "Bill Clinton and Al Gore go into a Washington diner for lunch. As they read the menu, the waitress comes over and asks Clinton, 'Are you ready to order?' Clinton takes a gander at the shapely waitress and says, 'Yes, I want a quickie.' 'A quickie!?' the waitress disputed. 'Sir, given the controversial health of your personal life, it's not a good idea. I'll come back when you're ready to order from the menu.' Gore clocks her walk off then leans over to Clinton and says, 'Bill, it's pronounced, quiche.'"

"*Hah!*" Crossman shrieked, his aspect lighting up. "Dan Lebowski said you were apt to crack a good joke." Stopping, he turned dark again. "Gore is another son of a bitch who brought the White House into disrepute. Do you know, the trendy liberals call him Saint Al for all his do-gooder proclamations? The man makes me sick. He knows he can't deliver on any of his holier-than-thou green schemes, and making films to con the gullible young into trusting his bull is just plain, irresponsible, dogma-loaded propaganda, designed to scare and justify eye-popping taxation levels."

Recalling a confab from the family's summer tour, Fraser

quipped, "my cousin Barry might agree with you there."

"Well, Gore is so sanctimonious," Crossman criticised. "I can't abide liars and cheats, *par example* Gore and Clinton, especially when they use their potency to spread disinformation, and use White House security to conceal their sins."

"Have you heard the one about Hilary's revenge?" Fraser explored.

"No, but I'm sure I'm going to enjoy it."

"Bill Clinton steps out on the White House lawn in the dead of winter. Ahead, he sees, 'The President must go,' written in urine across the snow. Well, old Bill is pretty ticked off. He storms into his security office HQ, and says, 'Somebody wrote a threat about me in the snow, and they did it in urine. Son of a bitch had to be standing right on the porch when he did it.' The security guys stay silent, ashamedly staring at the floor. Bill hollers, 'Well dammit, don't just sit there. Get out and find out who did it. I want an answer, and I want it tonight.' The entire security staff goes to work on Bill's instructions. During the evening, his chief security officer sidles up to him and says, 'We have some bad news.' Clearly embarrassed, he pauses then adds, 'And we have some really bad news. Which do you want first?' Clinton says, 'Oh hell, give me the bad news.' The officer says, 'Well, we took a sample of the urine and tested it. Winds up being Al Gore's urine.' Clinton yells, 'Mother fucking son of a bitch, I feel so betrayed. My own Vice President. Well, what's the really bad news?' The officer replies, 'Well sir, it's in Hillary's handwriting.'"

"Haaa, ha, ha, ha…ha, ha," Crossman frothed. "Really good, Roger. It illustrates Clinton's mendacity is only superseded by his hypocrisy. What a bounder as you English might say."

"Oh, bounder underplays his mischievousness. There are much stronger words appropriate to describing him."

"Such as?"

"Cuthbert Ulysses Norman Trollope."

~ * ~

Later in the day, Metzer landed at Canary Wharf to get into sync with the Irish showdown strategy. A cross between the sinister Major Arnold Toht in *Raiders of the Lost Ark* and Colonel Hans Landa from *Inglourious Basterds*, he remained just as Fraser memorised from foregoing Anglo-German encounters. He even wore a monocle and had a weakness for leather and lederhosen, further cementing the Germanic comic figure archetype.

"Gut afternoon, Herr Fraser," he bayed, almost clicking his heels and breaking into a Nazi salute.

Put him in a wheelchair, the stock analyst imagined, and you've got a dead ringer for Doctor Strangelove incarnate.

"*Guten tag*," Fraser courteously reciprocated.

"Ah, alvays ze diplomat," Metzer felicitated. "But ve vill need to verk on your accent a little, if you are to get by in ze fatherland, er, I mean Germany."

Persevering with the bridge building, and staying with what little German he understood, Fraser enquired, "*Wie Ihr von Frankfurt zu Ende Flug war?*"

"Ah…you are soliciting how vas my flight over from Frankfurt," Metzer voiced, unashamedly touched by the Englishman's attempt to make him feel welcome. "Lufthansa flights are alveys un time," he stipulated. "Zhat is vhy I alveys fly with zem."

"We've booked you into the South Quay Square Hilton for tonight, where Milton Crossman is also staying," Fraser communicated.

"Excellent," Metzer proclaimed. "Vith zhat magnitude of efficiency, you must have German blood coursing through your veins?"

"I'm afraid not, Heinrich," he illuminated. "I'm pure bred English, the product of at least six generation's heritage."

"Don't vorry, Roger," Metzer sympathised. "No von is perfect."

Continuing in German from Fraser and English from Metzer, the give-and-take ensued encapsulating more logistics.

Lastly, Fraser enquired if the business trip would give the German pleasure. "*Gibt es ihnen vergnügen, ihren finger Ihr arsch zu durchstechen?*"

Puzzled, Metzer posed, "are you really asking me, if schiking my finger up my arse gives me pleasure?"

"Ah, something lost in translation there, Heinrich," Fraser uncloaked with more than a hint of discomfort at both the association and the *faux pas*. "Please accept my sincere apologies."

"Like I said," Metzer reaffirmed with an air of growing superiority, "no von is perfect."

~ * ~

Mustering the Dublin bound troops together for a conclusive briefing in one of The Firm's executive meeting rooms, Fraser made the necessary introductions, Crossman taking an immediate dislike to Bradley Purnell.

"So, Brad," he sneeringly grouched, "you're one of Bembridge's bum-boys?"

"Yes…I mean no, Mister Crossman," Purnell gabbled. "Mister Bembridge is my uncle."

"*Oh*, a touch of nepotism, hey," he censured before issuing him a decimating stare. "Makes your position even less tenable."

Not replying, Mad Milton's vitriolic remark heightened Purnell's embarrassment in the company of his seniors.

"And, what's your role in this enterprise?" Crossman examined.

"I'm to observe what's going on, and execute duties at Mister Fraser's discretion."

"Just along for the ride then, hey?"

Residing tight-lipped, Purnell's antennae told him the New Yorker was not exactly his *numero uno* fan.

"Hhmm," Crossman grievously uttered. "Just keep your mouth shut in the meetings." He leant forward imparting foreboding ruin. "*Clear?*"

"Yes, Mister Crossman."

Unexpected and unprepared for, Fraser realised Mad Milton's

reputation for being intolerant of anything not to his liking could surface out of nowhere. Clearly capable of making the most intemperate remarks, he cerebrated how the American might react to some of the unorthodox whimsies of doing business in Ireland, his biting attack on Purnell contrasting sharply with the gracious funster, who only hours earlier had been such genial company at the House of Commons. Unaware of any historical impasse between Bembridge and Crossman, Fraser put his mood transformation down to not liking a junior player on the Dublin bound team.

To some extent soulmates, Ricky Henshaw had always got on very well with Heinrich Metzer, compatible regimes for handling delinquent brokers forging not quite a brothers-in-arms cabal, but more a despots-in-arms connection. Often Metzer gave his counterpart tips on effective disciplining, and his latest casehardened methods for making sure the Frankfurt team were always attuned to his brain patterns.

"You know, Ricky," Metzer cooed in his usual icily cold, brooding voice, "vot really is persuasive to maximise performance is ze *fear* of failure, und vot zhat vill mean for a trader's future career. It is vot I play on all ze time to make sure ze traders are always maxed out."

"Must drive them to the brink of breakdown?" Henshaw proposed.

"Oh, yes, but, zhere is a plentiful supply of villing candidates to take ze place of those collapsing over zheir trading screens. Ve, er, take zem down, und replace vith another dealer."

Startled, Henshaw squawked, "*really*! I'm not sure we could circumvent that in England, EU Human Rights Laws seeing the perpetrator in court."

"Ah, zeese EU dictats alveys get in ze vey of effective management methods," Metzer moaned. "In ze fatherland, er, I mean in Germany, ve make all ze right noises about compliance with EU laws, but—" Desisting, a sinister smile developed across his kisser. "Ve have vays around zhem."

"Mmmm," Henshaw murmured. "We tend to obsequiously comply with EU regulations and laws. I find it vexing, because no other country in the EU does the same."

Rubbernecking Crossman, the German catechized, "how is it for you in ze mothership, Milton? Does ze firm adhere to all of Uncle Zam's edicts in New York?"

Smiling, his own fractious philosophy naturally gravitating towards the direction of Metzer's thrust, he elucidated, "in the US, we have experimented with all kinds of incentivising packages to accomplish trader maximum fulfilment. Some ordain huge bonus's make for optimum discharge, but as you say, fear of failure or being tarnished with that brush is definitely a career limiter. Dealers know any black spots on their CV cogently means they are out of the game."

Jesum crow, Fraser conjectured*, this is the same as eavesdropping on a bunch of megalomaniacs, preparing their final solution for world domination.*

Signalling to gain their absorption, he prescribed in his usual clement business voice, "gentlemen, let's spend some cycles going over our strategy and schedule for the Dublin trip."

Going through each of the planned meetings, the team visioned out the pros and cons of the potential investments, then ran over specific strategies safeguarding an auspicious position for The Firm.

Gifting corporation tax breaks to businesses for the past twenty years, as a means of creating jobs and bolstering the economy, the Irish Government esteemed they were on a winner, the migration of blue chip sized companies' European operations to Dublin booming. Amongst the new arrivals were telecoms manufacturer Baker Finch, Wellman Enterprises, a player in the off-shore petro-carbons exploration market, one of the world's largest suppliers of electric machines, Kaufmann Vogel Electric, and Dresdner Fuchs, a specialist in rolling stock and locomotives. All Firm targets, the latter two were of German origin, hence the Obergruppenführer's inclusion on The Firm's team.

Taking advantage of the tax breaks, companies channelled revenues from as many of their worldwide production sites into Dublin as trans-continental company laws allowed. Some used Ireland as an assembly and distribution centre, but the expansive bulk of baseline manufacturing dwelt in other parts of Europe and the Far East. Hence, most of the jobs created were unskilled blue collar, clerical and middle management functions. Aware of the Euro-crisis and subsequent economic downturn, the Irish Government pledged favourable consideration on those companies seeking investment in return for commitments to increase jobs for skilled blue-collar workers, meaning setting up plants in the Republic.

All the ascribed companies used Whately & Waterson for investment banking services. A local independent brokerage house with a strong pedigree of achievement over half a century, they had become one of The Firm's business partners, demonstrating themselves to be reliable, loyal and astute professionals, well-versed in the peculiarities of doing business in Ireland.

Whately & Waterson's primary business centred on hedge funds, the axiomatic business to business reason why they had been engaged as The Firm's investment services partner in Dublin. Part of a fifty-plus, world-ranking, financial, big hitters community subsuming ABN Amro, BNP Paribas, Citibank and Commerzbank AG, Whately and Waterson had a suite at the heart of the Dublin international financial services centre in an enclave at North Wall, adjacent to the River Liffey.

To revitalise the economy, the Irish Government intended to channel investment capital loans directly to business, on the proviso any company taking advantage of the cash incentive injected an equivalent amount of private equity. Investment banks, namely The Firm, came into the reckoning as a source for private sector financing. Quite rightly, the Irish Government concluded private sector involvement not only shared the risk, it also helped ensure success by virtue of the laws of capitalism. Fifty percent of the investment loan would be interest free, the balance subject to normal investment banking commercial terms and conditions. In principle, a very attractive accord for those participating in the venture, the Irish Government found an inexhaustible source from the private sector willing to play ball.

Whately and Waterson sounded out the four manufacturers regarding beefing up their capabilities in Ireland, some even contemplating piece-part manufacturing using the investment package on offer. Everyone agreed to take meetings with The Firm's lieutenants to discuss possible finance for the fifty percent of the investment needing to be acquired from the private sector.

Whately & Waterson senior partner, Kieran Kavanagh, had booked The Firm's contingent into the Fitzwilliam Hotel in York Street for three nights. Albeit the meetings were tabled to take place over two days, Fraser foresaw from antecedent Irish trafficking to allow at least one day of contingency, really meaning recovery from copious Guinness and Jameson inhalation the Irish fed business envoys virtually as soon as they set foot on the Emerald Isle.

~ * ~

Fraser's foremost exposure to Irish hospitality happened just a few months after joining J P Morgan. Dispatched to Dublin to validate investment viability with the Port of Dublin Authority, an organisation responsible to the Irish Government for all shipping and air freight infrastructure developments, in a trice his plans became compromised.

Met at Dublin Airport by one Seamus Sheehan, a name Fraser subsequently found to be almost impossible to pronounce after a few sherbets, Sheehan had been called in by J P Morgan to act as their intermediary and local agent for the Port of Dublin Authority business. Instead of going to the Custom House, a neoclassical eighteenth century government property, dripping in tradition and oozing muscle to meet Phelan O'Neill, Sheehan's prime contact at the Dublin Authority, he whisked Fraser off to The Mercantile, a small hotel with a measureless bar to meet O'Neill for lunch, before allegedly they went on to the Custom House.

Bridges were built between the Union Jack and the Tricolor, but little of their three-way palaver centred on the financial services landscape, let alone the Authority's business requirement. Lunch came and went, as did the afternoon and the entire evening with O'Neill, Sheehan and Fraser slowly getting blitzed on various Irish alcoholic concoctions.

Fortunately for Fraser, Sheehan had booked him into The Mercantile, so his newly bagged Irish drinking buddies poured the Englishman into his bed for the night. Waking the next morning with a hangover as capacious as Dublin Bay, it took Fraser a few minutes to reconcile his whereabouts and why he was in Dublin. Having also booked rooms at The Mercantile for the night, his hosts met Fraser for a very late brunch. Plainly completely wasted, O'Neill and Sheehan suggested deferring business until later in the day. Readily acquiescing to the notion, brunch transfigured into another meeting with Mister Guinness and Mister Jameson, the threesome falling into another alcoholic haze, the preconceived second day's official meeting failing to materialise.

After a comparably booze-ladened dinner in the evening, Sheehan scurried to the gents to relieve himself. Not reappearing, O'Neill and Fraser searched the lobby and the bar, but Sheehan could not be found. Exhausting all other possibilities, they went to the men's room and heard snoring coming from one of the traps. So sozzled after nearly two days of exhaustive drinking, their companion had passed out during a download attempt. Resorting to desperate steps, the pair called in The Mercantile's security staff to break down the trap door to get Sheehan out.

Needing therapeutic recharge, on the way to his room Fraser said to a porter he'd met the previous day, "I need a shower."

"I never take a shower, sir," he rejoindered. "I always have a bath. You get too wet in a shower."

Thunderstruck by the incongruity, Fraser blurted, "but…"

"Yes, sir?"

Familiar with Irish logic and the hopelessness in arguing its irrationality, Fraser muttered, "nothing."

Ultimately taking place at the Custom House the afternoon of the third day, two and a half days late, the formal Port of Dublin Authority meeting went off without a hitch, the business finalised to the satisfaction of all parties.

Feeling like he had drunk Ireland dry, later Fraser checked into the Aer Lingus desk at Dublin Airport, homeward bound for Blighty. Above her check-in position, the lady clerk had erected several large posters of the Aer Lingus Short 330 regional airliner made in Belfast. Staunchly Irish, she told him, Aer Lingus were about to retire their Short 330 fleet for replacement Dutch Fokker 50s. Very uptight about the prospect, she proudly betokened the posters and cawed, 'I'm not taking down my Shorts for any Fokker.' Still inebriated, Fraser didn't really take in the unintentional gaffe. But a few days later, the irate Irish lady arose in the forefront of his mind, and he howled at her incendiary comment.

Chapter 17: Dublin Knights

At the crack of dawn the next day, Fraser and his cadre were outbound from London City Airport on a BA flight to Dublin. Though early morning, some of the more licentious bog trotters couldn't resist the alcoholic temptations on sale from cabin service. Much to the amusement of non-Irish travellers, for the undivided flight, as soon as the seat belt sign went off, they summoned the trolley dollies and consumed beer and spirits to the tune of *Amhrán na bhFiann*, meaning The Soldier's Song otherwise known as the Irish national anthem.

While the revelry ensued, Fraser sat next to Henshaw discussing the business ahead of them.

"I hope Milton doesn't use Americanisms with the Irish," Henshaw bluntly supplicated. "They've enough of a test comprehending normal English business terms, so god knows what they'd make of New York slang."

"Yes, the up-to-the-minute version of the American to Irish dictionary lingers in a constant state of flux, and its author has still to get past 'A.'"

"If he talks about 'nitch' markets," the trading floor sales manager cautioned, "when he really means 'niche' markets, it will really throw them."

"And not wishing to offend," Fraser envisaged, "they'll probably start using the term, 'nitch.'"

"Once that happens, it will be as per a dose of the clap, wellnigh inconceivable to eradicate from their business word set."

"Unequivocally."

"Misinterpretation can be fatal in business transactions," Henshaw professed. "I've seen it happen before, and it can get very ugly. When The Firm sent me to Mexico to handle a joint undertaking with New York, on the way to downtown from the airport, I saw huge billboard signs every quarter mile containing a depiction of an alluring senorita, pouting and shaping up very sexy, with the strap-line, 'Support national shafting week.' Of course, straightaway I deduced it profiled a government sponsored campaign to encourage procreation, and had visions of all these wetbacks seeing the ads and rushing home to do the business with their wives."

"*Crikey*!" Fraser bellowed. "I'd have come to the same determination."

"Turned out national shafting week referred to a crusade to solicit monetary contributions for sinking oil drilling shafts."

"Wowee, an exemplary example of misunderstood local phraseology, assessed in let's say, the more conventional interpretation of the word shafting."

"Quite."

"It's the same as Jasper Carrot's dispute in Los Angeles," Fraser cited.

"Oh, how do you mean?"

"When Jasper became eminent in the late-seventies, he set up house in LA and found a new set of septic mates. They were relaxing on a veranda overlooking Lincoln Boulevard when Jasper saw a car coming up the street with the license plate inscription, B-O-L-L-O-C-K-S. Pronto, he broke into laughter, much to the surprise of the septics. Gawking at him open-mouthed, they wondered why."

"Of course," Henshaw recognised "back then, the California Department of Transport permitted any unique plate identification."

"Mmmm. So, one of the septics yelped, 'Hey Jasper, what's so funny?' Jasper responded, 'The car's licence plate.' Swapping baffled gawps, the septics shrugged their shoulders. 'What about it?' one of them probed. Jasper smirked. 'It's B-O-L-L-O-C-K-S as in bollocks.' 'Yeah,' another one of them queried, 'so what?' 'Well,' Jasper clarified, 'you know, bollocks!' The septics stared at him like he's from another planet, Jasper realising the jokester must be an Englishman, because the term bollocks wasn't widely known on the West Coast. So, inventing on the cuff, he told them, 'Bollocks is English for…zits.' 'Ah, we get it,' the septics verified. Then Jasper thought, can you imagine if these septics had acne, came over to Blighty, walked into a chemist's and boldly balloted, 'Have you got anything for these bollocks all over my face?'"

"Very good, Roger," purred a radiating Ricky Henshaw. "You come out with these stories at the drop of a hat."

"Yes, I often think I lost my true vocation."

"Oh, enlighten me."

"I should have been a *Jackanory* story reader," Fraser disclosed.

"Jeepers, unarguably it'd suit you," he joshed.

"Yep, I can just see myself sitting in the same chair as the illustrious Alan Bennett doing A. A. Milne renditions."

"By the way," Henshaw began, changing the spotlight, "have you noticed Milton has got one hell of a Randolph developing on his honker?"

"Yes. Yesterday I perceived it must be the light shining off his beak, but today as spots go, it's beginning to take after a belisha beacon."

"Let's crave the Irish don't seize upon it, or Crossman could become the butt of a few jokes. You know how ruthless they can be with peoples' facial irregularities."

"I do," Fraser countersigned sparkling. "And Mad Milton wouldn't see the funny side."

"For some illogical justification," Henshaw explained, "in recent years, I have always associated Randolph Scotts with James Cordon Bleu." Evaluating Fraser had not connected with the name, he stopped. "You know, the fat, smug git in *Kelvin and Tracey*."

"Oh, yes," Fraser testified. "That's out-and-out garbage."

"What, my appraisal of Cordon Bleu?"

"No, no, you're correct on that score. He is a fat, smug bastard, with his own self-grown zit kingdom. It's the so-called sitcom that's really self-indulgent rubbish, filled with non-entities and fallen hangers-on. What superb actress Alison Steadman is doing in it, I'll never know.

It's the equivalent of dumping Jack Nicholson in a cast of zombies to enact a Tennessee Williams masterpiece."

"Yeah," Henshaw braced. "Fat, smug bastards must be fashionable at the BBC."

"For sure. And have you discerned, anyone deemed fashionable, you know, one of the namby-pamby, nauseous, let's boost each other's ego brigade—"

"You mean for instance," Henshaw cut in, "that talk-show twat Gervase Honda and his self-ingratiating guests?"

"Yeah, you've got it. Somehow, they're allowed to flatter themselves with the most despicable acts of self-flattery and anti-social misdemeanours, in particular tax avoidance, yet those same PC zealots vilify others for the same act."

"You're right, Roger," Henshaw affirmed. "And—" Waggling a critical finger he carped, "fat boy Cordon Bleu's smugness hit the heights of self-indulgence in *The History Boys*, one of my held dear films and plays."

"Charlotte and I went to see the stage play at the Lyttelton. We found it astounding, and the film rendered the same distinction." Grimacing, Fraser annexed, "but of all the young actors in both the play and the film, Cordon Bleu abides as the least talented, yet he's become an unworthy kahuna."

"As you said, fat is fashionable, along with ugliness, specifically at the BBC, but it's not so much I find Cordon Bleu's fatness objectionable, it's his leery smugness, and the supposition he's A-list guest material, when in actuality, he's a talentless mediocrity."

"Blimey, you expressly describe what the BBC are facilitating; inferiority over real talent, inelegance over beauty, ineptness over intellect."

"Yes, but why?"

"The perpetual pandering and dumbing-down to the lowest common denominator. Long-gone are the days of trying to elevate audience zest for precocious dramas and PC-free current affairs programmes and documentaries. Those empyrean heights of excellence have been replaced by the ubiquitous no-quality reality show, endless PC soaps, and the aggrandizement of failed minor celebrities in cheap game shows."

"Yeah, it's the price paid for allowing Holy Joes, resident in Islington, to run the national broadcaster."

"*God*, what a savage attack," Fraser jubilantly praised. "Who shall we rubbish next?"

~ * ~

Dissimilar to Fraser's original stopover in Dublin on behalf of J P Morgan, Whately & Waterson's Kieran Kavanagh met The Firm's detachment at the airport, keeping them on the straight and narrow from the off by stressing they reached their first appointment promptly.

After Fraser made the introductions, Kavanagh took him aside, while the others were faffing around with their luggage.

"Now tell me, Roger, what profit margin do you foresee from this initiative?"

"Well, Kieran, I'd say between ten to twelve percent, but the deals struck will be largely up to Milton Crossman."

"You mean, that feckin' guy with a feckin' growth, where his feckin' nose should be?"

"No, no," Fraser contradicted. "That *is* his nose."

"What!" squealed the staggered Irishman. "Is he a Jimmy Duranti impersonator?"

"I can assure you, it's not a growth. What you see is his actual snoot with a fast-developing zit perched on the end."

Shimmying his napper, Kavanagh blasted, "*rubbish*, no one has a feckin' snout like that."

"He does."

Establishing solid credentials as a shrewd businessman, and socially very good company during visits to The Firm's London HQ, Kavanagh had attuned himself to The Firm's MO and the idiosyncrasies of cardinal executive players, principally Luther Bembridge and Toby

Chalcroft. Meeting Henshaw and Fraser on several occasions, a steadfast business relationship had been founded, uppermost with Fraser, who invited him down to Hazelwood for a weekend and introduced him to the delights of Kappa Corinthians. Reciprocating in kind, Kavanagh furnished tickets for the Ireland-England Six Nations match in Dublin. Popular in the bullpen, many of the Essex boy traders such as Pierce Finlay and Trevor Evans adjudged him to be a hotshot, not appreciating much of his Irish rhetoric and wit took the piss out of them. Lapping it up with a fork and spoon, they left Fraser and other analysts shaking their heads conjecturing, how could The Firm's future be placed in the hands of brokers, not having the gumption to decipher they were the butt of the Irishman's jokes.

Kavanagh and The Firm's 'Dublin Knights' team, as Toby Chalcroft had dubbed them, met with Kaufmann Vogel Electric and Dresdner Fuchs during the course of the morning to verify their investment requirements and agree a next set of aims. Being responsible for the German speaking territory of Central Europe, Metzer led on behalf of The Firm. As usual, though attempting to be gentle and amicable in English conversing meetings, nonetheless, his menacing presentation, dominating manner and the loaded way he asked questions signifying riposte content must align perfectly with his anticipations, had the Kaufmann and Dresdner mediators recoiling in his presence.

Augmentedly on tenterhooks by the Obergruppenfûhrer's dictatorial stance at Kaufman Vogel Electric, Kavanagh whispered to Fraser, "who the feckin' hell is that guy?"

"Ahh, I take it you're referring to Heinrich's somewhat robust approach?"

"*Robust*!" Kavanagh blustered, his peepers opening to their extremities with disbelief. "He comes across like a feckin' all-conquering Panzer Division, marauding through downtown Dublin."

"He's very good at his job," Fraser cheerfully advertised.

"He'd better be. Those two Kaufman fellas don't look exactly feckin' enamoured with your feckin' friend Heinrich. Someone ought to feckin' well tell him the IRA is still active south of the border, and they do take on civilian contracts, if the price is right!"

"Mmmm," Fraser capitulated. "I'll see if I can get him to dampen his temperament a bit."

Regardless of Fraser's conciliatory call to Metzer, and the Obergruppenführer's promise to lighten his delivery, the Dresdner Fuchs emissaries suffered the same silky smooth but sinister onslaught, not daring to argue with Heiny baby, for fear of winding up hanging by their genitals with piano wire.

"Und of course in ze Fatherland, er, I mean Germany," Metzer budded, crowning his response to the Dresdner Fuchs business plan for the requested cash injection, "ve expect maximum attainment, und payback un our investments. Zhose failing to deliver are severely punished." Burning satanically at the Dresdner spokesmen, his monocle almost fell from its resting place between his eye socket bone and temple, fleetingly magnifying his optic, and making them jump up in their seats. "Failure vill not be tolerated, und zhose found guilty of inadequate fulfilment, vill be dealt vith harshly," he added before finalising with, "I credit I make myself crystal, gentlemen."

Impressed by the no-nonsense dictum, Mad Milton whispered to Fraser, "boy, I wish I had a whole passel of Krauts like Heinrich in the Big Apple, to replace those felonious dealers from Brooklyn and the Bronx. We'd sure as hell take New York by storm then."

"Quite," Fraser judiciously replied, surmising it'd also spark off World War Three.

Feeling Kieran Kavanagh's hand on his arm, he faced him.

"B'jesus, Roger," the Whately & Waterson man bickered. "If this feckin' guy doesn't shut the feck up, there's going to be another feckin' uprising on the streets of Dublin, *ala* Easter 1916. Who the feck does he think he is, Hitler's grandson?"

"Funny you should say that," Fraser approved.

Terminating their workload for the day, the afternoon saw Kavanagh and the Dublin Knights attend Baker Finch, Crossman's Randolph nearing full bloom as the meeting commenced. During the reciprocity, Fraser dialled the Baker Finch negotiators were transfixed by the developing mini volcano on Mad Milton's muzzle. A regal specimen by normal benchmarks, with the addition of the bulbous spot, categorically it resembled a fairy cake with a cherry on the top, the hypnotized onlookers unable to drag their vision away.

After the Baker Finch team had delineated their schemes requiring inward investment, the Dublin Knights delved into the opportunity.

"So, gentlemen," Crossman hatched, "in summary, you want to beef up the existing manufacturing capability at your Dublin plant and need capital investment for the purpose."

Baker Finch Financial Director Feilim Flynn had become so absorbed in studying the New Yorker's schnozzle, he barely heard the digest, his co-partner, Production Director Riordan O'Shea nudging his arm.

"Hhmm," Flynn groaned, not realising Crossman's outline had been addressed to him.

"Feilim, the gentleman wants to know," O'Shea reiterated, "if the reason we need the investment is to beef up our fabrication capacity."

Pulling himself out of his nasal obsession, Flynn blundered out, "oh yes, Mister er, er…"

"Crossman," O'Shea sharply prompted.

"…Crossman," Flynn awkwardly echoed. "It certainly is the proverbial driver."

Crossman and Flynn kicked the business draft around a bit more before Ricky Henshaw came in with some further queries.

"What are the timescales for the investment profile?" he canvassed.

"We need it as soon as possible," Flynn positively asserted, fully cognizant with the meeting objectives once more. "Baker Finch is the telecoms leader in network router technologies, but our parent company in England knows the competition is catching up fast. We need to grab as much market share with our products before *par exemple* Siemens and Ericsson have their latest offerings in production."

Sustaining his audit, Henshaw educed more qualifying data

before Crossman reacquired command by overviewing some of The Firm's investment references in telecoms, embodying AT&T and Cisco Systems. Capping the pitch, Fraser outlined some investment model options, then talked about The Firm's telecom's proficiency in the UK with Orange and Cable & Wireless. A typical bi-directional custom and part of the *de facto* mechanism required for both parties to feel each other out before agreeing a way forward, eventually it led to common ground and a mutual accord before segueing into some Baker Finch investigations about The Firm's Irish business experience.

Lapsing into staring at Mad Milton's ever growing and incandescent volcano again, Flynn cross-examined in an unfocused voice, "does er, does The Firm have er…" Fearing his ally losing application, and coming out with an unfortunate remark about Crossman's swelling hooter, O'Shea cleared his throat, the action neutralising Flynn's inducement. "…does The Firm have any traffic with other telecoms manufacturers in the Republic or Northern Ireland?"

A pump awaited by the Dublin Knights, invariably tabled on the basis of a clash with local business interests, they had prepared accordingly.

Henshaw had the response but before he could reply, out of the blue, Bradley Purnell, sitting quietly in observation mode up to that juncture, as he had done at Kaufmann Vogel Electric and Dresdner Fuchs, chimed in with, "oh yes, we have bonds in play with A B Steadman in Cork, and Holhurst Technologies in Belfast."

If looks could kill, the burgeoning rage developing into a tsunami on Mad Milton's mug would have vaporised poor Purnell on the spot. Expeditiously, the Ayatollah's nephew fingered he'd made a mistake, a grave mistake. In business, the seller never says more than is necessary, and always keeps his cards close to his chest, preferably, until the ink is dry on the contract.

Accepting he'd have to intervene quickly, or he envisioned young Bradley being returned to his Uncle Luther in a coffin, embossed with the American eagle on the lid, and the phrase, 'Couldn't keep his mouth shut', splashed in blood across it, Fraser adjudicated, "what my colleague meant to say is, The Firm does have some existing business linkages with various telecoms manufacturers in the Republic and Northern Ireland, but they are no longer active. The investments with both A B Steadman and Holhurst Technologies are closed."

"Ah, I see," Flynn inveterated. "So, The Firm has no on-going conflicts of interest?"

"Not in Ireland," he underwrote. "Of course, we do have on-going telecoms equipment sector investments in other parts of the globe, but I'm sure you will agree, it's a normal business discipline."

"Yes," Flynn concurred, clocking O'Shea for solidarity. "We do understand."

"Besides," Fraser certified, "we erect Chinese walls between investments in the same market place to retain mutual confidentiality."

Notwithstanding Fraser rescuing the situation, Mad Milton had become incensed, snorting like an enraged bull, making his Randolph glow even more intensely, giving warning of a possible eruption. Sensing the cataclysm and expecting to be spray-coated in hot milky white puss at any moment, Flynn and O'Shea nudged their chairs aside from the negotiating table cowering under the threat.

~ * ~

When evening came, The Firm's team gathered in the Fitzwilliam's bar, Crossman immediately rounding on Bradley Purnell.

"Hey, lightning," he sarcastically reprimanded.

Curling up into a ball in reaction, Purnell's ingrained sense of survival drove his body to provide a minimum form factor to the forthcoming assault.

"I thought we agreed, you'd keep your mouth firmly shut during business negotiations."

"I'm very sorry, Mister Crossman, I don't know what came over me. I just felt compelled to serve Mister Flynn's moot point, because I knew the answer."

Towering over the errant gofer, resembling Hercules dwarfing the

Earth, Crossman advocated, "next time, if there is a next time, don't say a word unless one of the grownups expressly permits you to unseal your mouth…*clear*?"

"Clear," he parroted, sinking further into his minimal body shape. "If you'll excuse me, I must go to my room for, for…" Abandoning the sentence uncompleted he exited the bar.

Taking the New Yorker aside, Fraser urged, "easy on the lad, Milton. He's not here by choice. He's here at Bembridge's insistence."

"Hhmm, might be so," Crossman acquiesced, foam still leaping from his discharging mouth, "but keep him from underneath my feet."

Scowling, Crossman began walking away, leaving the stock analyst pondering about the American's foremost blast at Bembridge's nephew in London when guessing Purnell's junior status drew his disdain. Now he reopened the assumption.

"Milton," Fraser commandingly brayed.

Twisting sideways, he marked the Englishman.

"Is there something I should know about, pertaining to you and young Bradley?"

Narrowing his croakers, he stepped towards Fraser. "Let's just say, there's some history between Brad's uncle and myself."

Lowering his gaze, he admitted, "I know Mister Bembridge has a habit of rubbing people up the wrong way, but why take it out on Bradley?"

Plunging out of his pent-up anger, Mad Milton consented, "yes…you're right. The boy didn't make a heavyweight deal busting slip."

"Can you possibly share with me," Fraser desired in his most polite voice, "what the inhibitor is between Bembridge and yourself?"

Reflectively, his vein changed to remorse, even regret, echoing an aberrant nun in the confessional box. "Let's sit over there," he proposed, designating a couch area adjacent to the bar.

Settling down, Fraser in his best listening mode, endeavouring to act as the holy father, Crossman laid out the source of his discontent.

"I shouldn't really be telling you this, but since you have a personal recommendation from Dan Lebowski, I will trust you not to breathe a word of what I am about to tell you to another living soul."

"You have my word, Milton."

"Eons ago, well before you joined The Firm, Bembridge came to New York to discuss the carve-up of various global accounts. The Firm's regional organisations in the Americas, EMEA and Asia Pacific were all under review, regarding revenue recognition shares and responsibilities. I made the call for one prestigious blue-chip player to be run out of New York. Bembridge challenged it, saying the account had more revenue generating opportunities in his neck of the woods, and should be run from London." Suspending his account, Crossman became sanguine. "I concede Bembridge's appraisal held water, but the crux of the conference hinged on arbitrating the most efficient and effective ways to manage The Firm's top-drawer global clients. Some were best led by London, some by Frankfurt, Hong Kong, Sao Paulo etc, and some best led by New York. All those taking part had assented on every single global account, before Bembridge dug his heels in about the one I'd made the business case for, being led out of the Big Apple." Breaking off, he duly postulated, "no doubt you know how he can flare?"

"Oh yes," Fraser notarised, wondering if he should tell Crossman about his theory apropos the Ayatollah metamorphosing into a lizard killing machine, but gauging the gravity of what he formulated precluded satire.

"Well…Bembridge lost his rag and got very spiteful with me. He brought my track record into dispute, and in general denigrated my successes." Ceasing his memory trawl momentarily, the New Yorker surged into an atypical crushed comportment, Fraser sensing the retention still hurt. "I'm a hard man, Roger, capable of taking a lot of stick, but what Bembridge said, and it was in front of The Firm's executive board including the CEO and the Chairman, really infuriated me. I took so much, then retaliated in kind and flew at Bembridge…nothing physical, but the verbal reprisal became perceptibly fierce."

"I see," Fraser acknowledged, tempted to entreat if the Anglo-

American dual had gotten him the nickname, 'Mad Milton', but once again deciding to be discrete.

"After this client account had been critiqued and sanctioned to be a New York jurisdiction by the board, Bembridge became even more volatile. Since, our rapport has been curt to say the least."

"Mmmm," Fraser suspiciously whimpered. "Tell me, do you speculate Bembridge deliberately made young Bradley a member of this team, just to get at you?"

"Huh, it wouldn't stupefy me. Hell, everybody embracing Bembridge knows I can't stand halfwits, and with all due deference to young Brad, he's never going to be the sharpest knife in the business box, is he?"

"Maybe, but he's still young," Fraser defended. "Sometimes ugly ducklings metamorphose into handsome swans. If the Bembridge family leash is taken off him, Bradley could flower and become a player."

"Maybe," Crossman yielded.

"I'm beginning to see Mister Bembridge's hidden agenda," Fraser perceived, "but all the same, with respect, taking out your frustrations on Bradley is not worthy of a man of your position and obvious talents."

"Yes, you're right, Roger," he licensed, his inflection bordering on the apologetic. "I'll try to curb my temper with him."

Later, after a sumptuous dinner and enough Guinness and Jameson to loosen everyone up to the edge of shedding all inhibitions, The Firm's troupe of busy businessmen retired to the bar again and ripped into recounting stories.

Meanwhile, Crossman's zit had built to summit proportions attracting a lot of attention. Infatuated by the mini Mount Vesuvius, even the Fitzwilliam's waiters lost their concentration dispensing beverages, bottled mixers poured down shirt collars instead of into glasses, and soda misaimed at shirts rather than into whisky tumblers. If Mad Milton did feel self-conscious about his conk addition, he hid it well, any inkling of being the centre of amusement for all and sundry, skilfully concealed. Apparently unconcerned and thoroughly chilled out, notably since Fraser kept refreshing his glass throughout the evening, he could have had a zillion zits on his honker, without a care in the world.

Preoccupying the New Yorker in grandiose tales about Germany being The Firm's premier revenue bearing region in Europe, Crossman opposed Heinrich Metzer's claim by stating it was only so if England's lion's share contribution was discounted. Countering, in the Obergruppenführer's jaundiced standpoint, he argued England rested as non-European, and should be attributed to the Americas region.

"After all, Milton," he fostered, "England is ze fifty-first state."

"Oh, very good, Heinrich," Crossman complimented. "They'd love that in New York."

"Anyvey," Metzer tagged, not really taking in the American's comment, "you should see ze troops. I mean ze traders goose-shtepping, er, I mean valking in step to ze beat of ze drum." Beaming, his countenance blossomed with Germanic pride. "It is a vonderful sight to behold, mien führer, I mean, my vice-president."

So blissed-out on Jameson and past caring about the Obergruppenführer's vision for rekindling Germanic world domination, Crossman blithely retorted, "you don't say."

"Oh yes, zhere is nothing a German broker cannot do," he meticulously avowed. "Ve have ways of driving zhem to peak performance."

"You do it in the traditional German way then?" Crossman posed.

"Yes, indeed," Metzer confidently validated. "Everything from ze rule book and by ze numbers."

Does it encompass sex? he conjectured, before asking, "are you implying your techniques ought to be applied throughout The Firm?"

"It vould not ve difficult, mien führer, er, excuse me, I mean Mister Vice President. Ve vould enforce ze German model vith a video conferencing broadcast on ze Firm's intranet. Everyone vould be required to tune in. No exceptions."

"*Holy cow*, I can't see The Firm going for it, Heinrich," Crossman forewarned, more than ever perplexed about the German's veracious and disturbing dreams of unrestricted dominion.

Metzer's glorification of the fatherland continued, Crossman caught between diplomacy and his instinctive desire to pull the ripcord, and exploit his seniority to supersede the ghastly dialogue, markedly so as the Jameson soporific effect lessened.

At length, Fraser, Henshaw and Purnell heard the strains of the German national anthem coming from the pair, Heiny poking at Milton to join in a few lines.

"*Deutschland, Deutschland,*" Metzer sang, while waving his hands under his chin in an attempt to get some rhythm into it. "*Uber allies, uber alles in der Welt.*" Stopping, he blared, "now, Milton, together."

Joining in, Crossman mused, *the only way to get this God damn, sausage eating, sauerkraut smelling, Marlene Dietrich fetishising Kraut of my back, is to appease him, but Chamberlin did that with Hitler, and look what happened next*!

Nevertheless, he took the expedient route to extricate himself from being invaded.

"*Deutschland, Deutschland,*" the pair sang. "*Uber alles, uber alles in der Welt.*"

"Gut," Metzer enthused, pleased with the duet. No longer caring about his Nazi inferences, he predicted, "ve will have you in ze jack boots and ze lederhosen before you know it." Cocksure Mad Milton had softened to his vision of the world, he sleekly interrogated, "und have you heard ze one about…."

Still observing the fanfare, Fraser footnoted, "looks like Heiny baby is toiling to make Milton into a stormtrooper."

"Yes," Henshaw bolstered. "He'll be covering him in little swastikas and awarding him the Iron Cross next."

"Erm," Purnell began, "if you'll excuse me again, I have to call home."

"Is that why you withdrew earlier on?" Fraser solicited.

"Yes. This might be silly, but my mother still worries about me. Calling earlier, I only got the answer phone."

"Don't be troubled by it, Bradley. All mothers worry about their offspring."

Smiling, he chirped, "thanks, Mister Fraser."

"Isn't it about time you called me Roger, at least when we're off duty?"

Elated, he warbled, "can I?"

"Of course, and that's Ricky over there."

Henshaw raised a friendly hand to him.

"Best to keep on addressing Milton as Mister Crossman and Heinrich as Herr Metzer," Fraser appended. "Informality with the young does not come easy to them."

"Of course, Mister Fraser, er Roger. Back soon."

As they watched Purnell walk off, their eyesight became drawn by the German, still deep in a one-way conversation with Crossman.

"*Himmel*!" Fraser mocked. "It's a good job the waiter didn't ask for our orders at dinner, unintentionally mimicking the *Fawlty Towers* sketch, or the Obergruppenführer would have told him, 'Orders must be obeyed at all times.'"

Sniggering, Henshaw marked Crossman's burgeoning nose addition had developed. "Good grief," he burbled under his breath, "Milton's taking on the guise of a crazed macaw with that multi-coloured mountain not far from the final eruption on his schnoz."

"Indeed," Fraser favoured. "I'm contemplating handing out umbrellas to protect innocent bystanders from the puss ejaculation when it strikes critical mass and bursts skywards."

"Do you remember the scene in *Close Encounters* where Richard Dreyfus is fabricating a plateaued edifice in his kitchen to represent the UFO landing pad at Devils Tower in Wyoming?"

"I do."

"Well," Henshaw gingerly recapped, pointing at Crossman, "it seems Dreyfus has been hard at work sculpturing a congruent structure on Milton's snout."

"Yeessss," Fraser mischievously upheld, grinning at the Trading Floor Sales Manager's observation. "With hindsight, we should have videoed on a mobile the evolution of Milton's giant zit to the apex at which it eventually explodes. It'd lend a mesmerizing spectacle to the London operation, but—" He grimaced. "Albeit Milton's volcanic nature, I admire him, so it'd be unkind to abuse his unfortunate nasal supplement."

"Hhmm, I'm not so sure," Henshaw disputed. "But as you say, his bark is worse than his bite."

~ * ~

Converging together, the two Dublin Knights groups with Purnell rejoining the throng ventilated about investment banking mythology and the larger than life virtuosos' it sometimes created.

"Of course," Henshaw substantiated, "the gold standard for double-hard bastards must be Clark Jefferson."

"For sure," Fraser reinforced. "A very formidable gentleman."

"Phooey, you understate him," Crossman rectified. "When it comes to top-of-the-pile flyers, you'll find the name Clark Jefferson in Webster's Dictionary next to the word, legend. To say he was an overnight sensation is an understatement. Hell, he ripped up the rule book and re-wrote it."

Fabled maverick New York stock trader Clark Jefferson left The Firm at the onset of the millennium in search of new adventures. Though in presentation the classic, all-American business archetype, clean shaven and with a Cary Grant hairstyle, beneath the surface gloss laid a natural eccentric and a nonconformist by choice. Not quite a freak, nonetheless he did often tend towards anomalous behaviour, baffling both confederates and customers.

A Harvard man, joining The Firm in the late nineteen-seventies, he laboured to make himself a shed load of money as a broker, his reading of stock markets and people unsurpassed, enabling him to stay at least three steps ahead in the game. Incontrovertibly, he knew what investors would do before they knew it themselves, and how markets reacted to a prevailing economic atmosphere, way before the stock index moved. By age twenty-five, The Firm had tendered him numerous management posts. Declining all of them, instead, he chose to preserve the stock trader station, giving him the latitude he wanted to do his own thing.

Recognising early in his career they had a blue bird winner tallying as unmanageable using mainstream routines, The Firm gave him free reign to come and go as he pleased, knowing he'd blow apart his quarterly targets by ten to twenty times. Every quarter, The Firm hit him with some astronomical goal, reasoning even if he achieved one tenth of the number, it'd be unparalleled, only for Jefferson to pull off the miracle over and over. Also condoning his eccentricities, for example, coming into the office in Bermuda shorts, or using one of The Firm's Learjets for impromptu trips to Las Vegas, he became fireproof.

By age thirty, he had accumulated enough capital and income from investments to keep him, his ex-wives and brood of brats in yachts and mansions for the rest of his life. Bored with stock trading, he sought another job with The Firm. Not wanting to lose their powerful piece of manpower to a competitor, they gave him a VP of global futures grade. Rumour had it, he held the highest paid, non-executive appointment in financial services worldwide, but by then, money no longer motivated him. In fact, it never did. Ascribing money to be merely a tool used to fuel the game he played, to Jefferson, his remuneration equated to a symbol of his luminary standing.

Seeping into the public domain, his eminence mushroomed. Frequently on the cover of *Time* magazine and courted by television to give guru-equivalent pronouncements on the state of the stock market, his star rose in leaps and bounds. Basking in global futures for the next ten years, it gave him the scope to do his own thing, whilst concurrently accomplishing all his delegated Firm objectives with commensurate ease. During this period, the eccentricity snowballed, his persona even more unconventional and just plain weird. He also developed a hard, often bordering on sadistic side, many anticipating brought on by excessive white line fever and recurrent bouts of taking on all-comers in Tequila slammer contests. Sagacious to his unassailable status, he bludgeoned people into his way of conceptualizing, made enemies outside The Firm, and became the focal point of exposé reporter investigations.

Some tattled Jefferson had a Howard Hughes karma, replete with peculiar foibles and curious habits, but so long as the goose laid golden eggs, his often-bizarre antics and madcap indiscretions were swept under the carpet, The Firm's all-pervasive potency on Wall Street and in Washington ensuring his peccadilloes never saw the light of day.

Quitting investment banking with The Firm all together, he launched his own independent financial advisor company, with a suite on Liberty Street, right in the heart of New York's financial district. Now and again, he wrote a leader for the *Wall Street Journal* and guested on TV chat shows, but beyond the guild image, he became more and more reclusive, vacating the running of his business to a management team he had personally selected.

His screwball buffoonery and cranky misdemeanours intensified. Intoxicated with his own success and no longer protected from scandal by The Firm's Praetorian Guard, he found himself at the centre of shameful articles in the opening pages of the *New York Times* and the *Washington Post*, his celebrated star no longer in the ascendency. Howbeit, bad publicity meant nothing to Jefferson, and his legions of admiring clients just brushed it off as rich man singularity. So long as he did the business for them, they couldn't care if he porked Hilary Clinton, many coveting he had done to so scour the sourpuss smirk off her smug face.

"Clark Jefferson," Crossman uttered again, clearly flooded in fond remembrance. "Now there's a name to conjure with, and as you say Ricky, he was, and probably still is, what you Brits call a double-hard bastard."

"Yep," Henshaw commended, "criticism and hard knocks just bounced off him."

"Who is this Clark Jefferson?" Purnell grilled.

"Yes, who is he?" Metzer endorsed. "I don't fink I am familiar with ze name either."

"Ah, he was before your time, Heinrich," Fraser extolled. Augmenting Crossman's homage, he enumerated, "there are insufficient superlatives in either Webster's or the Oxford Dictionary to adequately describe the irrepressible Clark Jefferson."

"Clark Jefferson," Crossman re-repeated with almost idolatrous reverence. "They don't make them like him anymore. Last I heard, he'd been in a collision with a fast-moving Chevy."

"Oh yes," Henshaw ratified, smirking. "I heard a few strands about that."

"Irrefutably," he resumed, "the Chevy came off worse."

"Vot vas Jefferson driving?" the Obergruppenführer enquired.

"Oh, he wasn't driving," Crossman cited. "He was walking down the middle of 5th Avenue when it happened. The Chevy nearly took him out, but just as it neared him, he rotated and raised his right hand as if he were a traffic cop with ultimate jurisdiction over all road users. Screeching to a halt, Jefferson proceeded to batter the Chevy with a baseball bat he'd just bought."

"What about the driver?" Fraser catechized.

"Ohh, allegedly, he was so fazed by Jefferson's surprising Babe Ruth emulation, he couldn't get out of the Chevy. He cowered in his seat, beholding him pounding the bodywork until it was totalled."

"Did the cops attend?"

"Yes, they did."

"What did Jefferson say to them?"

"He apologised, saying he didn't know what came over him, and threw five, ten-thousand-dollar bills at the frightened plaintive to cover costs."

"Wow," Henshaw quacked, bursting into a gladdened smile. "He really is a double-hard bastard, isn't he?"

"Just as I told you," Crossman corroborated. "But the casual violence came about more through frustration rather than annoyance with a fast-moving Chevy."

"How do you mean, Milton?" Metzer quizzed, with his psychopharmacology background always fascinated by anything involving psychotic behaviour.

"Well, on the last occasion I actually spoke to Clark Jefferson…" Glowering, he tried to recall the specific date. "…must have been March

2005. He ambled into the Four Seasons where I wined and dined some clients. Analogous to a reject from *Baywatch* or should it be Babe-watch, never could tell the difference, he'd dressed in the style of a Hawaiian beach bum, rather than a penthouse on 5th owning, peeking out over Central Park, soaring with the eagles, money markets celeb." Hesitating, he shook his head, as if still not quite trusting what he had seen. "Anyway, he had his entourage of long-legged, Jean Paul Gaultier suit wearing PA's with him, and a flock of sycophants he consented to hang on to his shirt tails, because they amused him. He took a booth for his clan, then ordered at least fifteen-thousand dollars' worth of *cordon bleu* dishes and fine wines. The maître d didn't even bat an eyelid during the process, never mind offering him a tie."

"Hah," Henshaw jeered, "living the kooky lifestyle to the full then?"

"Very much so. I had a few words with him as we were departing. He jumped up like a jack in a box when he saw me coming, rushed forward, grasped my hand, shook it, then much to my embarrassment, announced to his disciples I was one of the few people in investment banking playing the game properly. We talked for a while, but then I had to re-join my guests. He said he'd call me, and we'd chew the cud over a few bottles of Bollinger, but…I never heard from him. However, from what little he did convey, it seemed evident he remained frustrated with the shortcomings of the money markets, and took his vengeance out on anything happening to cross his path. Hence the later Chevy incident."

"You've not seen him since?" Fraser pressured.

"No. I heard he'd gone off to Nevada to try and outfox the casinos with some method or algorithm he'd devised to predict the turn of the roulette wheel, or the sequence of falling poker cards. He did just fine until he decided to go swimming with his car in Lake Tahoe. When the feds showed up, he claimed he'd been chased by Reno casino gangsters. You see, he'd already been invited to quit Las Vegas by the mob."

"You mean, his gambling technique verked?" Metzer drilled.

"Yes, Heinrich. Verked, I mean worked, too damn well. It's why he had to vamoose and neared becoming a candidate on the Mafia's

Greatest Hits show."

~ * ~

At breakfast the next morning, Crossman submitted, "judging by some of Heinrich's ultra-pro-Fatherland discussion topics last night, and his general Hitler-fetishist demeanour, I'm evaluating he is not too tightly wrapped."

"Oh, Heiny's all right," Fraser advocated. "Sometimes he just gets a bit too carried away underpinning his *bone fide* paradigm. Behind the menace he emanates, he's a consummately pleasant fellow."

"Then how do you account for all this German national anthem stuff, the leatherettes and lederhosen, and the brutal way he treats his staff in Frankfurt?"

"Take it all with a pinch of salt. He's stuck nursing the archetypal stamp of Germans people have worldwide. For logic only known to him, he feels predisposed to ceaselessly make the sentiment reality." Ogling at Henshaw, Fraser beseeched, "what do you think, Ricky?"

"I agree. I know people working for him, and most say the menacing stuff is artificial, just a front he puts on to insulate himself from the world at large and conserve the estimation he is intimidating. Granted, he plays the part well, and for the uninitiated, he can be quite overwhelming."

"But why, Ricky?" Crossman probed, his timbre urging explanation in cogent terms.

"Well, let me put it into perspective. I've acquired a reputation for being tough with the sales team in London, and it's true." He mugged Fraser. "Right, Roger?"

"Oh, yes, irreproachably. Ricky is not one to cuddle and coax the dealers, tickle their tummies to make them laugh, or take them to see the wanky boy band of their choice."

"Quite," Henshaw sanctioned, proud of the tribute. "Heinrich knows he is capable of creating stupefying affections, and he sees me as his opposite taskmaster in London. For this motive, he gravitates towards me. I'm his comfort zone for what he believes to be an ally authoritarian figure. But, during the instances we meet, I play up to his perception of me by giving him chapter and verse apropos how I have scared the living daylights out of delinquent brokers. He tries to top it by giving me his advice regarding optimising trader attainment through the power of fear. I don't know if he knows I'm playing up to the persona, or whether he suspects I judge he's perennially in role play mode. Nevertheless, it does serve to foster good relations between the London and Frankfurt bullpens, so no harm done."

"I see," Crossman responded. "Only I got the distinct intuition, he wanted to recruit me into his own version of the Hitler youth movement…only for senior managers."

"Yes, he's tried that one on me in the past," Fraser merrily publicised. "Too much Guinness and Jameson got him visioning out his blueprints for world domination. He does the same thing under the influence of schnapps in the Fatherland, er Germany."

"Okay," Crossman espoused. "So, the next time he says, and I quote, 'I can see zem now, marching down Vall Street, er I mean Karl-Marx Straße,' I should assume he is fantasising?"

"Absolutely," Fraser assured.

A few hours later, The Firm's team and Kieran Kavanagh were in parleys with Financial Director Foghan Slattery and Engineering Director Barra Molloy at Wellman Enterprises.

With Mad Milton's zit heading out on its countdown to a monumental explosion, as soon as the Wellman directors met the New Yorker, they both became rapt by his snout appendage. Every time Crossman moved his head, their blinkers traced the object of their fascination. Even when Slattery summarised the plans for Wellman's investment, he kept on failing to complete sentences, as if already musing, *if that thing bursts, we're all going to get encapsulated in milky white heat, and we need to take some precautionary measures for our own safety*. Seeing his colleague faltering, Molloy terminated most of his unfinished sentences for him.

Henshaw, Metzer, Purnell and Fraser also foresaw the worst.

During a lull in Slattery's patter, Henshaw whispered to Fraser, 'Investing in sou'wester outfits would have been a prudent idea, particularly the caps to protect bystanders from the imminent zit blast'. While the conjecture ensued, Crossman sat impassively absorbing Slattery's message or simply maintaining his cool.

Realising that if left to Slattery, they were going to be there all day, in the end Molloy took over communications.

"Gentlemen," he yammered, riveting their attention." Perhaps I can add a few salient points pertaining to our drafts for scaling up Wellman's engineering projects, so as to give you a feel for where the investment capital will be used."

"Please, go ahead," Crossman encouraged.

Profiling the off-shore equipment utilisations they had in mind, Molloy recorded some state-of-the-art wellhead valve and actuator device clusters designed to operate under inordinate seawater pressures, and a giant platform-housed pumping station accommodating a massive diesel-engine-driven pump array.

"In terms of meeting end user needs," Fraser registered, "what's so special about this oil exploration paraphernalia?"

"Ah, I'm glad you asked, Mister Fraser," Molloy saluted. "In all probability your scrutiny is induced by investment risk factors?"

"Precisely."

"One of the mammoth headaches for oil production is continuity of supply breakdown caused by wellhead malfunctions or the platform pumping station breaking down. All exploration companies, embodying Shell, BP and Exxon use run and standby systems, but it's very expensive. Our revolutionary methodology builds redundancy into a single entity to accomplish the same run and standby facility, but at a much-reduced price. If we can perfect this craft, Wellman Enterprises will steal a march on our competitors."

Impressed by the science, Fraser tabled more investment verifications, as did Henshaw and Crossman, the discourse then moving onto the investment quanta and ROI timescales. In principle, the prospect seemed sound, until Bradley Purnell tapped Fraser on the forearm, bringing his attention to the latest oil exploration live news feed he monitored on his laptop, the denoted item certifying Stewart & Stevenson Oil Tools of Houston were about to unveil a new off-shore oil production pumping system, approximating the Wellman Enterprises' solution. Keen to inform his comrades, Fraser swivelled the laptop so Crossman, Henshaw and Metzer could see the live feed.

"Is there a problem?" Slattery polled.

"Mister Slattery," Fraser delicately called. "Is Wellman Enterprises heedful of any competitors making apparatus for the market that your latest development is intended to address?"

Exchanging an uneasy glance with Molloy, Slattery proclaimed, "there are some remedies available at present, but they do not furnish the price-performance advantages our scheme will have."

"What about Stewart & Stevenson Oil Tools?" Crossman tendered.

"Ahh—" Arching his cheeks up at the suddenness of the knock, Molloy's expression reminded Fraser of Caesar Romero playing The Joker in the Batman tv series. "Are you studying their deep-sea production commodity?"

"We are," Fraser settled. "There's some news on the oil exploration live feed website."

"Stewart & Stevenson are aware we are engineering a revolutionary technique," Molloy explained, "and they're campaigning to transmit the hint they have a mechanism in place already."

"Mmmm, this is not as open and shut as we derived it might be," Henshaw voiced. "We'll need to make a few enquiries before advancing."

Mutually agreeing to suspend negotiations until The Firm had surveyed the Stewart & Stevenson merchandise more thoroughly, the meeting ended, Wellman Enterprises taking a plea from Fraser to contrast and compare their offering with the American competitor's appliance for The Firm.

Just as they were shaking hands and the Dublin Knights making ready to skedaddle, Mad Milton's zit finally erupted, sending showers of creamy puss over Slattery and Molloy.

"I know you have some reservations about the investment," Slattery quipped, "but there's no need to amplify your proviso with a volcano erupting impression."

Staring at the mess Molloy added, "we'll have to bring in an industrial cleaning team to mop up the fallout."

"*B'jesus*, Roger," Kieran Kavanagh whispered to Fraser. "I'm going to be known as the feckin' man, sponsoring the feckin' grand exploding zit fiasco, all over the feckin' Dublin financial district!"

~ * ~

On their way over to Whately & Waterson for a wash-up meeting, Fraser applauded, "well, young Bradley saved the day there."

"Yes," Crossman graciously concurred. "Outstanding Brad, that'll get you a case of beer the next time you're in the Big Apple."

Exhilarated, Purnell radiated with ecstasy.

"You'll be able to tell the Ayatollah, er, your uncle," Fraser adjusted, "you made a valuable contribution to the business."

"Does this mean I can join the bullpen team in some capacity?" trilled the jubilant gofer.

God, Fraser cogitated, *once they distinguished his Bembridge connection, the Essex boy traders would have him for lunch, Purnell suffering daily bouts of japes and jokes.* Nonattributable to any identifiable dealer, they were cute enough to ensure when ripping into a victim, it became generic and non-ascribable.

Peering at Purnell with an air of caution, Henshaw caveated, "well, I wouldn't get delirious just yet. We'll see."

Fraser discriminated it echoed him aiming to put Heather off from owning a pet gerbil, and about as probable as Piranha Brothers Manny Goldberg handing out free tickets to an al-Qaeda fund raiser at his eldest grandson's *bar mitzvah*. In reality, neglecting his uncle's mightily influential leverage, if Purnell had a future at The Firm, the accounts department beckoned to be his destination.

Re-examining the business, the Dublin Knights and Kieran Kavanagh deduced the trip had been a success. Apart from Wellman Enterprises, the three other investment opportunities were secure. Consequently, the climate became upbeat, celebration in the air. Punctuating the hit came down to the team employing tried and tested investment assessment models of Germanic origin, Obergruppenführer Metzer gleamed with elation, Crossman raising his eyebrows in refreshed consternation about his apparent superiority complex. Delighted with the outcomes, Kavanagh promoted the endeavour rendered a significant win-win for The Firm and Whately & Waterson, though he did whisper to Fraser, goose-stepping krauts and puss-exploding septics were not incorporated in The Firm's next stopover to the Emerald Isle. Glinting in response, Fraser shrewdly merited that often business handiworks were populated with far-out characters, but only the end result counted. Predicting The Firm's corporate investors jumping at the chance to participate in the last vestiges of the Euro bale out fiasco, Henshaw got into the act, albeit, he did temper his enthusiasm when Metzer gladsomely branded two-thirds of the revenue would be accredited to Frankfurt, until the Wellman Enterprises opportunity could be resolved.

Renewed with confidence, even young Purnell revisited the scene of his revelatory oil exploration competitor discovery several times, too many for Crossman's liking. Having to shut him up, Fraser whispered to him, he prophesied the esteem he had built up in the American's good books instantly reducing to zero, if he persisted in replay mode.

Bringing some degree of proportion to the Dublin Knights bubbling achievement, the 'explosive in more senses than one' New Yorker reproached, "before we all get on cloud nine sucking each other's dicks, there's some more work to be done. What say you, Roger?"

Remembering Henry Jacques had incongruously emitted the same phrase, he set forth, "well, speaking for myself, I've never sucked anyone's dick. I even find it difficult to suck my own, but Milton does have a point. A few more checks and balances need to be made before we can be unreservedly sure they are investment revenue bearing opportunities."

"I agree," Kavanagh endorsed. "We're expecting Baker Finch, Kaufmann Vogel Electric and Dresdner Fuchs to have feckin' answers to the feckin' issues we raised tomorrow morning. Providing the data we requested is feckin' satisfactory, by noon, we should be in a position to give the feckin' investment go signal to them."

"Right," Crossman approbated, acknowledging Kavanagh's remark as the Whately & Waterson man immersed Metzer and Henshaw in more consultation. Gawking at Fraser, he ticketed under his breath, "what does this word 'feckin' mean, Kavanagh uses in every sentence he utters?"

Smirking, Fraser avowed, "I'll tell you later, Milton, when we're on the plane to Blighty."

Because the weather endured clement, after finalising the Whately & Waterson business at the international financial services centre, Crossman suggested they walk to the Fitzwilliam Hotel to collect their baggage. His concomitant knights agreeing, they boldly set off.

Crossing the Liffey into Moss Street on the south side of the river, an inconclusive wrangle broke out as to the best route to take to the hotel, many options proposed but few seconded.

Lastly, Ricky Henshaw advanced, "why don't we ask a local?"

"Good idea," Fraser justified.

Reconnoitering around, he saw a man coming across their path. "Excuse me," he requisitioned in a gregarious voice, "could you possibly direct us to York Street?"

Rubbing his chin, caked in bristles and the vestiges of a mussels in Irish cider lunch, the man probed, "York Street, is it, sir?"

"Yes, York Street."

Contemplating further, he foraged up and down Moss Street, twice. "Well, sir, to get to York Street, I'd not start from here, if I were you."

Peeping at his cohorts, Fraser clocked their mouths had become unsealed in disbelief at the dotty Irish logic, for once even Obergruppenführer Metzer dumbfounded.

Furrowing his brow, he cooed, "I see…well, er, where would you start from?"

"To get to York Street, sir," the man enlightened, "the best place to start from is Castle Street."

"Castle Street," Fraser aped, screwing up his features in abject astonishment.

"Yes, sir. Unmistakably, the best place to start from to get to York Street is Castle Street."

Gaping at his companions again, they appeared equally perplexed by the route master's instructions.

"And, er," Fraser hesitantly interrogated, "how do we get to Castle Street, prey tell?"

Gazing up and down Moss Street for a second time, the man rubbed his chin again, a combination of spent bristles and mussel fragments falling to the ground. "Well, sir, I'd not start from here, if I were you," he earnestly counselled.

And the process went on, and on, and on, and on.

Chapter 18: Roger's Shagging Maria Sharapova!

Christmas and New Year approached. In the Fraser household it meant readying for family guests staying at Hazelwood during Yuletide week, or they travelled to either Charlotte's or Roger's parents for the celebrations. Also an occasion when brother Colin and his family came south from Headingley to join their Fraser brethren, and cousins Peter and Barry and their families descended on Roger's parent's house or Aunt Jemina's house, traditionally, the festive season had become a forum for a massive family get-together. Often raucous soirees', lubricated with gallons of mulled wine and fuelled by tons of mince pies, they donated many treasured and memorable moments to the entire Fraser clan.

In terms of work celebrations, apart from the rare executive shindig like Bembridge's summer party at Cheyne Walk and the annual company outing, Christmas Eve was the only time when The Firm let its hair down, employees warranted the most outlandish japes and misdemeanours without reprimand, let alone being presented with their P-45s.

Getting in tune with the crimbo season, most of The Firm's London offices were decked out in Christmas trees and glistening decorations, Bembridge and his associate executives making their usual arrangements to lay on a massive spread of choice quality foods and fine wines to keep the workforce happy. An occurrence for furtive as well as festive frolics, everybody looked forward to the blowout. Customarily, people meshed in one-off snogs in stationary rooms, the more daring, usually meaning the traders, dropped their pants, sat on photocopying machines, and sent high-fidelity, colour pictures of their derrieres picking out every nook and crevice, to all and sundry. Turning blind optics and deaf lugholes to the goings-on, insightful executives and middle-managers understood the jovial activities released pent up frustrations and aggressions, all good for team morale.

~ * ~

Fraser had some relatively minor capers to complete before Christmas Eve, the most tricky being final negotiation of equities and commodities traffic with Milligan Danby, a middleman investment house advising their clients which investment banks offered the best options for maximizing returns, their market testing identifying The Firm were currently *numero uno* in the equities and commodities investment stakes.

Involved with Milligan Danby treaties in the past, Fraser differentiated the company to be fastidious and protocol obsessed in all their transactions. Based on the outskirts of Batley in a large manor house once owned by Victorian industrialist Sir Titus Salt, on previous calls he had combined the business with swift excursions to Headingley to see brother Colin, and Leeds to call on cousin Barry. Regrettably, there'd be no slack in the timescale on this appointment allowing for such happy conjunctures. Because of their commendable triumph in the equities and commodities markets, Ricky Henshaw assigned the sisters, Jasper Gilham and Todd Charnock, otherwise known as Beavis and Butthead, to represent the bullpen at Milligan Danby.

A no-nonsense, straight-talking Yorkshireman, brooking no debate when it came to doing business with Milligan Danby, the Firm's team were set to meet with Tom Braithwaite, Director of Commodities and Equity Securities. Paralleling Charlotte, Braithwaite had graduated from the Brian Clough School of pre-prepared negotiation. Professedly a stiff proselyte, allowing business partners some cosmetic latitude to discuss investments, he then brought the boom down, heralding his way was the only way, and had no hesitation making it evident that if the business partner didn't approve, they knew where the door was to be found.

On their flight up to Leeds, Fraser instructed the sisters to listen diligently to Braithwaite. Being in the business for at least a thousand years, he had forgotten more about investment banking than they'd ever know.

"A heavy duty player then?" Charnock postulated.

"Take it from me," Fraser advertised, "they don't come any heavier."

"So," Gilham queried, "how do you want us to play it, Roger?"

"Smile and nod, and if you must spout, make it in agreement with whatever he is saying. Remember, this is virtually a done deal. Milligan Danby has already pre-selected The Firm based on our daily equities and commodities trading figures. All we have to do is play ball and the contract is ours."

"We will, Roger," the sisters attested in unison.

"And above all," he flatly accentuated, "be straight, like red-blooded males and *please*, no limp handshakes or effeminate gestures, like you did when you met the Big Lebowski."

"But we *are* men," they steadfastly purported, again in unison.

Tutting, he gave them a sideways goggle.

Just as Fraser retained from their preceding meetings, Braithwaite's craggy, uncompromising demeanour had been safeguarded. Corresponding to a coiled rattlesnake, ready to strike without warning at anyone he even remotely hypothesised might give him an argument, he emanated intense swagger, significantly so during initial introductions when he set eyes on the sisters, then gaped at Fraser as if to say, 'What have you brought with you, a couple of Larry Grayson doppelgangers?' Though extremely competent and gifted dealers, Bevis and Butthead tended to come across as Southern Jessie's, no matter how much they tried not to.

"Alright, Roger," Braithwaite sanctioned, his voice paved with resolute vigour, "let's get down to business."

Sketching the Milligan Danby investment profile and their client's requirements, he stressed his aspirations of The Firm. Steering the response, Fraser delineated why The Firm was the best option, by detailing equities and commodities market accomplishments over the last three quarters, the sisters supplementing examples of their own trading attainments. Satisfied the rhetoric tallied with his market testing findings, Braithwaite then buzzed Fraser to chart The Firm's futures strategy in terms of volcanic-yield equities and commodities, the axiomatic reason why Toby Chalcroft had sent the stock analyst on the business call. Appreciating Fraser had a good Milligan Danby track record in terms of stock market predictions, Top Cat premeditated 'playing the Roger card' as he called it, guaranteed sealing the deal.

"So, you think South East Asia will develop across the board?" Braithwaite tabled.

"Well, I'm not going to pretend the region will crank out the same explosive earnings it did before the recession kicked in," Fraser confided, "but of all the emerging ultra-modern technology geo-regions, conspicuously in telecoms and energy research, South Korea, Indo-China and Japan are in the vanguard."

"What about the European and American telecom product suppliers?"

"We'll subsume them into the investment portfolio," he authenticated. "But their across the board earnings peaked in 2009-10, and some of the European mobile phone suppliers are a bit shaky right now, the only exception being the rise of 4G mobile phones and networks in Scandinavia. The next wave will be dominated by Asia-Pacific. They invent nothing, but are excellent innovators, hence the gains will be larger than from Europe or the Americas."

"Agreed, but I assume," Braithwaite qualified, "The Firm will make a mixed investment to lower risk?"

"Of course, Tom. We never rely on a single worldwide region for any type of futures investment. It's always been a bedrock Firm strategy, not just lately sequent to the severe recession."

"Hhmm, good," he okayed.

All went swimmingly well until Braithwaite outlined his generic vision for the Milligan Darby investments portfolio over the next two years, Todd Charnock feeling predisposed to contest the plan. *Oh no*, Fraser cerebrally bemoaned.

Recoiling at the notion, the tyke entreated, "teach your grandmother how to suck eggs?" Affronted, his veneer flamed with vitriol. "I've been making investments and analysing stock markets, for longer than when your mother had an unfortunate urge to oblige your father, and you became the fruit of their sordid union."

"But, Mister Braithwaite," Charnock pleaded, "I'm only trying—"

"*Trying*!" he interrupted, coming to the boil. "Don't you presuppose I checked and double-checked all my brass tacks before taking this meeting?"

"Er...yes," he nervously wailed.

"Then don't question me, boy. Not now, not ever."

Setting the tincture for the residue of Braithwaite's dissertation, the contretemps had Charnock shrinking in his seat, his co-sister refraining from taking up the defiance. Astutely waiting for his temper to fade, Fraser recovered the status quo in his own inimitable way, issuing some smoothing words, and promising Charnock would be subjected to some penance for his brazenness at Canary Wharf.

With the covenant content agreed and only needing a counter-signature from Equities Director Toby Chalcroft, Fraser collected together the contract papers and nominated they went for lunch to celebrate the transaction at Zucchini, a swish Italian restaurant in Batley.

Howbeit placated by Fraser's redress to Charnock's outburst, the Yorkshireman tarried broody and puffed-up, noticeably when his spiers fell on either Beavis or Butthead.

"Great balls of fire, slick traders, they look more like Butch and Gay Dance," he reproved under his breath more than once, the sources of his malice taking heed and behaving like choirboys for the remainder of the encounter.

Wary he rarely forgave easily, Fraser crusaded to soften Braithwaite's sombre mood by using the lunchtime break to talk about things beyond the world of investment banking.

Reprising his love of God's own county, Fraser eulogised, "you know, Tom, we have some amazing countryside in Kent, especially on and around the North Downs."

"*North Downs*," he dismissively taunted. "They're nowt but foothills compared to the Pennines, lad. But I fancy it's in-keeping with the smallness of namby pamby Southern Jessies.'" Glaring at the sisters, obviously suspecting their sexual orientation might not be as presumed in the sovereign principality of Yorkshire, and thereby they should be burnt at the stake, he murmured, "mmmm."

"But, Tom," Fraser objected, "I'm not a Southern Jessie as you so indelicately put it. As you know, Cheshire is my birth place."

"As far as I'm concerned, anybody from outside Yorkshire is a Southern Jessie, …encompassing you rich folk from Cheshire."

"But, Tom," he bleated again, "I'm a man of meagre means, with a wife, three children and a rugby club to cosset."

"Aye," the irascible tyke accepted. "But you're a clever lad, and you'll be very rich one day. Anyway—" He made a reconciling mug as if conscious of taking out his enmity of the Beavis and Butthead on Fraser. "Has your work taken you to any foreign climes since we last met?"

"As a matter of fact, I had to deputise for Toby Chalcroft at the 2011 FinTech conference."

"Oh aye, and where was that held?"

"Exotic Montevideo," Fraser proudly informed.

"*Montevideo*," Braithwaite blasted. "Montevideo's got *nowt* on Batley, lad."

"I didn't say it did, Tom."

"Montevideo, huh." Folding his arms contemptuously he asserted, "I bet Montevideo can't claim to have a world-renowned Wheel Tappers and Shunters Social Club."

"But Tom, that was a fictional television programme from the mid-nineteen-seventies."

"Rubbish, there's been a Wheel Tappers and Shunters Social Club in Batley since George Stevenson brought the railways to South

Yorkshire. Any similarity to the TV variety show is ambiguous. Anyway, that show was based on the Batley Variety Club." Jabbing Fraser's arm with an outstretched finger, Braithwaite extolled, "I bet they've not got a club in Montevideo that can boast the likes of Shirley Bassey, Tom Jones and Ken Dodd on their top rank roster."

"Quite right, of course not," Fraser conceded, not wishing to put the Milligan Danby contract at risk, whilst cogitating, *not sure how Ken Dodd and the Diddymen would go down in Uruguay's sophisticated first city.*

Shaking his head, Braithwaite uttered, "Montevideo, *huh.* Montevideo's got nowt on Batley."

~ * ~

Following the Yorkshire witch trials escapade, the second outstanding task Fraser had to cap centred on progressing a settlement with Kvaerner Masa-Yards Oy, a Finnish ship builder seeking investment capital from The Firm for a new fleet of ocean-going cruise ships. In light of the recession, The Firm had been very careful rating risk for capitalisation running into the hundreds of £millions, fail-safes put in place to recover the investment at key milestones in the ship building programme, and danger to capital investors belt and braced with a derivatives artifice to spread the investment risk further.

Part of The Firm's valuation process, earlier, Fraser and his compeers visited Kvaerner Masa at Turku and Helsinki. After the business powwows had been concluded, senior members of the ship building company took them out to dinner, a normal enactment of courtesy during such engagements. Notwithstanding, they did not forecast the succeeding all-night vodka drinking session, Fraser and co the recipients of hangovers as big as Boston in the morning and longing they had never ventured near a *Finlandia* vodka bottle.

As a counterpart to the business, the Fins were coming to London to validate The Firm from their angle, and to talk to English shipyards accessing investment funding from The Firm over the past forty to fifty years. At their bequest, Analysts Department PA April Harrington arranged accommodation for the Kvaerner Masa posse at the Cumberland Hotel. With Christmas just around the corner, the Fins wanted to be close to Oxford Street for personal shopping.

Acting as their host, Fraser had also been booked into the Cumberland for the night of the day the Fins landed in London. As a precursor to the subsequent day, when they'd assemble at Canary Wharf for Luther Bembridge and Toby Chalcroft to give them the grand tour of the London headquarters, his charge became softening them up to make them receptive to The Firm's overtures.

Picking up the Kvaerner Masa taskforce from the Cumberland in the early evening, Fraser taxied them over to the Belvedere at Holland Park for dinner. Several bottles of *Château Montaiguillon, Montagne St Emilion* and a half bottle of *Remy Martin V.S.O.P* were rifled through during the evening, everyone consigned to merriment and light-heartedness.

About to bid his clients goodnight before retiring at the Cumberland, the Fins told Fraser the time had come to commence serious drinking. No matter what protestations he made, they failed to relent. Ensconced in one of the quieter ground-floor ante rooms, the Fins practically sat on him to make sure he stayed for at least a few nightcaps. By one in the morning, with his alcohol meter registering full, Fraser managed to slink off, leaving the Kvaerner Masa crew to indulge in attempting to drink the Cumberland dry.

When the alarm clock went off at 6:45, Fraser felt like an entire Panzer division, probably headed by Obergruppenführer Heinrich Metzer, had steam-rollered his entire body. Worse still, his brain banged around his cranium as if Wayne Rooney stood inside using it for penalty practice. After a long shower and a short shave, he wandered down to the restaurant in search of breakfast. To his bewilderment, as he passed the drinkers' afterhours anti-room, he saw the Fins still inside, still making whoopee, and still draining the Cumberland of its last remnants of spirits. Calculating *today is going to be an unadulterated wash-out*, Fraser envisaged the Fins eventually falling over, and spending the day in the horizontal position.

Cogitating how he could convincingly explain the no-show of the Kvaerner Masa delegates to the Ayatollah and Top Cat, by eight he had checked-out and climbed into a taxi taking him to the Isle of Dogs financial district. Much to his confoundment, with only minutes to go before the appointed time to take the shipyard envoys up to the executive floor, he heard a knock, knock on his hideaway door, and three smiling Fins stepped in, their deportment as sober as judges.

Geez, Fraser inwardly averred, *these guys must have the constitution of an ox and in place of human organs, an internal combustion engine.*

~ * ~

Concurrent with the London Stock Exchange closing business trading at 12:30 pm, The Firm's 2011 Christmas Eve party kicked off. Mirroring the Pope giving apostolic blessings to the masses and making merry with lesser beings, Bembridge and other board execs plus all the senior directors, Toby Chalcroft inclusive, came down from the lofty heights of the executive floor to dispense benediction, their annual pilgrimage into the heart of The Firm's operational and business management areas becoming the hub of light mockery among those with a satirical yen.

As 'Pope' Bembridge and his ecumenical council glided into the bullpen, Fraser overheard Douglas Kellet, an old-school broker in the twilight of his career, crack to confederate stock jockey Anton Devereux, "any moment he'll be swinging a vessel containing holy burning essence before him, making the cross sign to his underlings, and reverently enunciating, *Benedicat vos omnipotens Deus, Pater, et Filius, et Spiritus Sanctus.*"

Simpering, Fraser cerebrated such an outlandish and astute observation could never emanate from the mouths of any of the Essex boy traders.

Snagging Kellet's gaze, he translated, "may almighty God bless you, the Father, and the Son, and the Holy Spirit,"

"Quite correct, Roger," Kellet validated. "I see you've not forgotten your grammar school Latin."

"I've retained some, but in this case, it's resultant from a childhood occurrence I recounted at a recent dinner party. An old Catholic friend of mine could recite the apostolic blessing verbatim. In a superficial attempt to convert us Christians to Catholicism, he said it so often, some of it stuck."

"Mmmm, I'm Presbyterian myself," Kellet stipulated, "but I've always had a penchant for Catholic Church architecture and decoration. In comparison, protestant churches are sterile and dull."

"I couldn't agree more," Fraser affirmed. "I've been invited to several catholic services and they were majestic, largely because the inside décor and the pomp of the ceremony were inspiring, whereas on the infrequent occasions I go to our village C of E church, the interior is lifeless and bare in comparison."

"Decidedly, we don't get wonderment from supercilious Rowan Williams on the steps of St. Paul's or at Canterbury," Kellet criticised.

"*Hah*! Not long ago, one of my friends alleged something similar when a group of us were proposing candidates for Room 101."

"I know I shouldn't say this, because it's disrespectful," Kellet prefaced, "but Williams is a super-king-sized, politically motivated twat."

"Yes, that appraisal became our conclusion as well."

As the festivities hit full-throttle, the analysts and dealers were joined in the bullpen area by colleagues from equities research, underwriting and mergers & acquisitions, over and above a few stragglers from accounts and IT support, curious to understand how the main players of The Firm's business let their hair, and sometimes, pants down.

Jacking-in his analyst duties in favour of indulging in *Mercury Domaine Meix Foulot 2008* and Colston Bassett stilton, Fraser joined Henry Jacques, Dennis Passmore and Pension Fund Manager Oscar Giddins on the trading floor, swapping stories about client investment banking episodes, and corporate entertainment galas they'd been to over the years.

"Glyndebourne took some beating for sheer ambience and aura," Passmore remarked, "but top of the pile for me remains a production of *Oedipus Rex* at Covent Garden with some clients from the FMCG investment sector I chaperoned."

"Oh yes," Jacques strengthened, "without doubt, the Royal Opera House is one of my highlights."

"What did you see, Henry?" Fraser enquired.

"*Cosi fan Tutti*," he pealed, "with some execs from Lindley Mayhew."

"The construction group morphing into Frankland International?" Fraser quizzed.

"Mmmm."

"When did it occur?" Giddins broached, like Fraser presuming it hailed from the other side of the millennium.

"When you and Roger were still in short trousers."

Lubricated by overconsumption of *Mercury*, the foursome continued to recap refined culture instalments from yesteryear until the confabulation revolutionised into sporting bashes.

"Did any of you guys go to The Firm's client function at Wimbledon in 2005?" Giddins cross-examined.

"Yes, me," Fraser inveterated.

"Of course," the amiable pension fund manager acknowledged. "Then you will recall the Maria Sharapova incident?"

Giddins referred to a noteworthy-investor corporate jolly, co-hosted by Fraser, himself and other firm appointees. On the championship's opening day, Fraser escorted a group wanting to watch the first-round Maria Sharapova versus Nuria Llagostera Vives play-off on one of the outer courts, Giddins and his guests also at the same contest. Right from the off, it became obvious virtually every male spectator attended the match purely to drool at the delicious, delectable Miss Sharapova. By game four, Fraser noted, instead of heads swivelling left and right tracing the ball, the wolves, Giddins and himself included, stared exclusively at Maria. They also espied that some women in the crowd couldn't take their snoopers off the Russian beauty either. 'Must be lesbians,' Fraser had razzed. Then, they spotted the odd man not fixated by Maria in the least, tracking the trajectory of the ball, Giddins gauging, 'They must be woofters.'

"Every spellbinding shake," Fraser specified. "There is eye candy and then there is Maria Sharapova. Irrefutably she drew some beat. Though during the contest, I conjectured for the sake of preserving onlooker hearing, the court officials should really have handed out earmuffs to protect the inner ear from Maria's x-certificate howls and screeches when she struck the ball."

"Quite. She made more noise than a busted chainsaw."

Sucking in breath, he ratified, "that's an understatement. Her yelps and cries were ear piercing. I also surmised being Maria's boyfriend must be an ear-threatening experience when they're on the job. If she makes the same noise during the act of love making, the boyfriend has probably been turned deaf."

"Changing the subject slightly," Giddins begged. "Did you know men think about sex every twenty minutes?"

"Oh, I think that's an under-estimation. It's more like every ten minutes, certainly in my case."

"Are you a sex maniac, Roger?"

"I'll let you into a secret," he offered, drawing close. "All men are sex maniacs."

Unbeknown to them, the very name Maria Sharapova had heads rapidly craning in the direction of the conversationalists, particularly those of the Essex boy traders.

"What's this then, Roger?" Lawrence Springs piloted. "You've not been having a secret love affair behind Charlotte's back, have you?"

"Certainly *not*," he blared, aghast at the inflammatory inference.

"What was that about Roger having a love affair?" Trevor Evans polled.

"He's been playing find the sausage with Maria Sharapova," Springs roared.

"*No, I haven't,*" Fraser angrily protested.

Joining in, Landon Boyce, yet another tactless Essex boy broker shouted across the bullpen to a festive flock of his Essex brethren getting blue sky blonde on *Dom Perignon*, "*hey…*" They whirled to the yowl of his familiar guttural voice. "…Roger's shagging Maria Sharapova."

"*What*!" Fraser cried, increasingly perturbed by the accelerating false gossip.

"Give her a portion did you, Rog?" shouted someone from their midst.

"Certainly *not*," he bellowed.

Gathered together in a clique reminiscent of the three witches from *Macbeth*, and probably uttering, '*When shall we three meet again in thunder, lightning or in rain?*', by the time the jaw-dropping news reached April Harrington, Bembridge's PA Marcia Knight and man-eater Alice Vaughan from HR, it had become, 'Maria Sharapova is having Roger's love child.'

As prognostication grew *vis-à-vis* Fraser's shocking extra-marital avocation or vastly-esteemed bedpost notch, dependent on the reviewer's take on morality or envy, the furore spiralled, people swapping Fraser stories and reciting his intimacy history from school onwards, most of it invented on the spot but nevertheless dynamite in its impact. Not unknown for luminary Lotharios from the turbo-powered world of investment banking to indulge in salacious goings-on of the carnal kind with corking celebrities and even page-three girls, howbeit previously sanctified for unequivocal fidelity to his wife, Fraser's purported dalliance created a groundswell of intrigue and speculation. Suddenly, quite rational people became feverish with talk about his 'Mister Clean' persona being a shroud for a covert life of debauchery and lust. Others more versed in the ways of the dark side, asserted Fraser had a Dr. Jekyll and Mister Hyde split identity, at night the stock analyst come trouble-shooter donning a black cape and top hat before cruising East End backstreets Jack the Ripper fashion, seeking out ladies of the night to satisfy his lustful appetites, before dispatching them to oblivion with a surgeon's lance.

Heaving with buzz, the bullpen became Fraser tittle-tattle central, every insignificant phrase he had voiced of a sexual nature during his tenure at The Firm brought to the surface and amplified to the brink of righteous heresy. Feeling like Father Urbain Grandier in Ken Russell's *The Devils*, Fraser could already see himself tried by The Firms' inquisitors and consigned to the cleansing flames.

Just as Fraser's consternation breached full tilt, Toby Chalcroft strolled into the bullpen area. Shouting above the crowd din, desperate to stop the front page headlines in the *Financial Times* or god forbid, *The Wall Street Journal*, he wailed, "I am *not* shagging Maria Sharapova, as Landon so indelicately put it, and on no account is she having my love child."

Nudging Fraser, Henry Jacques alerted him to Top Cat's presence.

Aiming a half-envious, half-critical shine at Fraser, TC chastised, "Roger, I hope you've not been using your trouble-shooter brief to promote Anglo-Russian relations beyond normal business decorum."

Wrinkling his nose defensively, Fraser whimpered "Toby, I've never even met Maria Sharapova, let alone gained carnal knowledge about her."

~ * ~

Unabated, the commotion about Fraser and Sharapova went on until Lawrence Springs retreated from his fellow tameless clan members, and accidentally on purpose poured a glass of bubbly over Sarah Williams, the well-endowed accounts secretary who had chased Dave Stratton around the office in the summer for imitating Nigel Brooks' predilection to get his Bristol rovers on her massive mammaries. Sucking in air sharply as the liquid drenched her tight blouse, Sarah treated the Essex boy traders to an instant wet tee-shirt competition, before chasing after Springs with the forethought of soiling all his future Christmases permanently.

As her chest swung along to and fro during the pursuit to the sounds of the Beatles *I Don't Want to Spoil the Party* coming from the background PA, Trevor Evans wisecracked, "I didn't know she could juggle those in sync with music."

Just when Fraser perceived the Maria Sharapova controversy had died away, Alice Vaughan sauntered up to him, and chirped in her catty but suggestive voice, "so, Roger, what's Maria like in bed?"

Call-back of more employee embarrassing accounts and extra-curricular shenanigans dominated contentions around the bullpen, their lucidity exacerbated by everybody downing an endless conveyor belt of champagne and fine wines, and gorging themselves silly on the sumptuous spread.

Ambling unsteadily headlong, like two Dionysian disciples plastered on ambrosia, Brendan Kirkman and Pierce Finlay, two of the most inarticulate users of the Queen's English, and probably the worst examples of barrow-boy Essex dealer mentality, parked themselves beside Giddins and Fraser.

"Allo, you two poshens," Kirkman squawked in his own inimitable way of dovetailing into two-way communication. "Enjoying the bash, are you?"

"Kirkman," Giddens admonished, "Roger and I are not *poshens*, as you so indelicately put it, but if you're intimating we enunciate clearly and concisely, compared to you feral beings from east of Dagenham, then yes, we do express ourselves appropriately and with clarity."

"Yeah, that's right," Kirkman reiterated, "poshens."

Grinding his teeth, Giddins gibed, "do you actually speak English?"

"*Huh*," he brayed, flustered by the unsubtle syntax.

"You know," Giddins tested, "an inflected language, characterised by modal verbs, and based on a proto-indo European foundation."

"Huh," Kirkman grunted again, still not recording the put-down, and coming across as vacant as a dimwit failing the two times table.

"Ere," Finlay babbled, identically nonplussed by Giddins' rapacious outburst. "Wot 'ave you two bin up to lately then?"

Before either Giddins or Fraser could answer, Finlay charged off, spewing out his own communal rundown. "Socially, I've bin shaggin' as usual." Suspending to yawn, displaying his twenty-two-carat gold fillings, he then hiccupped. "As many birds as I can, not in your league of course, Roger…Maria Sharapova, wow."

"I keep on telling you," Fraser bemoaned, "I am not having an affair with Maria Sharapova."

Unconvinced, Finlay leered then gleefully guffawed. "Yeah, right, heh, heh, we'll give you the benefit of the doubt, wink, wink. Anyway, I sometimes fink there aren't enough birds in London to satisfy my hungers."

"Ere, Pierce," Kirkman blabbered, so drunk he swayed around congeneric to a sozzled tailors' dummy on speed, "I'll 'ave to give you a lend of my gal Shirley. She goes like a steam train, 'specially when I'm pumping her."

Appalled, the construct of Kirkman on the job with the waif-approximating Shirley or any other female, made Giddins and Fraser grimace with nausea. Gawping at each other, they shook their heads, sighed, and tutted their disapproval, neither Finlay nor Kirkman detecting the revulsion. Too far gone on the ecstasies of *Dom Perignon* to book any sign of condemnation, the trader's chin-wag waxed into further congratulatory on-the-job bombast needing no audience to uphold its momentum, until Medwin Mottershead, a petulant and snappish high-roller with Firm business partner Luxborough & Simonson bubbled to the summit of their staccato patter.

"I'll tell you wot," Kirkman threatened, "if Motorhead gives me anymore verbals, 'is time won't be long on this Earth."

"Yeah," Finlay agreed, "he deserves a solid kickin' for all the fuss he made when that Spence-Harding share price 'eaded south. I mean it wos his fault, not mine."

Inclined to put the Spence-Harding debacle into perspective, Fraser said, "you two might consider Luxborough & Simonson took a pounding on that stock, and, The Firm were no saints over shared losses. Motorhead as you so quaintly call him balled Pierce out because he was at least partially culpable of mis-reading the stock in play. Besides, Mottershead is on his way up and he's got an elephant's memory. You two don't want to be in his future firing line, so I wouldn't engage in the blame game with him. He can be really nasty."

"Wot do you mean by that, Roger?" asked Kirkman

"The bloke's a real James Blunt."

"Wot?"

Bemused by Kirkman's failure to comprehend the cockney rhyming slang, he tried again. "An Anthony Blunt."

"Huh."

His befuddlement approaching overload, he couched, "a Cuthbert Ulysses Norman Trollope."

Kirkman hunched his shoulders.

Correspondingly dumbfounded, Giddins blasted, "a cuntasaurus rex."

"Oh, you mean he's a twat."

"*Yessss,*" Giddins and Fraser both chimed.

Now cognisant with the probable downside of incurring Motorhead's displeasure, Kirkman and Finlay formed a huddle sharing counterattack ploys should the Luxborough & Simonson ramrod fall upon them.

"If we walk off," Giddins whispered to Fraser, "do you figure they'll even notice?"

"Probably not." Staring at the loquacious pair, rattling on about the square root of nothing of any significance or consequence, he denigrated, "where there's no pulse, there's no sensation."

Chapter 19: Christmas at Fraserville

Christmas Day morning in downtown Fraserville found Charlotte and Roger preparing for their guests; his parents Don and Angela and his Aunt Jemina. Dressed in the spirit of Christmas, Charlotte had clad herself in a short, tight-fitting Santa rig with high heels, the seductive outfit always something Roger set great store in seeing over Christmas week. Complementing her festive costume by transfiguring into a paragon of illustrious society chic, he had attired himself in a black dress suit, white dress shirt and a red bow tie.

"Now, Roger," she point-blank decreed, "let's have no bouts of drunkenness or bad language today."

Genuinely mystified, he advanced, "I don't know what you mean."

"Of course you don't," she whined. "You were so far gone on wine and spirits last Christmas Day when we went to the candlelight evening service, it doesn't surprise me you can't remember."

"Oh, yes—" Partially distinguishing the chapter, he winced. "Ouch, of course."

"Fancy asking the Vicar of Saint Paul and Saint Peter's Church, if once he had baptised and confirmed new-borns, if he ever saw them again?" Flaunting an admonishing governess stance, she placed her hands about her hips. "*Really*," she venomously crowed, "Davina will never forgive you."

"I'm sure the vicar has forgotten all about it," Roger countered, stimulated further by Charlotte's unintentional dominatrix persona, but refraining from begging to go to the bedroom to continue the role play.

"Besides, Valentine reckoned it was indispensably witty and poignant."

"*Phooey*. Buckingham is not like Kent," she repudiated. "People up there are far more traditional and conservative in their attitudes." Scowling, she censured, "and then you had the audacity to ask the verger, if he had ever contemplated roller-skating down the aisle with the collection plate when Sky Sports transmitted live football, so parishioners could scoot early." Her lour intensified. "That really took the biscuit. I've never been so embarrassed in all my life."

"Your father allotted it to be a good idea, and I don't recall Davina being in the slightest upset."

"Yes, well, often what my parents say is entirely different to what they think," she contended. "Even more blasphemous, you then had the effrontery to ask the vicar, if the Anglican clergy were allowed a dispensation to bury the bishop, sink the squirrel and baptise the hairy font at Hogmanay! *Really*, Roger."

Deciding to throw in the towel to his lambasting, Roger whinnied, "message received and understood, darling."

Hearing the kitchen door unfastening, they gave Wendy kindly smiles as she came in wearing the Karen Millen cocktail dress and high-heeled court shoes they'd given her for Christmas. In keeping with the blithesome function, she had tied her mass of long, wavy blonde hair up into a regency style, and the gold necklace and pearl earrings she received for her seventeenth birthday adorned her above the shoulders.

"Oh, darling," her mother proudly extolled, "you do look beautiful."

"Thank you, Mother," she blessed, gleaming endearingly at her.

"Well, Roger," Charlotte prompted, "are you going to acclaim our eldest daughter?"

Still enthralled by Wendy's entrance, her father walked over to her. Coming out of his trance, he kissed her on both cheeks and felicitated, "you looked your supreme best on your birthday, but since then you've grown even lovelier. You're really stunning, Wendy."

"Oh, Dad, Mum," Wendy budded, tears forming in her peepers, "you're so loving to me. Thank you again for the Christmas gifts."

"You are very welcome, my dear," her father assured.

Hearing the tail end of the palaver as he entered the kitchen, James yawped, "you're not going to get all mushy, are you?"

"Good lord," his mother retorted. "Wouldn't do you any harm to loosen your tender side occasionally."

"Oh, I've got all that to come, Mother," he fended with a playful grin. Turning to Roger, he inducted, "Dad, this MP3 player you and Mum gave me for Christmas."

"What about it?"

"Can I download MP3 files from a laptop onto it?"

"Yes, I'd think so."

"What I really mean is, can I download some of your MP3 music files onto it?"

"What?" Roger exclaimed smirking in disbelief. "You're not ditching the Arctic Monkeys and the Killers in favour of the Rolling Stones and Led Zeppelin, are you?"

"Yeah," James upheld, nodding like a berserk rocking horse.

"*What!*" he vigorously repeated with enough incredulity to imply his son must have been subjected to an epiphany rendezvous. "To use a famous Victor Meldrew expression, 'I don't believe it.'" Glinting at Charlotte, her jaw dropped as if to indicate her own amazement. "Finally seen the light have you, my boy?"

"Yeah, well, hah. Jeremy Payne's elder brother is really into music. He declared all the new bands have produced rubbish over the past ten years, and we revere his opinions."

"Oh, a realist, is he?" Roger plumbed, raising his eyebrows in recognition of the notion. "Even a visionary?"

"I'd not go as far as that, but he investigated nineties Brit Pop. You know, bands comparable to Oasis, then prospected seventies punk with the Clash, and in due course found the Rolling Stones and Led Zeppelin."

"On a voyage of discovery, is he?" Roger teased, his simper of contentment growing.

"I suppose so, but since then, Jeremy, Neville Matthews and Billy

Swan have been banging on about second-generation English rock music, and I just want to find out what all the fuss is about."

"Ah, peer-group pressure," he discerned.

Chagrined he'd be tarnished with the sheep-replicating, follow the leader brush his father always cawed about, James didn't authenticate the supposition out of hand.

Clocking his reticence, Roger avowed, "by all means, you can have access to my magnificent accumulation of gems."

"You don't judge I'm just pursuing the pack, then?"

"In this paradigm, no," he defended. "Truth is absolute, and in this instance, Jeremy's elder brother has stumbled onto it, and is spreading the gospel, just as I consider converting everyone into a Liverpool FC apostle, is doing God's work."

"*Really*, Roger," Charlotte bawled. "Anyone would think you were a saint."

~ * ~

First to make it to Fraserville, after the usual Christmas morning hugs and kisses, succeeded by the traditional giving of gifts all round, some even useful to their recipients, Don and Angela settled down in the lounge with Heather.

"What did you receive from your parents for Christmas, Heather?" Angela investigated.

"Well, Grandmother, I'm growing out of my stuffed animal stage, so I got an astronomical telescope and a two in one globe, as well as some clothes and other things."

"What's a two in one globe?" she balloted.

"It's two globes. One is the Earth by day, the other Space by night."

"I see. Are you developing an interest in the stars?"

"We did the Solar System at school, and Mummy told me more about it. Then I found out some more on the internet."

"So, Father Christmas obliged you?" Don tendered.

"Oh, Grandfather," Heather stressed, "there's no such thing as Father Christmas or Santa Claus."

Flabbergasted their youngest granddaughter alleged some chubby chap from Lapland, dressed in red and white with black boots, and who parked his reindeer-powered sleigh on the roof before coming down the chimney to make requested deliveries, didn't actually exist, Don and Angela exchanged puzzled glances.

"Hhmm," Don replied. "How do you know Father Christmas does not exist?"

"Last year, Adelaide Perrett from school told me she found her Christmas presents on top of her parent's wardrobe. So after I told Mummy and Daddy what I wanted for Christmas this year, a few weeks later, I found the telescope and the two in one globe in the airing cupboard, along with some gifts for Wendy and James. That's when I knew Adelaide had been right about Father Christmas not being real."

"I see," he acknowledged. "You really are growing up."

"Last year I thought it possible anyway, because I woke up early on Christmas morning and found Daddy putting presents around the Christmas tree. He jumped when he saw me. I asked him what he was doing, but he couldn't give me a passable explanation, apart from saying recovering the glass and dish containing refreshments for Santa, after he brought our gifts down the chimney."

"Hhmm," Don neighed, "you weren't persuaded then?"

"No."

"Why, Heather?" Angela probed.

"Because on Christmas Eve, I saw Daddy drinking from the same glass and taking a mince pie off the same plate."

By midday, Aunt Jemina had joined the Fraser clan. Peppering the dialogue with quotations from literature and religion, she attached her own unique brand of elucidation and enlightenment to proceedings.

Sat in the lounge, the entire family, encompassing the junior Frasers, talked about how the year had worked out for each of them, replaying situations either to attract sympathy or impart a fountainhead of amusement.

"I do so cherish these traditional family get-togethers," Jemina opined. "They always bring out stimulating and worthwhile discussion topics."

"Yes," Angela legitimated, "uppermost on festive intimacies like Christmas Day."

"It's a time for the women to cook and the men to eat," Don remarked.

"Here, here," Roger piped up. "Sums it up very nicely."

"Yes, fine if you don't have to cook," Charlotte caveated.

"Here, here," Angela and Jemina backed in unison.

In tune with the hearty riposte, they all broke into laughter, Christmas boosting release from all anxieties and bolstering a convivial, tolerant atmosphere. For the Frasers, Yuletide had long become an opportunity to make light of life's absurdities, and pour scorn on the outside interfering world affecting their lives for the residue of the calendar year. Somehow, it had burgeoned into an unwritten law, if they were in a Fraser household, whether it be Don's, Colin's, Roger's or Aunt Jemina's, nothing became galling or problematical, everything up for lampooning and satirising, with no sacred cows or special exceptions.

Outside the bounds of Christmas, Don's incendiary mock comment might have drawn a piercing rebuke from the lady members of the family, but under a festive habitat no one came under attack for expressing normally contentious sentiments.

"These jamborees," Jemina opined, "have become a vital forum for embracing the human condition in all its many splendid guises."

"And," Angela supplemented, "exploring the outer limits of pathos."

"Well, incontrovertibly, they drive the dynamic range," Don appended. "From mince pies to plump poultry and out of body experiences challenging the laws of nature, we must have covered just about every theme imaginable over the past fifteen or so years, certainly since Wendy came into the world."

"My, everybody is so philosophical today," Charlotte exalted. "Makes you want Christmas to go on forever, or make every day like

Christmas Day."

"For sure," Roger agreed. "And we've got you at it, as well. It's a treasured hope, darling."

"Christmas with family and relations just seems to bring out the best in me," she advocated. "I can even see the funny side of what you said to the vicar and verger of Saint Paul and Saint Peter's Church last year."

"When are you going up to Buckingham to see Valentine and Davina?" Angela solicited.

"The day before New Year's Eve," Charlotte confirmed.

Coughing, Roger gabbled, "providing I don't have to go into the office."

"Off course," Don attested, "Friday 30th December is the ultimate trading day of 2011."

"Precisely, Father. You never quite know what might happen during year end week. It really depends on how the markets are reacting to prevailing economic climates."

"What will happen to your Buckingham plans if you have to work, Roger?" Angela grilled.

"Either Charlotte will ferry the kids up to Buckingham in the MPV, and I'll take the beamer in the evening, or we'll all go up early morning on New Year's Eve."

"Are you happy with the arrangement, Charlotte?" Jemina queried.

"Over the years, I've become accustomed to Roger's work commitments, so yes, it is satisfactory."

"I will positively know if I can take the thirtieth off by mid-week," Roger warranted. "By the way," he augmented rubbernecking Don and Angela, "what time are Colin and his family arriving at Tatsfield on the twenty-seventh?"

"In the late afternoon," his mother advised.

"Oh, good, I'll be home from The Firm no later than six o'clock, so we'll be with you by seven. Presumably Peter and his family will have already landed?"

"Yes, we expect them mid-afternoon along with Jemina."

"Superb," Roger enthused, "enough Frasers amassed under one roof to tender a challenge to Doris Johnson's dominion over London."

Reconstituting 2011 junctures, the interlocution delved into recounting highlights or lowlights, dependent on the commentator's point of view. From Roger's lexicon of controversial occurrences, his desire to tear down airy-fairy exhibits and make a massive bonfire of them when the family visited the Royal Academy of Arts Summer Exhibition, and his misinterpretation of the term 'dongle' mistaking it for a gentlemen's member were retraced, much to everyone's amusement.

Also coming under the laughter microscope, Charlotte's New Age food fallout from the Age of Aquarius event attended by Roger and her, climaxing in guests cringing at the sight of the witch's brew placed before them, and how she had narrowly avoided being arrested for fighting a woman from the Greenwich Park Tree Preservation Society were studiously replayed.

"I still have the video of Mum doing her Sugar Ray Charlotte impersonation," James trumpeted with a contented leer.

"*Yes*," his mother maddeningly validated. "When I do get my hands on that inflammatory film short, James, your life will not be worth living."

"You're not going to feed us lupines and lentils for Christmas Day lunch," Don put forward, "are you, Charlotte?"

"No Father-in-law, darling, I have relented on my ambition to make this house a meat free zone, and in the interest of tradition, we'll be having the usual Xmas goodies."

Relieved not to have to crunch their way through nutmegs and gruel, a tumultuous cheer went up by all concerned.

As usual, Christmas lunch became a jaunty splurge, everyone buoyant to the borderline of nearly floating above the table, either liberated by too much alcohol or too much laughter. Decamping from the dining room, their stomachs filled to bursting, they headed to the lounge for coffee, liqueurs and family recreation. Everyone had a party piece to enact, mostly renditions of traditional Christmas songs, Charlotte near to tears when Heather chimed out *Silent Night*, Don's unparalleled rendition of Coleridge's *Kubla Kahn* and Roger's interpretation of *Have Yourself a Merry Little Christmas* with Heather sat on his lap drawing warm applause.

An accomplished pianist herself, Angela had insisted Roger and his brother Colin learnt to play the piano at an early age. Both had lapsed after an initial term of tinkling the ivories with some aplomb. Nonetheless, having achieved economic stability, the brothers had invested in pianos for their homes for old-time's sake. Additional to Roger periodically playing the Broadwood & Sons upright in the lounge when he had the house to himself, Christmas had become a forum when the Fraser family and guests united around the piano to sing Christmas songs accompanied by Angela and Roger.

"Come on," Charlotte promoted, "it's that time of year again."

Knowing what she meant, radiant with expectation, everybody trouped over to the upright.

Always a strong proponent of the event, Aunt Jemina enquired, "what are you going to give us, Roger?"

"Oh, I'll let my mother inaugurate the programme." Flexing his fingers, he disclosed, "I'm not loose enough yet."

"Your fingers may not be," Don quipped, "but incontestably you've drank enough wine and spirits to take care of any performance inhibitions."

"Ha, ha. Perfectly true."

"What's it going to be?" Angela catechized, sitting at the piano.

Touching her grandmother's arm affectionately, Wendy suggested, "how about *Walking in a Winter Wonderland*?"

"Yes, that's a good one," Charlotte applauded.

Initiating the song with a flourish, Angela then nodded and the family launched into the old *tour de force*, before segueing into *The Christmas Song*, Roger changing the lyrics from *Chestnuts roasting on an open fire* to 'Brigit Hammond roasting on an open fire', even Charlotte amused, followed by *White Christmas* and *Blue Christmas*. Taking over piano duty for *I Saw Mommy Kissing Santa Claus* and

Lonely This Christmas, Roger then upped the tempo with *Little Queenie*, *What'd I Say* and a rollicking *Rockin' All Over the World*. Furthering the selection, Angela and Roger duetted accompaniment to more rock 'n' roll classics, the undivided family collapsing into fits of laughter at Don's Jerry Lee Lewis spoof and James's send up of Little Richard.

Materialising late afternoon, taxis took Don and Angela, and Jemina, to their respective homes. Waving them goodbye, Charlotte then went into the dining room. Surveying the table debris, she smiled at the remembrance of everyone gorging themselves silly on a flock of fowl, tons of vegetables and a Christmas pudding the size of Liechtenstein, all washed down with several vats of *Gevrey Chambertin* and *Muscat de Beaumes de Venise*. Hurling caution to the four winds, Roger in particular had indulged in red burgundy and white dessert wines to his heart's content. Conversely, not wanting to add unnecessary calories to her approaching size zero figure, Wendy had been more decorous with her intake. Equivalently conservative, Charlotte sustained her campaign not to overindulge in meat and sweet goodies, whereas James took full advantage of being allowed a few sherbets and had developed a very sozzled comportment by the end of the mouth-watering meal. Ever the paragon of animal rights, Heather castigated her family for endorsing the wholesale slaughter of wildfowl for the celebration feast, only eating a few slivers of turkey and justifying her ingestion on the basis there was nothing else to eat.

Shaking her bonce, her smile broadening, Charlotte evaluated her marathon work in the kitchen to have been very worthwhile. She couldn't wait for the next Christmas Day.

~ * ~

After everything had been renovated to a more sanguine state of affairs in Fraserville, the family clustered around the box in the lounge watching *The Great Escape* for the umpteenth time. Snoozing through over-alcohol consumption, Roger felt very chilled out, his jacket button undone and his semi-released bow-tie hanging down like a limp dick.

Then the front doorbell rang.

Lured by the chime, Charlotte exclaimed, "who on Earth can that be?"

Coming to his senses, Roger speculated, "probably a late Chrissie delivery."

"Don't be ridiculous," she dismissed.

"Maybe Daddy's right," Heather playfully posed, "and there is a Father Christmas after all, and he is delivering late Christmas gifts."

Smiling proudly, her father lauded, "verily, she is developing my vent for sarcastic humour, isn't she?"

Charlotte glowered in response.

Pricking up their ears, they heard the strains of *Oh Come All Ye Faithful*.

"Carol singers," James critically illuminated, his modulation indicative of putting the strolling minstrels in the same category as vermin and lepers.

"I caught a disturbance a few moments ago," Wendy flagged, "but I thought I imagined it."

They heard the doorbell ring again.

Going to the large bay window, Wendy drew back the curtain. "Oh yes, there are quite a lot of choristers."

"Just ignore them," Roger urged, very comfortable, content and disinclined to move from sitting.

"We can't ignore them," Charlotte contended. "They'll have seen the lounge and hallway lights on. You'd better go and answer the door, Roger."

"*What*!" he protested, "Why me?"

"Because you're the head of the household," his wife inflexibly told him. "And give them at least £5, not the paltry fifty pence you gave to the Chorale Society carol singers, before threatening to set the dogs on them if they showed up again…and Roger—" She tutted signalling her indignation. "Do up your tie and button your jacket."

"Yes, my little commandant," he cheeked, going into Basil Fawlty mode.

Cursing under his breath like Muttley giving Dick Dastardly heat in *Wacky Races*, he struggled unsuccessfully with his bow tie, the neckpiece still resembling a limp dick. He did however manage to button his jacket, much to Wendy's amusement and Charlotte's disgust. Setting off for the front door, still cursing, he mentally prepared what he'd say to the carol singers to make sure they never darkened his door again.

Opening the front door, the full thrust of *Oh Come All Ye Faithful* hit him agnate to a sledgehammer, parting his hair and nearly blowing him off his feet. Recovering from the verbal strike, he identified the Right Reverend Roland Reddick, the Vicar of Saint Giles Parish Church, where all the Fraser children had been baptised. Surrounded by four, deep-piled rows of crooners, indubitably hard to fit onto the Royal Albert Hall stage, the vicar stood to their front, looking more like a stormtrooper captain than a clergyman, Roger recoiling at the prospect of their massed ranks.

"Good evening, Mister Fraser," the Vicar shouted in a jovial manner, his companion singers prolonging the hymn at an ear-splitting storey of decibels. "And a very happy Christmas to you and your family."

"Good evening, Vicar," Roger blared, poking his ears to stop them ringing as *Oh Come All Ye Faithful* grew to a crescendo.

"Who is it?" he heard Charlotte shout from the lounge.

About to reply 'the vicster', he thought better of it. Instead he hollered, "it's the Right Reverend Roland Reddick."

Appearing on the scene within a microsecond, as the final strains of the hymn came to an end, conjuring up visions of heavenly angels slowly moving into place behind the choir to complete the biblical scene, Charlotte gawped aghast at the adoration spectacle, Roger conjecturing Superman could not have made the short distance from the lounge to the front door any quicker than his speedy wife.

"Good evening, Vicar," she greeted in her most refined voice.

"Hello, Missus Fraser," he genially responded, before frowning. "We haven't seen you at Saint Giles recently. I do hope you haven't been unwell."

"No, no," Charlotte stuttered. "I er, I er…"

Seeing his wife about to commit the cardinal sin and lie to a vicar about her absence from church services, Roger intervened. "Vicar, would you and your brethren care to come inside for some Christmas cheer and a warm up?"

"Oh, very generous of you, Mister Fraser." Gleaming around the ranks of his door-to-door choir service ensemble, they all nodded. "We'd be delighted to accept your hospitality."

Opening the front door to its maximum reach, still soused Roger hung on its latch to support himself, as a regiment of fully-armed and ready, burbling, bubbling carol singers stepped inside, Charlotte hustling them into the lounge.

"Jesus!" James let slip. "We've been invaded by the god squad."

Horrified by her son's insolence, Charlotte threw him a mortifying gloom designed to turn him to stone, James cowering under its harmful rays.

With the Right Reverend Roland Reddick and his band of Ken Kesey echoing merry pranksters assembled in the lounge along with the Fraser family, akin to over friendly sardines packed and ready to be shipped, the toe-to-toe gathering necessitated the unlocking of the connecting double-doors into the dining room by Wendy, allowing everyone to breathe in again.

Deciding on mulled wine to warm up their guests, Charlotte poured twelve bottles of *Château Moulin Eyquem* into a super-large source pan. Adding cloves, cinnamon sticks, lemon and orange juice, brown sugar and *Smirnoff* in the right proportions, she brought the concoction to just below boiling point then dispensed the brew into a giant punch bowl and distributed twenty-four glasses of mulled wine to everyone apart from Heather, who told the vicster she lingered tea-total. Raising their glasses, the carol singers felicitated each other and the Frasers with Yuletide salutations such as, 'Happy manger happenings', 'Let the Magi make merriment', 'Here's to shepherd's washed feet' and 'May the archangel's force be with you', few apart from the last Roger understanding. Whilst Charlotte and the children engaged their guests in discourse, Roger greedily gobbled down the mouth-watering beverage, before sneaking away and helping himself to another glass.

Logging her husband's ruse, on his return to the fray Charlotte pulled him aside. "Don't you think you've had enough?"

"No, no, no," he opposed. "I'm just getting started."

"You must have drained at least a bottle and a half of wine during lunch, and I stopped counting how much port you had after the sixth glass."

"Well, it is Christmas, darling, a time to let your hair down and lose your inhibitions."

"I'd say you lost your inhibitions during the pre-Christmas lunch aperitifs."

"Ha-ah, ha-ah. A corking line" he aggrandised. "Wish I'd said it."

"Roger," she chastened, "just don't show me up in front of the vicster, er, the vicar."

"Of course not, my sweet."

While the mobile choir told the Fraser children about their carolling escapades, the vicster took on Roger and Charlotte.

"Hhmm, this is delicious, Missus Fraser," Reverend Reddick rejoiced, a satisfied grin spreading across his bulbous face. "Is the mulled wine recipe your own?"

"It's a traditional Buckinghamshire country recipe my mother gave me," she proudly explained.

Taking another sip, he proclaimed, "oh, it's tremendous. Reminds me of what we assume in folklore to be a seductive witches brew. Very moreish."

"Well Davina should know," Roger uttered under his breath, not in the least conceiving of ill towards his monster-in law.

"What did you say?" Charlotte piped up.

"I said," Roger mis repeated, "well, country folk know best."

Boring at him, she rejected with gusto, "no, you didn't," suspecting he had rendered something else, but gave him the benefit of the doubt under Christmastime conditions.

Recognising the need to move the conversation on before Charlotte changed her mind, and he'd suffer a future tongue lashing for his off-the-cuff derision, Roger quickly blustered, "Vicar, that hymn you were singing, *Oh Come All Ye Faithful*."

"Yes," he cautiously replied, cerebrating what his host might say next.

"The Liverpool Kop used to sing a variant of the hymn." Suddenly, Roger burst into full song. "Oh come all ye faithful, joyful and triumphant, oh come ye, oh come ye to An-Anfield. Come and adore them, they're the Kings of Europe, oh come let us adore them, oh come let us adore them, oh come let us adore them, Liv-er-pool."

By the conclusion of the football anthem, all the choristers had switched their attention to the LFC devotee's impulsive display. Aghast, their mouths had flopped wide open.

"You've got quite a good voice there, Mister Fraser," the vicster extolled. "Have you ever considered joining the Saint Giles Parish Church choir?"

Not directly replying, instead he snapped out, "there's another one we used to balls up, er I mean, get the words incorrect to at junior school."

"Oh, yes," Reddick painstakingly allowed, further placating his host.

"*Roger!*" Charlotte admonished, but by now having had more than his fair share of alcoholic beverages throughout the day, her husband barely heard the reprimand.

"Yes, a variant on a hymn containing the line, *hosanna excelsis*," Roger testified. "Some teenagers, including my elder brother Colin, were still wearing Chelsea boots, so the line became, 'Hosanna in his Chelsea's.'"

"*Roger!*" Charlotte cried out again, giving him a dig in the ribs he barely registered in his inebriated state.

"Oh, it's quite alright, Missus Fraser, the Church is used to having its tail pulled," the vicster lamented. "No harm done. We do have latitude for humour you know."

Startled by the allowance, Charlotte giggled nervously.

"As it happens," Reddick assertively docketed, pinpointing Roger with a vehement stare, "I'm a Chelsea aficionado."

"Well, somebody has to be," he blurted before laughing at his own pun. "Do you know, Vic, erm Vicar," he reflected, still smirking, "shrouded in the minutiae of the mid-nineteen-eighties…" He hiccupped. "…occasionally, I used to go to Stamford Bridge with my mate Steve Hunt. Like you, he underwrites the dark side. At the time, Chelsea had less patronage than Fourth Division Leyton Orient, and the ground had become festooned with tumbleweed and the ghosts of the 1970 Chelsea FA Cup winning team. Club Chairman Ken Bates used to meet Steve and me at the turnstiles and ask, 'And where do you lads want to stand today? As you see, there is plenty of room,' and that was just minutes before kick-off."

"You don't say, Mister Fraser," the vicster granted, attempting to pacify his over-confident host.

"Yep. At one match, I said, or rather shouted to the next patron at least twenty yards from my position, 'Crowded today, isn't it?'"

Irritated, the vicster fended, "hhmm, very drool, Mister Fraser."

"Hah, ha…ha, ha, ha," Roger guffawed, past caring about etiquette and respect for the cloth. "I anticipated you'd see the funny side, Vic, er vicster, Vicar."

Undiminished, the vicster baiting went on, Roger soliciting Reddick if he had ever been tempted to play Batman dressed up in his full vicar's uniform replete with cape, and could it be true there are some questions Google can't answer, but the church can? Extending his witticism, he even asked the Right Reverend, 'How many Calvinists does it take to change a light bulb? None,' he pronounced rejoindering his own puzzle, 'God has predestined when the lights will be on,' before breaking into uncontrollable laughter, the vicster not joining in. Worse, he then had the impertinence to canvass if Reddick had a gigantic picture of Father Ted above his bed he mooned over every night, the vicster correcting, 'Wrong denomination.'

"Off course," Roger bragged, swaying around on his feet, his blinkers invoicing tank nearly full of alcohol like in a *Tom and Jerry* cartoon, "I'm a titanic aficionado of the episcopal parallels."

"You mean, parables."

"Yes, parallels," he misquoted again. "My favourite is when Joab got a cob on with the Philistines and slews them with the arsebone of a giraffe."

"That's not a parable. It's from Judges, and you'll find it's Samson, and he slew an entire army with the jawbone of an ass."

"Right," Roger conceded, hiccupping again. "Knew it had something to do with arsebones and asses."

Levelling up the abuse, the vicar downed his fifth, filled-to-the-brim glass of mulled wine, and went on the offensive.

"Right, Mister Fraser," he declared. "The gloves are off, and I used to do a bit of boxing in my youth."

"Oh yes…" he sluggishly verbalised, dazed by Reddick's boast.

"Yes. I used to box for the Parish of Saint Bartholomew's Church, Birmingham."

"Ahh," Roger postulated, "explains the curious nasal accent you sometimes lapse into at church services."

Glaring, Reddick clucked, "what's the difference between an investment banker and a pigeon?"

"Beats me."

"A pigeon can still put down a deposit on a new Porsche 911 Turbo."

"Oh, very good, Vic," Fraser enthused, not even bothering to square Reddick's shortened job title.

"Here's another one about your ghastly industry, Mister Fraser. How do you define optimism?" Before he could reply, Reddick gladsomely told him, "a banker ironing five shirts on a Sunday."

"Yes, I like that one as well, Vic. Pretty good."

"And in conclusion," the vicar pushed, enjoying himself without restraint. "What does a hedge fund manager with no fund to manage say?" He paused. "Would you like fries with that, sir?"

"Best one of the lot, Vic," Roger complimented, slapping him on the back, the Vicster nearly regurgitating his mulled wine. "I never realised churchmen had such keen wit."

Seemingly *ad infinitum*, the church versus investment banking, ostensibly good versus evil banter went on, the vicster losing more of his inhibitions and customary parish protocol as he resolutely drained glass after glass of mulled wine. Meanwhile, his carolling colleagues also became equally sloshed, singing songs from the latest pop charts requested by Wendy, James and Heather. Stood on the sidelines, Charlotte monitored both sets of entertainment, ready to take policewoman control action if the need arose.

An hour later, arm in arm, Roger and the vicar were singing rugby songs and swilling down more mulled wine.

"You know, Reverend big dick," Roger began.

"It's *Reddick*!" the vicster vociferously revised.

"Whatever. You know," he acclaimed, putting an arm around the clergyman's shoulder in a token of burgeoning friendship, "you religious dudes are not bad company, once you get the bugs out of your rear ends."

"Very gratifying to know, Mister Freezer."

"It's Fraser, actually."

"Quite."

"I'll tell you what I'm going to do, Reverend big dick—"

"Red dick," the vicar corrected, emphasising each syllable.

"Right, sorry, red dick," Roger copied. "I'm going to make a recommendation to Kappa Corinthians apropos your services be called upon to bless our pitch and sprinkle Holy water on it before every match. What'd you say, Vic?"

"I'm flattered, Mister Freezer—"

"Fraser."

"I suppose," the vicar pressed, "you'd want me to kiss the ball as well?"

"Now there's a thought," he bayed with relish. "You don't think it'd be a little kinky?"

"No."

"Mmmm, I can see there's a walk on the wild side tendency to you, Vic."

Thereafter, the Right Reverend Roland Reddick and his band of very merry funsters withdrew, the vicster saying as penance for his unmitigated impudence, he'd expect a sizable collection plate donation from Roger in the New Year. Unabashed, Roger responded saying, since we're in the age of cyberspace transactions, would he accept American Express?

~ * ~

After Wendy, James and Heather retired, their parents cleared up the improvised ecclesiastical party train wreck.

"You've developed quite a penchant for going after the clergy at Yuletide, Roger," Charlotte pealed almost approvingly.

"The Right Reverend big dick, erm red dick, gave as good as he got," he claimed. "And I howled at every one of his investment banker gibes."

"That's as maybe," she refuted. "But it was inexcusable to make jokes about his Brummy accent, especially now when he is doing his best for the parish."

"Oohhh, hogwash," Roger denounced. "The vicster enjoyed the verbal fisticuffs as much as I did. I'd not be surprised if he gave me a capacious rebate on the trillions I've poured into Saint Giles over the years."

"Wishful thinking," she remonstrated. "Your treatment of the vicar approached the disgraceful—"

"Don't tell me," Roger interrupted, holding his hands up to acknowledge the grave misdemeanour. "I'm in the doghouse."

"No, not quite," she amended. "If not for Christmas, you'd be spending tonight in the spare room with a dunces' hat on your head, but—"

"Yes, yes?"

Beaming at him, she glorified, "you were extremely funny. You didn't see me, but behind the vicar, I sniggered at your demolition of Chelsea Football Club."

"Ah-ha," the clergy destroyer thundered out. "So…Roger Fraser finally gets his just desserts at year's end, hey?" Holding his arms aloft in a gesture of triumphalism, he bellowed Tarzan-style, "*yeeesssss*."

"Doesn't mean to say the sentence for your reckless onslaught will not be deferred to another date."

"What?" he retorted, his victory smile souring. "What do you mean?"

"Well, my darling, the letter of the social law has to be recognised, even in festive times. I'm holding your punishment in abeyance until after New Year's Day."

"Nnnnnrrrhh," Roger moaned. "Just when I daydreamed immunity from getting the rough end of the pineapple awaited me."

"And I give you fair warning," she annexed. "If you step out of line when we're in Buckingham, and commit any more social misdemeanours, particularly with the clergy, I can promise you will be in for such a pranging, you'll be lucky to get one pass out for your rugby club shenanigans in 2012."

"So…it is the doghouse blues again?"

"I'm afraid so."

"You are a heartless—"

"What?"

"Nothing, darling," he blathered, fuming and about to add more before suddenly seeing his metaphorical kennel on the horizon.

About the Author

Clive Radford began writing at school, then university but mainly through subsequent life experience.

His poetry has been published in numerous poetry magazines such as *The Journal, The Cannon's Mouth, Poetry Monthly, Poetry Now, Storming Heaven, Poetry Nottingham, Scripsi and Modern Review*, plus in many compilations by United Press.

A series of his short stories and poems have been published by Ether Books. The Arts Council has sponsored publication of his novels *One Night in Tunisia* and *The Sounds of Silence*. His contemporary satire *Doghouse Blues* was number one in Harper Collins Authonomy chart and has been awarded gold medal status. It has been published by Black Rose. His spy thriller *Zavrazin* has been published by Triplicity Publishing. Its companion sequel 'Nexus Bullet' is published by Ex-L-Ence Publishing. His three-book series *Disclosures of a Femme Fatale Addict* is published by Wild Dreams Publishing.

His science fiction novel *Maggie's Farm* and suspense-thriller *Incident at Lahore Basin* are published by Rogue Phoenix Press.

One Night in Tunisia, Zavrazin and *Bullet* have all been converted into three-act screenplays.

The *Zavrazin* screenplay is under contract with Story Merchant/Atchity Productions for film production.

Wild Dreams Publishing re-published *Disclosures of a Femme Fatale Addict* as a deluxe edition, May 2020.

Rogue Phoenix Press will be publishing his satire *Doghouse Blues 2* in March 2021.

His work has a distinctive voice setting it apart and appealing to those fascinated by intrigue and who question status quo accepted views.

Also by Clive Radford
at
Rogue Phoenix Press

Incident at Lahore Basin

Whilst on business in Pakistan, ex-RAF officer and businessman Dale Latham comes close to death when his helicopter is downed by a ground to air missile. Hospitalised, he meets Chanda Govinda, a persecuted Christian Indian and helps her escape across the Pakistan-India border. Although there is no evidence linking Latham's involvement with Chanda, Muslim zealot police chief Aman aims to imprison him.

With his top-secret knowledge, HMG fear Latham will end up in the hands of Pakistani intelligence. MI6 agent Ross Hunter is dispatched to appraise the situation, and if necessary, liquidate Latham. When Latham is abducted by terrorists, Hunter rescues him, saying that Aman set him up for the ultimate fall. Without evidence, Aman is forced to allow Latham to leave Pakistan, avoiding a bullet from Hunter.

Chapter 1: Tempest

Flameout! Pilot Wing Commander Dale Latham's Tornado zoomed groundward. As the aircraft stalled, rolled and flipped over into a spiral dive, its altimeter decremented at an astonishing rate.

He had to act fast. Initiating the engines start-up procedure, he managed to engage one RB199. Singing into life the turbofan generated thrust, allowing Latham to push the stick forward making the aircraft nose down, then increase throttle setting to full power. Miraculously, the Tornado settled, enabling him to apply back pressure to the stick levelling the wings, the aeroplane regaining steady-state flight, Latham recovering altitude as he tried to ignite the second RB199.

Approaching RAF Lossiemouth, backtracking from a combined RAF-Luftwaffe sortie over the Rhineland, navigator-weapons officer, Flight Lieutenant Harry Beaumont, warned of severe hailstorm conditions ahead. As the Tornado slowed from supersonic speed and descended from 30,000 feet over the Moray Firth channel, she hit the inclement weather. Far worse than expected, a freak set of climatic conditions had conspired to generate the mother of all storm clouds, cumulonimbus building a trail blazer of epic proportions.

As the Tornado passed beneath 15,000 feet, she encountered heavy rain and tennis-ball- sized hailstones, the contaminants ingested into the engine's inlet ducts leading to dual-turbofan flameout.

Whilst Latham struggled to re-start the second RB199, Beaumont contacted Lossiemouth Air Traffic Control, advising their predicament. Asked if the Tornado wanted to register a Mayday call, Beaumont answered in the negative. Confident of Latham's flying skills, he knew the pilot would be reluctant to pull the ejector seat handle, releasing the canopy and sending both aircrew into space, abandoning the Tornado to crash into the Moray Firth.

Latham had never lost an aircraft. He certainly did not intend to let the £14m fighter-bomber end up in the drink. Albeit, the second engine refused to spark into life, further ingestion of the life-threatening hale defeating his attempts. Though capable of flight on a single engine, prudence dictated under the tempest onslaught, having both turbofans operational equated with minimising further danger. Gaining height, the Tornado rose above the cumulonimbus wrecker, permitting the second engine inlet duct to clear of ice debris. Sustaining the re-start protocol, at last the stagnant RB199 burst into life, the gained extra thrust making the aeroplane nose-up. Deciding not to risk landing at Lossiemouth through the storm, Latham called RAF Leuchars, requesting permission for an emergency landing.

South of Lossiemouth by 90 miles, Leuchars allowed the Tornado to land without any further troubles, her aircrew reporting the flameout incident, and staying until clement weather prevailed over the Moray Firth locale, allowing then to return to Lossiemouth.

Beaumont's assessment of Latham had been spot-on. Wholly aware that the UK taxpayer owned the platforms he carried out missions on, spanning his RAF flight career, Latham had made it his business to ensure any aircraft allocated to his charge remained in one piece from take-off to landing. A trait inherited from his father; a sense of responsibility in all matters came to dominate his life from an early age.

Sometimes the quality resulted in gladness and fulfilment, whereas on other occasions, it got him into hot water, his innate sentiment to duty subduing imperilment factors.

Also by Clive Radford
at
Robue Phoenix Press

Maggie's Farm

Cody and Carolyn Redford enjoy a carefree lifestyle in Kent County, with friends Gavin and Melanie Maynard. In Cornwall, the Redfords encounter a soothsayer predicting a bleak future for mankind. The foursome then notes some unexplained changes in the behaviour of wild animals and migrating birds, giving credence to the prediction. When a terrorist outrage in South Africa leads to further major atrocities in Israel and India, détente finally fails. Global nuclear war is sparked off by an unforeseen source, resulting in the superpowers exchanging H-bomb punches like drunken boxers. In the midst of survival, Cody Redford becomes aware of the artificial insemination and incubation (AI2) programme, an initiative hatched in the Cold War years to store the sperm of prominent scientists with the objective of using surrogate hosts to factory farm children in a post-holocaust world. Though appalled, nonetheless, he resigns himself to supporting the programme, unaware of the significant down the road consequences to the nature of human life.